Daughter of Calamity

BY ROSALIE M. LIN

Daughter of Calamity

Daughter
of
Calamity

ROSALIE M. LIN

TOR

First published 2024 by Tor
an imprint of Pan Macmillan
The Smithson, 6 Briset Street, London EC1M 5NR
EU representative: Macmillan Publishers Ireland Ltd, 1st Floor,
The Liffey Trust Centre, 117–126 Sheriff Street Upper,
Dublin 1, D01 YC43
Associated companies throughout the world
www.panmacmillan.com

ISBN 978-1-0350-1126-1 HB
ISBN 978-1-0350-1127-8 TPB

1 3 5 7 9 8 6 4 2

A CIP catalogue record for this book is available from the British Library.

Designed by Devan Norman

Printed and bound by CPI Group (UK) Ltd, Croydon, CR0 4YY

Visit **www.panmacmillan.com** to read more about all our books
and to buy them. You will also find features, author interviews and
news of any author events, and you can sign up for e-newsletters
so that you're always first to hear about our new releases

FOR MICHELLE

Daughter
of
Calamity

CHAPTER ·ONE

Every Friday, I deliver the bones the way my grandmother taught me, with my shoulders down and my chin held high.

"Be proud of my art," she said, so I strut down the alleys of the Old Chinese City with her package wrapped in brown paper, wearing my pride like an ostrich feather fan behind my head.

The way night unfolds in Shanghai, like a sigh against a mirror, makes the city harder and harder to read as the hours crawl by— the bluish gas lamps above the fortune tellers' stalls, the hooves of a slaughtered cow swinging gently over the pebbled sidewalk, the large wooden mallet falling with quiet thuds onto a sheet of peanut brittle. Everything is muted, like the beginning of a dream. As I catch the bloodshot eyes of the pork butcher eating noodles behind his stall, I begin to think the streets are inhabited not by warm bodies, but by ghosts.

Past the blinking neon sign for a Turkish bath, the man I'm looking for is sitting on a crate beside a fruit stand in the crumbling wall, smoking a cigarette. As he draws his hand away from his mouth, his fingers glint silver in the washed-out moonlight.

The first time I made this delivery, I was twelve years old, and the fruit seller was just a teenager. "You see his hands?" my grandmother whispered in my ear, as I hid behind her with wide eyes that did not know what to make of the flashing neon and blue smoke. "Those are not the hands of a boy who chops pineapples all day."

I held out my trembling hands made of flesh, and he used his silver one to place a yellow rind in my palm, the sticky juice running between my fingers. There was no other word to describe the honey in her voice except pride, but it wasn't until many years later, when I watched him slip a dagger between the ribs of another man, that I understood what those hands were for.

The man drops the cigarette from between his silver fingers and crushes it with the heel of his leather shoe. After so many years, he can read my relationship with my grandmother from the brooding slant of my eyebrows. "You've been fighting with her again, haven't you, Jingwen?"

The thin fragrance of dragon fruit swirls in the cold December air.

I shrug my shoulders, which are bare below the short cap sleeves of my qipao, and hand over the package. "I'm going dancing later. Let's get this over with."

The fruit seller peeks inside the package, marveling at the assortment of bones, and pours its contents into the large brass scale meant to weigh fruit. When he stands, the hilt of a sabre peeks over his shoulder, wrapped in gray-blue leather. "Lots of arms," he observes. "Not that many legs."

"Legs aren't in fashion right now."

Xiao Lei is a gangster in the Society of the Blue Dawn. Not too many years ago, he gave up his own right arm—flesh, bone, and sinew—and lay on a table screaming as my grandma cast a mold of his flesh in steel, and sewed his nerves together, the old and the new. "You know what they miss the most?" my grandma told me, the corner of her mouth lifting like we were sharing an inside joke. "The lines on their palm."

The scale wobbles back and forth a few times and steadies.

"Twelve kilos," Xiao Lei says. "You sure you want to be paid in yuan today? The Mexican silver dollar is the highest-valued currency on the market."

I roll my eyes and thrust my hand out, palm up.

Xiao Lei pulls a wad of paper bills out of his pocket, licks his thumb, and begins to count.

"Nine hundred. You know, I see the way you look at me. Just because I'm a gangster doesn't mean I'm trying to cheat you."

His silver finger brushes against my palm, and I expect the cold kiss of steel. But Xiao Lei's hand is warm. Despite his plea, I count the money anyway while he watches me. "Still, if you were an ordinary boy, you'd be taking girls out dancing on Friday night. Not pretending to sell fruit while doing whatever it is you're doing."

A gentle fog begins to engulf the alley, like a watercolor brush being dragged across parchment, warning of dawn rain.

Xiao Lei leans his elbow against the crumbling wall, smirking a bit. "Liqing tells the gang you would make an excellent physician if you chose to become her apprentice. You certainly have the flair for it."

"She told you to say that." I tuck the bills safely into a pocket I've sewn into the waistline of my qipao, so I don't lose them later at the cabaret. "I'll pass the money along to her. Good night, Xiao Lei."

He grins, leaning his shoulder against the alley wall. "You don't realize how good you have it, dancing the night away without second thoughts about your grandmother's world. Don't you ever get curious how the cabarets can still shine when this city is up to its neck in darkness?"

The mist refuses to clear, hanging in the alley like hot breath on glass. I suddenly wish I'd worn a wool coat.

"It sounds like you're talking about some fairy-tale myth. Not Shanghai." There's a British banker I danced with last week, who likes to pay girls with literal gold ingots to sit beside him and sip champagne. If I hang around here any longer, he might choose a different partner tonight. "I need to go."

"Can I at least tempt you with a dragon fruit for the road?" Xiao Lei cradles one of the spiny fruit in his silver hand with a smirk. "Look, a rare species cultivated in Annam. They must serve this in your ballrooms, but do they tell you about the traders who scalp the price until a cactus-bloomed fruit costs more than a ruby? It's thanks to the Blue Dawn that you dancer girls get to nibble dragon fruit off crystal toothpicks."

Behind him, the bathhouse sighs, warm steam pulsating out of the giant steel vents.

Standing against the brick wall, tendrils of mist and shadows dancing about him, Xiao Lei makes an imposing figure. In that moment, he's right. I do want to know more—where he takes the bones after I leave, the way he might smile when he draws his sabre with his silver hand. I allow myself to briefly entertain a dream of myself as a gangster's companion, sweeping through cabaret halls side by side with Xiao Lei, while the curious showgirls whisper about us behind their hands.

Quickly I remind myself that these evenings it's much more fashionable to sip champagne with one's pockets bulging with gold ingots.

"It's just a fruit, Xiao Lei."

He sighs, gazing down at the fruit in defeat.

"Alright, let me prepare this for you at least. Your grandmother insists the gang look after you. She has a disdain for the American diets that are popular in the tabloids." Xiao Lei slices the dragon fruit's white flesh open with an ordinary kitchen knife, the red skin curling back like a flame.

"Fine."

I perch on the edge of a wooden crate, taking care to smooth my qipao over my knees so the silk stays unwrinkled. Unfortunately, the chilly night air has already raised gooseflesh along my thighs.

As I watch Xiao Lei's silver hand glide through the night air, like a koi drifting along a riverbed, my mind wanders to my grandmother, depositing her delivery in my arms. She got her hair permed recently, white curls like the crests of ocean waves, which accentuate the sharp corners of her eyes. My grandmother likes to say that if I really loved her, I would show more interest in her work—more than begrudgingly ferrying a package of human bones across the city every Friday. But in the black markets of Shanghai, all goods change hands, flesh to silver to flesh, until you forget where they came from originally. And I've never found the thrill in flirting with danger when there are easier ways to enjoy life.

On Friday nights, I dance at the Paramount.

The entire ballroom shimmers like a mirage—white woodwork and crystal panels that echo the light like waterfalls. The orchestra is from Havana, but they play the latest American jazz, chandelier light swimming in the shells of French horns and sousaphones.

Before the long row of mirrors in the performer's room, I smooth the wrinkles out of my qipao, which is the color of sea foam, with a high slit that runs up my thigh. Of the three clubs I dance at, the Paramount has the richest foreign guests and the gaudiest drama. When the manager hired me, he stressed that he wanted us to be "Chinese flappers," whatever that meant, so I don a headdress woven from gold beads, with a fringe that swings over my eyes when I turn my head.

I am dabbing red color onto my lips with my middle finger, when the chair beside me is yanked back by a dancer wearing a velvet circlet adorned with a peacock feather.

Zenaida Minsky, who is renowned in the cabaret scene for her violet eyes and red-brown curls, brushes aside the ripped stockings and stray pearl earrings on the makeup table to rest her elbows on the surface. She blinks dreamily at her reflection. "Jingwen, can you believe this? Nastasya joined a circus in India, with elephants and fire breathers. Now she dances on top of an elephant! Oh, I'm so mad at her. She should have taken me with her!"

Her gently accented English is sharp to my ears. I remind myself that within the cabaret's gilded walls, there is a different game we play. We duel not with silver hands or leather-wrapped sabres, but lips that shine with rouge like blood.

"Zina, you wouldn't like India," I assure her in English.

Zina sighs, her long lashes fluttering like the wings of a moth in firelight. "I want to go somewhere tropical, where the dancers balance fruit baskets on their heads and the cocktails are adorned with pineapples and bananas. I'm sick of the oily air in Shanghai."

I move on to applying blush, leaning back to avoid smattering the mirror with powder. "You can barely stand the heat of a Shanghai summer. Don't even think about somewhere tropical."

"Oh, but the waves and the ocean—oww!" Zina yelps and cowers suddenly.

Arina Lashkova, the oldest dancer among us, has just twisted her left ear. "Oh please, Zina, wipe that frown off your face. Your head is so empty, you couldn't balance a pineapple on it if you tried. You only dream of it because you're from the snowy wasteland of Harbin."

Both Zina and Arisha claim to be exiled princesses, their families driven out of Russia by the Bolsheviks a few decades earlier, and Arisha—with her pale blue eyes and silvery hair that glows white before the incandescent bulbs—I could almost believe.

"I'm from Moscow," Zina retorts.

"No, *I'm* from Moscow. You were born in a poor Siberian railroad town."

We are interrupted by the creak of the dressing room door, and Li Beibei sashays in wearing a gold qipao embroidered with orange chrysanthemums. Beibei has the largest breasts of any girl in Shanghai. Her specialty is a belly dance with a snake, wearing nothing more than a beaded brassiere and a loincloth. She is only twenty, but she has already landed two men in prison and one dead in a gun duel over her affections. There is a rumor that she can cure men's cancers with just the undulations of her hips and the smirk on her face.

Beibei elbows her way between me and Zenaida, where she beams, her lips ready to spill perfect English. Although Beibei is a country girl who moved to the city to be a nanny for two British children, she quickly found her fortune in the dance halls like a fish discovering water. "Didn't you all hear? The son of Claud Harrington will be at the cabaret tonight."

Zina and I exchange an annoyed glance in the mirror.

"You mean Claud Harrington the lumber magnate?" Arisha never passes up a chance to show off her knowledge of Shanghai gossip, which she cultivates through the meticulous reading of every tabloid in town.

Beibei plants her hands on the makeup table between Zina and me, showing off a large Padparadscha sapphire on her right hand, gifted by an Indian patron. "Yes. His only son and heir, Neville, will be here tonight with his cousin Daniel, who is visiting from France. I came to let you all know that he's going to be dancing with me, so you all be sure to stay away."

"Go to hell, Beibei," Zina retorts, glowering through her thick eyelashes and wide eyes.

Beibei leans her hip into the makeup table, uncomfortably close to Zina and me. I can smell the gardenia perfume she wears, her painted eyebrows shining like fresh ink on a calligraphy scroll. "Do you want to challenge me?"

Zina folds her arms across her chest, the movement causing her chiffon dress to slip from her shoulder. "You know, I'm done taking your shit. You think you're better than everyone just because you have to wear imported bras."

"Stop it," Arisha insists, smacking her in the ear again. "It's not civil to fight like this on the dance floor. We'll scare the guests."

"Exactly," I pipe up. "That's why we do it in the dressing room. There are no guests here. I'm not afraid of you, Beibei. What are you going to do?"

Beibei flicks open a silver lighter adorned with trumpeting vines, the flame glowing with a menace between her fingers. She smirks in a way that reveals none of her teeth, yet I can't determine if the gesture is sweet or menacing.

"You wouldn't dare!"

But just in case, I grab a hairpin adorned with golden leaves to arm myself in response.

The door creaks open again, and a man's blond head appears in the crack.

It's the ballroom's manager, a former flautist who was fired from the Paris ballet when he eloped with the prima ballerina. The girls whisper that his nose is crooked because the prima ballerina's husband broke his flute over it, but if you visit the Turkish bath on the Rue de Consulat on Sunday evenings, you'll see he enjoys having his shoulders scrubbed by a particular Russian bath girl who has the same delicate chin as his lost paramour. "What do you airheads fight about all evening?" he demands. "I can't hear the cook explaining his idea for a wine-basted lamb shank dish. Please—keep it down."

His head withdraws once more, and the door slams shut.

"He's right, what are you four fussing about?" asks Huahua, a younger dancer recently poached from the smaller Majestic Club, who had been powdering her cheeks in a corner and pretending she's too good for us. She's new, but she too thinks she should be the queen.

Beibei tosses the lighter back on the makeup table with a deep, husky laugh. "Fine then," she says, and without even raising her voice, she has garnered command over the entire room. "I propose a contest. Let's settle this once and for all. Whoever can bring the richest date to the annual Firefighters' Yuletide Ball at Christmas will get first choice of any dance partner for the next *year*. And all the rest will have to cater to the winner's wishes—bring her champagne, massage her shoulders, even paint her toenails if she asks."

The entire room hushes, as we picture ourselves in that position.

"Don't you think you're taking things a little far, Li Beibei?" Huahua asks, her hands covering her mouth.

Beibei narrows her eyes, the chrysanthemums sewn into her dress glowing like suns. "We waste so much energy fighting, don't you think it would be simpler to objectively acknowledge that one of us is better than the rest?"

I cut in. "Deal. But if you lose, you have to leave the Paramount."

I'm talking to Beibei, who attempted to mix poison oak into my rouge the first night I was hired and whom I have considered rival number one ever since.

She studies me like one of those decorative plants with monstrous, jagged leaves, which she is trying to decide if it is genuinely alive or woven from plastic.

"I won't lose." She spins on her heel with a dramatic flourish, her crystal earrings trembling in her wake.

"Jingwen!" Zina hisses, elbowing me sharply in the ribs. "She's going to win!"

"No, she's not," I say, without taking my eyes off Beibei's back. "I've studied her for years. I know what makes her tick, and I know how to break it." I lean in closer so that I might whisper my wisdom in Zina's ear, but she flinches and holds a hand up to push me away.

"Don't whisper to me like that, Jingwen. We're enemies now. For all I know, you might be lying to manipulate me."

Arisha, busy fastening lavender pearls at her earlobes, laughs ironically. "If you want to win, Zina, then you better hire a literatus to rewrite your Moscow story. At this point, you couldn't even convince a five-year-old child to believe it."

And so, the prize is set the way decisions are made in the Sin City of the East—on a whim.

I size up the other dancers in the room. Seducing the right boy from the foreign concessions meant several weeks of steak dinners, maybe an ermine trim coat. But now, the deal has sweetened and grown more poisonous. I don't care so much about having the other girls paint my nails and fetch me champagne. I just want to bathe in Beibei's wide-eyed jealousy when she sees I've beaten her. It should scare me more than it does. Because winning is a sport that has long amused my grandmother.

The door flies open and the Paramount's manager leans his head in again. We all cover our ears as he whistles with two fingers. "Alright, girls, doors open in three! Jingwen, why does your hair look like you've been running in a horse race?"

"It does not!" I scrunch my short, curled hair in my fingers to make the waves bouncier, before hurrying onto the dance floor after the other girls, just as the orchestra has started to play.

Immediately, Zina is swept away by a German stranger with a red beard. I hear her spinning her usual yarn, about her childhood in a palace in Moscow. Arisha is chosen by a Chinese banker, a friend of the Paramount's investor, who has a thing for tall, willowy blondes. I dance with a law student from Fudan University, who has come to see me twice in the past fortnight.

"Vilma," he says, using my stage name. "You don't mind that I am not rich like the other men here?"

Although we are both Chinese, he chooses to converse with me in English, the fashionable language of the times, and so I respond in kind.

"No, after all you'll be a lawyer someday." I lean into his embrace, so that I can search the ballroom over his shoulder for Neville Harrington, the lumber magnate's son.

Wheels of colored light soar across the maple floor like heavenly chariots, the sprung floor giving way underfoot like we are walking on clouds. My fellow dancers drift by in the arms of rich men, their necks arched like swans.

"Do you think I'll be a good lawyer?" my partner asks.

"You are an expert at questioning me." I giggle, and he laughs along.

"The university girls are all so sullen," he sighs. "And they don't know how to dress. I can't imagine marrying one of them. How old are you, Vilma?"

A few feet away, Arisha's partner twirls her under his arm, and she sneaks a glance across the dance floor. Two young men have just arrived in fur-trimmed coats, and the manager shows them to a reserved table with the best view of the orchestra and dance floor. Arisha may have spent countless hours studying every rich heir in Shanghai, but all I had to do was study her.

"Seventeen," I respond, although I am actually twenty.

My law student partner perks up. "You're my sister's age. My mother thinks she should get married soon. Think about it, if we were married, you and I could spend every night dancing in each other's arms."

"That would be lovely." I affirm his fantasy as I watch Neville and cousin toast with aged Merlot.

The soft croon of the trombones fades, and the first dance of the night ends.

I draw away, but the law student does not let my hand go. "I could only afford one dance ticket tonight, but I don't want to let you go."

I kiss him on the cheek and gently untangle my fingers, before he can ask for a free dance. "I'll wait for you next week."

The key to stealing patrons from Beibei is to act fast. Charm them into buying so many dances up front they never get the chance to notice her full lips and large breasts.

"Don't forget me, Vilma!" my lawyer-in-training calls after me.

I saunter across the dance floor, my bare arms brushed with cool light that turns them to the likeness of blue jade. Arisha's partner refuses to relinquish her after just one dance, and as her shoulders drop in disappointment, I run the last five steps to where Asia's wealthiest lumber heir is recounting last Sunday's Canidrome race to his cousin.

The beads on my headdress catch the light from the gilded lamps on the tea table, creating a dazzling storm of gold rain on the white wood floors.

The young men break from their conversation, hypnotized.

"Good evening," I say, brushing one leg behind the other in a small curtsy. I'll have to hazard a wild guess which one is the millionaire's son. Like the Sunday dog races, it takes a dash of luck to make a fortune. I pick the one with the dark, curled hair and pointed chin, who is wearing a tan vest and a gray bow tie. There are less lines on his forehead, so perhaps he's had less to worry about in his life. "You must be Neville Harrington."

He leans back in the couch. "How did you know?"

I smile and tilt my head to the side, setting the beads in my headdress aquiver like aspen leaves. "All the dancers know you are coming today. They say you're so handsome, the tabloids are raving about it."

The lumber heir laughs, a curl of dark hair bouncing above his eyes. "Really! I guess I should start reading the tabloids. Which one?"

I blink. "Oh, I meant it as a compliment—"

"Daniel," Neville says, turning to his companion. "Do you read the tabloids? Have you ever seen me in one? I feel as if that's the sort of thing my mother should have told me about."

"I think she was speaking figuratively," Daniel agrees, setting down his glass of wine.

A spray of cold wetness dashes over my chest, and I barely have time to gasp before the breath is crushed from my ribs. I inhale the overwhelming aroma of gardenia perfume, as I am knocked to the floor. I reach for the edge of the table in vain and succeed only in knocking my head against it, the black trellis rug scraping my knees raw. Beibei lands on top of me, a cocktail glass still clutched in her hand.

I want to wring her neck, but Neville extends his hand down with a gentle frown.

"Are you alright, miss?" he asks, helping Beibei to her feet.

Beibei gasps and covers her small cherry mouth. "Oh, I'm so sorry!" She gathers a napkin to dab at the wine spatters on his sleeve, tears shining in her eyes. "I'm so clumsy. How can I ever make it up to you? The only payment I have to offer is a free dance."

The lumber heir, his eyes glued to the curve of her breasts, grasps her agitated fingers to still them. "No need to fret. My father will buy me a new shirt. What is your name?"

She tucks her chin meekly and blushes. "Beibei."

He hands her a handkerchief from his pocket, and she sniffles as she dabs at the corners of her eyes.

"Beibei, please don't cry. I'll gladly dance with you."

As he leads her away to the dance floor, she turns over her shoulder and twists her face into a sneer.

I catch Daniel Harrington staring at me over the edge of his wineglass. As I watch, he sets the wine down and clears his throat.

Maybe he has some money, but dancing with him at this point would just affirm that I'm second best to Beibei. After all, I didn't come to dance with the cousins of millionaires. I came to dance with the millionaires.

Slowly, I watch his eyes rove to the wine stain on my hip, and he looks away.

Defeated, wearing a stained dress that won't be easy to clean, I kick off my high heels and sink into the nearest couch. There is an unattended drink resting on the tea table—an amaretto bourbon garnished with lemon peel. I have just about downed the whole thing when a man dressed in a slender evening suit stops in front of me. The shadow of his homburg hat falls over the couch like a palm frond over a pond at midnight.

"The night is still young," he says, removing the hat and taking the seat opposite me. "Why are you sitting this dance out?" Presently, he removes the glasses from his face, folds them, and puts them in a pocket.

The man's accent is American, his face boyish but lined with crow's-feet.

I make a show of sipping from my near-empty glass, torturously slowly. "My company costs six dance tickets," I tell him, when I finally set the glass down.

He draws all the tickets out of his breast pocket and lays them out on the table. "They're yours."

I sweep up the dance tickets, slightly suspicious of how easy it's going.

"What's your name?" he asks.

"Vilma," I say. "You?"

"Dr. Bailey Thompson," he responds. "From New York. I'm new to Shanghai. Shall we dance?"

He offers me a hand to lead me onto the pale, wheaten dance floor. Doctors aren't lumber heirs, but I'm intrigued by his aloof confidence. So, I place my fingers in his.

The orchestra plays a forlorn violin melody that blossoms into a mischievous piano rhythm. Our first dance is a tango. I rest my fingertips gently on Dr. Bailey Thompson's left shoulder. He smells of musk and sandalwood, earthen aromas that feel at odds with the metropolis of Shanghai. We sashay through the crowd, a languid, playful rhythm like a hunting cat.

"What kind of doctor are you in New York?" I ask.

He smiles down at me, crow's-feet crinkling around his eyes. "I'm an obstetrician."

"Do you make a lot of money?"

He dips me back suddenly, toward the floor. The blood rushes to my head, and I bite back the urge to gasp. By instinct, I've arched over his arm like a swathe of silk. From the top of the Greek pillars around the dance floor, colored lights brush over my skin like warm, roving moons. Layers of white and black fly across the gilded walls like swan wings. The doctor pauses as if he is holding my head under water, smiling faintly. I can feel the ends of my hair brushing the hardwood, his warm breath on my forehead.

When he brings me back, I twirl away from him to hide that I've lost control of my breath.

"I deliver babies," the doctor answers finally, gathering my waist in his arm. He is a good dancer. I guess he must've spent a lot of his nights dancing in New York City.

"And Shanghai? What brought you here?"

The doctor grins coyly. "I decided to try my hand at business."

The violins suddenly race to a climax. The song is coming to an end. In a daring move, I wrap my leg backward around his waist in an arabesque, and he leans to the side, carrying me with him. I trust him to support my weight, as I bring my gaze to meet his over my shoulder. Around us, the few sitting guests gasp and applaud. I see Zina covering her mouth in shock.

The doctor tips me back onto my feet and bows with a cool incline of his head.

I am panting like I've nearly drowned in the depths of the Huangpu, but my cheeks are flushed with a thrill I've never felt before. My glee deepens when I catch sight of Beibei grasping Neville's arm, her spotlight stolen.

The next dance is a jive. I can tell the doctor is competitive. He wants to tire me out. I return the favor, galloping around him and showing off my flexibility. The gold beads of my headdress fly around my face, like a swarm of gold scarabs on a white sand dune. On the crowded dance floor, the faces of the other taxi dancers are contoured by shadows. Usually, I can out-dance my lawyer admirer easily, and that makes it boring. Dancing with the doctor is thrilling because he knows all the latest dances like the samba and the Lindy Hop, and he's quite experienced. I forget for a moment that this is all an illusion I've created, and he's believed.

When the six dances are over, the doctor buys me a green, iridescent cocktail and leads me over to a couch. There is a gleam of sweat in his black hair.

"You're more of a flapper than any of the girls I've danced with in New York City, Vilma," he tells me. "It's because you've got the touch of Shanghai in you. Kissed by the devil."

I sip the cocktail he bought me, as the throaty growl of the trumpets rumbles in my breastbone. I've never had this drink before. The taste is faintly floral, making me think of white jasmine flowers, dusted across the window seat of a French Concession mansion. Although I'm flattered, I'm not stupid enough to believe an angel has fallen into my lap tonight, without requiring a fight.

I cross one leg over the other, leaning back into the cushions. "Let me guess what kind of life you led in New York City."

The doctor laughs deep in his throat. "I like this game already."

He lights a cigarette and offers me one. I eye the label etched on the worn paper pack. *Chesterfield,* it says, *just as pure as a glass of water . . .*

I draw a cigarette out between my index and middle finger, showing off my fresh-painted red nails as he lights it. I hate the way the smoke stings my throat like fire, but I am a cabaret girl after all, and part of our trade is to smoke and drink with the guests.

"You cheated a lot in medical school," I guess.

Bailey arches his eyebrows in response. "Oh?"

I relax into the cool, gray smoke. "Instead of studying your books and your cadavers, you were out dancing. Doctor, I don't think you have any reverence for formulas and diagrams. You strike me as the type to make your own rules."

He angles his chin toward the shadows and exhales, blowing smoke up to the ivory fleurs-de-lis etched into the ceiling. "What makes you think that?"

"Your arrogance." I grin a little. "That and the way you dance.

You strike every move at the edge of a beat so that each step is almost late. It means you like to push boundaries."

"You're not wrong."

On the dance floor, a Lindy Hop ends with a triumphant crescendo, and I bring my hands together to clap with the other seated guests. I notice the crimson polish I've used to paint my nails has a sheen of glitter to it, only visible when I hold my fingers at a particular angle.

"My turn." Bailey smirks. "Let me guess about you. You're a liberated creature of the night—sleep in the day, dance to your heart's content when the moon is out."

I sip the light green drink. "Wrong."

He frowns, drawing a thumb across his chin. "How could I be wrong?" he asks gently.

I smile and straighten my back a little more. "You don't understand Shanghai yet. But once you understand Shanghai, you understand the rest of the world."

"Those are grand words to proclaim," the doctor exclaims, as if I've told him the sky is actually red. "Nonetheless, I concede your victory. You've piqued my curiosity. What do you do during the day then?"

"I train as a chorus girl for the East Sea Follies, the Paramount's in-house revue company." I tap the ashes from my cigarette into a porcelain tray adorned with naked women and seashells. "It's a different sort of dancing—not the kind where I spend the night with handsome, foreign doctors, sipping pretty drinks."

Bailey chuckles. "Ah, a cabaret star. I should've guessed. The dance halls aren't sophisticated enough for you. You want to be an actual artist."

I feel my cheeks warming as I take another drag on the cigarette. "It's not so simple. Shanghai is a monstress, and she feeds on money. Those of us who have lived here our entire lives are practiced in the art of bottle-feeding this city."

"Surely though, performing in the Paramount's in-house revue would rake in a lot of riches, no?" He leans down, running his fingers over his five-o'-clock shadow in contemplation.

I regret bringing up the revue now. That's the last way to seduce a client—by bringing up how you are a member of an actually-failing dance troupe.

"We don't have as much draw as the Russian and American troupes with professionally trained ballet dancers," I admit. "When we perform *Swan Lake*, we can only draw an audience of sixty, but when the Kukolka Dance Ensemble performed *Swan Lake* last winter, they filled an entire theater." I kick my shoes off and draw my legs up under me. "Enough about me now. What kind of business do you do?"

The doctor smiles as his eyes rove over my calf, under the sheer layer of my tights, like he is admiring a rare, silver pheasant behind a wall of ivy. He must feel like he's won, having prodded too deeply into my personal affairs. "That's a secret," he says.

I collapse back into the cushions, my cheeks swollen with embarrassment. "With so many secrets, you fit right into Shanghai."

He is staring right at a table of gangsters through a forest of twirling white legs and flying silk. Their bodies glisten with silver modifications like aspen boughs in the moonlight, as they pour maotai into glass liquor cups. Bailey raises his glass of whiskey to his lips and misses. "Well then, it seems I made the right decision to come to Shanghai," he muses. "New York was getting quite boring."

Across the dance floor, a girl screams.

At first, nobody hears her over the orchestra except me and Arisha, whose ice-blue eyes I catch above the feathers and curled tresses twirling on the dance floor.

"Stop!" Arisha shrieks.

The white legs and flowing silk of the dance floor scatter like dead leaves swept in a dust storm. In the eye of the storm, a young girl crouches in the middle of the dance floor with her knees splayed, covering her face with her white hands. It's Huahua, the flirtatious sixteen-year-old dancer who has only been with the cabaret for four months. As she sobs, the pearl strands in her ears and the gold bracelets on her wrists vibrate with the same frequency.

Arisha gets to her first, elbowing aside the nosy onlookers, who are clutching each other in fear and confusion. I leap over the tea table and rush to Huahua's side.

"What is it?" Arisha demands.

Although a few nights ago Huahua stole a Japanese accountant I was wooing, and just a few months ago Arisha tried to sabotage her hiring audition by smearing butter on the dance floor, in that moment I fear for her. I see Huahua the way patrons must see us—interchangeable, and I can't shake the feeling that whatever happened to her could've easily happened to me.

Huahua shakes her head and sobs louder, tears dripping into the collar of her qipao. The other taxi dancers have gathered around us now.

Arisha wrenches Huahua's hands away from her face. The entire ballroom gasps at what they see.

Where Huahua's mouth used to be gapes a hole, deep as an abandoned well buried in the springtime field of her face. Fresh, bright blood flowers against her skin like poppies blossoming in winter snow.

Someone has cut her lips away.

My heart begins to thud very loudly somewhere high in my skull, each beat sending the world asway. It must be a prank, and Huahua will emerge any second now from behind a mask, giggling at how she's fooled us all. Such an act of mutilation doesn't fit with the gilded, ivory-paneled walls—such an act of mutilation isn't even possible.

The manager emerges from the crowd and swears loudly in French. "Get her out of here!" he yells at us dancers. "Don't leave her where the guests can see!"

As several other dancers rush to Huahua's side, I look into her eyes, searching for the girl who had so confidently bested me just a few nights ago, but they are glassy with shock. Her face swirls with shadows that aren't made by the ballroom's chandeliers.

Then, buried under the hands of the other dancers trying to drag her to her feet, she tilts her chin suddenly and meets my gaze. A cold shiver claws down my spine. Her brown eyes are desperate—trembling with a hollowness that feels like an accusation—that I have chosen to stand aside and watch.

"Hurry!" the manager shouts. "I said get her out of here!"

And then the other dancers lead her away.

I feel a warm touch on my back. I have forgotten all about Bailey Thompson, who appears at my side, expressionless. "Well, it appears we must cut this night short." He takes my hand and bows. "I look forward to dancing with you again, Vilma."

And he presses his lips gently to the back of my hand.

As he vanishes into the crowd, I run my hand through my hair, untangling the wild knots that have settled from all our dancing. Too much has happened too quickly.

A frenzied, hot pounding begins in my chest, like my heart is a butterfly trapped within the prison of my ribs.

I run outside the ballroom to gulp the night air, which pierces my lungs like ice. My fingers leave white indents where I've gripped my thighs. I'm not sure I believe it—that I just saw a dancer with her lips cut away—seamless where the privacy of her mouth bled into the shadows across her face, almost artistic in the execution.

Slowly, I raise my head as if I expect to find the world changed.

A convertible drives by with its top down, and Zina Minsky stands in the backseat, giggling maniacally while clutching the hand of a man in a dark suit, her hair streaming behind her head.

"Jingwen!" she calls to me, waving her arms overhead. "Jingwen, look I'm flying!"

Across the street from the Paramount, a single plume of smoke rises from the courtyard of the Jing'an Temple, its darkened red and gold pagodas sleeping in the shadows. Although it's past midnight, the temple's front gate remains swung open in a foreboding invitation. But no one is going in. Instead, a mix of tired, drunk club-goers revel under a string of cheap lanterns flickering under the temple's vermilion walls, pawing through cheap trinkets and

perfume sachets heaped on rickshaw carts. Softshell blue crabs sizzle on rusted stoves, dusted with sliced chilis and spring onions,
before they pass into velvet gloves and into dainty red mouths.
What they don't know is that the crabs are fried so hard to conceal
how the flesh has gone black inside.

The city laughs on.

With each pulse of neon on the Paramount's blinking face, my
heartbeat dulls in my chest.

A girl may have lost her lips tonight behind the Paramount's
ivory doors, but the streets remain merciless with their dazzling
lights and drunken splendor.

The weight of the hundred-yuan bills in my pocket grows heavy.
Before I can go to bed tonight, I'm supposed to turn the money
in to my grandmother before she locks her clinic doors. I imagine
Beibei tossing her head with her signature scoff, pearl-studded pins
glistening in her hair. *There's no point ruminating on the meaning of
things,* she often chides us. After all, we get to go home early tonight
without being fired.

Everything I saw tonight is just a glitch, I explain to myself.
And what was one glitch in the rhythm of our connected, beating
city, which stops for no one?

CHAPTER TWO⊙

My grandma's clinic lies in the attic of a piano bar on Blood Alley, in the bowels that lie between the groomed, sleeping towers of International Settlement and the French Concession.

In the hellish blue alleys that run under the Bund's distinguished consulates and banks, neon lamps illuminate the faces of courtesans and gangsters, who are smoking cigarettes in the shadows. Outside a dive bar, a group of boys in white uniforms—sailors in the American navy—nudge each other and whisper behind their hands, nodding at me. But on the other side of the street, a group of silver-handed gangsters from the Blue Dawn are keeping watch, steel sabres ready to be drawn at any second, making the sailors think twice about going after a Chinese woman.

Inside the Cabaret Volieré, merriment and abandon overflow like the foam atop a mug of beer. The Texan pianist is playing honky-tonk with his callused fingers on a peeling, out-of-tune grand piano, occasionally missing notes due to the broken keys. Knockoff absinthe, made in some British swindler's bathtub, makes its rounds on brass trays. Everybody is drunk. The dresses are falling off the shoulders of the taxi dancers, who are lying across the laps of their patrons, their makeup smudged.

I run up the stairs behind the piano, past the couples tangled in each other's skin on the second-floor lounge, to the closed door at the very top of the stairs.

The clinic, with its steel sink and gleaming operating table, is empty. Tendrils of warm sandalwood incense dance through the air like souls, rising from a small shrine in a corner of the room. A pile of offerings—oranges, apples, and a small pineapple—lay heaped

before a Nuo opera mask, a lacquered ebony face twisted into a grimace, with flaming red brows and a tiger's whiskers.

As I approach the shrine, incense crawls after me like a summer
insect, creating a halo around my head, and I bat the smoke away
with my hand. "Go away," I say, although it's just smoke.

Near the clinic's window, a steaming kettle of black coffee rests
on a low sandalwood table beside diagrams of musculature and
anatomy. The window is wide open, silk curtains fluttering in the
breeze.

I arrange my high heels neatly under the windowsill and climb
outside, onto the rusted fire escape. Down below, a couple of gangsters look up, cigarettes between their teeth. I smooth my dress
down to conceal my underwear.

Yue Liqing is standing on the roof, leaning over the parapet,
wearing a flowing blouse made of patterned silk. A strand of her
curled, white hair dances in the night air.

"Waipo!" I yell from the fire escape. "What are you doing?"

She holds her hand up to silence me. "Breathing," she says. "Jingwen, don't you feel like the night air is haunted sometimes? It's
beautiful."

In the distance, nightclub signs twinkle like paper lanterns floating down a stream. Automobiles glide up the avenues like a school
of goldfish. The fog I had noticed earlier that evening has lifted.

"Waipo, I brought the money."

Liqing's eyes open slowly. "You're also late. You were caught up
dancing with some new paramour, weren't you? That's why you're
wearing that ridiculous thing on your head. Your mother was exactly the same in her youth."

I reach up and realize I'm still wearing the beaded headdress.
"There was an attack at the cabaret." I comb my fingers through
the beads to untangle them from my hair. "Waipo, you always
know everything that happens in Shanghai after nightfall. What's
going on?"

Liqing exhales one last time, the warmth of her breath lingering
in the air, and she descends the fire escape, her surgeon's hands

steady on the rails. At odds with the rest of the urban decay, she is wearing black-and-white cloth slippers, a relic of her childhood in the countryside.

In her clinic, she pours a mug of coffee. We sit across from each other at the table, both of us kneeling. When the mug is nearly full, I reach for it, but Liqing slaps my hand away.

"The first cup is always for the spirits," she responds, setting it between us.

I sigh audibly, but she ignores my exasperation. With a deep breath, I prepare to launch into a rant about Huahua and her missing lips, but I bite my tongue before I start. Liqing's shoulders are relaxed, her eyes closed as she inhales the coffee steam. If I say anything now, she won't hear it. So, I gesture to the shrine instead, trying to appease her obsession with ghosts and demons. "The mask is different from the one you had a few hours ago when I came for the bones."

Liqing fills a second mug of coffee. "Ah yes, that mask was meant to ward off the spirits of my hateful, long-dead in-laws. This one is meant to repel the pig-faced ghost."

The vines of smoke dance toward my outstretched finger, hissing like a viper, and I draw my hand away. Liqing nudges the coffee toward me, and I take it as my cue to start.

I suck in another deep breath. "Someone cut Huahua's lips from her face. It happened like lightning. One second everyone was dancing, including her, and then she screamed and her lips were gone. I don't know how to describe it—she wasn't even bleeding that much. Her face became a sort of moving shadow."

"That is gruesome," Liqing agrees, "but hardly the strangest thing I've heard about this city."

"Even now, I wonder if I imagined it. Maybe I'm just going mad."

My beaded headdress lies discarded on the old carpet—crown jewels under the Paramount's sparkling chandeliers, but cheap junk on the floor of my grandmother's clinic.

The lines around Liqing's mouth deepen. "Shanghai is a wild

animal. Her cruelty lies in her capitalistic nature. If you choose to become a cabaret girl, then you should be prepared to deal with the consequences."

"It wasn't something I asked to happen!"

"No," Liqing says, a stiff edge to her voice. "It's not your fault Shanghai is dangerous. But there are only two types of people in this city—puppets and puppeteers. Cabaret girls, whose fates are tied to the men who dance with them, are puppets." She touches her hand to her breast. "Jingwen, I am a puppeteer, pulling strings to turn the world my way, and that's why I have always implored you to follow in my footsteps. I wish you would become my apprentice and leave this world of puppets behind."

She sits before me, smiling as if she knows me better than myself, and I want to tear her diagrams and anatomical maps and scatter them about the clinic like ash.

"Oh, stop making this about you."

I cannot erase the image she's put in my head—that we are dolls in a shop, waiting for customers to pinch our cheeks to test whether we're made from porcelain or rubber. Huahua and I were never friends, but I won't stand to see her insulted like this. Not because I think Liqing actually cares about a mutilated sixteen-year-old girl from a no-name town in Jiangsu Province, but because we aren't really talking about Huahua. We are talking about me.

"I don't want to be your successor," I tell Liqing, my voice rising. "Stop trying to drag me into it. I know you asked Xiao Lei to annoy me about it tonight. Do you know how exhausting it is, having the two of you breathing down my neck every time I see you? I don't have to keep visiting you and doing your dirty work."

I stand up, accidentally stepping on the beaded headdress. The fake pearls crunch under my heel with an unpleasant sandiness.

At my threat of leaving, Liqing raises her voice as well. "Jingwen, I'm only trying to save you. How much longer are you going to play dollhouse with your life? You're too old for this."

I tower over her—the woman who took me in when my mother could no longer care for me, who let me run wild around her clinic when I could still barely walk. "When you say puppeteer, what you mean is *criminal.* It makes my skin crawl just to think about the way you trade human bones like cheap rubies. Mama is right. You're the most selfish person I've ever met. No wonder she never wants to see you."

Liqing's eyes harden like the roots of a thousand-year-old tree at the mention of my mother. "How dare you," she says.

I storm for the door, but before I can push it open, there is a loud knock on the other side. The shadow of two leather shoes lurks in the crack underneath the door. In the distance, drunken laughter echoes. I have totally forgotten we are not alone. In fact, we are in a house of merriment. If I close my eyes, I can hear the inanity of a cakewalk being pounded on the piano.

Liqing twists around. "Who's there?" she shouts.

I back away from the door and whatever lies behind it.

A man's voice answers, smooth as amber cognac being swished in a glass. "Madame Yue, I bring an inquiry for a patient."

Liqing's brows furrow. "Dr. Yue," she corrects him. "At any rate, I don't operate on Englishmen."

I hear the man's hand on the doorknob a second before it happens—he pushes the door open. I scramble toward the shrine, as if the grimacing idols housed within can protect me.

"My client is American," the man says, sweeping the fedora off his head as he bows. "A lady, in fact."

He straightens, his beaming clean-shaven face a stark contrast to the growling demons decorating Liqing's walls. His suit is so neatly pressed he looks two-dimensional, like an advertisement in a newspaper. At odds with his demeanor, he is wearing a polka-dot tie.

"Who the hell are you?" Liqing asks.

The man bows again. "Who I am is not important. However, I represent a client seeking a novel procedure that has never been performed before—one that has the potential to catapult you toward fame in the West and beyond. You could make history, Madame Yue."

"I've already made history."

"Western history," the man clarifies.

"Fine, describe the procedure."

The man produces a brown package from his inner pocket and unties the red velvet bow on top. He unfolds the paper like a child unraveling a stolen candy and holds his hands out to us.

Two plump, red crescents, curled like mandarin orange slices, rest upon the paper. "My client desires a new, softer kiss."

"Those are Huahua's lips!" I lunge for the package, which the man lifts out of my reach.

"Your hands are not clean," he explains, his red mustache twitching in a smile. "If my client acquires an infection due to your dirtiness, you may rest assured I will have you pay for it."

"Those are my friend's lips! Are you the one who attacked her?"

The man extends his palm toward my grandma with Huahua's mandarin-slice lips still resting upon the brown paper, like a waiter proffering a platter of venison steak. "Madame Yue, what do you think?"

Liqing's eyes are filled with a shining intensity, like oil set ablaze by a torch. "Get out of my clinic," she says quietly.

The man lowers his hand just a bit, seemingly unfazed.

"As you wish," he says finally. "If you change your mind, I'm open to negotiating a price." He produces a business card from inside his vest and lays it facedown on a table by the door.

With another little bow, he walks backward out of the door and shuts it behind him.

In the silence he leaves behind, I hear can hear every breath of mine. They seem to echo off the walls of the clinic.

"Weren't you going to go, Jingwen?" Liqing says softly.

I stride up to the tea table, where I dig the wad of banknotes out of my pocket and set it before her. It sits there like a dead animal run over by a rickshaw and left to rot in the street.

"You're going to call that man back, aren't you?"

Liqing's eyes narrow, and she clenches her hands beneath the edge of the table. "What do you think?"

"I think you are."

When she doesn't say more, I pick up a turtle shell lying on a bookshelf, carved with spidery runes. A large crack runs through the middle, splitting off to one side.

"Don't touch that," Liqing says.

I roll my eyes as I set the turtle shell back down on the shelf.

A flood of exhaustion suddenly hits me, the way it usually does as I'm walking home from the cabaret barefoot with my heels in my hand, as taxis dart past me blaring their horns. It's the feeling of being invisible, of realizing you're but a single honeybee in a crawling hive, who matters very little in the grand scheme of the world.

"I think you're going to call him, but I hope you don't," I say without looking at her.

And I walk away.

CHAPTER THREE

My name means, "the silent ripples in water."

In Mandarin, the lingua franca of the Old City, it's 靜紋, pronounced Jingwen. Liqing named me. Every time it rains, when mist shrouds the piers like a fur stole and black umbrellas bob in the street like diving bells, I think about the circumstance of my christening. In Shanghai, the ripples in water are never silent. Even the rain that drips off the eyes of the door-guarding lions comes with its own pa-la, as it pools under their paws quivering. Water is how eleven nations forced Shanghai to her knees and sliced her skin into concessions, when they came across the sea in their steam-powered ships and razed her city walls.

Liqing talks about a day when the sun never rose in the forty-fifth year after the Partition of Shanghai, when the carriages stopped on Bubbling Well Road and the horses tore their stirrups in terror, and in the darkness below the piers, the waves lay still. That was the day the Mother of Calamity, the goddess who had watched over the city since its founding, fled with her entourage of winged tigers and leopards across the sea—when she saw how the Western powers had carved her beloved city into a mosaic of babbling tongues and different-colored eyes. And a city without a god, Liqing reminds me, is nothing more than a ghost city. She named me after that day so that I would never forget, that someday Shanghai would need its goddess back, and there might be no one.

In Japanese, my name is Shizuko. I'm not a poet, but I believe that every time you rehome a name in a new language, it loses a piece of its heart. In Chinese, my name sounds wistful, like the first two words of a Tang Dynasty poem. In Japanese, it sounds like the shape of an ocean wave, the angry kind that rushes at the shore during storms. The Japanese army came to Shanghai last winter, after they captured Heilongjiang, Jilin, and Liaoning in the northeast. Their presence has lingered in the bands of long-bearded ronin who roamed the farmlands in the outskirts, torching barns suspected of harboring rebel bases. Some say there's a war brewing on the horizon, and we should all gather our things and flee south. But no one's really running.

In French and English, my name is Vilma. After Vilma Bánky, the Hungarian actress. The Paramount's manager named me because he thought "Jingwen" wasn't sexy enough. This name is newest to me, like leather gloves that haven't been broken in. For my twentieth birthday, the manager gave me a framed photograph of Vilma Bánky in *The Son of the Sheik,* being dipped back into a kiss by the male lead. I've placed the photograph on my nightstand, where I study it sometimes, but I don't feel like Vilma Bánky.

In Shanghai, everybody wears multiple faces. Even the streets have more than one name—the temples, the banks, even the Paramount. Some mornings when I walk home alone at the break of dawn, I think about how terribly lonely it is to live in a place like that—a place where you can never really know anyone.

It may be hard to understand then, why nobody leaves the Sin City of the East, despite all the warning signs. But you see, the Shanghai I was born into had just entered its Golden Age of dancing and jazz. And there was no feeling in the world like soaring across the dance floor in imported silks, drowning in flying lights and the croon of trumpets, night after night, believing the morning would never come.

Six days a week, I drag myself out of bed to practice with the East Sea Follies, a ragtag troupe of taxi dancers from the Paramount who have banded together in our desperate need for a second salary. Our latest choreographer is Madame Evgenia Tsoy, a former ballerina of the Russian Imperial Ballet. As a refugee in Shanghai, she has grand visions of remaking the ballet out of whatever troupe of girls she can find, even if they are vedettes and burlesque performers. The latest punishment she has devised for unpunctuality? Footwork drills in a handstand for the entire duration of the warm-up. I much prefer taxi dancing, but unless you're Li Beibei, who can afford to throw her dance tickets off the edge of bridges just to watch them float down to the water, dancing with a salaried troupe is a necessity.

So, while Beibei inevitably sleeps in, no doubt dreaming of Neville Harrington's promise of a summer getaway to Qingdao in her silk-curtained canopy bed, I wake up late and do my makeup while slurping half-dissolved cocoa powder, my window thrown open for the morning sun. As I'm applying lipstick, I hesitate with my upper lip only half colored.

The carmine lip rouge looks like blood. Quickly, I wipe my upper lip on the back of my hand, smearing red all over my knuckles. But Huahua didn't bleed messily.

I turn away from the mirror.

My dappled shadow breathes heavily on the wall.

I throw open my window as far as it'll go before the pane gets stuck. There's a prayer of some sort going on at the Daoist shrine across the street, monks in black robes chanting scripture while shaking tambourines. The aroma of fresh crab shell pie floats into my room, and I crave the escapism afforded by a mouthful of pork and spring onion rolled in hot shallot oil. But the smell is quickly overtaken by that of soap flakes, as the elderly woman next door begins slapping wet underwear onto a laundry line outside her window.

Forget it then. I won't wear lipstick. With one last pat of rouge on my cheeks, I toss my coat over my leotard and fly out the door.

Unexpectedly, there is a package lying outside my door, which I nearly trip on—a rectangular white box embossed with a sheer pink ribbon. I tear the top off and brush aside the layers of tissue paper. A qipao lays nestled within, a designer dress spun from dark blue silk, with white, gold, and black fans hand-sewn in a daring geometric pattern. There is a little white card with a hand-scrawled note, folded into the middle of the dress.

I've made an investment you might find interesting.
—*Bailey*

I clutch the dress to my chest, burying my neck in pillowy silk. It smells like a department store, the kind I could wander around in for hours but never afford a single dress from.

I wonder how he found me in the sprawl of shikumen tenements stacked like a magician's castle made from cards. But with enough power, you can find anyone trying to hide in Shanghai. Power was like a fire juggler's ball—something thrilling to play with for a short while before you got burned. The art of it was knowing when to let go.

I imagine the way Beibei's smirk will slide off her face when she sees me wearing it tonight and laugh out loud, prompting a cat who is grooming his flank in the stairwell to turn his head and hiss. The memory of Huahua's mutilated figure dims, outshone by fiery poinsettia wreaths at the Firefighters' Yuletide Ball, which I sweep under arm-in-arm with Bailey, who just happens to turn out richer than Neville Harrington. I dwell on the shocked anger that courses through Beibei's veins.

I nuzzle my face into the silk again, to remind myself all I have to gain.

I arrive at the Lyceum's attic studio fifteen minutes late.

Between the splintered wooden rafters and dusty windows, a gaggle of cabaret girls have assembled with bloodshot eyes and tousled hair, masking their yawns under their hands.

The door shuts behind me with a bang.

I glance around wildly, but Evgenia is not here yet, which means on this glorious, auspicious day, I am spared. I scamper to the back of the studio like a roach, hoping to go unnoticed.

In the cozy, sun-lit studio, we should be doing our warm-up

stretches, but instead everyone is splayed on their bellies, poring over the morning's newspaper.

"What's going on?" I ask.

The lead dancer, a girl named Rongyu who has the best ballet technique in the revue, but is not very good at flirting, holds up the newspaper. "There's only one line about Huahua's attack in the *Shen Bao,* and nothing in the *North-China Herald.* Personally, I think it was an ex-lover or a pervert. That's the danger of being too successful as a taxi dancer—you're exposed. I prefer to secure my livelihood through my actual dance prowess."

I snort behind my hand.

Rongyu's eyes rove across the studio and land on me. I break into a dainty coughing fit that gives me just enough plausible deniability to recuse myself, but across the studio, Arisha and Zina's eyes dance with mirth.

"Laugh if you'd like, but you're just jealous I'm the only one among us who's ever taken *real* dance classes." There is something uncannily familiar about her smirk, right down to the bright red Tangee lipstick Rongyu is wearing. In fact, I know a girl who likes to wear the same shade.

In recent months, I have met more and more girls on Yuyuan Road who are trying to impersonate Li Beibei. It's been unnerving at times, to turn a corner after a tired night of dancing and spy three girls on the sidewalk wearing the same black velvet qipao Beibei wore to the Cathay Hotel's Venetian Masquerade last summer, smoking the same Craven A cigarette, laughing with the same arrogant scoff. It's almost as if they know they can't outcompete her, so they've decided to morph into a version of her. None of them are good at it yet, but I dread the day I cannot tell who the real Li Beibei is anymore.

Around us, the girls set down their newspapers, excited for the drama to escalate.

I know how to prod Rongyu where it hurts. "Right, and the only reason anyone dances with you, Rongyu, is because you tell dirty jokes when you're drunk. You're no Li Beibei, no matter how hard you try."

Rongyu looks like she's about to slap me, but at that moment the door bangs open, and Evgenia arrives, wearing a shin-length belted coat with fur cuffs. She is not alone. A young Russian boy follows closely behind, leading a spotted mule, and another young Russian boy behind him, hugging a cage containing two emperor tamarins.

The troupe falls silent.

Evgenia claps her hands. "Why aren't you warming up?" she demands in shrill English.

"Someone's lips were cut off in the cabaret last night," Zina pipes up, shrinking back as if Evgenia might strike her.

The director waves her hand. "You can live without a pair of lips. During the Bolshevik Revolution, the peasants guillotined the royals in the streets. This is not important right now." Evgenia yanks a collapsible chair out from under a mountain of our bags, dusts it off, and falls into it with her legs crossed. "I want to see Act 1, Scene 2. Hurry now."

We are supposed to be practicing the vaudeville operetta *Tuileries Park,* about a swan who witnesses an affair in a public park and is brought to court as a witness. The swan testifies against the lovers, who then murder her upon the bedewed park lawn at midnight. During the court scene, monkeys with cymbals dance upon the bar, and for no apparent reason at all, Arisha will perform a provocative contortion act upon the spotted mule's back.

"I know we've rehearsed this for four weeks already," I hear Zina whisper in Arisha's ear, "but I still don't understand the plot."

Arisha grimaces as we line up, dust and bits of hair clinging to our pink nylon tights and white leotards from sprawling on the floor. "There isn't one," she explains patiently. "More people will come see a show if it has dancing girls *and* monkeys imported from Brazil. By the way, Jingwen, your tights are ripped."

I rub my legs together self-consciously and yank my skirt lower. "Stop looking at my legs down there."

The music starts, an innocent flute melody full of airy tremolos and breathy scales.

Rongyu, playing the Swan, mimics rising out of water. She gasps in delight at meeting the sun and shakes her wings, shedding invisible water droplets. Her character, a botched tribute to Mikhail Fokine's masterpiece *The Dying Swan*, performs a sexualized, ballet-inspired dance with much flapping and leaping. I doubt any of the drunken audience will ever get the reference, but that's not what they came for.

Cue the chorus.

I flit out from the imaginary wings with the other chorus girls, a flock of cygnets, our arms spread daintily by our sides, and we circle Rongyu with a series of playful leaps en pointe.

"Cut!"

I halt mid-leap, facing the door, and Zina barrels straight into my chest. "Oww!"

I cradle my head in my hand, stars exploding before my eyes, as the scene in front of me swims into clarity.

There is an old man with long disheveled hair and a beard standing in the doorway, holding a snake walking stick and beaming with delight. I rub my eyes a few times to make sure I am seeing clearly.

"Hello, everybody," he says in Mandarin, with a cheery wave.

Evgenia uncrosses her legs in shock. Her thin eyebrows, which have almost disappeared from her plucking them thinner and thinner all the time, knit together. "Who are you?" she responds coldly in English.

"My name is Sui Feng," he replies, continuing to speak in Mandarin. "I will be the new director for the East Sea Follies, replacing you."

There is a collective gasp around the rom. Even the mule handler drops the apple he is feeding his charge. The chewed red fruit rolls through patches of sunlight broken by the spaces between the windows and comes to a stop at Sui Feng's feet. The mule neighs in protest.

"Excuse me?" Evgenia says, her voice becoming so stern chills run down the back of my neck. I can't help but picture Evgenia ordering Sui Feng to perform footwork drills in a handstand, and I accidentally giggle out loud. Arisha elbows me in the ribs, and Evgenia shoots me a death glare.

Sui Feng turns to look at me as well, his eyes lingering on my face until I step behind Zina to hide.

"The Paramount Ballroom has been bought by a new investor, and the old owner, who appointed you, is gone. I am in charge now." He makes a grand, circular flourish with his arms and points them at the door. "So I suggest you leave, before I call the police."

"I don't believe you," Evgenia says.

"I have the papers here." He produces a folded receipt from his pocket and holds it out for Evgenia.

Several of the girls standing up front squint in an effort to see how much they are worth on paper.

"You see his outfit?" Zina whispers to me. "Plain brown baggy shirt and trousers? There was a man who dressed like that in my hometown—I mean, the place I moved after my family moved to China—Harbin. He was rumored to be a *dragon* in disguise."

"Or he could be a Daoist immortal," I chime in, thinking of the bewhiskered, trident-waving guardians of the shrine by my home.

Evgenia snatches her handbag off the ground, and the door shuts behind her with a *bang*.

Sui Feng clears his throat loudly.

"Is there a dancer here named Vilma?" he asks.

Silence greets him. I wish the other girls would stop giving me away with their hostile glances.

"She's right here!" Zina declares loudly.

I elbow her sharply in the ribs.

"That's me, sir." I cower from his piercing, unblinking gaze.

"That can't be your name."

"I'm also called J-Jingwen."

I stutter accidentally and curse myself for it. Jingwen is the name I've worn since I was born, yet it feels unnatural asking a revue director to recognize it—as if I've worn a Qing Dynasty aoqun to the Paramount's costume contest and expected to win first place. Perhaps all my nights dancing on Yuyuan Road have changed me.

Sui Feng claps. "Ah, Jingwen! You will be the new leading lady of the East Sea Follies. It was a personal request of the Paramount's new owner." He kicks the half-eaten apple back at the spotted mule and the tamarins. "Now get rid of those creatures, please. They stink."

In the front row, Rongyu immediately bursts into tears, but nobody comforts her.

My head spins with the events of the morning. I recall Bailey's note, the soft texture of silk against my neck. All this time, I had thought he was referring to the qipao. But no—Bailey Thompson has bought the Paramount Ballroom, and by association, the East Sea Follies.

Slowly, I feel myself grinning.

Sui Feng paces the length of the studio's mirrors, as the mule and monkeys are led away. "You have been corrupted by the capitalist nature of this city!" he declares passionately. "Look at all of you flapping around the stage with these circus animals. You are the official revue of the city's most notorious cabaret, and you choose to squander your talent like street acrobats. It's a waste, I say!"

He bangs his walking stick on the ground for emphasis.

"I will show this city how it's done. We will perform a Chinese folk dance, showcasing our country's rich history and mythology."

"But nobody will pay to see that," one of the girls pouts.

"Oh, is that what the Russian lady told you?" Sui Feng cocks one eyebrow, amused. "Why should we only perform what our friends in the concessions are familiar with? The dancing tradition of this country is no less decadent than that of France and England. They want to see a burlesque? We'll give them a traditional water sleeve dance. They want a tango? We'll give them a fan dance. After all, I bet the gods from their countries don't know how to dance."

Although he is wizened and un-modern, this last remark rings with a certain flamboyance. Deservedly, it's greeted by silence. I like Sui Feng, I decide. In another life, he would make a winning cabaret dancer.

He beckons with one finger, and with some hesitation, we take a few steps in. Dust sparkles in the sunlight of the studio. I can smell the tingly scent of jasmine shampoo in the girls' hair.

Sui Feng clears his throat and spreads his hands like he is clearing fog from a window. "Once upon a time, there was a feral goddess who lived on Mt. Kunlun, at the western edge of the world. Bored of her immortal peach gardens and jade palaces, she decides to visit the Black Cat cabaret, which flourished in Shanghai in the 1920s. There, she embraces the sinful life of a cabaret girl—drinking with sailors and dancing until the sun rises. She even falls in love with a pianist from New Orleans, the birthplace of jazz! Completely enchanted, she refuses to go home. The Heavenly Court, wishing to bring her back to Mt. Kunlun, sends an envoy to find her in Shanghai." He beams. "The show will be a fusion of modern jazz and folk dance. We will hire musicians from New Orleans to perform the score. No donkeys or monkeys. Now, would you pay to see that?"

I glance around the studio to assess the other girls' reactions, which are all deadpan. Sui Feng might be a madman, but I'm almost scared to admit I like his ideas. A traditional Chinese goddess in a fashionable nightclub, a modern twist on the old—alternately, a vintage twist on the modern. We could start a new movement like Cubism.

I could see the French literati debating it hotly in the cafés, women with tall feathers in their hair lining up to see our show with breathless curiosity.

"Jingwen," Sui Feng says out of nowhere.

I jump. "Yes, sir."

"You will play the Feral Goddess." He points at a spot in the center of the floor. "Stand here."

The other girls scurry out of the way. Zina shoots me a sad look, as if one of her paramours has taken her hunting for a date, and I am the first deer to be released. My fate is their wildest guess.

Sui Feng reaches into his pocket and produces a wooden flute with the head of a gourd, which he waves through the air. "I'd like you to forget everything you learned from Evgenia. The hardest part of this training will be to reshape your minds. Currently, you all think like ballerinas, factory machines that move without thinking. Instead, I want you to dance like a waterfall upon a small hill, responding to every slightest shift in the direction of the wind." He brandishes the flute. "This instrument is called a hulusi. I am going to play a tune, and I want you to pretend I am a street performer and you are a cobra. Ready?"

He plays a smooth, low melody like the call of an owl.

"What, I—"

Sui Feng widens his eyes and dips his head emphatically, indicating I am supposed to begin dancing. I look to the other girls for help, but they stare back without blinking. None of them know what to make of him either.

I lift my arms by my sides and pirouette.

Sui Feng keeps playing, his head bobbing to the rhythm, so I lift my front leg in a kick and leap forward. I am not sure how to impress him, so I decide to attempt the fouette turn sequence from *Swan Lake,* which our company has only performed once, starring Rongyu. As none of us have real ballet training, and only fifteen audience members attended *Swan Lake,* I realize as I begin that I am more likely to injure myself. A look of horror crosses Arisha's face as she realizes what I'm about to do.

"Cut!"

I stop with my arms still poised overhead.

"You are doing ballet," Sui Feng says, brandishing the hulusi through the air. "I didn't say to do ballet. I said to pretend you are a cobra. Do cobras dance ballet?"

"No, sir."

"Start again. And stop looking at yourself in the mirror."

Sui Feng poses again with the cucurbit flute and continues the owl call, before building to a flowing tremolo that resembles a bubbling creek.

I undulate my arms experimentally, and sway from to side like a cobra facing its master. I can't actually recall the last time I had the patience to stop and watch such a performance in Shanghai. Abruptly, I decide to fall to my knees. Unsure what I'm doing, I flex my feet and writhe on the floor. Rongyu's face contorts into a grimace. Evgenia would have hit us by now for dancing the way I am.

But Sui Feng laughs through the flute. So I keep going.

The hulusi's call grows panicked, like the cries of a songbird being chased by a falcon. I thrash my arms wildly and roll over the scuffed hardwood floor, acquiring quite a few splinters in my thigh.

"Okay," Sui Feng says.

The company holds their collective breath.

He repositions his fingers along the pipes. "Now I want you to pretend you are a pit viper."

I attempt to tuck a few flyaways back into my bun. "Sorry, I don't know what that is, sir."

"Bright green snake with red eyes and forked tongue? The type of thing they sell in jars on Nanjing Road for five thousand yuan?"

"I—don't pay attention to the snakes for sale in the apothecary."

He ignores me and exhales softly into the mouthpiece.

The hulusi tune he plays is warm and lazy, like the shape of soft, green slopes in the Inner Mongolian grassland—which I've only ever seen in paintings.

I stretch an arm out tentatively and flap my hand like a snake's tongue, while being sure to hold my fingers delicately. Around the room, I can sense the other dancers' eyes boring into me like wooden screws, aghast at my outlandish performance. None of them know how hard I am working to channel every bit of focus I can muster into imagining I am a green snake in a scammer's basket on Old Tibet Road.

At last, Sui Feng sets the hulusi down.

"Very good!" He claps his hands. Zina is the only one of the dancers who echoes his applause. Sui Feng holds my shoulders from behind and pushes me forward, into a slice of blinding sunlight. As

I squint, he tells the company, "This! This is what I want from all of you."

Once he lets me go, I collapse in a corner of the studio.

Was that really Chinese folk dance?

The aftershock of the choreography feels foreign in my limbs, as if I've spent my entire life molding my body to fit inside a square box, and now I'm being asked to lie inside a triangular one. It's quite strange when I think about it. Within the Paramount's walls, I sell my Chinese blood like a novelty, yet there's nothing Chinese about the way I dance.

I sink down against the floorboards, content to watch as the others are now tortured by this crazy old man's whims. He calls them to the center one by one, and asks them to dance like all manner of things—snakes, birds, even a feather buoyed in a stream.

When the rehearsal is finally over, the other girls and I buy crab shell pie from a street stand, wrapped in our thick wool coats and knit mittens.

"Well, that was strange," I mutter, sinking my teeth into the flaky pastry.

"Do you think he's a pervert?" Zina asks, using her pie to warm her hands. "I'm not sure if I feel envy or pity for you, being the lead."

"Personally, I pity you." Rongyu blows on her steaming pastry.

I burn my tongue on hot oil and fan my mouth. "We're cabaret girls in China. Yet none of us know anything about Chinese folk dance."

Rongyu shrugs. "I mean, I guess."

I cozy up to her, jubilant at how she must be withering inside. "Now I know how you feel being the lead." I find I'm grinning as I chew another mouthful of pork and spring onion. "It certainly feels good."

All this because I charmed a mysterious American doctor on a whirlwind of a night. I understand how Beibei must feel now, about to shape men like clay under her long, red nails. Liqing was wrong. As a cabaret girl, I can be the puppeteer too.

Around the corner, we pass by a young boy holding a wooden flute, sitting beside a straw basket.

"Wait," I tell the others, and I run back.

The boy, who has been sitting with his back against the wall, watching us eat our pies, stands up and flashes a mischievous grin. "Ten yuan to charm the cobra."

I throw a coin into his hand.

CHAPTER FOUR

onight, I am going to dance with the new owner of the Paramount Ballroom, and I shall relish watching the other girls' souls
leave their bodies when they see.

Just the thought is enough to make me giddy.

I spend four hours getting ready in front of the mirror, as diluted
incense smoke from the Daoist shrine drifts through my window.
Although I've never believed in demons and ghosts, the aroma reminds me of my childhood running wild in Liqing's clinic, back
when things between us were simpler. There aren't many night
temple-goers, but with each offering to the shrine's animal-headed
gods, the flavor of incense changes, from cassia cinnamon to al-
oeswood to camphor. I know them all by heart.

I've put on the dress Bailey sent, which clings to my hips like a
second skin, and I can't help standing up and turning before the
mirror, admiring how thin my waist looks. My makeup table is
littered with crumpled tissues, each bearing a stain the shape of
my lips, in different colors—berry red feels too cold, pink is too
girlish, orange makes my skin look sallow. Eventually, I settle on
a deep brick hue, which draws out the brown in my eyes. As I dab
away the imperfections at the corner of my mouth, I think about
Huahua again, huddled in the center of the vast dance floor like a
bird with broken wings, predators circling her carcass.

Arisha said it once—if you wish to survive in this world of ours,
it's best not to dwell on others' pain.

I ride the tram up to the Paramount, whose crystal mien appears
to receive starlight sloshing from the heavens. The foreign playboys,
smoking cigarettes in their black cars while they wait for the doors

to open, wink and tap their ashes onto the sidewalk. I cross the street, shifting into that other skin of mine as I near the cabaret's front doors, my body washed in the Paramount's icy glow. Within these throbbing walls, we live a recurring dream that begins anew each time the sun falls.

There are poinsettia wreaths adorned with giant bows fixed to the columns in the main ballroom, a new addition to herald the celebration of Christmas in the foreign concessions next month. The waiters are wandering the halls carrying trays of warm chocolate liqueur, which a few of the dancers are tasting, their cheeks flushed as they giggle. A team of janitors run across the dance floor, pushing long mops. The maple floors gleam like the top layer of a brûlée. I can almost convince myself the previous night's ending no longer matters. After all, I almost have Bailey Thompson in my pocket, and he is the key to a new world.

From the bar, I order a green chartreuse cocktail, similar to the one Bailey gave me, although I can't quite figure out what he asked for, and I plop down in the same velvet couch we shared the previous night. As the orchestra begins to play, crystal-studded violin bows swaying together, I smooth my dress over my knees and practice my opening line.

With excitement: "Mr. Thompson, I knew you'd come! Thank you for your gifts, I can't repay you enough."

With no change in expression, slightly hard to get: "Mr. Thompson, I didn't know you were such a vaudeville fan."

With a mischievous grin and a wink: "Mr. Thompson, an interesting investment you've made, indeed!"

I trip over the English words "interesting" and "investment" and utter them to myself a few times.

The guests pour through the halls, receiving their complimentary demitasse of velvety chocolate with gasps of delight. The first dance is a foxtrot, a sly saxophone melody which moves the dancers around the oval dance floor in a tide of white legs and dark coats. I scan the crowd, looking for Bailey's black homburg hat. Instead, I spot Arisha dancing with the same German banker who always comes to see her, her silver hair glowing lavender under the spotlights. Beibei, known for her obnoxious entrances onto the dance floor, is nowhere to be seen.

A second dance passes, and then a third. I glance down and realize I've drunk more than half of my cocktail, and it's only a quarter past ten. Perhaps Bailey has run into a friend or associate, and he is distracted by conversation. I decide to look for him, taking care to arrange my fingers around the stem of my coupe glass.

Drink in hand, I wander the perimeter of the dance floor, under the poinsettia wreaths where the business executives are enjoying prime rib and trading gossip about their factories. The rich aroma of horseradish gravy makes my stomach growl.

A hand touches my waist.

I flinch and spin around, my lips tingling, but it's just Neville Harrington, a broad smile on his young, princely face.

"I never got to learn your name last night," he says. His cologne smells like flowers, his touch light like air.

An unexpected twist of events. I flutter my eyelashes, smiling with as much enthusiasm as I can muster. "Vilma," I tell him.

"Neville," he says, dropping his hand back to his side. "You are beautiful, Vilma."

The din of forks on white plates clatters around us like applause.

I know I should jump on my opportunity to steal him from Beibei—say something clever to seduce him, but I'm unable to think of anything. An awkward silence blooms, and he fiddles with his wristwatch.

"Do you like greyhounds?" I ask, remembering his tale of the Sunday Canidrome race.

"Yes," he responds.

Silence falls between us again.

Just then, three waiter boys emerge from the hallway, juggling a gigantic, three-tiered cake the size of a large chandelier. As I watch in horror, they make a beeline for us, knocking over wineglasses and crystal vases on all the tables in their way.

"A gift for you, Mr. Harrington," they chant in unison, setting the cake down on the floor. One of them is sweating down his forehead.

Swirls of cream rest atop the cake like naked breasts, dusted with silver sugar.

"Surprise!" Beibei bursts out of the center, throwing cream and silver glitter into the air.

I spin away to avoid having a second dress ruined. Neville, on the other hand, bursts into laughter and claps his hands. "That's brilliant!" he exclaims. He dips his fingers into the cake and tastes it. "Oh, it's very good!"

Of course she would.

I watch like a fool as Beibei plants a kiss on Neville's cheek, giggling madly, and he leads her away to the dance floor, dollops of frosting shimmying off her body onto the carpet. The waiter boys are left to haul away the uneaten cake, their arms and chests smeared with cream.

With a sigh, I return to my couch, where I upend my glass upon my lips. In my two years of dancing, I've never finished a drink this fast before. It's shameful for a cabaret dancer, who is expected to entertain guests until the sun rises. I cross my arms and slouch into the velvet cushions, as Beibei goes twirling by with Neville Harrington, again and again. She is wearing stunning red heels with ghillie laces that are impossible to ignore, the leather so shiny they could be wet with blood.

My lawyer friend is not here to see me either.

Like rain streaking a dusty window, my earlier excitement washes away. Now I feel stupid for spending hours getting ready, believing I had won Bailey Thompson over so easily. Perhaps Liqing was right about us cabaret girls all along.

I picture invisible strings connecting Beibei's wrists to Neville's, and I try to figure out who is pulling who, but the chartreuse makes me too dizzy to concentrate. And then Beibei drags Neville off the dance floor in front of me, and he dips her back in a passionate kiss, the crown of beaded silver flowers almost slipping out of her hair.

I can't even blame her for gloating.

My shoulders hung in defeat, I retreat back to the dressing room. A scented candle flickers romantically on the makeup table, a reflection of the flame swimming in melted wax. Even the ballroom is taunting me.

I blow the candle out, and the flame's last protest lights up my reflection in the mirror. In my frustration, I've somehow smudged the kohl liner on my right eye. I grab a towel and wipe all of it off—glitter, rouge, and sweat coming off in my hands. Alone, I shed the mask I wear.

Hot, restless despair fills my chest. I need to get out.

I drape my coat around my shoulders and slip out a door the kitchen workers use to take their smoke breaks, into the cold night. Ordinarily, I'm not the type of girl to skip shifts, but I'm in a strange mood tonight.

Along the ballroom's side, a straggled crowd hangs about the sidewalk to cool off from all the dancing, flushed cheeks and a night breeze that pierces like needles. I spy Zina working extra hard to charm a handsome man wearing a suit of green-brown tweed with billowing trumpet pants—trademarks of an unruly Japanese "modern boy." There is a flash of red along the sidewalk, and my heart races instantly. Two girls stand several strangers apart, smoking cigarettes while flirting with two different men, wearing the same red ghillie-laced heels Beibei wore. It makes me angry that's she's everywhere, and she seems to do it so effortlessly.

As if one of the girls can sense me watching her, she turns over her shoulder suddenly. I don't look away in time. We meet one another's gaze across the night. With a start, I realize she is a foreigner, with blue eyes like the sea and freckles dusted over her cheeks.

I don't know why I'm holding my breath—everyone is so lost in their own world, they wouldn't notice a dancer without her makeup playing truant.

Nonetheless, I can't shake the feeling I'm being watched from all sides.

I turn around a few times before I see him. It's a hawker across the street, who winks at me over towers of steaming bamboo baskets, piled higher than his own head.

"Osmanthus and rose-flavored rice cakes!" he calls cheerily, spreading his arms wide.

The steam rising from the baskets creates a mirage, bending the night into new, unfamiliar shapes. Behind him, the Jing'an Temple's pale vermilion wall stretches toward the sky like a looming predator.

I deliberate on my temporary freedom—my sad consolation prize for losing to Beibei tonight—which gives me strength or stupidity, and I decide to cross the street.

The hawker breaks into a wide smile when he sees me coming.

"How much for an osmanthus cake?" I ask.

He winks again. "For you, only one yuan."

I hand a small coin over, and he slips me a dainty golden cake carved in the shape of a diamond.

The next cart over is piled with glass snuff bottles, hand painted with cherry blossoms and rippling clouds. The merchant, who is reading *The Crystal,* tosses the tabloid over his shoulder when he sees me and begins rummaging through the pile. "This one is perfect for you."

He holds up a small, heart-shaped vial between his thumb and forefinger, painted with a swan gliding through lily pads.

For some reason the energy on this side of Avenue Haig, the street that separates the Jing'an Temple from the Paramount, feels different. I can't place what it is, but I feel it in the air—something fluid like a sky in a dream.

I squint at the vial. "Why?"

Pleased he has caught my attention, the merchant flashes a sly grin. "This perfume vial holds historical significance. It contained the poison that the late concubine Zhao Feiyan drank to commit suicide, the day she was stripped of her eventual title of empress. You can have it for four hundred fifty yuan."

I shrug. "Never heard of her."

The merchant shakes his head like there is water in his ears. "What! Don't you kids know anything about history anymore?"

I turn to go, and he follows me, weaving through eager merchants showing off silk fans and bronze platters of lotus roots stuffed with sticky rice, dripping with hot flower syrup. He waves the painted vial above the crowd. "Wait, wait, wait. Don't go just yet. Did you know Concubine Zhao became the empress? She was just a common dancing girl, but rumors say she practiced witchcraft and harnessed the power of a deadly goddess. She killed the sons of the other concubines."

I stop short, feeling offended by the story. Was he trying to compare me to Zhao Feiyan? "And why would I care if Concubine Zhao did any of that?"

His grin overflows with glee. "Because you're a dancing girl. In the old days, when girls chose to enter the palace, it was nearly always a death sentence. Yet hundreds of girls shed their blood within those red walls at the hands of other girls, all because they wanted a shot at becoming the empress. And that"—he nods at the Paramount, dripping light—"is another palace."

I think of Huahua again, with a bloodied pit in her face. The merchant flashes a grin, but under the swinging lanterns, his face cracks open like old stone.

I am suddenly glad we are surrounded by drunk young men and scantily clad girls with flowers in their hair—fragments of the Shanghai night that feel familiar to me.

"Why would I buy your vial after you've told me such a horrible story?" I chastise the merchant. "Leave me alone."

I bite into my osmanthus cake and spit it back out into my hand. It's not real, but coarse sponge cake dyed with orange food coloring.

I toss the whole thing into the dirt.

Without my noticing, the merchant's chased me before the

Jing'an Temple's main entrance. The temple's tall bronze doors rise to the sky in a yawn, spiked knockers resting on heavy rings. The darkness inside begs to be filled, the air cold but somehow inviting.

When I exhale, my silvery breath is drawn toward the velveteen darkness between the doors.

It's not like I have anywhere to go.

I have embarrassed myself waiting for Bailey, and now I have the rest of the night to squander. It's strange now that I think about it. I've danced across the street from the Jing'an Temple for two years now, yet I've never been inside. Most nights I don't even notice it. I've visited every other cabaret along this street and the next, and yet I've never visited the Jing'an Temple, which has stood for hundreds of years, before Shanghai ever tasted opium or jazz. Where better to escape from the modern chaos of Shanghai than inside an old temple?

As if I am a leaf drifting on a stream, buoyed by the chance stirring of a breeze, I slip through the doors.

The temple's courtyard spreads out before me like a snowy plain, glowing blue along the tops of the walls where the Paramount's neon residue clings like lint, unable to penetrate the temple's heavy shadows. Incense burns in a singular bronze burner in the courtyard's center, sending long tendrils of fragrant smoke toward the moon. I stroll past barren trees hung with hundreds of red-tasseled numismatic charms, which tremble in the wind like they are haunted. I wonder how there came to be so many, where there are no visitors to hang them.

On the courtyard's four sides, the worship halls have their doors swung wide open like brothels vying for customers. Pale red light seeps through the dark bronze doors, and in the glowing caverns I see the golden outlines of Buddhas and bodhisattvas—giant sleeping effigies who have lost their relevance in the Age of Glitter. I climb the stairs to the Mahavira Hall, which houses a colossal Buddha carved from white jade, crowned in gold. The old, red silk prayer cushions are pockmarked by the weight of many knees, although the hall is empty now.

Why didn't anyone rob temples, I wonder, when there was no one guarding them? A slice of the Shakyamuni Buddha's forehead might be enough to afford a mansion.

On the Mahavira Hall's other side, a circle of monks has gathered under a chestnut tree, lying in a sea of gold coins and ingots and drinking spirits. I recognize a bottle of Gordon's gin, which must have been bought from the Paramount's kitchen. They stare at me as I pass, a bewildered expression in their eyes.

I walk along the temple's tall red walls. Although I strain to hear, the laughter on the other side cannot penetrate the painted teak. For all I know, I've transported to a different world. Below the skyline, soft golden roofs glisten faintly in the moonlight, guarded by a pair of roaring phoenixes. I've arrived at the Guanyin Hall, shrine to a tall bodhisattva carved from camphor wood, her fingers delicately poised in a Buddhist hand symbol.

A cabaret dancer dressed in fine silk kneels on one of the cushions, gold tassel earrings trembling as she bows upon the prayer cushion, her palms flat on the red silk. A pair of black velvet heels peers out from under the hem of her qipao, which is silver-blue with embossed white peonies.

I would've thought she was a ghost if the buoyant way she carries herself was not immediately familiar to me.

"Ma," I say.

She tents her fingertips and glances over her shoulder.

"Jingwen, what are you doing here?"

"I didn't know you were religious."

My mother looks me up and down, and I do the same for her. She looks younger than I remember, her recently trimmed hair curled in a fashionable bob about her ears. "That's a really nice dress," she says.

"Thank you. It was a gift from a guest." I lift my dress to step through the doorway.

My mother winces as I place my weight on the raised threshold, the point of my high heels clacking on the painted wood.

"Sorry," I apologize, remembering that in the olden days, stepping on the threshold meant you were stepping on a dragon's neck. And it was not auspicious to insult dragons.

Up close, the goddess looms even taller. The expression on her face is uncannily lifelike, her eyelids fluttered shut like she's deep in slumber.

A platter stacked high with dragon fruits and other exotic-looking goods rests at her feet. I wonder if it's left out to rot, or if the monks add it to their treasure horde when the last worshippers have left.

"Do you know the goddess?" my mother asks me.

I stare into the goddess's face and marvel at how anyone could look so serene in the turbulence of Shanghai. "Guanyin Buddha, the Goddess of Mercy. Every old lady in Asia has a statue of her in their bathroom shrine."

Beside the effigy lies an ornate glass box, where worshippers are encouraged to toss ingots and coins as offerings. Guanyin's is full to the brim, although I still have not seen any worshippers aside from my mother.

My mother sits back on her heels. "Goddess of Mercy," she scoffs, and an expression of scorn clouds her delicate features. "Just like how the gangsters call your grandmother the Bringer of Fire. Names are worthless, Jingwen."

"What do you mean?" I gaze upon the goddess's gentle mien, tranquil as a sea devoid of waves. If that face is not the epitome of mercy, I didn't know what is.

My mother shifts her weight on her ankles. "The Buddhist Guanyin was the daughter of a cruel king, who ordered her to be executed. In the afterlife, she defied the guardian of Hell by playing music, and flowers blossomed all around her. The King of Hell was so shocked he sent her to the Fragrant Mountain, and she became a saint with a thousand arms."

My mother narrows her eyes a bit saying this, as if the Goddess of Compassion has somehow deceived her. "But the Taoists know her as a goddess of destruction—a demon who wandered the side of a mountain destroying villages before she attained enlightenment. They call her Xiwangmu, the Mother of Calamity. In the Hindu Temples, her name is Durga, the tiger-riding warrior queen who slayed cruel kings to free their subjects. The people love her because her violence is an expression of love. What do you think, Jingwen? Can violence be love?"

I look into the wooden statue's eyes. Her eyes are closed, her lips chiseled into a sigh.

So this is the Mother of Calamity who dances at the fictional Black Cat cabaret in our show—one and the same as the boring, enlightened Guanyin, whom mothers install in their sons' dumpling shops for good luck.

In Shanghai, even statues wear multiple faces.

"You seem awfully distrustful of a goddess you've chosen to pray to," I remark to my mother.

My mother laughs under her breath, and I can hear her world-weariness rattling in her lungs. "In Shanghai, you shouldn't trust anyone."

My mother was one of the first cabaret dancers Shanghai ever had. The Paramount's manager tells me she was the Li Beibei of her day, but I can't imagine that now as I gaze upon her gently lined face and tired eyes. I wonder if someday we will all wither away like the creatures that used to live in seashells, leaving behind nothing but a pretty porcelain husk.

An awkward silence blooms in the space between us. It only takes the blink of an eye, and we are strangers again.

I walk up to the pyramids of fresh fruit, delicately arranged at Guanyin's feet. In the center, elevated on a wooden altar, lies a plate of mangosteens.

I pick up one of the smooth, purple fruits.

My mother frowns. "You're not supposed to touch the offerings."

I look from the mangosteen in my hand to the goddess with her eyes closed. "Guanyin has expensive taste. I've only ever seen slivers of mangosteen in cocktails. Doesn't it grow somewhere in the south?"

That's when I notice a scroll pinned under a pineapple, with flaming calligraphy inscribed down the center.

An Offering to the Mother,
Courtesy of the Court of Exiles.

"What is the Court of Exiles?"

Before my mother can answer, a low whistling drifts through the open doors. I recognize the song immediately. It's a jazz tune that failed to be a hit in America but has bloomed in popularity in Shanghai.

Xiao Lei walks into the worship hall, holding a tin can of kerosene in his silver hand. Ignoring us, he approaches the pile of offerings and pops the cap off. Still whistling, he pauses for a second to regard the Goddess of Mercy. And then he upturns the can and drizzles the kerosene over the fruit, without a care for the world. I don't even realize how tense I've been until I see how relaxed he is. My mother and I watch, stunned, as he empties the entire can over the goddess's feast and shakes it to ensure he's gotten every drop, dark oil staining the altar silk and pooling on the floor.

Then, he lights a match and hurls it into the pile with gusto. The deathlike silence of the temple is shattered by tall, orange flames, which lick at the goddess's knees, so alive I forget it's dark outside.

"What are you doing!" I exclaim, rushing up to meet him. "Those fruits are expensive!"

Xiao Lei steps back to admire his work, his arms folded over his chest. "And I'm a fruit seller, aren't I, Miss Jingwen? Your grandmother has arranged it—you can have a free mangosteen whenever you like."

My mother glares at him. I guess Liqing never arranged for her to receive free mangosteens from the Blue Dawn.

"You've burned a goddess." I hate the edge of panic that has entered my voice. I think of the Mother of Calamity from the Black Cat razing the city, before I remember that our show is merely fantasy.

The fire eats through the pineapple rinds, and the awful stench of burning sugar begins to fill the air. I hold my coat sleeve up to my nose, but Xiao Lei steps closer to the flames. As the goddess continues to sleep, he reaches his silver hand out and sticks it through the fire. My mother gasps behind me, but of course Xiao Lei's silver flesh does not burn.

"Fuck the goddess," he retorts, drawing his hand back. Clutched in his fingers is the burning scroll, the beautiful calligraphy running and morphing in the flames.

My mother and I glance at each other. I can tell she is uncomfortable with the ease of my banter with the Blue Dawn gangster. If I'm a reluctant stowaway being dragged through the Shanghai netherworlds by my grandmother, my mother was never allowed to even participate.

Xiao Lei closes his fist, crumbling the scroll into blackened ashes. "I've been asked by your grandmother to personally escort you home. She says it's not safe for you to wander the streets alone at this hour."

"I've told her before, she's not allowed to bother me while I'm at work."

He tosses the empty oil can aside. "Sure. But you're not at the Paramount anymore. You crossed the street." He dusts his hands off, as if he's finished some gardening. "I'm meeting a friend for drinks at one a.m., so let's get this over with."

I turn over my shoulder at the door. The statue of Guanyin stands, her eyes still closed, wreathed in flames. Yet the fire drifts about her like water around a pier, without breaking her skin.

"The statue isn't burning," I observe.

Xiao Lei waves his silver hand. "That thing is so old, I wouldn't be surprised if the wood was petrified."

My mother suddenly elbows her way past us, her dainty heels clacking on the temple floor like gold-filled shoes on a carriage horse's feet. I catch Xiao Lei's eye—his eyebrows are raised and he is smirking.

"Ma," I call after her.

Having crossed the worship hall's raised threshold, she bunches her skirt in her hand to descend the stairs from the hall. I try to come up with something to say as she hurries down the steps, but I'm too slow.

"You didn't have to gang up with Liqing against her," I chastise Xiao Lei as he strides toward the exit as well, a leisurely bounce to his step. As the flames grow hotter, I have no choice but to follow.

"Your grandmother earned my respect."

In the distance, my mother's silhouette melts into the incense-muddled night, like water soaking into velvet.

CHAPTER FIVE

Xiao Lei leads me so deep into Shanghai's bowels, I'm not certain I could find my way out on my own. He's too comfortable in the ruined maze, occasionally leaping onto rooftops and running along the raised edges, his feet as light as air. I walk alone on the ground, passing little shops selling hand-carved jade figurines and colorful perfume sachets. My shadow swells and fades around the soft gas lamps.

It would've taken us five minutes to get home in a cab, but taking cabs is evidently beneath the Society of the Blue Dawn, who pride themselves on their ability to navigate dusty, tight passageways.

"How did my grandmother know where I was?" I ask the darkness above me.

"She always knows where you are," Xiao Lei answers from up high, leaping from the lion-shaped cornerstone of one roof onto the eaves of the next.

"That's not a violation of my privacy at all."

Xiao Lei doesn't answer. We pass a Turkish bath, which sighs through its vents, huge billows of warm steam rolling into the alley with a tight hiss.

I won't give up so easily. "Why do you do what she asks? She's just an old lady who would probably crack her head on the cement if you pushed her over. Why does she hold so much power over the Blue Dawn?"

This time, Xiao Lei leaps off the roof, landing beside me with a gentle stirring of the night air. "Because she made us as powerful as the gods."

We pass under a shikumen gate, carved with snarling dragons who I fear might come to life at any second.

"But there are no gods here to compete with."

Xiao Lei laughs, slowing down so that I can keep up. "It's not a competition, Jingwen. If the Blue Dawn did not run this city, the foreigners would bleed Shanghai dry like a sacrificial cow, after which they'd move on to the next shining metropolis—Hong Kong or Saigon maybe? There would be no dancing and parties for you."

I roll my eyes. "You make yourself sound noble. Yet you also sell the bones of your fellow gangsters on the black market. Is the black market in one of these alleys too?"

Xiao Lei's shoulders begin to shake.

"What's wrong?"

Then he turns around, and I realize he's laughing. "You think the black market is a physical market?"

My cheeks grow hot. I'd pictured the gangster underworld like a Saturday fish market, with rows of bones and organs piled in reeking mountains on wooden boxes of ice, the metallic scent of blood piercing the morning air. My ignorance only affirms the naïveté Liqing has always accused me of, which I'm sure she has complained to all the gangsters about.

"You can make fun of me, but I know it's not only bones and opium that get sold. I know there's a trade for dancers' lips."

I only say it because Xiao Lei thinks I'm naïve, but I regret my decision instantly.

The gangster keeps walking, but his shoulders suddenly stiffen. "That's very specific. Why dancers' lips?" he asks, his voice dangerously soft.

I hesitate, having not expected to touch a nerve.

"A man came by the clinic last night, asking if Liqing would sew a pair of lips onto a rich foreign woman. I think she only said no because I was there." I should let it go. It's not important when I have Beibei's contest to win. There are always duplicities attached to the Shanghai night, and meddling doesn't make them go away. "Do you know a man who sells dancers' lips?"

The words slip out of my mouth anyways. A small shiver crawls up the back of my neck.

"No, I don't know a man like that," Xiao Lei responds, briefly turning over his shoulder to meet my eyes.

It's simple to tell from how he searches my face to assess my reaction before he turns away.

"You're lying."

There is more life around us now. We pass a second-floor Japanese teahouse, where a girl dressed as a geisha dances with a fan. A lonely food stall in the middle of the road advertises hotpot on a flickering neon sign, strings of pork belly and cabbage baking under warm lights. A lone customer stares into a steaming bowl, his eyes sunken with exhaustion.

Finally, Xiao Lei sighs. "Do you really care about this? I thought you only cared about gentlemen who pay you gold ingots to sit by their side."

I don't know how to answer.

He kicks a pebble in the middle of the road. "There's a bar on Blood Alley, called the Dove House, where business deals are frequently made between gangsters and foreigners. Go there if you want to find the answer to your question. Now let's stop talking about this."

We walk in silence for a while, my thoughts swimming with the perfume merchant's warning about palaces and bloodshed. And now I can't help but picture Huahua's lips wrapped in delicate, brown paper, cradled in the lotioned hands of a stranger she's never met.

Xiao Lei stops in his tracks suddenly and holds a finger to his lips. I come to a rest at his shoulder and hold my breath.

A low twang echoes from the depths of the alley, beginning like the dying reverberations of a temple bell on the New Year, and growing louder. I rack my memory for a calendar of Daoist and folk holidays, which only Liqing celebrates in the depths of her clinic.

Glass bursts along the silent storefronts likes ocean waves

crashing upon a shore. A hawker and his customer scatter into the night, and in the second-floor teahouse, porcelain shatters.

Meanwhile the note continues to sing, as if someone has flicked the blade of a sword with a single fingernail, and the melancholy note has become trapped within the layers of time, vibrating and spreading in heavy, metallic ripples.

A copper-skinned young man with long, flowing hair bunched behind his head emerges from the far end of the alley, playing a mouth harp shaped like a small silver fan, which he is strumming with his right hand. He is dressed strangely, in loose, baggy clothes and leather boots. As far as I can tell, both his hands are made from flesh. Yet this new stranger's presence pops out of the night like a firework—an audacious violation of the precariously groomed Shanghai evening.

Xiao Lei grabs my arm. "Get out of here, Jingwen," he mutters. He is breathing hard.

But I can't tear my eyes away. In the space of a breath, I have been transported back to the Paramount's wheaten dance floor, only this time I am standing in the audience. The streetlamps become the roving spotlights I am used to bathing in. But this time I'm left in darkness, and upon the stage, worlds away and utterly bored of his mesmerized audience below, stands this stranger with his flippant self-assurance—which could rival Li Beibei's.

He lowers the mouth harp, a grin on his face. There is a dimple on one side of his face, which inflects like the skin of a cocktail pierced by a crystal toothpick. Yet just like the crystal toothpicks of the Paramount, which are polished until they are sharp enough to glide through flesh, his grin signals a thinly veiled threat.

"Xiao Lei," he says, with an expert twist of his neck that sends a ripple down his ponytail like a fan unfurling. "You burned my offering to the Mother Goddess. That was very rude."

"Nalan Zikai, I thought that might have been you I saw a few nights ago." Xiao Lei steps around me and draws his sabre, the blade singing with a flat vibrato in the cold. "Jingwen!" he hisses at me.

Recovering my senses, I stumble into the doorway of a locked and shuttered apothecary, glass crunching under my toes. The musk of dried herbs seeps through the old walls.

This stranger, Nalan Zikai, raises a mouth harp and plays a note that ripples like a drop of rain falling into a still pond. I become aware of the cold suddenly, the air in the alley condensing into thin tendrils of cold mist, which swirl around his ankles to the rhythm of the harp's vibrations. Through my breathless state, I remember to feel afraid. This is my grandmother's world that I have been stupid enough to wander into, and I can't find my way out without Xiao Lei's mercy.

The mist churns and separates, and settles into the shape of a wolf, which walks along the parapet above the shops. Its bristled fur is made from coils of smoke, its claws no more than mist.

Zikai grins up at his opponent with a glint in his eyes that is uniquely cruel.

"Go back to the Court of Exiles," Xiao Lei growls.

I recall the flaming note in Guanyin's offering pile, crushed in his silver hand. Slowly, the pieces fall together in my mind.

Zikai stretches his neck, teasing a strand of hair out of his eyes. "I came a long way. That would be a waste."

He is close enough now that I can count the silver ribbons in his hair. Objectively, he looks ridiculous—long hair is out of fashion even for women these days, but there is a piercing sharpness about his green eyes that makes me feel like I'm gazing straight into the eyes of a tiger. Dangerous, but softly beautiful. Like an ache. Instinctively, I take another step back, before my hands press into rough brick behind me. He plays another note, this one vastly uncomfortable, like a knife scratching down porcelain, and the wolf stalks closer, dwarfing the moon as it walks along the city line.

Xiao Lei watches the wolf, his eyes narrowed with what might be amusement. "The last time I saw you, it took you hours to call the wolf."

Nalan Zikai snickers under his breath. "I have always striven to become the best, no matter what it took—unlike what you've done. Instead of cultivating your strength, you chose to sell your body to that hag. Look, you've even bleached your skin to fit in with the foreigners."

Xiao Lei laughs in response. "The sun was too harsh in Hulunbuir. I left our heritage behind and became something that transcends humanity. No matter what you do, you're still just a horse boy from Inner Mongolia."

And then the wolf flies into the air, its mist body shimmering against the wind.

Xiao Lei raises his sabre, and the moment they meet, the sabre sings, vibrating like a plucked zither spring. The Blue Dawn's sabres are made from Heavenly Steel, ancient relics my grandmother claims are left over from the age where gods and demons blessed the weapons of warriors. I notice a few shoots of young clover, growing from a crack in the road, shrivel and die.

And then the note changes as the blade disappears into the wolf's flesh. Long streams of smoke pour out of the wound and blossom toward the neon skyline. I mourn the loss of its beautiful existence, which thrums with the same unignorable magnetism as its master. But Xiao Lei twists the blade, and the note inflects, the wolf unraveling from the ghastly music that bursts from its chest—until the mist has been completely swallowed by the light of a hundred cabarets on Nanjing Road.

Zikai bites his lower lip in a sneer.

Advancing slowly, Xiao Lei raises his sword and touches the very tip under his opponent's chin. A thin line of fresh blood rolls down the side of his neck, shining like a gem in the otherwise shadow-washed alley.

"Leave Shanghai. Do you hear me?" Xiao Lei speaks softly, but each syllable carries the weight of a blow. Although Nalan Zikai is half a head taller than him, Xiao Lei's shoulders are wide and powerful.

His opponent bares his teeth, a thread of crimson disappearing into his collared shirt. I think of the ghostlike strings that hold numismatic charms in temples. "This wasn't a fair fight. Not when you're part machine. It's not natural."

Xiao Lei reinforces his grip on the sabre, his forearm glowing pearl blue in the moonlight. "I don't have to be natural to be powerful."

"You aren't the powerful one. The old lady is." Zikai smirks in spite of the blade at his throat. "Leave her and come back to us."

Xiao Lei laughs with disdain. "For what? I heard the Court of Exiles wants to bring the old gods back to rule Shanghai, but they don't know how."

"Is that what she told you?" Zikai snorts. "Power is what she really wants, and she's afraid the gods would take it from her—"

"What do you mean by that?" I ask, emerging from my hiding place.

There is a frightening silence, as they both turn to stare at me. My heart thuds in my ears. For a second, I despair that even the dress Bailey gifted me is not extraordinary enough—I just want him to notice me. I am not used to being plain—to being ignored, and it makes me feel weak beside his brilliance.

On the Cathay Hotel's rooftop bar, some partygoers are shooting actual fireworks into the night, fiery peonies and green chrysanthemums blossoming in the sky.

Nalan Zikai's eyes widen, as if he is registering my presence for the first time.

I feel naked standing before him, and suddenly embarrassed, as if I am waiting for him to pass judgment. Although we don't know each other.

"Are you a gangster?" he asks with a curious tilt of his head—even though the motion causes a second tributary of red to run down his neck.

"No, she's a cabaret dancer I was escorting home." Xiao Lei shifts his body to block Zikai's view of me.

"I'm Yue Liqing's granddaughter."

Zikai, still pinned under Xiao Lei's blade, twists straighter, the way a wildcat does when it spots a mouse in the shadows.

A pang of delight flutters through my middle that he's registered my presence. I even feel a thrill at the petrifying revelation that I am about to be hunted. For a second, I don't remember what to say, before I remember that his tense exchange with Xiao Lei held meaning to me. I shape my words into a controlled whisper the way I've learned to at the Paramount, to claw back a semblance of control. "What did you mean, my grandmother's afraid the gods will take her power away? What did she do wrong?"

Zikai starts laughing, his voice booming in the otherwise silent labyrinth of alleys. "Where to start? Before she came to Shanghai, she stole—"

"Shut up," Xiao Lei says, lifting him by the shirt and slamming him into the wall, "or I'll drive this through your throat. Jingwen, this has been enough. I'll take you home now."

The rational part of my brain knows Xiao Lei is protecting me, but there is a new, hungry part of me that just wants him to move out of the way, so that I can study the silver ribbons in Zikai's hair and the musculature of his bare throat, tight under the sabre's tip.

Zikai, wincing, cracks a smile. "Ah, yes. Yue Liqing makes silver limbs for her gangsters so they may escort the cabaret dancers home. A noble cause—I see now why you traveled all the way to Shanghai from the grasslands of Hulunbuir."

Xiao Lei releases him roughly.

"Leave and don't come back," he repeats. "I spared you this time because we grew up together. Next time I'll really kill you."

Nalan Zikai dusts out the wrinkles Xiao Lei has left in his shirt. The display is arrogant and rebellious—everything the Blue Dawn's gangsters are not. "Even Liqing's own granddaughter recognizes she's a criminal. I would reconsider, Xiao Lei, before the Court of Exiles decides you're their enemy too."

He leaps onto the alley wall and sweeps his arm around his waist in a deep bow to me. On either side of him, the flashing lights of hotels and department stores graze the sky, dwarfed by his unfashionable clothing and bewildering style. The Shanghai I know feels so far away. Zikai lifts his head with a flourish of his ponytail and winks with a flirtatious smirk, before dropping to the other side of the wall.

The slanted perfection of his smirk remains burned into my mind.

Xiao Lei sheathes his sword with a dramatic stroke. "I thought you said you weren't interested in your grandmother's affairs."

I fight to hide my sweeping disappointment that we are alone now. I desperately set to work convincing myself that he is just another strange, fascinating glitch of the Shanghai night. Something to admire for ten minutes and forget.

I fold my arms over my chest. "I'm not," I protest, even as I study the dense, cold air above the parapet where the wolf had walked. What scores to settle could Liqing possibly have with a man from Hulunbuir who calls wolves out of the air?

Xiao Lei starts walking again and beckons to me gruffly over his shoulder. "Don't talk to Nalan Zikai if you see him around town. He may seem charming, but he'll be the death of your grandmother. Trust me, you don't want to live in a Shanghai where the Court of Exiles has brought their gods back. It would be worse than the foreign consuls."

I thrill at the thought of seeing Zikai again, before I banish the thought from my mind. It strikes me suddenly how naïve and stupid I've been this whole time, to allow my fascination to get the better of me. It's Bailey Thompson who has handed me my future on a silver platter, after all.

"I told you already," I snap at Xiao Lei, not bothering to conceal my annoyance. "I have no plans to get involved in my grandmother's affairs."

"I'm relieved to hear it."

High above the alley, two identical green fireworks burst into life, dancing like Nalan Zikai's eyes.

CHAPTER SIX

Sui Feng says I am to perform the dance of the Qingniao, a long-feathered bird as dark as the night itself, which lived in the center of the sun and served as the Feral Goddess's familiar.

"When the goddess was hungry, Qingniao flew over the ocean in search of exotic berries," Sui Feng explains, spreading his arms before him. "When the goddess came to Shanghai, Qingniao posed as a gargoyle atop a hotel during the day, and at night when the city came out to play, she would fly between the towers to admire the brassy, geometric spires, with the goddess possessing her eyes."

We are sitting in a circle around Sui Feng in the pleasure garden of the Alexandria Club, in the shadow of a burbling fountain with a cherub in the center. During daylight hours, the garden feels like an abandoned relic of a long-dead European empire, devoid of patrons kissing and making love under the palm trees. Instead, the winter sun pours between the golden forsythia branches, onto the carefully pruned arrangements of soft apricot ranunculus, orange Moroccan roses, and silver-green mint, which have been imported from Marrakesh or picked fresh in the Himalayan foothills, and kept alive in the dead of winter at an expensive cost.

If you did not know we were a dance troupe under the direction of an eccentric old man, we could pass for lazy water nymphs sunning around a fountain in the land of eternal summer.

"Jingwen, what do you think of the story?" Sui Feng asks, coming to a stop before me. His shadow blocks out the sun, which swells around him like an eclipse.

"It's very good," I reply.

He knits his eyebrows together.

I clear my throat. "Sorry. I meant—the Mother of Calamity used to be a demon before she was a goddess, so it makes sense that naturally, she would be drawn to Shanghai."

My story is greeted by silence. The palm trees wave their fronds in the winter sun.

Sui Feng strokes his beard, the sun swelling behind him until I have to look away. "Very interesting. I was not expecting you to be so familiar with the goddess's past. What do you mean, naturally she would be drawn to Shanghai?"

I feel like a rambling drunk, parroting my mother's story about Guanyin Bodhisattva. "The foreigners call Shanghai the City of Demons. Well, I think the Qingniao represents the goddess's past—the demonic darkness that always lives inside her, even after she has attained enlightenment. The Qingniao flies to Shanghai because it identifies with the sin of the city, and the Mother of Calamity can't help but follow."

I want to wince from how painful the silence is—the way Zina is staring at me wide-eyed like I'm crazy.

Sui Feng jabs at the sky suddenly, his finger catching on the edge of a palm frond. "That's right! When she comes to Shanghai, the cabarets and temples become one. The worship of the Mother of Calamity as a goddess and a dancer become one and the same identity. By portraying her—in venerating her through your dancing—you all become the goddess yourself."

He nods in a triumphant manner. By now, many of the girls have tired of his eccentricity. Zina stifles a yawn behind her hand, and I bite my lip as my throat muscles ache to yawn with her.

Sui Feng doesn't seem to notice. "Do you know why I have brought you here?"

Rongyu beams from the lip of the fountain. "Because where better than a garden to practice the art of dancing!"

To my annoyance, she is wearing the same yellow tweed coat that Beibei wore several nights ago at the Paramount. I want to hit her, as I remember my embarrassment at being stood up by Bailey and outshone by Beibei, after I spent hours dressing up. I can't help but wonder, what if last night, Bailey and I missed each other in the Paramount, but he was dancing with Rongyu the whole time instead? I realize how precarious my position is, when it was never truly earned.

To my relief, Sui Feng ignores her. "There are peacocks in the garden," he explains. "The historian Zhuzi believed the legend of the Qingniao was inspired by a melanistic peacock that lived in the forests of Yunnan Province, while the historian Muzi believed the Qingniao was actually a white peacock who wandered the fabled Mount Emei only at night—"

Arisha taps my shoulder, frowning. "Is it just me, or does he actually believe these things he's saying are real?" she whispers in my ear.

I can't help smiling as I'm reminded of Liqing and her oracle bones and nuo masks. But then my stomach sinks, when I remember how we fought.

"—anyways," Sui Feng is saying, "I want you to observe the resplendent fowl in this garden and learn how to move like peacock, dance like a peacock, *breathe* like a peacock—so convincingly that even the peacocks cannot tell you apart from their own kind. Remember that by portraying the Qingniao, you are welcoming the goddess's spirit into your own bones. This may be a nightclub, but I want you to transform it into a temple. I will require a demonstration at the end of the morning."

He flaps his hands at us, telling us to go.

I must admit, he's bold to request transforming a nightclub into a temple, when my mother was the only worshipper in the Jing'an Temple last night. Rather, his suggestion feels like the peony-lined road to bankruptcy.

We split up amongst the garden. I follow a stone path onto a slope of terraces overhung with date palms and pomegranates, the main path splitting into small coves nestled amongst the leaves to encourage illicit affairs. In the summer, the garden must be a paradise of lush, green forest, like the Hanging Gardens of Babylon. Some of that luster has been lost in the winter sun, but nonetheless, for a second, I'm able to convince myself I have left the grime and glitz of Shanghai. Perhaps this is the paradise Zina Minsky dreams of dancing in, which she won't shut up about. I hope she's happy now.

None of the other girls have chosen this section of the garden. I imagine that in the evening, the path will glow with orbs of soft light, moths colliding in the tangles of ivy that dangle above the wooden benches. At the end of the path, a manmade waterfall spills into an ornate black pool. I kick my left shoe off and dip my toe into the cold rush of water. It makes me laugh.

Through the velveteen splashing, I hear a soft squawk. It's coming from the other side of a living wall of forsythia and ferns. I slip my shoe back on and lean closer, softly feathered leaves caressing my cheeks. Indeed, I can hear the low cooing of birds.

I hold my breath, as if I'm about to dive underwater, and plunge my arms through the brush. The dried branches catch in my hair and leave tiny scratches on my face and arms. I emerge into a solitary, circular lawn, surrounded by a wall of pruned bushes. A single peacock, drinking from a tiered fountain carved from black marble, stands in the center of the lawn.

For a moment, the peacock and I stare at each other. Its back feathers are mauve in color, a single patch of iridescent green on the back of its neck. A hen, I realize.

The peacock loosens its wings and makes a half-hearted charge at me, chattering, and I take a tentative step back.

"Truce!" I declare, slowly extending my arms in a flowy wave, so that I can dance with it.

The peacock emits a high-pitched squawk and launches itself after me. I clap my hands over my ears as I flee back through the wall of plants, tearing branches and ferns as I go. The peacock comes crashing through the brush, its large feet padding expertly through the moss, as I slip and stumble back down the terraces.

I run all the way back to the fountain where we started.

Rongyu, perched on the fountain's edge, snorts as she fans herself with a fallen palm frond. She has shed her yellow tweed coat, which is draped precariously over the fountain's edge. Without it, I notice details about Rongyu's face—her gently cleft chin and beauty mark—that have been smothered under Beibei's likeness for weeks.

I dust plant matter off my leotard, which has been smeared with a nasty green stain. "You try it," I dare her. "You've just been sitting there."

Craning my neck, I search for Sui Feng around the garden. Where is he when I need him to see Rongyu slacking off?

Rongyu tosses the palm leaf aside. "Alright, I will." She marches up to the peacock, which has begun to graze in the shade, and twines her arms above her head, like she is belly dancing.

The peacock stamps its feet, chattering madly. And then it barrels toward her like an arrow, its head lowered and wings lifted to balance the weight of its torso. Rongyu scrambles up a plum tree, showering me with crumpled, brown leaves, while the peacock circles down below, squawking.

I laugh as loudly as I am able to.

"Shut up!" She glares through the branches.

After two hours, Sui Feng calls us back to the fountain. Most of the girls have brambles in their hair, small cuts on their necks and wrists.

"That was impossible," Zina retorts, shaking her head to coax her red-brown curls out of her eyes. There is a scrape on her cheek, and her fingers are bleeding where a peacock bit her. "How can he call this dancing?"

"I would like to see your progress," Sui Feng says.

Our collective efforts in peacock charming have lulled four of the birds to the fountain, two males and two females, who strut back and forth anxiously.

Sui Feng extends his arms behind his body and shimmers his fingers like a peacock's tail. The larger male bird stops pacing, observing him through sharp brown eyes rimmed with white feathers. I wonder how such a beautiful creature could have so cruel a beak. Holding the peacock's gaze, Sui Feng bends at the waist and undulates his arms in the likeness of a bird taking flight, and I'm inclined to believe he really does have wing bones.

Zina gasps and grasps my shoulder. Slowly, like a burlesque dancer opening a fan behind her back, the peacock spreads its tail. Sui Feng slows down his wingbeats so that we can see the intricate movements he is making with his wrist and fingers to create the illusion, and the peacock turns in a circle, trembling its tail feathers.

"How is he doing that?" I whisper to Zina, whose violet eyes are round as Daoist talismans.

Sui Feng drops his arms back to his side and beams. "Now, show me what you have learned."

The entirety of the East Sea Follies turns to stare at me. If I am truly deserving of my title as lead dancer, I will volunteer as the first to have my eyes gouged out by a raging peahen. I stand a safe distance away from the smallest bird and experimentally wave my arms around. It ignores me.

Sui Feng claps his hands. "There's four birds, what are the rest of you waiting for?"

I feel better when the other dancers surround me, in case someone like Bailey Thompson happens to walk along the bridge overlooking the gardens, I'm not the only girl undulating her limbs like a madwoman at an apathetic peafowl.

The peahen finally takes notice of me and decides to march in my direction, picking its feet up like a soldier parading in a brigade. The brown feathers of its crown waggle in the breeze, somewhat ominously.

"*Oww!*"

My head collides painfully with something hard and hollow-feeling. Without realizing it, I've backed into Rongyu, who is dancing with the larger male peacock. The bird squawks and continues to turn left and right with its shimmering train, which Sui Feng convinced it to reveal. I wouldn't be surprised if Rongyu later tried to pass it off as her own doing.

"Watch it," she hisses.

Just then a furious peacock cuts across the path, and another girl hurtles past us, but the heel of her laced sandals catches on mine, and I feel my balance swiftly toppled from beneath me. I grab for anything I can hold and seize Rongyu's leotard.

All of us fall in a heap in the neatly pruned rows of pink tamarisk and violet creeping thyme. I manage to stick my hand in peacock shit. In that moment, it suddenly strikes me how ridiculous the whole situation is. I cannot help it—I burst out laughing. A few of the other girls stare at me bewildered, sticks and imported earthworms in their hair, before they too, begin to laugh. Even Rongyu, who has only ever sneered in my view, chortles behind her hand.

I start laughing and I cannot stop, my belly spasming and tears flowing from my eyes. With a start, I realize this is the first time my laughter has felt genuine in many months, and it makes my chest sore to laugh like this. Rongyu doubles over, her coat slipping into the fountain, and in that rare moment, I see us like a voyeur peering through the window of our lives. We are the untouchable girls, drunk on our youth in the glamour of Shanghai, like the wild maidens in Greek paintings who wear ivy in their hair and dance in streams flowing with wine. And the only souls in the universe who understand the feeling are the others.

Through my tears, I catch sight of Sui Feng's expression.

"Silence!" he bellows.

We shut up instantly. In spite of the ridiculous circumstances—the sunny garden we have illegally broken into on the order of a bewhiskered old man, blue-crowned peacocks strutting about the lawn while they shit and squawk at leisure, our dirt-smeared faces and torn uniforms as we ruin thousands of hours of expensive gardening—I am more terrified than I ever was facing Evgenia.

"You think I'm a bumbling old fool, eh?" Sui Feng marches toward us, his hands planted on his hips.

Above the garden, the skies suddenly darken, gathering dark gray clouds rimmed in fiery gold, which churn and roil like the sea. The sunny garden we chased peacocks in vanishes, replaced by a dark, monochrome world of shadows and coldness. A deep, groaning rumble begins high up in the heavens.

Rongyu inhales sharply. I find I've instinctively latched onto Zina's elbow.

Sui Feng, who appears to have been clenching his teeth, rubs his jaw.

"If you are serious about this, you will do better," he says, more softly. "In your free time this week, wander into the wilderness and channel its spirit. I will ask to see the Dance of the Qingniao again next week."

And then the loud rumbling stops. The clouds split apart, allowing the sun to spill its bright rays back into the garden. I catch Zina rubbing her eyes, desperately hanging onto the last wisp of a cloud before it scatters, leaving a clear winter morning.

"Did he . . . make that happen?" Zina asks, as we rise back to our feet. The grass has left wrinkles in my thighs and forearms.

Rongyu flips her hair in our faces, catching Zina in the mouth. "Don't be ridiculous. He's an artistic director, not a magician."

And like that we return to being enemies once more.

Another few nights pass, but Bailey still doesn't come to see me. Every night when I return home from the Paramount, I pull the white box out from under my bed and ruffle the layers of crepe paper aside, to run my hands over the dress he sent—soft silk and boldly-colored fans catching under my fingertips. When I think back to the lone conversation we had, I can no longer recall the timbre of his voice, although I remember his deep, lulling laugh.

A wave rises in my chest, that might translate into panic. Neville Harrington has come to dance with Beibei three times this week already, and Arisha has found a Kuomintang general to shower her with bouquets of lilies. I'm falling behind, and I never even found out how wealthy Bailey actually is.

I visit Guanyin Bodhisattva again, on a tired night when the sky rages with brightness, and the only thing that stands out is the sunken darkness surrounding the Jing'an Temple. The wind is wilder tonight, the red wooden talismans beating against gnarled branches with sharp clacks. Tonight, the monks are nowhere to be seen, although I think I spy a golden ingot buried between the roots of a gingko tree.

Guanyin Bodhisattva meditates alone tonight. The wooden statue towers over her lonely room, her eyes closed, unscathed by fire. My neck aches from looking up at her. There is a new plate of fruit on the altar at her knees, which has softened from sitting out for too many days, the flesh growing pulpy and brown.

The wind sweeps through the tall, open doors, lashing my hair around my face. The statue's hair does not move, carved from fragrant camphor wood. I stay, gazing up into her gentle smile, until my fingers become numb from the cold.

On the nights when I'm not dancing, I end up looking for Sui Feng's wilderness. I'm not sure what the point is, trying to appease a madman who thinks he can make me into a star, but I haven't stopped thinking about the Mother of Calamity, turning the heads of every sailor and prince in the Black Cat, and Guanyin Bodhisattva in her shadowy cell, put on show like a prostitute, smiling serenely into the night.

After a few nights of wandering, I end up on a university campus by a large, empty road. I spend a few minutes just standing at the edge of the road, the soft, golden fields of weeds trembling before me under a light breeze. A river flows between the fields, the water a deep azure that borders on black. I close my eyes, until all I hear is the rattling of the milkweed husks and the lazy sloshing of the river.

I wade through the yellow fields in my leotard, tiny thorns and leaf edges getting caught in my tights. Farther in, two rows of tall, still trees lean into each other from either side of the river with their bare, tangled branches. There are a few short bridges that span the river's width. On the farthest bridge, I can make out the dark form of a university scholar sitting under a lamp with a textbook.

I kneel in the moonlight, at the edge of the dark river, and practice flapping my arms like wings.

I hear a laugh in the stillness.

It's coming from the trees above me.

I grab a rock from the dirt field and hurl it into the branches. It snaps a few twigs, before clattering back down in front of me. Following it, an arrow whistles down through the air, and embeds itself beside where the rock has fallen. The shaft is adorned with green feathers.

Nalan Zikai, the green-eyed boy from Inner Mongolia, laughs from the trees above.

Of all the destinations I might have guessed the night would lead, it would've never been to him. I blink furiously to confirm he is really lounging in the trees above me at this strange hour of the night, my heartbeat rising behind my ears like a wave.

"The Dance of the Qingniao," he muses, twirling a second arrow between his fingers.

"How do you know?" I ask.

He grins through the dried twigs. Like the first time we met, his presence takes up the entire night—his enthusiasm much too alive for the hustling, impersonal Shanghai pace. But I am a cabaret girl well versed in the study of personalities, and tonight I've come guarded against the magnetic effect he has. I choose to study him like an artwork in a museum instead—his high ponytail falling carelessly over his head and his fingers draped loosely on a branch, his elbow hanging down by his neck.

There is a haughty note to his voice when he speaks next. "I have studied martial arts and shamanism my entire life. I'm very familiar with the Feral Goddess. It's sad that here in Shanghai, you nightclub girls reduce the complicated history of an ancient legend into some sad, erotic fetish."

I bite back a scoff at his words.

He is the type of person, like Beibei, who thinks they can get away with saying anything they want because they are charming. It's a characteristic I've only ever seen in cabaret dancers, and I can't deny it fascinates me that a vagrant warrior from the grasslands could display the same attitude. But I am a professional too. I've resisted Beibei my entire stay at the Paramount, and I won't be soft for him after he has discredited my entire livelihood.

"The cabaret show tradition is rooted in the art of seduction and heartbreak," I inform him. "You can conjure wolves, I can conjure fantasies. These nightclub girls you speak of are capable of terrible things."

Zikai's green eyes dance with confrontation.

"Oh, is that so? I've studied with half-saints in the north and battled tigers in the west, on my way to becoming the most powerful shaman in China. You know, out in the martial arts world, it's not like here where your gangsters are all men. There are women who fight, in colorful silk robes with long, elaborate hair—"

"Long hair went out of fashion ten years ago," I cut him off.

He narrows his eyes, looking faintly amused. Perhaps because he himself has the longest hair I've ever seen, gathered high above his head. "Alright, well, what have you done in your life worth mentioning, then, city girl?"

I rest my hands on my hips and hold my chin high. "I danced with the owner of the Huarui Bank once."

He starts laughing again, so hard the entire tree is shaking.

The entire night falls away under his pretty, laughing face, but this time it annoys me more than anything.

My cheeks grow hot. "He still sends me fruit baskets every now and then. Last year, I got to have lychees on Christmas day."

Zikai clutches at his chest, his shoulders still shaking. "Oh, a fruit basket you didn't have to pay for. What a glorious achievement."

I glower at him through the dried branches. "Why don't you come with me then? I'll introduce you to some girls, show you what they're capable of."

Zikai howls with laughter, barely able to form words. "Thank you, but I didn't come to Shanghai to dance in pleasure houses. I have business to do."

I am so angry I would scramble up the tree and slap him if I could. "Then go do your business. I'm trying to concentrate."

In the river, his reflection arranges itself to face away from me. The rustling in the branches falls silent. Our whole interaction has been infuriating, but I ventured this far for a reason, and I won't let him distract me from it.

I take a deep breath to refocus and make a small wave through my wrist, the way a peacock's neck flows when it looks up at the sky. In the still waters, I imagine my wrist's shadow is the peacock herself, stirring in her nest at the first peek of moonlight.

A loud twang rings into the night air, sweeping through the tips of the goldenrods. High above me, Zikai begins to play his mouth harp. The deep reverberating notes stir a chain of ripples through the water, breaking my reflection.

I stop undulating my arms. "What are you doing?"

The branches crackle, and I'm showered by broken twigs. Zikai raises his eyebrows. "It's not your garden. I'm allowed to do whatever I want here. You showed up after me."

He plays a scintillating tune, quivering with yearning. The melody belongs somewhere pastoral, at the edge of a mountain or waist-deep in a river. I comb bits of twigs and a caterpillar out of my hair and move to the other side of the bridge, away from him.

But I can't concentrate while he is playing.

The melody is otherworldly and soul wrenching. Beautiful isn't the right word—it makes the field seem a lot vaster, as if we are the only two humans in an immense wasteland. It makes me yearn for the comfort of the pulsing lights and warm bodies on Yuyuan Road.

After a while, I walk back and stand directly beneath him—him in his carefree, high-handed attitude, so antagonistic to the artfully constructed performance I have perfected for my every blink.

"Do you really believe the Blue Dawn bleaches their skin to look like foreigners?" I yell over the echoing refrain of his mouth harp.

The tune fades into the wind. Zikai lets his arm relax, the small, fanned instrument hanging loosely in his fingers. He grins and flicks his head, indicating I should look to my left.

Something cold and heavy brushes against my cheek, not a breath but the absence of a breath. I turn my head to find myself staring straight into the dark, empty eyes of the mist wolf, who is snarling in my face. I stumble back against a tree root and clutch at the tree to steady myself.

Zikai laughs from up in the branches, his devious eyes flashing between the branches.

The wolf shakes its head and paces around the trunk, its tail flicking.

"Want to see a new trick I'm teaching her?" Zikai asks.

There is the ringing of metal against metal as Zikai draws his scimitar. He flings the sword into the air, rather lazily. Time seems to slow down as the blade tumbles down, inverting once, then twice. Out of nowhere, the wolf launches from the ground to meet the sword midleap, catches the hilt between its teeth, and flings it around.

The sword flies toward me but I don't have time to react. Cool ice brushes my neck as the sword flies past my chin. The blade quivers in the tree beside my neck, singing with a pleasant note.

I close my eyes and lean my head back against the tree, my heart thudding.

"That wasn't necessary," I breathe.

Zikai leaps down from the branches and yanks the scimitar out of the tree. The blade flies past my face again, taking a few strands of hair with it.

Up close, he is almost an entire head taller than me.

"I don't care whether the Blue Dawn actually bleaches their skin," he hisses. "Although, you know, you have something in common with Xiao Lei. Both of you have lived in foreign-occupied Shanghai for so long, you're neither foreign nor Shanghainese."

"I don't bleach my skin." I tuck the now shortened strands of my hair behind my ear, but they won't stay. "Are there other martial artists who use the dark arts to summon wolves out of smoke?"

"They aren't dark arts," Zikai retorts, his green eyes flashing. "The Tengri shamans of Inner Mongolia believe that all living things have multiple souls. Some souls perish with the body upon death, but the shadow soul is free to leave. In the Violet Thistle

Sect, where I grew up, we learned to bind the shadow souls of animals who died on the plain. It's true there are others from my sect, but we're from the far north. I can't imagine why they'd come here."

I take a step back, surprised at his sudden wrath.

He continues. "Anyways, you city people are just like the higher-ups in the Court of Exiles. Anything you've never seen before is an inferior, dark art. I'm the first disciple of an Inner Mongolian sect to ever be accepted into the Court of Exiles, and I'll show them what a shaman with Tengri blood can do. It was fun sparring with you, but I'll leave you be to bowdlerize the historic dance of an ancient legend. That's all there is to Shanghai in the end—butchered folk dances and cute drinks with paper umbrellas."

With a small bow, he sheaths the scimitar and begins to walk away with his wolf.

I resist the sudden, bewildering urge to reach after him. It's not that I desire him—his pockets are empty of the gold ingots I like—but his presence is overwhelming, like a dazzling stage light that has cradled my bare limbs through a performance, suddenly switched off.

I decide I'm not done with him yet. I'll show him cute drinks with paper umbrellas. "You know, I bet I can outdrink you."

He pauses midstep, spins back around as I knew he would, his pride getting the better of him. "Excuse me. Along every wanderer's highway, from the Altai Mountains in the north to the golden temples of Xishuangbanna in the south, I've drunk with bandits and madmen. Maybe even one or two gods."

"But you ever try gin made in a bathtub?" I'm smiling now, reaching for my coat, which I've draped over a nearby log. "Absinthe from a glass fountain?"

Zikai narrows his eyes. A strong breeze ripples through the field, bowing the heads of all the golden rushes. He straightens. "Alright, then. I challenge you to a drinking contest."

CHAPTER SEVEN

And so I bring the shaman from the Court of Exiles to Blood Alley. By now, the shadowy street has come to life—a sea of warm bodies and low voices under a row of European-style buildings punctuated by cheap, flashing signs. In the empty spaces under torn awnings, the artificial scent of men's cologne mixes with that of blood.

Nalan Zikai lingers in the doorways of the bars, which gape like smaller, hungry mouths. Strings of holiday lights line the dark entrances, glowing like pearly teeth. Occasionally, one of the mouths will exhale blue-gray cigarette smoke, and down a short, black throat, we watch drunk sailors in white uniforms turn laughing girls under their arms, both partners stumbling against the walls.

"So, this is where dancer girls do their drinking?" Zikai asks me.

Electricity races through the veins in my wrists, bared to the cold. "Yes," I lie, although I've never set foot in any of the bars in Blood Alley.

Like voyeurs gazing through the orifices of the drunken city, I take him down the street, pausing to peer through fogged windows and doorways—curtains the bluish gray of a liver, a table of laughing courtesans beating like a heart. We pass under the Cabaret Voliéré, where a trapeze dancer hangs from a suspended hoop in the second-floor window, washed in a lavender glow. Somewhere in the attic above her, Liqing is burning incense in offering to yet another nuo face, maybe the one with blue skin and a monkey's features. An odd sense of rebellion fills me as I stare up at the fire escape where she liked to sit and inhale the night air. We have not made up from our fight, and now I am sharing a drink with the enemy.

It is a thrilling game to play.

A door slams shut like a snapping pair of jaws, and we freeze, caught in a huff of its breath, which smells like sweat and imported beer.

Zikai inhales sharply.

This deep in the alley, the streetlamps from the main roads cannot reach the storefronts. Rather, the pulsing neon dances across our bodies like faded candlelight, cutting Zikai's face into shadowy squares. Before an older bar with pockmarked wooden doors, a slender white dove in a gilded cage hangs under the awning.

As we approach, the bird chirrups and hops from the floor of the cage onto its perch.

The sinews in Zikai's neck tighten, and I delight in surprising him.

"This one?" I suggest.

And then I catch sight of the bar's name, flashing on a neon sign.

The bird tucks its head under its wing to preen the feathers there, and a singular white feather drifts down, swaying from side to side as if to tease us. Zikai reaches his hand out, almost trancelike, and catches the feather between two fingers. "It's your world," he says, examining the feather in the light. "I'm just your guest."

"Do you know what the letters say?" I indicate the pulsating white sign.

"No," he says, squinting at the English letters.

"The Dove House," I read, as I push past him and grab the handle of the heavy metal doors.

Zikai puts his hand on my shoulder.

I still under his grip, which is firm but warm.

"Do you see this?" He holds the feather up to the sky, so the neon shines right through it.

"Yes," I breathe. I glance from the feather to him, a childlike wonder etched across his high cheekbones. "What about it?"

"The quill of the feather isn't hollow. It's not real."

I turn to observe the dove again. It swivels its head around to regard me and opens its beak in a scream. This time I stare down its throat at the sea of silver gears that turn inside it.

"You seem surprised," Zikai observes, before yanking the door open.

A new type of smoke pierces my lungs, sharper and more herbal in aroma than the kind that wafts from cigarettes. Everything in the Dove House is washed in darkness except the bar, above which a hanging lamp illuminates the black wood counter like a magician's stage, expertly set with black napkins folded in the shape of calla lilies. Behind the counter, glistening decanters of spirits line shelves made of the same black wood, which spirals and curves in the popular geometric fashion, punctuated with tasteful accents of white.

There is laughter in the darkness. Through the smoke-filled air, I can barely make out carnations in dark hair and white fedoras. Despite the lack of gilded ceilings, the patrons are dressed no less nicely. With each blink of my eyes, the scene before me shifts, like gears turning in the belly of the dove. The flash of a silver ring against a lowball glass. A man's hand resting on the sheer pantyhose encasing a woman's leg, for a second before she turns her body away. There is a sweet, drunk smell hanging in the air, of peanut shells, watermelon slices, and smoke.

I am uniquely aware of Zikai's presence behind me, his green eyes wide as he admires the mottled assembly of bottles on the wall, the jewel-toned shine of their labels. I find I'm smiling. The thrill of entering this wholly new world pierces me like a shard of glass, like I am breaking rules I did not know I was living by. This is not the type of bar to which I belong, but tonight it is the world upon which I am a host and Zikai is my guest.

We slide onto mahogany barstools at the counter. The mechanical bird swiftly leaving my thoughts, I suppress a laugh behind my hand because Zikai looks so out of place, with his high ponytail and baggy clothes.

The bartender, who is pretending to shine already-clean glasses with a black rag while eavesdropping on a nearby conversation, raises his eyebrows to indicate we have his attention.

"The absinthe fountain," I request.

The bartender smirks and slides the glass back onto a rack hanging from the ceiling. His forearms are inked with flying hearts and swallows, which are faded into his skin. In the space of a single blink, he has set a muddled, green glass bottle upon the counter with a dirty brown label. The absinthe itself is followed by the absinthe fountain—a globe of iced water nestled atop a gold post, which towers over the bar like a streetlamp illuminating a dark alleyway, fixed with an ornate pewter spigot. Beads of condensation roll down the sides like tears.

"What, this is a lamp," Zikai remarks. He swipes his finger down the middle, wiping away the dribbling water. "How are you supposed to drink out of it?"

The bartender sets down the remaining accoutrements with the care of a mortician laying out his dissection tools: two flared lip glasses, a silver spoon, and a small glass pot of sugar cubes.

"With this." I pick up the silver spoon, which has grilles carved in the figure of a sleeping fairy. "I'll show you how the literati of Shanghai drink."

As Zikai leans over my shoulder to observe, the ends of his hair gently grazing my bare shoulder, I lay the spoon over the glass and gently balance a sugar cube over the grilles. And then I uncork the decanter of absinthe, releasing the sweet aroma of anise into the air.

I pour the absinthe like tea—in imitation of a phoenix bowing her head three times—before I realize I've messed up. A quick glance at Zikai confirms he hasn't noticed. Hiding my grin, I force my wrist to be still, and a slender waterfall of olive liquor drips onto the sugar cube and through the spoon, crystals of sugar fluttering through the grilles like snow. Once enough absinthe has swirled to fill the bottom of the glass, I move the glass under the fountain and twist the spigot to a slow trickle.

In Shanghai, even the drip of cold water into absinthe is not silent. Water dribbles through the grilled spoon like rain off the parapets overlooking the city streets, dancing upon the absinthe's skin like raindrops in the Huangpu River. The effervescent green lightens by a single degree with every drop.

When the cocktail has achieved a pale olive color, I twist the spigot off.

"That's a lot of work just to water down your spirits," Zikai complains as I hand him the glass. He raises it to his lips, but I place my hand over his to stop him.

"You have to drink slowly. It's how the artists do it."

He snorts and closes his eyes, long lashes brushing his cheek. As he drinks, he lifts a pinky from the glass—perhaps for dramatic effect, or perhaps because he truly does fit in with the flair of Shanghai, despite his odd fashion sense. I fight back a smile because I find him truly fascinating.

For a moment, Zikai is completely still as he savors the green fairy.

I find I'm leaning in to study the details of his expression. He has a mole beside the corner of his left eye, and his eyelashes are unusually long for a boy. Both features, which might be considered feminine by traditional beauty standards, create his air of mischief. I can't figure out what he's thinking, and it drives me a bit mad.

When he opens his eyes again, he makes a grimace. "This tastes like licorice cough syrup."

I snort and begin to mix another glass for myself. "No, I saw the way you closed your eyes. You liked it."

"I did not," he insists.

I tilt my glass back a bit too far and manage to inhale a bit of absinthe, which stings the membranes in my nostrils. Zikai sets his glass back down, looking alarmed, as I burst out coughing. Absinthe runs down my cheek and under the collar of my leotard, cold like a shard of ice, but I wave my hand to indicate I'm fine.

"Let me help you." He reaches out with his thumb and wipes a drop of absinthe from my chin.

I freeze under his touch, caught in the way his loose shirtsleeve falls down his forearm, the way he smiles just a little bit when he touches me.

A saxophone begins to play a swooning melody out of the darkness behind us.

Clearing my throat, I lean my elbows down on the polished black wood, as a pleasant warmth spreads through my belly. The absinthe, of course. The counter, oiled so thickly it shimmers like water, displays the slightly flushed faces of a young man and a young woman—one dressed like a bandit from the paintings hanging in Liqing's clinic, the other wearing a white leotard under a heavy wool coat.

Zikai twists to one side and rests one arm on the counter, facing me straight on. "So, you've never introduced yourself. Tell me who you are."

I smile as I continue to sip my absinthe. I decide I won't look at him anymore. It's safer that way. "My name is Yue Jingwen. Born and raised in the beautiful city of Shanghai. Lead showgirl of the East Sea Follies, dance hostess at the Paramount Ballroom."

He touches his hand to his chest. "Zikai from the great clan of Nalan," he announces. "Shamanist cultivator from the Violet Thistle Sect in Hulunbuir, appointed to the Court of Exiles at the Yearly Gathering of Half-Saints in Shambhala City. Wanderer and appreciator of fine spirits and slightly charred lamb satay. Destined to someday hold the title of Highest Cultivator of the Middle Kingdom."

I laugh into my glass. "You say that a lot, don't you."

"Only if people ask."

Zikai and I set our drinks down simultaneously. He wipes his mouth on his sleeve. Then, slowly, he grins, as if we have been sharing a secret joke all along. "I have a deal to propose to you."

I can tell he's been waiting for this. Suddenly, I remember to be wary. If Xiao Lei's words hold any truth, then Zikai wants something from me. And Xiao Lei had warned—Zikai had that maddening quality that made you want to give him whatever he asked for.

"What is it?"

The shaman from the Court of Exiles reveals his mouth harp, which he wears around his neck, and begins to toy with the fan-shaped keys. "I overheard your conversation with Xiao Lei the other night. You have suspicions your grandmother is sewing the lips of your fellow dancers onto rich foreign women."

I fold my arms over my chest. "And?"

Zikai flicks the mouth harp with his pinky nail, and a soft, wobbling note drifts against the trombone melody. "When wealth and glamour are the currency that drive a city, humans will do depraved things to each other. That's why the Court of Exiles believes that gods should rule Shanghai, not gangsters. The Blue Dawn is growing too arrogant with their silver limbs and far too comfortable with foreign power, as all of Shanghai has become."

"You're accusing us of selling out to the West." As the absinthe seeps into my head and my bones, the floating trombone melody tingles against my skin like fur-lined gloves I am slipping on. I can't fight the lightness in my head, which makes me feel like I am floating.

Zikai downs the rest of his absinthe in a single gulp. "There were less bodies in the Huangpu River before the concessions. The Blue Dawn turns a blind eye to most of it, so long as they have their gold and their wealth."

I tilt my head back and finish the rest of my drink, just like him. "Yet the other night you left an offering to Guanyin Bodhisattva, who herself disobeyed the gods and played music in hell. Sounds like hypocrisy to me."

Behind the bar, the mottled assortment of jewel-toned labels glistens against white glass, more brightly than before. Zikai rounds both our glasses up and splashes another round of absinthe into the bottom. I lean over to assess the accuracy of his pour. He's a fast learner.

"Guanyin earned her enlightenment. Your grandmother stole from a god when she was young. That's how she's able to perform those surgeries, you know."

He twists the pewter spigot on the fountain, and iced water

drips over the grilled silver spoon, washing sugar into the shimmery green fairy below, louder than the bartender shaking a cocktail over his shoulder, louder than the chatter in the bar.

I shrug. "So? The world is not a fair place. One time, I fell asleep on the tram and my bag was stolen. My tap shoes were in my bag and I needed them for a Sunday matinee show, but I couldn't afford to buy another pair. So I swiped the pocket watch of a patron I danced with. I don't have any regrets because I needed the money more."

Zikai narrows his eyes as he passes my glass back to me. "You've spent too much time in Shanghai. Honor means something outside of this city."

The gentlemen sitting beside me get up, tipping their felt hats back over their heads, and a new pair of gentlemen replace them. The cologne they wear is slightly different—more chemical, more serious.

I shift my shoulders forward and talk to the wall. "You think my grandmother should be dead because she made the Blue Dawn powerful, and instead a bunch of gods should control Shanghai. Xiao Lei says you don't even know how to summon the gods back, so what's the point?"

"If I wanted her dead," he explains, "she'd already be dead. All that is to say, I don't actually want her dead."

My head spins as I try to untangle his words. "It's too late for riddles. Just say what you mean."

Zikai's grin widens. "I want Wang Daojun, the leader of the Blue Dawn, dead."

"So kill him then."

He spreads his hands out on the counter. "I want it to look like Yue Liqing killed him."

My grandmother's name spoken from his lips should not surprise me, but it does—a stark reminder that despite Zikai's laughing manner, he still came to Shanghai on the orders of a dangerous faction, to harm my grandmother.

I turn to face him straight on.

"If you haven't figured it out yet, I'm suggesting that I want you to kill him, and frame your grandmother." His eyes have a fiery red-brown center, rimmed by the soft green of faraway hills.

For some reason, I feel a little hurt—that for a moment, I'd forgotten the circumstance of our meeting and let my guard down. But of course, we are not here to enjoy absinthe and trade banter. He wants something from me—I am just relieved I'm not stupid enough to give it to him.

"You're absurd," I tell him. After all, I am a cabaret girl through and through. Detachment is my fondest strength.

He spreads his hands out on the counter. "We've known for a while there is a succession crisis within the Blue Dawn. After Wang Daojun dies, the rest of the gang will fracture until they are too small to matter. The simultaneous assassination of Wang Daojun and the removal of Yue Liqing from power would permanently dismantle the Blue Dawn, clearing the way for the Court of Exiles."

When I don't respond immediately, Zikai raises his glass in a toast to me, his head tilted toward his shoulder. "You feel guilty because your friends' faces are being carved to pieces, and it eats you alive to be torn between them and the woman who raised you. I've given you a way out. Frame her for Daojun's death, and she won't be able to operate a clinic without the Blue Dawn's support. She doesn't even have to die. You win and I win."

I burst out laughing because he thinks he knows what matters to me.

"They're not my friends."

Zikai studies my face with a frown. "But it bothers you anyways."

When I continue to laugh, Zikai wrests my empty glass from my hand. I've finished another drink without even noticing. His fingers are warm and dry when they brush against my wrist. "Consider my offer. She wouldn't be physically hurt in any way, not with her sense of cunning. Just . . . intellectually maimed."

He pops the cork off the absinthe with his thumbnail and spills another fresh dash of the green liquor into my glass.

I try to imagine what they would look like. Wang Daojun, the beloved leader of the Society of the Blue Dawn—dead on my grandmother's operating table, surrounded by paintings of gaping-mouthed demons and angry gods. My grandmother, a strand of her white hair dancing in the wind coming through her open window—blamed for the kill.

"She's no ordinary physician. She'll just find the patronage of a new gang."

"The Court of Exiles will act faster than that. We'll take over the city before she can try. I'm not worried about it." Zikai smiles. "It's just that Wang Daojun's too careful. Nobody can get close to him except your grandmother."

"And how do I know the city will be better off then?"

"Anyone is more trustworthy than a Shanghai gangster."

He has forgotten about my cocktail sitting under the fountain, the absinthe now leaping over the edges of my glass onto the counter. I snatch my glass away.

Zikai sighs and begins to mix a second cocktail for himself. In the center of the bar, a spotlight flickers on, like an interrogation light. A few of the patrons, laughing over an entire row of empty cocktail glasses, lift their hands to cover their faces. Particles of dust, like the down shaven from a feather, dance in the light beam.

The scratched-up record of a quiet tango melody begins to play. And then a large birdcage, gilded with the same gold leaf as the one outside, lowers from the rafters in the ceiling. There is a girl sitting on the perch within the bars, a dancer swathed in white ostrich feathers, who folds her body backward as the birdcage continues to descend from the heavens, two large fans gripped in her hands. Her shadow spreads its wings on the wall, like a live dove. I am mesmerized by her movements, which flow in a way I could never achieve, even under the tutelage of Sui Feng.

The birdcage has almost lowered to the floor. It twists around in midair to reveal an open door on the other side. The dancer grips the golden bars and swings her body up so that she is standing on the perch, the fans spread behind her like wings. For a moment, she stares out into the audience, and I meet her eyes across the white beam of light.

Except she doesn't have any.

Beneath the blunt fringe cut across the forehead, two sunken blossoms of darkness tremble against the ivory foundation painting her skin, profoundly empty. Across the empty space between us, and bits of dust swirling in the air, her attention seems to linger for a second in my direction, and then she turns away from me, bringing the fans around her body.

It's a girl like Huahua.

I drop my glass, which shatters on the floor of the bar. My heartbeat quickens under my ribs, a dull pounding I can hear over the frenzied tango music.

The audience roars, although there is a snarl buried in their calls, that sounds more like a sneer. She is a circus freak to them, I realize, and they love it.

"So you were lying," Zikai says softly beside me. "You've never actually been here before."

I don't understand how he can remain so calm. "Did you see? She's missing her eyes."

Zikai pushes his drink across the bar, with a nonchalance that is maddening. "Right, but you aren't friends, so it shouldn't matter."

I take a deep gulp of his absinthe, wondering if all this could just be a dream. The faint taste of licorice coats my tongue like a layer of cotton. I can't watch the girl dancing in the birdcage. If she opened her mouth and screamed, I begin to fear, would her stomach be full of gears as well?

Applause breaks like a wave upon the eerie tango music. The act is over. As if a vise has been removed from my chest, I find I can breathe again. The girl has left, and the birdcage is hoisted back up into the rafters, swinging wildly on its rope now that it's lost the weight of the dancer.

"Interesting performance," Zikai notes. "You think your grandmother will sew her eyes onto some rich lady's face too?"

"Stop."

I raise my voice, just a bit, because I am scared. I wonder how much Xiao Lei knew when he told me to come here. The more I think about it, the less I know what is scarier—the fact that Hua-hua is not the only girl to have lost a part of her face, or the fact Xiao Lei knew about it, and what that might say about Yue Liqing and the Blue Dawn. And then I notice a blur of light in the corner of my vision.

The faceless girl has come to the bar, white ostrich feathers blinding in the otherwise muted darkness. I turn my body away in an attempt to deter her, without much success. Even Zikai is staring at her.

I feel her breath, warm against my cheek. She is standing so close. "You're Yue Jingwen, the dancer from the Paramount. I've seen you there."

With no choice, I force myself to look at her.

She stands like she is staring right at me, but I don't know how she could, without eyes. The shadows on her face appear to move, like they are alive.

"Not many dancers with faces come to the Dove House. I thought I'd never see one of us again."

"I don't know you," I tell her.

"But I know you." She smiles, although the expression feels empty without her eyes. The shadows on her face obscure her lips. "Did you come here to help us?"

I can't shake the feeling I am staring at her through a thick fog. "What could I help you with?"

She touches her hand to her breast. "My name is Usugi. I danced at the Carlton Cafe, where you were a coat girl three years ago. Five nights ago, I was drinking with a few of the other dancers—I wasn't even dancing with a man—when I was attacked. The only thing I remember was a loud roar, like the clap of thunder, and the next thing I knew, my eyes were gone. It didn't even hurt." She runs her fingers through her hair, a small action I've seen many cabaret girls do—when they're nervous, when they're lost, when they don't know what to expect. "This bar—this is where all the faceless girls go."

I can't help but stare into those two blossoms of darkness on her face, which have no bottom. "If you really don't have eyes, then how can you see me?"

She tilts her head to the side, a mechanical, doll-like quality to the movement. "I don't know."

Suddenly, she places her hands on my face. A flash like electricity courses under my skin. I jerk away from her.

"You have to help us," she says to me.

The shadows across her face twist and roil like storm clouds.

Usugi lets her hands fall back to her sides. "You don't have to talk to me if you're scared. Huahua—she danced at the Paramount too. She's here as well. Do you want to speak to her instead?"

"Huahua is here?" A wave of emotions washes over me, which I am too panicked to dissect properly—sadness that we could not save her, relief that she is not alone, guilt that I chose to stand by and watch as she was dragged away.

Usugi beams, an eyeless smile that only feels hollow. "I'll go get her. I'm sure she'll be happy to see you."

She spins on her heel, navigating the aisles between the tables as if she has not lost her vision at all.

"Wait—" I try to stop her, but she has disappeared.

Zikai leans against the counter, holding his chin in one hand. "Not the way the night was supposed to go?"

"No," I admit. "Not at all."

Suddenly, the absinthe's effect strikes me. High above, the single light bulb hanging over the bar becomes so bright it hurts my eyes to look at it. When Zikai turns his head, I see two of him, one smiling and the other pensive, eclipsing one another. I remember the story of a French poet going mad after an afternoon drink of absinthe, who started to see green fairies in his study. Maybe the girl without eyes has been nothing more than a figment of my imagination.

But then Usugi returns, pulling another girl by the wrist. This girl I recognize immediately, all dolled up in a powder-blue corset and lilac satin tutu. She looks like she's dressed for a circus act, a hair comb decorated with a golden sun pinned in her hair.

She runs up to me, her heels clacking against the linoleum floor. "Jingwen, you came to see me. I'm so grateful."

Huahua's face swirls with shadows like the interior of a clamshell. Her words are loud and heavy, without the pillowy cushion of her lips to soften them. There is nothing of the betrayal that twisted her face when we last met eyes across the dance floor.

I suddenly feel sick to my stomach. The only real memory I have of Huahua was her first night at the Paramount, when I took advantage of her naïveté to steal every partner she tried to dance with, so she had no choice but to dance with a man with extraordinarily sweaty hands. She left the ballroom crying that night, because the reality of her dream was nothing like what they advertised in the tabloids.

I don't know why it hurts so much to see her now. Like I told Zikai, Huahua and I were never friends.

"You're going to help us, right?" she says, smoothing her tutu nervously down her thighs. "You have to. We've heard rumors that your grandmother makes silver limbs for the Blue Dawn. She's the only one who can fix us. Ask her to make us new lips and eyes."

Behind her, Zikai is drinking another preparation of absinthe with his eyebrows raised. The two dancers ignore him, forming a tight half circle around me. But I know he's listening to every word.

I wish I could say something comforting to Huahua, but it's like I've suddenly forgotten how to open my mouth. It's the words she has chosen, as if she and Usugi are broken dolls in a collector's shop, and they want my grandmother the puppeteer to repair their strings before they are set in the window for display.

"How did you end up here?" I ask her after a long silence.

She tucks her gently waved hair behind one ear. "The Paramount's manager fired me after my lips were taken. I wandered the streets that night until I met the Dove House's manager. She's a really nice British lady, and she let me dance here. It's the only thing I have left. The dancing."

The shadows across her face move more quickly, and she grips my hand in both of hers, her nails stinging against my skin. "Do you promise you'll help us?" she asks, her chest heaving slightly with the effort of her grip.

Zikai's gaze bores into mine over her shoulder.

I turn from Huahua to Usugi, dressed in dollish finery with whorls of darkness and dried blood on their faces.

"I promise."

Huahua releases me, and I glance down to see little crescent moons pressed into my wrist and the back of my hand where her nails gripped my flesh.

"Excuse me." A man in a dark gray suit has come up to us, his hands resting casually in his pockets. Huahua turns around to see what I'm staring at, brushing a stray curl from her face with her slender fingers.

The stranger is handsome in a dangerous way like Bailey, the type of person who hides secrets under his good looks. He flashes a captivating smile. "May I have a dance?"

I open my mouth to respond, but he's not looking at me. He's looking at Huahua.

"First dance of the night costs two tickets," Huahua says, sounding uncannily like myself.

The man offers two tickets on his palm, and I can't help but recoil. His arm is burnt, the flesh shiny and raw, with errant patches of silver melted into his skin. The flesh is bruised purple and yellow around these silver splotches, as if the body has reacted to their presence like a pox. Three of his fingers are missing, the stumps melted with uneven knobs of silver. It looks like a botched version of my grandmother's surgery.

"What happened to your arm?" I say, hoping he'll reveal more.

But Huahua pockets the tickets and takes his hand. She winks

at me as they glide away. "I learned that trick from watching you—
you're good at inventing tricks to ask for more tickets. It works
beautifully."

I gape after her.

There is no room for a dance floor in the Dove House. Instead,
the guests have taken to dancing between the tables, bumping
against the low backs of couches and the corners of the tables. The
spotlights are too bright, making too stark a contrast against the
black walls and the black-stained wood.

Usugi leans her hip against the bar, her head tilted in wonder.

"Patrons like him," she explains to me, "they come for us." There
is an ethereal quality to her voice, as if she's on the border of dreaming. "They don't find satisfaction in the clubs on Yuyuan Road,
like the one you dance at, or the one I used to dance at. The girls
there are too bright—it's too much for them. Some people like the
darkness."

She traces her fingers lightly over her neck, as if in wonder at her
own predicament.

I watch Huahua dance the tango with the shadowy stranger,
her tutu fluttering against her thighs. The netting of her tights
seems to glow like veins. Her partner dips her back, his scarred arm
supporting her back, and her face draws in the light above until the
entire room seems to darken. I can't look away because I can see
now why it's entrancing.

Another patron comes and leaves with Usugi. As I watch her
dance, I can read who she once was—a fiercely individualistic and
opinionated dancer—the type who wouldn't feel insecure around
Beibei. There is an airy, floating quality to her steps now, as if the
same dancer is lost in a forest of mist. She pauses facing me, and
her face dapples and morphs under the light, like I am looking at
her through the mottled shadows of a gingko tree, the leaves quivering in the wind.

"So was there always a market in Shanghai for dancers missing
parts of their faces?" Zikai asks out of the blue, setting his drink
down.

I shake my head, breaking out of a trance. "No. It's like it blossomed overnight or something."

If anything, I should've learned by now. In Shanghai, there is a market for everything. As long as something is for sale, someone will buy it.

Zikai's eyes are narrowed at Huahua's partner and his blotchy silver arm. "It looks like there are some surgeons trying to become your grandmother as well. A lot of men are going to lose their lives on the operating table."

"She didn't ask them to copy her."

"Yes, but people want what's fashionable, and the Blue Dawn's silver limbs are fashionable right now."

Huahua spins under the stranger's arm, drawing the light into herself like a garnet on a rotating cushion, displayed in a sunny shop window. Around them, a hundred faces stare from the walls and the floor. The harsh spotlights make it seem like they are disembodied, floating in the dark air like clouds.

Zikai grabs my wrist, his fingers burning against the nail marks Huahua left there. His eyes cut like shards of green glass. "Remember," he says, "you win and I win."

CHAPTER EIGHT

You win and I win.

Zikai's words still echo in my head when I bolt up in bed the next morning. The night has left me with a hangover, my skull heavy like it's packed with down. My memory drifts to the stillness of Zikai's face as he sipped absinthe, long eyelashes brushing his cheek with nonchalance and the mole beside the corner of his eye—the way I had let my guard down and believed for a second that we could be friends. I dig my nails into the sides of my head to dull the ache.

Outside, a water boy is arguing with his customer under my window about money, their raised voices penetrating the brick nonetheless. The squeaky wheels of a rickshaw trawl past, flying over potholes in the road. I drag myself out of the bed and throw open the screen, so I can hear the mundanity of the street more clearly.

The blue, grimacing face of a demon outside the Daoist shrine greets me, and I am tempted to make the same face back at it. There are no faceless girls in the Old City, just aunties sweeping dead leaves out the doorways of their shops with stick brooms. I cradle my head in my hands, as my memories of the prior night swim back into clarity.

Huahua made me promise that I would help her. Was I really going to help her? There was a price tag attached to everything. Against my will, I imagine myself in Liqing's clinic, holding a knife at the bedside of the Blue Dawn's sleeping leader. In that moment, would I really be able to plunge the blade into a living man's heart?

I arrive fifteen minutes late again to the Lyceum, where the East

Sea Follies are rehearsing the first act of Sui Feng's operetta. The cold morning air numbs my headache.

When I push open the attic studio's wooden door, it releases into the lap of a man in a black suit, who is sitting against the mirrors with his arms crossed over his chest.

"Oh! I'm sorry." I squeeze through the crack in the door and drop my bag along the wall before I see who it is.

I am staring into the clean-shaven face of Bailey Thompson, who is reclining in a wooden chair, watching the rehearsing dancers like they are birds in a park, twitting amidst the trees. He is wearing a pair of stylish round frame glasses, a peaceful smile gracing his lips.

He catches the door and lets it shut slowly to not startle the dancers. There is a suave twinkle in his eye as he winks at me. "Ah, and here we have our leading lady, entering with style."

The air is filled with his cologne, a familiar, intoxicating blend of musk and earthen smells.

Sui Feng waves his arms overhead, cutting off the rehearsal. "Jingwen, you're fifteen minutes late."

They are rehearsing Act 2. After the Feral Goddess tastes the sweet sin of Shanghai, she embraces the lifestyle of a cabaret girl, even participating in one of the Black Cat cabaret's "cat dance" competitions, where dancers dress in feline masks and costumes and slink across the dance floor in their best imitation of a housecat. The Emperor of Heaven is humiliated. He assembles a conglomeration of deities to travel to Shanghai and bring her back: the Hail God, who sails the skies on a storm cloud; the Kitchen God, who wears a crown shaped like a trout; and the Insect God, who can summon storms of locusts with just the stomp of a foot.

Rongyu, who will be playing the Insect God, cannot stop complaining about how she wants a different role. She is wearing Beibei's signature Tangee lipstick again. "He summons locusts with his feet, it's so disgusting," she hisses in everyone's ear when she can. "I've never been late to a single practice, and Jingwen is late every time. I should have your part."

And yet, I am to be the Feral Goddess, who evades the Kitchen God by fleeing into a crowd of waltzing dancers and deters the Hail God by taking shelter in the Cathay Hotel, whose sleek, pyramidal spire proves impossible for hailstones to penetrate.

Each time Sui Feng calls for us to break, I sneak a glance over my shoulder and catch Bailey smirking at me. His gaze is sly, as if he can read what I'm hiding just by looking at me. I return a faint smile to communicate my reservation.

Where was he the entire last week? All those nights I waited for him at the Paramount, I thought he'd abandoned me. Why buy an entire revue to make me the star and then disappear?

I soon realize I am not the only one who has noticed Bailey.

A girl who recently joined the revue, whose name I do not know, misses her entrance three times because she is staring at him from the sidelines. When dancing nearby, Rongyu keeps careening off course, so that her skirts fly up in his lap, affording him the luxury of glancing at that space between her legs—covered, of course, by her leotard. Although I am dancing center stage, an ugly beast like a polecat rears its head in the bottom of my chest, irritated by a fly circling its kill. This is *my* kill, which will land me a date to the annual Firefighters' Yuletide Ball.

But Bailey never shows any hint of a reaction to these subtle flirtations, besides a slightly bemused smile. When I think he's not looking, I sneak a glance in his direction through the mirror, to find him staring straight back. He doesn't flinch.

So I challenge myself not to flinch either. After all, I was the dancer he chose to star in his show. The haze of sleeplessness hangs over me, but underneath, I feel that soaring sensation in my belly again, that I experienced when drinking with Zikai.

The rehearsal flies by with Bailey watching.

"I'm pleased you are finally starting to forget how that awful ballerina taught you to dance," Sui Feng says, beaming at all of us. He turns to Bailey—his flowing brown rags more raggedy than ever next to Bailey's trim suit. I've never seen a more unlikely pair.

"Now, girls, I'd like to introduce Bailey Thompson, the investor who has certainly saved the East Sea Follies."

Bailey rises to his feet, and with a boyish smirk, he bows to the revue.

A few of the girls blush and giggle behind their hands, because as showgirls we are used to patrons traveling across concessions and seas to fawn upon us, and Bailey's cool, disinterested manner makes a refreshing turn of events. But I don't react, because I am a professional of Beibei's caliber, and I've moved past the folly of romance. My real triumph is the status I would hold among the other dancers.

Sui Feng taps his fingers together in excited anticipation. "I believe Bailey has some news."

"Ah, yes." Bailey unrolls the newspaper he has been carrying under his arm. "Allow me to read an excerpt published in this morning's *Crystal*. 'The Firefighters' Yuletide Ball, the year's grandest ball and a celebrated Shanghai tradition, will take place at the Astor House on the twenty-fifth of December at 7 p.m. A special guest performance of the new vaudeville show *The Black Cat* will be given by the East Sea Follies.'"

He folds the newspaper up again.

One of the girls squeals behind her hand. All around, the dancers have dropped their jaws.

Bailey winks again, the slyness in his eyes enough to make most girls faint. "Make me proud, girls."

As we pack our bags, the Firefighters' Yuletide Ball is all the dancers are talking about.

"We get to go!" they keep saying. "Do you think they'll have papillons?"

Rongyu glances at me meaningfully. "I've heard some of you were stupid enough to challenge Beibei about the Firefighters' Yuletide Ball. Whoever brings the wealthiest date will hereby be the official Queen of the Paramount's backroom, with the right to dance with any patron she wants. So, who are you bringing, Jingwen?"

My competitive spirit ignited, I wheel around to face her.

"Someone you won't expect," I taunt her. "But I'm going to win."

Perhaps it's my confidence, but she draws back like I've struck her with my fangs.

A few nights ago, it was all I cared about—winning—but now, even talking about it suddenly makes me a bit tired. It's a bit silly, I guess, to put so much emphasis on petty contests when I've seen the world behind the Dove House.

"Do you think we'll really get to perform at the Firefighters' Yuletide Ball?" Zina asks, as she unlaces her dancing shoes. "I've heard only the best showgirls in Shanghai are invited to perform at the yearly foreign concession balls. At last year's Caledonian Ball, I heard the Scottish Society had peat moss delivered across the sea, which they used to decorate the hearths of the Astor House. The dancers were stealing bits of it all night since they would never have a chance to see Scotland otherwise."

Bailey and Sui Feng are discussing something in low voices, although it's impossible to ignore the way they stand—a stride of distance between them, Bailey's neatly ironed suit hailing from an entirely different era than Sui Feng's robes. They can't have been acquainted for long, and even now, they are not friends.

Sui Feng glances up, and I turn away before he can catch me staring. "I've only been to one foreign concession ball before. You'll love it, Zina. There are steaks for everyone, and the crystal chandeliers that decorate the halls are so heavy, if they fell, they would crush the skulls of a hundred dancers."

"Sounds like the setting of *Cinderella*." Zina giggles while staring over my shoulders. I know she is swooning over Bailey too, and immediately I feel the stirrings of jealousy in my chest. Zina has violet eyes and the pureness of an ingenue. *He prefers mystery,* I console myself. Biting my lip, I remind myself to stay mysterious.

"Come on, Zina. Don't stare."

I grab her arm and push her to the door.

"Vilma," Bailey calls my name.

I freeze in the doorway, my bag sliding off my shoulder. Zina covers her mouth in shock.

I spin on my heel slowly and brush past her, allowing the strap of my bag to slide down my arm until I am holding it on my wrist.

Bailey strides toward me, hands in pockets. "What are you doing this afternoon?" he asks.

"I was going to take a nap," I admit, smiling as mysteriously as I can.

"I'd like to invite you to tea in the French Concession."

A hazy picture crosses my mind, of Bailey Thompson sitting across from me in a restaurant along the Rue Soeur Allegre, an ermine scarf draped about my shoulders and my plate arranged with the prettiest sea urchins whipped into mousse, while Rongyu and Beibei gawk through the windows, condemned to watch without the strength to blink. Dabbing the corners of my lips with a red napkin, I turn to smile at them—the deepest torture I could inflict upon any of my showgirl rivals.

"I'd love to go."

He smiles. "Excellent. My driver can take us, if you'd like."

I turn around and wink at Zina. I'll show her how it's done.

Plane trees with twisting empty boughs, like ghost hands reaching for the sky, line both sides of Avenue Joffre in the French Concession. In the summer, broad, green leaves hang over quaint lingerie shops and cupcakeries, like a row of dollhouses under a jungle canopy. But in the winter, the wind blows through the spaces between branches with a cruel sharpness, the mannequins in the shop windows wrapped in scarlet wool and ermine fur scarfs.

Frenchtown stretches Shanghai into yet another shape—mothers in shoulder-padded coats pushing baby carriages with their green leather gloves while laughing to one another in French. The dizzying aroma of freshly baked cakes fills the air, little girls in frilled dresses and pigtails running ahead of their Russian au pair, buttercream smeared on their faces.

Bailey's driver pulls the black Packard Twelve against the sidewalk, in front of the Café Montmartre, a small café with teardrop-
shaped windows nestled in between a violin shop and a cupcakery.

The Café Montmartre is the type of establishment that holds
Tango teas on many a Sunday afternoon, which I've attended with
Zina and Arisha before. It's the type of bawdy literary hub where
French poets meet every evening at sundown to gossip about the
latest scandals within their circles—which literary genius has slept
with another's wife in revenge for spreading a bad word, and which
man is the latest to have won the affections of the tempestuous Li
Beibei, who can swing her voluptuous hips better than the girls
in the Moulin Rouge. It is here, in fact, that I once overheard the
recitation of a poem dedicated to Beibei, wherein a dashing young
poet compared her nether regions to the French national flower,
the iris. The poem achieved infamy in Paris itself a week later,
prompting a wave of curious socialites to voyage to Shanghai just
to confirm Beibei's existence with their own eyes.

Bailey holds the café door open with the seasoned politeness of an
older gentleman. I duck under the tinkling doorbells into the cozy,
well-lit café. The waitresses scuttle out of our way, carrying trays of
half-eaten cheesecakes and quaint, porcelain teacups.

I order a Hong Kong–style milk tea and a slice of tiramisu.
Bailey, who is sitting by the window, merely smiles at the waitress,
and she returns instantly with a slender brass cezve, from which
she pours a stream of amber coffee into a tiny porcelain cup. Bailey
picks up his Turkish coffee and leans back in his chair with a sigh.
Washed in the early afternoon light, he looks darkly handsome in
his gray suit and black suspenders.

"How have you been, Vilma?" he asks me. He presses his lips
together. "Or would you prefer I call you Jingwen?"

So he has been talking to Sui Feng about me.

I hesitate for a moment, caught like a fly on the jeweled web of
Shanghai's intricate politics. I consider the advantages each name
would bring me. Vilma conjures the satin whisper of Hollywood

scandal—an enticement he understands well from his nights dancing in New York, while there is nothing he can compare Jingwen to.

I recall the curious, scholarly way he'd studied me the night we met at the Paramount. *It's because you have a touch of Shanghai in you.*

"Jingwen," I respond, shifting in my seat, which is lined with imitation velvet that itches against my legs through my pantyhose. The waitress returns with a flower-patterned tray, upon which trembles a slender slice of tiramisu and my steaming milk tea. I pick up my teacup, and it shakes in its pretty dish.

With a leisurely sigh, Bailey relaxes in his seat and yanks the top button of his shirt loose to stretch his neck. A vivid hint of color pops out from under his collar. He's wearing a charm on a braided red cord around his neck. It's a worn silver coin with a hollowed-out center, carved with fiery letters—one character in each cardinal direction.

So I've guessed right.

"I like your necklace," I inform him, as I brush the lid of my teacup back to sip at my milk tea. "It doesn't exactly go with your suit though."

He touches two fingers to the pendant with a beam. "Ah, yes. A gift from a friend. A Daoist numismatic charm." He flips it over to show off the back, which is inscribed with the tarnished picture of lightning and clouds. It looks like the type of cheap talisman sold at the Jing'an Temple market.

I smile with a demure bat of my eyelashes. "Well, given how handsome you are, I'm confident that soon, all the businessmen in Shanghai will be wearing those."

A devilish glean lights up his face, and he winks. "Oh, they will."

There is a brief silence as I slide the lid back over my teacup, porcelain clattering between my fingers.

"You asked Sui Feng to give me the starring role. I can't thank you enough for that."

He smiles. "Don't thank me. My job is to make investments, and I saw a worthy investment."

"The dress too. I wore it that night. But you never came." I push the little gold tea tray away from me, making a point not to smile this time.

"I apologize deeply," Bailey responds gently. "I ran into some trouble with my new business."

He gazes out the window at the tree-lined street with a sigh. His side profile could belong on a cigarette advertisement, the type intended to seduce family men into the business of chain smoking.

I find I'm studying his every movement, my curiosity piqued by his coolness. Other men would be grasping at my hands under the table by now or brushing their knees against mine. Bailey does no such thing, although his gaze contains the sharpness of a scalpel.

"What kind of trouble?"

"Well, it's complicated." He adjusts his spectacles with a casual brush of his knuckles. "Nothing that would interest a showgirl such as yourself."

"Try me."

A faint smile tugs at Bailey's features. I dissect his charm apart. It's the subtlety in his facial expressions that make him handsome—as if he's spent his entire life resisting his feelings, but *I* alone have managed to tease a few out of him. I wonder if he practices in front of a mirror daily. "Jingwen, what do you know of the SMP?"

"The Shanghai Municipal Police?" I prod my fork into my cake. "They're the most corrupt entity in Shanghai."

He brushes his fingers over his chin, and a devilish smile breaks upon his expression, like I've amused him greatly. He leans over the table, the buttons on his jacket clattering against the glass edge of the coffee table, and whispers like we're sharing a secret. "Here's the thing—while traveling, a business partner of mine discovered a rare smoke leaf that grows at the peaks of certain mountain ranges in western China. When burned and inhaled, it produces a high like no other. Those who have tried it report feeling like they have become gods." He pauses for dramatic effect.

"What kind of gods?" I ask.

"Ancient Chinese ones," Bailey says. His fingers play with the charm around his neck absentmindedly. "I thought a drug like that might have exceptional popularity in America. But to harvest enough to make a profit—it would be very expensive. We'd have to hire camels to cross the desert and yaks to ascend the mountain, not to mention multiple guides to lead the way. So, I asked my business partner based in Delingha to send me a sample so that I could fund the expedition. And it just so happens to be that shipment was confiscated by the SMP."

Bailey drops the smile from his face, all business now.

"Jingwen, do you know what the SMP does with drugs they confiscate?"

"No."

He taps his cigarette against the porcelain ashtray and crosses his ankle over his knee. "Guess."

Officers of the Shanghai Municipal Police frequently pass through the Paramount on their late-night shifts, where they have gained a reputation for demanding dances from the girls without buying dance tickets. Almost every dancer I know prefers gangsters to police officers. But specifically, anytime the SMP is mentioned, I think of one officer in particular—a certain Raoul Smith, who has been dating my mother for two years. Raoul Smith, whose introduction into my life marked the beginning of the end of my relationship with my mother.

I envision my mother's boyfriend the first time I noticed him—a dark-haired British man with a slightly receded hairline, who helped my mother into a taxi one night outside the Neapolitan Gardens, the club she danced at. I had snuck into the courtyard with Zina and Arisha to see the ice sculptures they had imported from Harbin in the north, and she didn't know I was there. My mother and I were barely speaking by that point. As he guided her onto the mohair seat, one hand on her back, one hand on the car's door, he glanced up, and we met eyes across the garden. He didn't know who I was, and I didn't know who he was, but in that moment, I knew that I hated him with a deep, guttural burning.

There exists a myriad of ways to dispose of illegal drugs—you could burn them in the barren fields by the sugar factories of the city's outskirts, dump them in the ocean in weighted chests that sink to the reefs, dig up the half-rotted coffin of the ex-chairman of the Shanghai Municipal Council and slip them in the mouth of his skull. But none of them fit the veneer I saw in Raoul Smith—a man who was born with the urbanity of an English gentleman but the heart of a wolf—who would not hesitate to use that to his advantage.

"They smoke it themselves," I guess.

Bailey brings his hands together in a clap, grinning again like he can't help it. "Yes, I knew you would figure it out. Instead of patrolling the city and fighting crime, they lay about on the over-stuffed couches of their police station and get higher than the spires of the Park Hotel. At night when I walk past the old police station and see that green-tinged smoke floating from the windows, it fills me with a fury like no other."

He closes his eyes as he sips his coffee.

I lick rum-infused cream off my fork. "Actually, Dr. Thompson . . ."

The muscles in his throat ripple as he swallows.

"I can help you steal some of it back."

His eyes fly open. "What?"

The day I steal from the SMP, I've crossed into the territory I swore I would never touch. What would differentiate me from Liqing then, if I began to meddle with the gears that turn under the city's surface?

But I can't bear to be ignored again. I feel drunk on the way his eyes had followed me only in the Lyceum attic, while Zina and Rongyu clawed for his attention—and I can't bear the thought of another night primped up in my prettiest dress, drinking alone on a corner couch wondering if I'd only imagined everything. I need him to give me the Paramount upon a platter, so that my elation stops feeling like sand cupped in my fingers. I need Bailey to fall in love with me.

My heart sinks a little, but I can't help it. It's much easier to steal from the SMP than to help a girl like Huahua and Usugi. The inanity of our competition feels comforting now. No one really gets hurt fighting over rich playboys.

"This drug—it would make you rich, wouldn't it?" I ask.

Bailey raises his eyebrows. "Very rich, I'd like to think."

I rake my fork through the cocoa powder that dusts my tiramisu slice, gently as to not damage the cream beneath. "My mother's boyfriend is a detective of the SMP."

Bailey sets his empty coffee cup down on the table, and a waitress comes to refill it out of a silver kettle. "Interesting."

I continue, digging my nails into my palm under the table. "My mother is a dancer, and he sometimes comes to watch her dance. If he has the smoke leaf on him, I could steal it."

Steam rises from his fresh cup of coffee, like a veil between us. "That might not be safe for you, don't you think?" he says gently. "People like me can always flee back across the sea if I was hunted, but your life is tied to this city."

Yet the doctor's gray eyes dance with an invitation for mischief, and I swim in their sea, lost.

"No, I think it would be fun."

The words fall from my mouth before I have a chance to stop myself. I don't even know if I mean them.

"I didn't take you as the sort of girl who got excited by the idea of crime." Bailey folds his arms over his chest and leans back again. The sun has moved, and this time, his face is cast in shadow. "But I am the type of man who rewards my allies. If you do manage to steal back some of the smoke leaf, there's a gift I can give you that none of the other men in the Paramount has ever given a dancer."

The image of Beibei bursting from the cake shadows my thoughts. There is only one gift I need from him, but when the moment comes, I want him to feel like it was his idea all along.

He draws his wallet out of his pocket, slips a white business card out of it, and presses it in my hand. "Here's my number. I'd like you to have it."

I close my fist around the card, sharp edges cutting into my palm.

Bailey smiles genuinely, and I thrill that I've managed to tantalize such an intense emotion out of him. "Now, why don't we talk about something more pleasant," he suggests. "What's your favorite park in Shanghai?"

Outside, the sun has begun to set, a wash of orange that floods between the brownstones. Bailey lights a cigarette and exhales, the smoke fogging up the glass until I can no longer make out the branches of the plane trees.

CHAPTER NINE

My mother's name means "glass ocean." In Chinese, it's written 璃海, pronounced Lihai. Where the tender, gray waves of the Huangpu River meet the angry, green shape of the ocean, there lies a seam, where the tears, piss, and wine of the city gutters are washed away into the meaningless sea. My mother reminds me of the ocean, a dolled-up relic of bygone days, swallowed by nothingness, although I believe that once upon a time she was a river who could carve through rock.

On the next night I am not dancing, I walk through the narrow lanes under the Bund's forest of skyscrapers, the escalating spires with their roving lights projecting on the river, until I've arrived at the Neapolitan Gardens, where my mother has worked as a dance hostess for the last two years. The courtyard is open, patrons huddled around gas heaters under the broad-leaved palm trees that overlook the outdoor ballroom.

A coat boy dressed in all white takes my coat and exchanges it for a number, which I slip around my wrist. Goose bumps erupt along my bare arms as I wander through a marble colonnade, under rows of nasturtium hanging in woven baskets. It's that time of year again—in the main garden, tucked under arches covered in climbing roses, rest ice sculptures of rabbits and fairies with neon lights frozen in the center.

A three-tiered fountain splashes in the center of the path leading to the outdoor ballroom, cold spray peppering my bare arms. A dance is just finishing, dance hostesses leading their partners off the floor, cheeks flushed. Silvery female laughter rings in the trees.

I don't see my mother amongst them. She has always hated the industrial air in Shanghai, feared the sun might crack the skin under her eyes like old paper. And so I wander into the indoor ballroom, where a waltz is underway, the air terribly muggy after coming in from outdoors. But she is not there either.

After more wandering, I find my mother alone in the dressing room, lighting a cigarette at the makeup table.

I lean against the doorframe, not sure what to say after the awkward parting we shared at the Jing'an Temple. My dark blue qipao makes a harsh statement against the dressing room's pale cream walls.

She sees me first in the mirror behind the makeup table and hesitates, the lighter burning in her cupped hand. But then she decides she doesn't care and proceeds to light the cigarette.

"Ma," I say, as she sets the lighter down and grasps the cigarette between her fingers.

My mother is dressed in a pale lavender qipao and the same black velvet heels she was wearing at Guanyin's shrine. Under the warm dressing room lights, it's obvious she is much thinner than me, her diet a tightly disciplined menu of stir-fried lily bulbs and snow peas. Through her freshly painted makeup, I cannot tell her age at all.

"Jingwen, what are you doing here?" she asks.

"Are you dancing tonight?" I step inside and approach the makeup table.

"Yes," she tells me, her voice rising a bit, as if she fears my coming any closer to her. I meet her eyes in her makeup mirror, both our faces magnified. "You're not?"

"No," I respond.

My mother puts out her cigarette in an ashtray that is piled with a mountain of old, rotting cigarette butts and pulls a bronze compact from her makeup bag. In the mirror, I watch her dust more foundation over her cheekbones with a round brush.

We're not going to talk about the Jing'an Temple, it's mutually decided through silence.

"Will Raoul be coming tonight?" I ask instead.

The reflection of her eyes narrows. "Why do you care?"

Although she and Raoul have been dating for two years, he still hasn't invited her to live with him. He's a playboy, no children but plenty of ex-girlfriends my age.

He likes my mother because she was one of the original cabaret hostesses, the unreadable ice queen who ignored him for days when he was in his late twenties, but who will now follow him faithfully from club to club, while the old-timers *ooh* and *aah* at her continued appearance on the scene, as she slowly withers like a daisy in a vase. It's the power imbalance of their relationship that drives it.

I shrug. "There's no reason."

Annoyance twists her expression in the mirror. Finally, she turns around to look at me behind her.

"Leave me out of whatever game you're playing," she says. "I can tell there's something you want—your grandmother gets the same look on her face."

I've heard, from Liqing, that when my mother spends the night at Raoul's place, she'll wake in the morning before the sun is up, wash and redo her makeup, and slip back into bed, so that he will never get to look upon her bare, lined face. Anything to hide from him that she is forty-two years old, with a grown daughter.

I smile in a cold way, my teeth sharp against my lip. "Goodbye then."

Of course, I don't leave.

The halls of the ballroom are hung with imitations of French impressionist paintings of sunrises and lakes. As such, the ballroom feels mustier than the Paramount with her sleek angles and polished ebony. In the Industrial Age, paintings don't inspire the same awe as light shows.

While waiting for my mother to emerge from the dressing room, I accept a dance from a younger gentleman who I guess to be a factory manager, who attempts to pay me with dance tickets.

"I'm not a hostess," I tell him. "I'll dance with you for no charge."

He beams and eagerly leads to me to the dance floor, although I don't say much, because I am distracted thinking about my mother.

Liqing tells me I was born from a passion that lasted for one night. My father still writes to my mother sometimes from Hong

Kong, where he's married with a traditional-minded wife and two sons. He's never asked to see me, although I know when I was younger, he sent her money every once in a while. When I was a girl, I thought of taking a train to see him when I'd saved enough money—every dollar Liqing gave me for birthdays and New Year's, I tucked away in a little bronze box that I kept under my bed. But when I turned eighteen, I used the money to buy my first qipao, and became a dancer.

As I dance with the stranger, I wonder how the three of us fell from grace—Liqing, who cannot look upon her daughter's face without feeling ashamed that she has transformed into a foreigner's puppet, Lihai—who cannot look upon my face without feeling ashamed of her age, and finally me—infected by Liqing's pride but entranced by the worldliness of my mother's profession.

A sharp point digs into the little toe of my left foot, and I swerve slightly off balance but manage to catch myself before my partner notices. Nearby, there are two women dancing in each other's embrace, careening wildly as they try to turn under one another's arms at the same time. And one of them has stepped on me.

For some reason, the laughter of the taller girl strikes me as familiar. My factory manager partner guides me around in a circle as we dance, and I get a closer glance at the two women.

It's Li Beibei, in the arms of a shorter girl in a silver sequined dress, a red beret perched on her curly hair. Beibei stands out no matter what crowd she stands in, but it's the shorter girl I notice—who has skin the hue of cool sepia and dimples that give her a mischievous flair.

When the dance has ended, they retreat to a private table by the orchestra, and I follow.

The girl in the red cap has ordered champagne, which she and Beibei are drinking out of the wrong type of wineglass, while giggling uncontrollably. The little table is set with a rose-scented candle in the middle, which melts pink wax in a glass bowl.

"Beibei, what are you doing here?" I ask, more out of surprise than anything malicious. I am shocked to see her here without Neville Harrington in tow, and more than anything—I am shocked to see her enjoying herself.

She glances up at me. Her cheeks are flushed in a way I'm not sure is wholly the result of alcohol. Instead of a high-collared qi-pao, she is dressed in a short, fringed dress of a deep scarlet color.

"Oh Jingwen, it's you," she says, with a toothy grin uncharacteristic of her regular, seductive smile.

The girl in the red cap grins and extends her hand too. "Hello, you must be a friend of Beibei's. My name is Maia Kane."

Slowly, I grip Maia's fingers, and she shakes my hand. Her fingers are cold, a little sweaty.

Beibei drapes an arm around Maia's neck, huddling her close. "You must remember Maia! She sang at the Paramount a few months ago. Maia is from New Orleans, but she travels to different cities around the world singing jazz for the cabarets. Last week she was in Hong Kong, and the week before that, Venice."

Maia blinks at her companion fondly. "Yes, but I make sure to return to Shanghai at every chance I have, so I can go dancing with Beibei."

Beibei giggles and misses her pour of champagne. "Why are you staring at us like that, Jingwen? You think I'm just a fox spirit who eats men's hearts for dinner all the time? Come, have a drink with us."

I watch the stain on the white tablecloth spread like a flowering bloom.

Beibei grabs my hand and stuffs a wineglass in my palm by the stem. Maia clinks her glass against Beibei's, and the sound seems to ring across the ballroom.

"Drink, Jingwen!" Beibei demands, slamming her hand on the table.

And so I find myself drinking with Beibei, who is laughing so uncontrollably I begin to suspect she might be possessed. The night is young, and I'm already unsure what to make of it.

"What are you laughing about?" I ask Beibei after I have made it halfway through my glass.

She shrugs. "Life!" She hiccups, clearly drunk. "Don't you find life funny?"

At that moment, my mother emerges from the hallway where the dressing room is located. The young man who had danced with me earlier approaches her and attempts to ask her for a free dance, but she explains to him with a cold smile that her company will require one dance ticket.

Beibei wrests my glass away, and I allow her to pour me a second glass of champagne, laughing all the same as she does. "I see where you're coming from," I admit.

Soon, I lose count of how many glasses I've had. The whole time, my mother dances with different men, flitting in and out of the forest of white legs and pinstriped suits, all the while pretending to ignore me. Through the ballroom's window, I watch the dancers in the garden move out of sync to the orchestra music inside, gas heaters glowing under the rose-covered arches.

Shortly after a distant city clock strikes midnight, the soft chimes dovetailing the candle's flickering, I spot Raoul Smith amongst the crowd in the garden, sharing a beer with another foreigner. He laughs outside, dances a jive with a hostess even younger than I am, before he enters the indoor ballroom. A slight sheen of sweat shines on his forehead, a curl of his hair hanging loose over his brows.

Yue Lihai sails to him like a leaf in a stream, buoyed by a destiny she does not control. He dances once with my mother—a tango—and I find I'm analyzing their every movement. Raoul does not tease her with the sophisticated flirtations Bailey weaves into his leading, which all the more confirms to me that Bailey is the more sophisticated playboy, who must have danced hundreds of tangos in New York City while he was a doctor. When my mother leans into his embrace, she stops herself before she has truly tested her own weight, but when he engages her in a double-handed turn, she executes the turn more smoothly than I'm capable of.

They dance like they know each other, and it reviles me. Since the days Lihai used to sell champagne by the water, it's become cliché to look for a husband on the dance floor, although that's what they still do in Paris and New York City.

When the dance ends, I am secretly relieved I don't have to watch it anymore.

Raoul's throaty, happy laugh grates my ears from across the ballroom. He has moved on, talking to another foreign man. My mother hangs awkwardly around him, smiling in her demure, pretty way and sipping lightly on an orange cocktail, which she has barely dented.

That's when I notice it. Raoul takes a small packet of smoke leaf from his pocket and begins to prepare a cigar.

I bolt to my feet.

Beibei tugs at my elbow. "Jingwen, don't leave us yet. Maia just bought another round."

Maia uncorks a new bottle of champagne, and having accidentally shaken it, froth overflows from the top. She shakes it off her hands, landing dollops of it on Beibei and myself.

I shake myself free of Beibei's grip. "No, I have to go."

My mother watches me approach in horror, her eyes wide over Raoul's shoulder. Raoul, noticing my mother's expression, turns around searching for whatever's bothering her, until his gaze finally lands on me.

I fold both my hands at the edge of their table, rising over them like the Park Hotel spire over the older establishments of the Bund.

My mother grimaces. "Jingwen, I thought you were leaving."

I curtsy, facing Raoul directly. "I'd like to join for just a bit."

On the dais where the orchestra is housed, the pianist begins to play a cakewalk, coattails flying as he leans over the keys. I prefer the slim-fit suits of the Paramount's orchestra, personally. The rhythm kept by the piano is far too happy for all the deceit and heartbreak that happens in cabarets.

Raoul's companion eyes me curiously.

"This is Jingwen, a friend of Tiffany's," Raoul explains, and he doesn't sound happy about it. Tiffany is what he calls my mother in front of his friends. "She dances at the Paramount Ballroom."

"I see a resemblance," Raoul's companion notes. "You are—"

"Sisters," Lihai cuts in, refusing to look at me.

"Ah, well your mother must be the most beautiful woman in Shanghai," Raoul's companion muses, glancing from Lihai to me. "Both dancers. How wonderful."

An awkward silence falls between us, punctuated by the dancing candle flame and the rise and fall of our shadows against the impressionist paintings stacked on the wall.

"It's very wonderful," Raoul says, his grumbling voice indicating that my presence is anything but.

"Perhaps I'll go now," Raoul's companion adds, glancing meaningfully between my mother and me. I realize he thinks we are two sisters fighting over the same man, something which might turn him on, and if I had eaten enough beforehand to vomit on the table right there, I would have.

Raoul holds his hand up. "Before you do, let's confirm about Monday—"

My mother grabs ahold of me while Raoul is distracted, her nails digging into my wrist. "Jingwen, what are you doing here? I told you to leave," she hisses in my ear, angling her body so that Raoul cannot see the way her anger accentuates her wrinkles. I can't help but admire her, how practiced she is at this stupid art of eternally seeming pleasant in front of her lover.

I writhe out of her grip.

"That smoke is very fragrant," I say to Raoul. "What is it?"

"This?" His companion now gone, Raoul finishes rolling his joint and holds it up to the light to show me, twisting it between his fingers. "It's a new type of smoke I discovered. It's sweet, and it shines in the air."

I reach out to touch the joint, but Raoul pulls it out of reach. "Bold of you, a police officer, to smoke illicit drugs in public."

A look of panic crosses my mother's face.

"Is that what you think?" Raoul pockets the rest of the smoke leaf calmly. I take note where he hides it. "You, who delivers bones on behalf of Yue Liqing, Shanghai's most infamous black-market surgeon. Have you ever wondered where those bones end up?"

It never crossed my mind that Raoul might know what the Blue Dawn refuses to tell me. But of course—he's a police officer.

"Where?" I can't help myself.

He recognizes the hunger in my voice, and I curse myself for not hiding it better. "Ah, but you've annoyed me tonight, Jingwen, so I'm not going to tell you."

That's the thing I hate the most about him—that he treats me like I am twelve years old, when I'm a dance hostess of equal status to my mother. And she says nothing. Perhaps it is all a part of his fantasy to make her appear younger.

A feeling like an electric charge surges through me. I am almost shaking in my eagerness to spit out my next line. "You know what I've heard? The SMP has completely lost control over Shanghai. The Blue Dawn runs the city now."

Raoul doesn't say anything, but I see the anger threatening to burst from the shadows on his face. He raises his hand, perhaps intending to strike me. Cymbals crash in the orchestra pit, signaling the end of a dance, and the dancers on the floor rush to poise themselves like ice sculptures in the garden for the song's end. And they too lift their arms over their heads.

The entire ballroom hangs still for a moment, as the pianist plays his final chord.

I stare through Raoul's outstretched fingers like they are the peephole of a kaleidoscope, down a tunnel into the outstretched fingers of the first dancer pair on the floor, who are locked in an embrace of true passion, their arms twined and foreheads pressed together, and through their hands to the outstretched fingers of the next pair behind them.

There is a scream on the dance floor, which shatters the poetry of the moment. Those slender, poised fingers blooming in the air suddenly droop like wilted flowers, and the sylphlike giggles ringing through the hall, intricate as the flick of a nail against a champagne glass, dissolve into thin air like breath. Around us, pearl earrings tremble like decorative pinwheels in a child's hand. I flee from Raoul and my mother, toward the source of the commotion.

The guests are fighting their way toward the courtyard, fur stoles flying from porcelain shoulders and hats tumbling from disheveled heads. Like a doe running against her herd, I push closer to the fire, against my born instincts. There is a sinking feeling deep in the pit of my stomach. I've been here before, and the wound it opened never stopped bleeding.

In the center of the ballroom, the maple floors gleam like ashen fields in moonlight, around a lone dancer kneeling in the middle, holding her eyes with her blood-soaked fingers. The gold bracelets jangle together on her slender wrists.

I drop to my knees before her. "What did they take?"

Her chest heaves with panic. Slowly, she releases her grip, her fingers drawing down her face. Her nails, painted the fashionable red of the era, leave little white lines against her cheeks, which are shining with tears.

Shadows twist across her face, like ink that twines and dissipates from a brush dipped in water. Tiny droplets of blood, shining like jewels, freckle the area around her nose. But it's her eye sockets that stand out—two pits of roiling darkness on her perfectly made-up face where her eyes would've been, like impurities trapped in white jade.

Just like Usugi.

I imagine her dancing in the birdcage, the gold bracelets on her wrists glowing like miniature moons against the dark ceiling of the Dove House. I recall the glazed look that coated Usugi's face, as if she was imprisoned in a dream.

It's true that none of us have ever been friends. But under this sordid neon sky, we shared something. Without them, there would be no tide of velvet-cased heels and silk that carries us around the dance floor. The air in the cabaret would not buzz with life and madness. A single dancer is like a goldfish in a glass vase, swimming in endless circles against suffocating walls.

"Do you remember what happened? Think hard."

The girl shakes her head, lips parted in shock. "I was just dancing."

The ballroom has almost emptied completely. Instruments litter the orchestra shell like dead bodies, cellos lying on their faces and cornets hastily discarded on chairs.

"But was there any sound? Any smell? Do you remember what the guests around you might have looked like?"

"I think—I think it sounded like thunder." Her skin is blanched, purplish like she has been sitting in the cold.

"Jingwen, you should leave."

My mother's shadow flows over me, filling in the spaces between the dancer and me. There's something about her tone—more jaded than fearful—that tells me she's hiding something.

I rise to face her. "What do you know?"

We are the same height when we stand face-to-face, two snapshots of the very different eras we came of age in. Her hair is shorter, her lips painted in the bee-stung pout of 1920s Hollywood. Meanwhile, my lipstick is brushed so neat within the borders of my lips, the way machines lack the handmade imperfections of the decade before, and I've taken care to match my nail polish to my lipstick.

My mother shakes her head. "I'm not here to help you. I'm just warning you."

I search her face, and she won't meet my eyes. We even draw our eyebrows differently—hers a thin, breathy stroke, and mine the winged-out arch of the new decade.

"You have the same suspicion," I realize. "You think that waipo is involved."

An expression of pain crosses her face.

Behind us, the girl screams again. Raoul kneels beside her, flashing his badge.

"It's alright. I'm from the SMP," he says. "I'm going to take you back to the police station. We can call your family there."

The girl shakes her head violently. "I don't want you to call my family."

I try to maneuver around my mother, but she catches my shoulders, the lavender velvet of her gown shimmering like white fur.

"Don't," she says.

I am revolted by our closeness. All I can stare at is the thick foundation caked into the wrinkles under her eyes. "The other night, a man came into waipo's clinic and asked her to sew a dancer's lips onto some rich woman's face. We need to find out who that man was working for and whether she really did it."

"No, we don't." My mother is panting hard, the faint outline of her ribs pressing against the crushed velvet that encases her body. "I've spent my whole life trying to escape this family, until you brought everything back into the picture."

The silence that falls between us burns like a flame, consuming the oxygen so that we are left to gasp.

After a long time, I find the strength to speak. "Really? Are you just going to sit there prettily and smoke your cigarettes while all these dancers get their faces cut apart?"

"You don't get it," she says softly. She barely moves her lips when she speaks, but I can tell her teeth are gritting together. "You revere her, even though you fear her. She inspires that type of following in people. I know her better than anyone Jingwen, and you. Can't. Win."

She walks closer, looming over me like the wooden goddess in her shrine. The velvet-wrapped points of her high heels clack against the floor like claves. "You think you're protected because she needs you to inherit her art of surgery, or whatever she calls it. It's not because you're special—it's because she needed someone, and you were there. I was in your position once. She needed me to do something, and I changed my mind halfway. The price I paid was too much."

Her skin is pale like ivory, but I am convinced that underneath, Yue Lihai is a collection of roiling waves, dancing and pulsing against her bones. Perhaps they started as tears, but she's never let them fall, and over decades they've roiled and grown into a tsunami with nowhere to go.

All my life, I never paused to wonder how she came to dance in a cabaret. Did Liqing once groom her to deliver gangsters' bones as well? Was it a deep desire to be her own person that drove her out? Maybe I'm not better than her, like I've secretly prided myself my entire life. Maybe I'm the one who didn't get out in time.

"I think you're wrong," I whisper.

The look my mother gives me then—like I'm absolutely pathetic—twists into my chest like a knife.

Behind us, Raoul yells. I wheel around to find him clutching his face, where three gashes shine in his skin. The wheaten dance floor glistens under the spotlights, empty except for a tiny spray of blood at his feet, like scattered anemones rising from the snow.

The girl has run away.

I never even got to learn her name.

Through the ballroom's open doors, the crescent moon shines faintly in a clear sky. The garden is silent and empty.

Raoul starts toward us, but my mother draws her hand gingerly across his shoulder. "Let's just go, Raoul."

As Raoul turns to embrace my mother, I swipe my hand swiftly through the coat pocket where I saw him pocket the smoke leaf.

She turns in a storm of jingling gold bracelets and lavender silk, which seems to dissolve before me like a mirror shattering into flying bits. My breathing becomes very loud in my ears. I turn my wrist over and over, examining the bruises left by mother's thin fingers. Try as I can, I can't feel them.

I wait until they are out of earshot, and I draw the little bag with the smoke leaf out from behind my back. Despite Bailey's description of the smoke leaf, I am not actually holding a leaf. Rather, the substances resembles a flat, curled black fungus—so dark in color it shimmers green.

I pocket it.

I almost ask my grandmother what it all means, everything from the shimmering green fungus to the Blue Dawn's overwhelming hatred of the wooden statue of a sleeping goddess, and whether she's really involved.

For an entire evening, I sit on the roof of the clinic in Blood Alley, my high heels arranged neatly beside me on the tiles, breathing in the incense that wanders from the crack in her window. It's just incense, but it taunts me, sliding under my hair and forming hoops around my body like the Cabaret Voliere's trapeze—a constant reminder that I am never really free.

Through the roof, I can hear my grandmother's voice, conversing with a gangster. It's soothing to hear her, even if our last interaction was tense. I can picture her disinfecting her tools in boiling water, the sleeves of her blouse rolled up to her elbows. There is a soft, low voice responding to her.

I can't tell their exact words, but they are preparing a new patient for surgery. I begin to slip into a feverish panic, not knowing whether she is about to operate on a gangster or a socialite. It'd be easy to swing myself down onto the fire escape and peek through the curtains—she might not even see me in her concentration.

But I guess I'd rather not know.

"Hold on a second. There's a draft. It's not good for the patient."

My grandmother slides the window shut, and their voices instantly dampen until I can't hear them at all. The incense trail scatters into the purple evening air.

She probably knows I'm here—she's too smart, and I'm too naïve. But she won't call me out, and come Friday, when I arrive at the usual time to pick up her bones, neither of us will mention it.

I sit for a little longer, watching the neon signs flicker on one by one down Blood Alley, before sliding back down the fire escape until I've dropped in the narrow row behind the bars, where a few scullery boys are scraping white bass and asparagus shoots into a dumpster, while a kitchen manager calls for them to hurry up. None of them turn to stare, and I duck through alley after alley, drifting like a napkin dropped over the edge of a river cruise, until I realize I don't recognize my surroundings anymore.

The little street I'm standing in is gray, as if the color has been leached away by the sun. The roofs crawl over one another like fig roots fighting for territory, the polluted sky tiled in odd shapes in between the edges. A tall red sign rises over the collapsed roofs, like a larger-than-life numismatic charm warding off the surrounding neon. Two characters blaze down the center in white neon: 虹廟.

Hong Miao. The name means Rainbow Temple, but there is nothing colorful about the alley.

In the semidarkness, I make out a row of neat, dark shapes in front of a closed red door. They are folded bodies, bowed in supplication, holding incense sticks in their hands.

I've never noticed a temple here before.

It seems that after my first sojourn through the Jing'an Temple, I've awakened some type of curse. Now, I'm seeing temples everywhere, as if they are weeds growing out of the cracks between cabarets and Turkish baths.

At the sound of my footsteps, one of the worshippers straightens. She is wearing an elaborate, blue-beaded crown, studded with white pearls and red tassels that hang down to her shoulders. Her eyes are painted in brilliant red shadow, which rises at the corners like a bird's wings.

"You're a cabaret girl," she says, her gaze roving over my modern qipao and Western-style heels.

I study her in return—a red gown hemmed with golden bells, the sleeves wide at the wrists, turquoise beads dripping down her cheeks like rain. "And what are you?"

"A sing-song girl."

I've heard of her kind before.

She smiles. There is a beauty mark on her upper lip that would earn her comparisons to Jean Harlow at the Paramount. But in the sing-song houses, where the girls croon Peking Opera and caress stringed pipas on their laps, I can imagine the praises would be different. "My name is Yuechao," she says.

Her name means "musical waves."

I touch my fingertips to my collarbone. "Jingwen."

She makes an amused noise under her breath, as we acknowledge the mutual irony of our names.

Another of the worshippers rises to her feet and dusts her knees off with her large sleeves. She is dressed similarly, in floating robes with gold ribbons braided in her hair. Ignoring me, she briefly rests her hand on Yuechao's shoulder, before disappearing down the little street. Soon, she is washed in gray as well.

"What are you praying to?" I ask.

Yuechao points up beside the door, where I realize there is an old painting nailed to the wood.

I squint up at the portrait, faded by years of bright sun. I can barely make out a goddess in flowing white robes against a blue background. Maybe there is a lotus or some type of white bird with fanned feathers on its head. I can't tell—the details are obscured by a tangle of electrical wiring hanging over the painting. There are tattered red ribbons strewn across the wires, where it appears someone tried to pin them out of the way—but over time they have struggled loose again.

Nonetheless, it's easy to figure out who the goddess is.

It's Guanyin, the Queen of Compassion. My Mother of Calamity.

"But that's the door," I point out. "Why don't you go inside?"

She sweeps the curtain of turquoise beads from her eyes, with a patient smile. "Courtesans have come to this temple for centuries to ask for luck and prosperity," she explains. "It was a Buddhist temple during the Ming Dynasty, a family shrine constructed by a wealthy scholar who lived behind there." She points at the locked doors of a shop that now sells imported cigarettes, rows of small black boxes etched with silver letters lining the windows. "There were a lot of brothels on this street. Since then, it's become a Daoist temple, and the brothels have gone out of business. Many of the gods inside have changed, but she hasn't."

The girl raises her chin to admire the faded portrait. I look at it too, the smudged shape of white and blue paint, with faded black lines. It's nothing awe-inspiring.

"I'm going to go inside," I say.

Yuechao shrugs. "Sure. It doesn't cost money."

I press both my palms against the cool, red paint lacquering the door. With a gentle push, the door gives way with a soft creak, to reveal a small courtyard washed in velveteen smoke. I step over the threshold and catch the door against my hand to shut it softly.

A flared, pewter burner crackles in the middle of the courtyard, the tips of incense sticks glowing inside like ruby pins. There are a few worshippers standing around the burner, bowing with incense clasped between their hands.

Hong Miao is startlingly modest for a temple. There are only three rooms, filled with colorful, grizzled warriors like the King of the Underworld and the God of Wealth. Nonetheless, the flow of living bodies makes the courtyard comforting, a stark contrast to the unnerving quietness of the Jing'an Temple.

Everyone here seems to be in a hurry. A businessman trips on the burners in his hurry to fly out the door, spilling his briefcase onto the ground, which pops open to reveal rolls of cash. As he hurriedly gathers it in his arms, a mother rushes past him toward the God of Wealth, hushing the crying infant in her arms lest he drown out her prayers.

I wander past them into the main hall, which is dedicated to the original Guanyin from the Ming Dynasty, the style of the awning and filigree windows different from the other rooms.

There are a few worshippers praying to the goddess, lost in concentration. Silently, on either side of the door, two Blue Dawn gangsters are standing guard, their silver hands ready to fly to their weapons at any second. Their gaze follows me as I walk up to the altar.

I turn over my shoulder. "What?" I ask them, hoping to convey my annoyance. "It's not illegal for me to visit a temple."

One of them looks away. The other narrows his eyes. "We have other interests besides you, Miss Yue."

The answer makes me blush, as if I've inflated my self-importance. I spin on my ankle to face Guanyin instead.

The altar may have stood for centuries, but the statue representing the goddess has clearly been replaced. In this temple, the goddess sits on her altar with her arms drawn up before her, her body twisted to the side as if a doe has flitted by, and she has turned her head to watch it. The posture is mildly flirtatious, showing off the slenderness of her wrist and the arrangement of silver bracelets pressed to her inner elbow. Her statue is made of vibrant painted clay, flowing Han Dynasty robes emphasizing her waiflike delicacy. Unlike her plain, wooden incarnation in the Jing'an Temple, her hair is pinned in an elaborate updo, her robes open in a deep V over her breasts.

But in the most startling contrast of all, her eyes are open, laughing as if we have an inside joke to share. The eyes are paired with the face of an ingenue, her small, cherry mouth painted in a swooning gasp.

My mother says the Mother of Calamity was a demon once.

This statue looks like a dancing girl, who might dance with us at the Paramount. But if anything, all it proves is that Daoist temple decorators have a lighter heart than Buddhist ones.

I slip back into the little monochrome street. The girl in the beaded headdress is still praying, her hands clasped neatly under her forehead. A pattern of supplicant bodies has rearranged itself, suggesting that some of the sing-song girls have left, to be replaced by others.

"Yuechao," I say her name.

She lifts her head, the beads rippling in her hair like a field of wildflowers. "Yes?"

"What do you call her?" I ask, nodding up at the goddess's portrait.

"Niang Niang," she answers.

"Just Niang Niang?"

"Yes. It's what palace girls called the empress, and what the Jade Maidens of Heaven called the queen mother." Her smile grows sly. "She is the Patron Saint of Whores."

It shouldn't affect me, but I blush. "How did you become a sing-song girl?"

She laughs, perhaps slightly bitterly. "When I was four years old, my grandmother sold me to a sing-song house. From a very young age, I learned how to read Classical Chinese and memorized all the songs about the gods, so that I could perform them for the guests that visited us. That's how I know so much about Niang Niang."

"Is it true the Daoists see her as a goddess of destruction?" I ask, surprising myself by repeating my mother.

"Does it matter? Just like you and I are the same thing, they are also the same thing." She cocks her head to the side testily, daring me to challenge the comparison. When I don't, she continues. "Different identities are worth more in different times, to different people. Just like how several decades ago, poets wrote about how sing-song houses were the palaces of the night. But now it's the ballrooms on Yuyuan Road which light up the map like constellations, and girls like you rule the night."

I detect a hint of scorn in her voice. "Why don't you become one of us then?"

She squints, and all the beads and pearls arranged atop her hair quake like they are angry. "You mean a cabaret girl?"

"We don't have to know how to read Classical Chinese."

She makes a bemused noise in her throat, and her brow crinkles, but for a minute she doesn't speak. "Want to know about a dream I've been having recently?" she finally says. "I keep dreaming about a roulette wheel. It keeps spinning, and I wait for it to stop. I think it gets faster. There is no way to make it stop, without burning our fingers from the speed. You and I—we are both products of New Shanghai. And this city is obsessive, and fast. Once we start going down a path, no matter as a courtesan or a dancer, we can't stop. Not with pride and money at stake. We've forgotten how to slow down. All we can do is adapt and carve out a place for ourselves— maybe protect our sisters if we can."

I think about my grandmother, who started as a warlord's physician, treating routine wounds on the battlefield. And now she makes limbs out of silver at the defiance of the gods.

Perhaps that's what my mother tried to warn me of. Even now that there is a face stealer hiding amongst the guests in our cabarets, we still go back.

"If you change your mind," I tell Yuechao, "you can always find me at the Paramount. I could help."

I'm surprised at the words that come from my mouth. Why would I invite more competition to our doorstep, when Beibei is already a formidable rival?

But then I think about Beibei dancing with Maia, her cheeks flushed and a lightness in her step I've never observed before. We've watched each other so closely every night for the past two years, looking for flaws and hidden weaknesses—yet I don't know her at all.

That night, I dream of roulette wheels too—white and pink stripes on a spinning disk, shining so bright I can't see anything else. I hold my hand up to hide from the light, but it bleeds through my fingers.

I think of how I should walk away, but there is some small part of me which is mesmerized by the light. Maybe it's the part of my grandmother I've inherited. I should close my eyes, but I discover I can't look away.

CHAPTER TEN

E xactly a week later, I meet with Bailey at the Café Montmartre again, on the only night I'm not expected at the Paramount. I've dressed in the qipao he gifted me, a pair of kingfisher earrings trembling at my earlobes.

Bailey is sitting in the back again, against the window. The blue night outside hangs like a silk curtain, punctuated by white, glowing streetlamps.

"Hello, Jingwen," he says, taking off his hat, as I make my way through the bronze, spindly tables that crowd the café floor. "You look beautiful tonight."

There is a poetry reading happening in front of the hearth, a gathering of French literati and their young girlfriends splayed across plush couches, hearty flames crackling in the fireplace.

I march straight up to Bailey's table, where I place my hand, palm down, beside his coffee plate. "I've brought a surprise."

"Really?" He smiles, folds his hands in front of him. "I get the sense you're not the type of girl who likes to waste time. What is it?"

I lift my hand, to reveal the bag of smoke leaf I took from Raoul on the table—all but a pinky nail's worth, which I have kept in a corner of my makeup drawers, folded in a handkerchief.

"No way, you didn't really do it," Bailey says, sipping his coffee. His eyebrows are arched in surprise.

"I really did it." I tuck my hair behind my ears, showing off my kingfisher earrings.

He continues smiling in that reluctant way, studying me as if I am the centerpiece of a fountain he finds deeply interesting.

"Something about your expression signals to me you enjoyed stealing for me. Did you?"

I draw out the chair opposite him and plop down in it.

"This is what you do, isn't it?" I say, with a tight-lipped smile. "Go around metropolitan cities around the world enchanting unknowing girls into performing bad deeds."

A waitress comes and pours two glasses of red wine for us.

He laughs as he drinks, his hand lingering at the top button of his shirt. I know that under his collar, he's wearing his Daoist coin charm. "Think of me as the devil."

The wine is tart, stinging the sides of my tongue.

Bailey chuckles to himself, his gray eyes narrowed. "There are a few things I've learned about cabaret girls since I first started dancing with them in New York. Some women are looking for a husband, some are looking to get out of poverty. But I don't think either of these applies to you."

I drink my wine with a flippant toss of my hair. "I've never thought about it."

Which is a lie, of course.

In Shanghai, everybody is running from something. We all know that. But everybody is also running toward something. Only most of us don't know what we're running toward. I thought I wanted to drown in a sea of silver ingots, but if that was truly all I wanted, then why did I go to the Dove House that night?

Behind the coffee bar, a waitress begins to steam milk, an industrial growl deafening the pleasant tinkle of teacups.

"Why don't we try the smoke leaf?" I whisper.

I reach for the bag under the edge of his plate, but Bailey catches my hand. His fingers are warm and dry.

"An adventurous one you are," he says in a playful voice, but he doesn't smile this time. "That would not be a good idea."

Bailey slips the bag of smoke leaf out from under my fingers and pockets it deep within his vest, somewhere my fingers could never reach. Then he sets his empty wineglass down and pours himself another—the insouciance of a man who is trying to hide something.

The possibilities spin through my head—perhaps when smoked, the fungus allows one to selectively erase their memories, and Raoul wants my mother to erase her memories of me; maybe it extends the life of those who consume it, a magical elixir that the old emperors sought through dynasties; or perhaps it is just a tastier smoke than tobacco.

"What are you staring at?" he asks, hooking a finger around the stem of my glass to pour me some as well.

I smile a little now because the cards are in my hand this round.

"So, I brought you what you wanted," I tell him, trying to bring back the playful atmosphere. "What do I get in return?"

"Ah." He smiles again and jerks his head toward the street beyond the window. "There's somewhere fun I'd like to take you. Shall we?"

"That sounds lovely."

Bailey's Packard Twelve broods silently on the next street with the headlights on, his driver patiently reading a newspaper in the front seat. The danger rises through my chest like the bubbles in champagne. Maybe I do have a bit of Liqing in me after all, that desires to beat a challenge.

He pulls the door open with a crunch like bones breaking, and I slide onto the soft leather seat.

The automobile lurches forward.

"So where exactly are we going?" I ask.

"The Coeur de la Rose," Bailey says with a wink. "An exclusive gentleman's club."

"I've never heard of it."

"You'll like it."

We drive along the river for a bit, the headlights illuminating sampans bobbing on the dark waves like fireflies, brightened by lanterns on the prow. When the car stops, and Bailey opens the door onto the grand view of a short, seedy street near the Bund, I laugh.

He's taken me to Blood Alley.

Bailey offers me his hand and helps me out of the car. "What's amusing about it?" he asks.

"I know this street." I step on the sidewalk and twirl once, to indicate to him I have no fear of this dark street.

"Do you?" There's a twinkle in Bailey's eye.

At the street corner, a Russian man in a long overcoat is roasting fat, dark sausages on a charred grill, enveloped in a veil of thick, oily smoke. He is the only sign of life in the area. The row of gaping mouths that had sighed cool smoke at Zikai and me are closed, no hint of their glowing teeth.

After all, avenues like Blood Alley do not come to life until long past midnight.

I take care walking on the street in my white leather oxford heels, afraid to damage them in vomit or blood.

"But Bailey," I remark, as the driver pulls away, "there's no club here called the Coeur de la Rose."

"You'll know soon enough." Bailey smirks.

He walks up to the Fantasio Café, whose windows are darkened, the neon-lettering overhead switched off. The door swings open under his touch, revealing a cozy bar fashioned after an Irish pub. The underside of my oxford heels sticks to spilled beer that refuses to dry. A string of lights over the bar are switched on, but there is no bartender in sight.

"This way," Bailey sings.

He walks around the bar, to a small shrine buried amongst shelves of bitters and fine gins, the kind many of the locals like to keep in the backs of restaurants and street stalls, with a vessel of burning incense and the small bronze figurine of a goddess. Supposed to bring good business, or whatever. I stand on my tiptoes to see over his shoulder.

It's Guanyin Bodhisattva, of course. I'm not surprised, given her popularity amongst the older generation. This figurine of the Goddess of Mercy is carved from ivory, with curvy hips and pillowy lips that give her the appearance of an ancient, humorless pinup girl. Fitting, given she was made to watch over a sailor-run saloon. She could be the Mother of Calamity from our show, except that her eyes are hollow, leaving a cavity inside her skull that is dusted with ash.

I don't understand, until Bailey pulls a stick of burning incense from the vessel and holds it to the goddess's right eye socket. Then it dawns on me what he's doing. I've heard stories before from guests in the dance halls, about establishments like this in America during Prohibition.

"It's inside of another club?" I ask.

Guanyin's eyes light on fire, and the wall rumbles opens.

Some mechanism, built into the foundation of the Fantasio Café, turns its gears and pulls the shelves of bitters and spices apart, the shrine sinking deep into the chasm that appears.

Bailey sweeps his arm out, toward the dark corridor leading into the depths under the club. "After you, Jingwen."

I step into the chasm, and my heels make a noise on glass, like I'm walking over ice about to break. I grasp for the wall, and my fingers meet their own reflection. The corridor is paved with mirrors on all four sides. Animal heads, stuffed with cotton, line the walls, with soft candles lit where the eyes once were.

I run my hand over the velvet nose of a deer and through the mane of a lion whose canines are bared in a roar. The flickering of the candles is hypnotic, strangely alive.

The doctor stops behind me as I admire the giant feline, his hands in his pockets. I inhale his earthen cologne, which reminds me of the hunt. "I see I've managed to surprise you."

I turn my head, just a little, and I meet his gaze in the mirror. My red lips stand out in the silvery blue sea of glass like a target. We are everywhere.

"I've never seen anything like it." I draw my finger along the mirror, leaving a soft smear, which becomes reflected an infinite number of times.

At the end of the hall, two coat girls stand by a black velvet curtain, wearing identical low-cut velvet dresses, with a wreath of fresh flowers around their hips. "Members only," the one on the left says.

"Ah." Bailey produces a black card with flaming red letters from his wallet.

He shrugs his coat off his shoulders, and I do the same. I feel oddly exposed now in my qipao, as I watch one of the girls disappear through the swinging curtain with my wool coat.

"She's with me," Bailey explains.

The remaining girl nods and draws the curtain back, revealing a large, circular atrium padded with black velvet over all the walls, which extends over the domed ceiling like a starless night. Vertical neon lettering, in a language I can't recognize, drips down the walls, blinking red and blue. More animal heads, bigger than the ones in the hall, loom overhead, trapped in frozen screams—animals I've never heard of, with flaming manes and elaborate, tiered antlers, all with candles in their eyes.

Bailey sighs and glides down the stairs leading into the atrium, as if he has just walked into his summer vacation home. "It's so refreshing to be back."

In one corner, an expressionless band wearing leather masks beats on an assortment of horse-skin drums behind a row of candles, the vibrations pulsing through the floor. I can almost believe every living body in the Coeur de la Rose shares one heart. Our shadows rise and fall with the candle flames on the wall.

Bailey guides me through an expensive-looking arrangement of plush magenta couches, and we pass another guest in a stiff navy suit, who nods at Bailey. The face of his gold wristwatch catches the candlelight.

Bailey is watching me closely. "So, what do you think?"

I'm staring at the band, which keeps playing the same riff over and over again, a gallery of matte, nondescript masks. "This music—how do you dance to it?"

Bailey runs his fingers along the back of a couch, which turns a different sheen of red under his touch. The tantalization of a smile lights up at the corner of his mouth. "There's no need to dance."

The lightness in his voice sends chills down my spine. Because there is no rearrangement of Shanghai I can imagine where there is no need to dance.

He saunters through the maze of couches, and I follow, sometimes having to navigate the long way around a waved love seat or a slanted sofa. There are patrons sitting on the couches, but they're staring blankly into space, vapid smiles painted on their faces.

At the end of the atrium, a long sandalwood counter curves to form the shape of an eye. Behind the counter, a man dressed in an elaborate robe made of animal skins is dancing, bending forward and back at the hips like the bones are missing from his body, his hands outstretched like he can call forth the rain. Or the dead.

I know, without having ever seen a dance like that before, that he is a shaman like Zikai.

"That," Bailey explains to me, "is the bar."

The shaman is wearing a dusty mirror around his neck, from which hangs dyed and faded leather cords, in orange, green, and blue. A tall crown of curling yak horns wreaths his head, dripping with threads of black yarn.

There are indeed empty wineglasses hanging by the stem on an ornate wooden shelf that swings down from the ceiling, dangerously close to the shaman's horned crown. But aside from the hanging glasses and a honeycombed wall displaying gins and bitters, the Coeur de la Rose's bar pales against the presence of its bartender, whose aura rises like a multicolored sun, too alive against the black velvet walls.

"A bar?" I repeat.

When the dance stops, I catch a glimpse of the shaman's face. He is wearing a black leather mask, the mask's expression frozen in a scream. In the mirror that hangs over his chest, I see a mirage of my own face, clouded and unclear.

My heel rolls into something soft and rubbery, and I hear a light groan. With a gasp, I realize I've stepped on the forearm of a man lying on the ground, his tie pulled loose from being dragged around. The floor is strewn with unconscious bodies—mostly men, but also a few women in fluttering brocade gowns.

"What kind of drinks does he make?" I whisper urgently to Bailey.

"The drinks served here bend the senses," Bailey whispers in my ear, his lips close to my hair.

"Like opium?"

"Sweeter than opium." His breath is warm and soft against my skin. "Imagine a cocktail infused with the same bitters that shamans use to commune with nature spirits and the gods."

I glance around at a few half-empty glasses resting on low tables. Some of the cocktails shimmer with foil like a fish's scale, some are dressed with a dark substance that reminds me of oil spilled in the sea. But the emptier the glass, the less distinct the glamour—until all that's left at the bottom of some is a brown, watery sludge.

"I didn't know you were so familiar with shamanism."

He straightens his tie with a smile. "Ah, I chose Shanghai because she could offer things New York never could."

The shaman lifts his head suddenly, and although I can't see through the mask, I sense he is looking at me. The stitched white circles where his eyes should be bore into my vision. Time seems to freeze as we face each other from across the room, the mirror on his chest swaying side to side.

"Why don't we get a drink?" Bailey suggests, putting his arm around my shoulder lightly.

I force my jaw open to speak. "Of course."

We approach the bar slowly, and the shaman stops dancing. The cords hanging over his leather vest continue to swing, the candlelight reflected in the tight white leather stretched over his eyes.

"The menu," Bailey says, indicating a chalkboard hung over the counter.

There is only one drink on the menu: 组。

He smiles. "This drink is called Ancestry."

The shaman turns his back and begins spooning ingredients out of baskets and glass jars displayed on the black wooden shelves, ascending and descending a movable ladder so fast I get dizzy from watching. And then he is shaking the cocktail with the fury of a demon, his teeth gritted and his knuckles white with the effort.

When he slings the cocktail across the counter, light blue froth spills over the edge. I cup my hands around it, and the drink glows between my fingers. My skin tingles where the froth touches. When the alcohol evaporates, it leaves a trail of silver, like the mucus left by a passing snail. In that glittering residue, I see my own reflection upon my own skin, fractured into dust.

I turn the glass around in my hands. There is a dark silt in my cocktail that reminds me of the smooth, dark stones found at the bottom of riverbeds, which have lain unturned for centuries. It seems I am holding a serving of the Huangpu River itself, which has witnessed the dividing and conquering of Shanghai and caught her tears in its waves. If I close my eyes, I think I can smell the sea.

"Take a sip, and you'll experience your life retold," Bailey says, as the bartender passes him his own version of an Ancestry.

Bailey's Ancestry is a deep orange-gold.

I hold my own cocktail beside his to compare.

"They look different."

He points at me, and then himself. "We are different."

He leans his elbow down on the counter, as I raise my glass to my lips and taste the drink: 组, which floats across my tongue like the wisps of a cloud. Drinking the cocktail feels like possession—sweet and numbing like star anise and Himalayan silver mint have suffused through my body until I can't feel my own hands anymore.

I can't place the sensation, which reminds me of that soft, pink glow that paints the sky in Shanghai, in the hollowness just above the skyscrapers, where the neon melts into the industrial smog. It's the space between waking and dreaming, when anything is possible.

"And you thought you knew Shanghai," Bailey declares, triumphant.

A few sips into the cocktail, and I begin to hear the refrains of a forlorn zither tune, the strings loose and producing slightly flat notes.

I feel the warmth of Bailey's arm against mine, but otherwise I've left the cushioned insides of the Coeur de la Rose. Instead, I stand at the doorway of a teakwood temple, which floats upon darkness. Red tiles spill across the roof, the window panels carved with flowering omens.

I step over the raised threshold, to greet whatever god lies inside.

A younger version of my grandmother rests behind the altar, where the enlightened ones usually are. I see her sitting there with her legs crossed, her fingers forming a pretty Buddhist mudra. There is a golden ocean carved onto the panels behind her, molten waves rising over her head. Her eyes are closed, and a relaxed smile graces her youthful face. But behind her, the golden waves are blinding.

I hold my hand over my eyes to shield myself from the light.

"The cocktail's drugged," I breathe, shaking my head and sending my kingfisher earrings flying. I lean harder into Bailey's arm—hoping it can anchor me to the Coeur de la Rose.

"It's made by a shaman," Bailey reminds me, relaxing his shoulders as he takes a deep draught from his gold Ancestry, which sparkles so hard under the candle flames I have to close my eyes. "No other club in Shanghai has anything like it. But this is what Shanghai *could* be—the natural evolution that comes after dancing. Imagine if instead of a playground for illicit affairs, every cabaret was like this one—a place to experience the intoxication of shamanic magic. Dancing is inherently carnal, but I can offer something more. I can offer something *outside* the body."

"This club—*you*—"

I'm stammering, my attention fractured by the cocktail.

"Yes, Jingwen," he says. "Welcome to my club."

He turns his body gently, so that I cannot lean on him any longer.

I take another sip.

We are in a temple hall, but instead of worshippers, roses grow out of the cold stone floor, the blooms turned up to face my grandmother as if she is the sun. I am young again, and I run amid rows of carefully pruned, imported roses, stooping to inhale their fragrance: damask, bourbon, hybrid tea. They creep up the stone pillars like vines, studding the sacrificial altar with thorns.

I am not sure my grandmother is alive, so I shake her still body behind the altar. "Waipo," I call to her. "It's time to wake up."

But I'm answered only by the lonely melody of the out-of-tune zither.

The warm afternoon sun rises to flood the hall, drenching the entire hall in an ethereal glow.

"But I've never been here in real life," I say out loud, stretching my hand out to steady myself with the wall. The velvet fibers prick the tender flesh under my fingernails.

But the golden ocean behind Liqing's head is so bright, I can't see the dark velvet anymore.

"Not everything you know is a memory," Bailey says pleasantly. "Some things run in your blood. And I've found a way to bring them out."

Behind me, someone calls Bailey's name, and I'm hurled from the temple, as if I've left my body lying inert in the rosebushes, the stone floor pressed against my cheek—and suddenly I'm back in an underground speakeasy full of flaming, stuffed animal heads.

A tall, thin man wearing darkened glasses and a dark fedora has approached, clutching a fabric sack in his hands.

"Would you look at these bones, Doctor," he professes, holding the sack open. "Beautiful cocktails tonight, by the way. I'm listening to a two-hundred-violin symphony. My father was a violinist, although he passed away from cholera."

Bailey exhales in satisfaction after drinking from his cocktail. Behind him, a lion's head bursts into fire, wreathed by a mane of golden flames. The flames pulse in time to the soft harp rippling in the background. I'm convinced I'm imagining it, until one of the flower-wreathed coat girls comes with a watering can and upends it over the stuffed lion. The flames snuff with a dull sizzle, and water trickles down the velvet walls onto the floor, an element of profound sorrow added by the harpsichord.

Unaware of the burning lion's head behind him, Bailey leans over to examine the man's wares.

Tears of emotion streaming down my face, I peer into the sack with him. I recognize lots of arms, not many legs.

"Wait!" I exclaim.

In my head, a white-gloved hand takes a knife to the zither strings, which snap with a twang, cutting the zither-player's disembodied fingers, blood freckling the broad, wooden instrument like breakfast ketchup.

And my head is silent and empty.

Bailey and the man both stare at me.

"What are they for?" I ask.

The man dips his chin, and I know he's looking at me, although really all I see is my own reflection swimming in the dark shades he wears. Try as I can, I can't figure out why he is wearing sunglasses indoors.

He grins, his teeth blackened by smoke. With a glee that threatens to overwhelm him, he plunges his hand inside his coat vest and produces a small glass vial of lavender powder, which appears to shimmer when he turns it under the light. "Give me your hand."

I thrust my palm out.

He uncorks the vial and taps a smattering of lavender dust into my hand. "Do you wake up feeling tired? Do you have trouble falling asleep at night? Throw this elixir in your cocktail, and all your problems will be cured."

Even under the influence of the strange concoction in my cocktail glass, I hesitate before doing as he says. "What is it though?"

The man beckons for me to come closer, so I lean in so he might whisper in my ear.

"Powdered dragon bones," he says with a mystical lilt to his voice, and then he roars with laughter. I stumble back in surprise, the insides of my ear twinging. "Just kidding. They're arms and legs

I bought from that silver-limbed gang. I forget what their name is. Can you believe it? After they've lobbed their arms off, they have no use for the flesh."

He continues. "I use an animal-feed grinder to crush those bones into a powder finer than sand, throw in some pretty glitter, and then I stand in the middle of Times Square where the tourists abound. 'Confectioned dragon bones from the Orient!' I yell from atop a crate, and I can sell these vials at two hundred dollars a pop." He tries to sip his cocktail and ends up snorting it instead, flecks of emerald and gold flying out of his nostrils. "I'd like to get my product on the shelves of pharmacies and doctors' offices. Now, that's what Dr. Thompson here can help me with."

Bailey catches my arm to keep me from backing away any farther, and it's the only thing that makes me realize I've stumbled too close to the stuffed head of a horse, its blazing eyes about to set my hair on fire.

"Come this way, Al. I'll give you some phone numbers." Bailey produces a pen from a pocket inside his jacket, and the pair walks to the nearest plush couch.

I stay behind, gaping in shock.

Ever since I was a little girl, every time I strode past the flickering sign outside the Turkish bath, surrounded by blue smoke and invisible ghosts, I had carried the weight of Liqing's secret on my shoulders. As if there was a grave importance to the whole thing, and my reluctant sacrifice was enough to move worlds. But all I have been doing is ferry the raw ingredients of a tourist trap.

I wonder what Xiao Lei would say if he learned the bones of his forearm were sprinkled like sugar into the tea of tourists in New York City. I gulp down the remainder of my drink with a new desperation. It takes me a few seconds to actually swallow because my throat is numb. But then I wipe my mouth with the back of my hand, only to see my lips have left a trail of clumped, brown sludge.

I bite back the urge to scream.

"Jingwen." Bailey returns, his Ancestry almost depleted. A faint shimmer clings to the glass, but the dregs have similarly browned.

"Are you enjoying yourself?" he asks, that familiar svelte lilt return-ing to his voice.

I set my empty cocktail glass down on a high table and drag the back of my hand against the tablecloth in an attempt to wipe away the detritus.

I wonder what Bailey saw in his own vision, but his calm gray eyes betray nothing.

"I've never been to a club like this," I admit.

He raises his eyebrows, pleased. "Do you like my business model, Jingwen? Because you see, Shanghai is only a start. Once I have my hands on Shanghai, I'm going to build an empire. Think of what New York could become if I found more shamans like this one and opened clubs there—and then in Chicago, Atlan-tic City, San Francisco. You could be a hostess all the way across the sea."

The Daoist charm glints in the hollow of his throat.

In that moment, he appears as a stranger to me again, just an older American man with an expensive suit and a charming way of carrying himself. I shake my head, my kingfisher earrings trem-bling at my cheeks. No, he's been a stranger the whole time. I was the one who fooled myself into believing I'd opened him up and seen the gears that twist under his skin.

"Where did you find a shaman who was willing to become a bartender?"

Bailey wipes a drop of the brown sludge from the corner of his mouth. It clumps on his fingertips, before dripping to the floor. "Ah, last year I read in a medical journal about a British doctor burned out from his practice who journeyed into the grasslands of Inner Mongolia to find peace. He wrote about a transcendent experience local shamans could create using various rare flowers. I thought I spotted an opportunity to create a radical analgesic, so I came to China to find these flowers. But now that I'm here, I realize it would be a waste to use such beautiful substances just in times of pain. These shamanic drugs, when mixed with spirits and bitters, can create immense pleasure and escape. Our bartender here is the most entrepreneurial shaman I've ever met. I offered him a sum of money he couldn't resist, and here he is."

I glance over my shoulder at the bar, where I can barely make out the shaman's crown over a sea of dark homburg hats.

If all of Bailey's peculiar business deals can manifest in great fortune, then Bailey may have unseated Neville Harrington as the wealthiest date for the Firefighters' Yuletide Ball. But it feels like a curse now.

"Your ideas are certainly unique, Doctor," I say.

"Thank you, Jingwen. There are so many pretty things in Shanghai, it would be a waste not to share them with the rest of the world."

Far away, another voice calls to Bailey for another business deal. I realize that's exactly what the Coeur de la Rose is—a playground for these rich, foreign businessmen to share their plans to divide and conquer Shanghai. The shaman is just a pretty part of the décor.

Left alone, I wish the music in my head would come back, but it's faded away. I don't even remember what I'd heard, everything swallowed by the beating of those horse-skin drums, which vibrate under my skin, sending involuntary shivers up my shoulders. The neon writing on the wall appears to be shaking.

The first night I accepted Bailey's invitation to dance, I involved myself with a dangerous game, and I've stepped too far to get out easily. The only way left to go is forward.

I pace around the club, dragging my hand through the black velvet that encases the walls, until I come across a doorway hung with a red silk curtain, which flutters as if an open breeze is passing through a garden veranda. Curious about what lies behind the red curtain, I walk up to it. The silk flaps wildly before me, so much that when I hold my hand out, I have a hard time grasping the curtain to pull it aside.

A cold hand seizes my wrist from behind me. I let go of the curtain with a gasp.

It's one of the coat girls, a crown of burnt-orange marigolds resting atop her curled hair. She wags her finger at me silently.

"Why not?" I ask. "What's in there?"

She shakes her head. "It's not for you to see."

She grabs my wrist and pulls me back in front of the bar. There, she leaves me under a horned beast with flared nostrils and long whiskers—a beast whose mien I recognize grazing the walls of Liqing's clinic in a brush painting. I think of how humiliating that must be, for such a great creature to be reduced to a lampshade.

A sweaty, heady smell begins to fill the air. I observe the red silk curtain fluttering in the doorway, hiding something Bailey doesn't want me to see.

"Jingwen, there you are. Let's get another drink." Bailey materializes out of thin air, his pinky lifted from the stem of an empty glass.

"I—yes, let's go."

I draw my attention away from the fluttering silk curtain, and Bailey pushes through the crowd at the bar, calling each guest by name, until we have gained the shaman bartender's undivided attention. This close, I can smell a faint, gamey musk from the shaman's leather robes.

"Two more please," Bailey says, holding up two fingers.

The threads tied to the crown of ram horns shiver like rain. I find I'm almost dreading what he will produce—whether I will see a continuation of what I saw before, or something worse.

"Thank you," I say in Mandarin, wondering if he will respond differently. But it occurs to me he might hail from a region of China where they speak a different tongue.

He places the resulting concoction in my hands. The drink is svelte black without any garnishes—deeper and more velveteen than the sludge that coats the bottoms of some of the guests' drinks.

My hands are shaking slightly, so I lean against the wall to steady my elbow.

"It's different from the last one."

Bailey receives his own Ancestry, a spritely green that reminds me of the freshly cut grass in the Bubbling Well Cemetery, or a French Concession lawn. His smile turns wicked. "Go ahead. Try it."

We clink glasses.

Around us, the atrium has filled with more guests—herringbone suits and white hats with dark ribbons. Simultaneously, the coat girls are going around and placing flower crowns of hibiscus and magnolia around the necks of the burning animals. The fragrance of wildflowers grows sickening, like a rotting garden of paradise.

I taste my Ancestry.

The cocktail burns my mouth, a bristling heat that suffuses through my entire body, flickering behind my eyes like I've become a wild animal on the wall, flames pouring out of my orifices. The black drink coats my throat, bubbling like oil until I feel like I'm choking. I squeeze my eyes shut and force it down.

I hear the music again, this time a portentous orchestral score executed by flutes carved from giant, hollow gourds and animal bones—desperate air rushing to fill the empty space.

This time, there is a young woman ascending a blue mountain alone. The moon is red in the sky, and she stumbles over a twig lying in the path. In her arms, she cradles a swath of white cloth—a crying infant whose nose and ears have turned red from the cold. Wavering left and right on the path, sometimes dangerously close to the edge, the young woman presses on. It's my grandmother again.

Finally, she's reached the top of the mountain. In summertime, there might have been a garden with blue-throated bee-eaters and Mandarin ducks, but now all that remains is a cold, shallow pool, whose waters have turned a deep, jade green, surrounded by jagged rocks that tear my grandmother's feet and clothes. In the center of the jade pool, a stone altar glistens under the moon. The air contains the crisp fragrance of pine needles, although there are no pine trees on the mountain.

Liqing lays the bundle upon the altar, exposed to the stars, and the cloth falls aside. The baby thrashes and twists, crying from the cold.

The cry hurts my ears like a knife. Because I recognize myself, all alone now under the sky.

Bailey stuffs his hands into his pockets, as if we are about to go for a stroll in the park. "Why don't you be my date to the Firefight-ers' Ball, Jingwen?"

I am shocked back to the soft cavern of the Coeur de la Rose. "What?"

Bailey stands under the stuffed head of a European dragon with a scaly, flared snout, and the same candlelight appears to flicker in both their eyes. "I asked you to come with me to the Firefighters' Ball, Jingwen."

I shake my head to clear the cocktail's effect, trying to remem-ber what I'm supposed to say, what I'm supposed to do.

"I'd love to."

I rise to my tiptoes and kiss him. The act is mechanical, a script I am following because it leads to known victories. I don't close my eyes, and past Bailey's ear, I stare into the grizzly mien of a giant horse, whose long jaws are distended in a burning scream. The doctor's lips taste of ash and a faint sweetness.

Bailey opens his eyes and wipes his thumb across my lower lip. "Good." But he's not looking at me anymore. A steady smile breaks over his face.

"Ah, here's someone I would like you to meet, Jingwen."

Out of nervousness, I take another sip of the cocktail.

The drums beat along to my heart. The gourd flutes in my head rise in volume, hollow air rushing like angry waves to create a melody-less symphony. I hear a woman walking down the dais from the bar before I see her, the slow, calculated clicks of her chestnut leather heels and the swing of her hips. Her steps match my grand-mother's as she descends the mountain alone in my vision.

This time, I'm able to see her clearly. Unlike the wise, calculat-ing face I know, the Liqing in my vision is youthful and foolish. Tired and worn, with a gash along her cheek, but when I take a closer look, she is grinning, her shoulders down and her chin held high. Liqing never told me who my grandfather was, but I had inferred it from my mother's stories. He was a magistrate's son—a talented warrior with a sharp chin known for his integrity when it came to lawmaking. My grandmother, of course, had been bored out of her mind.

And then I see the baby again, still crying on the altar.

It's not me she left there in the pool.

It's my mother.

A tall woman wearing a moss-colored evening gown sweeps through the Coeur de la Rose. Her eyes are thin like a cat's, blanketed in smoke-toned shadow. The way she walks, with sloped shoulders relaxed and her slender chin lifted, makes it evident she's never had to look up at anyone. That's the way Liqing has always wanted me to walk.

With a warm smile, she kisses Bailey on the cheeks, no need to rise onto her toes. "It's so good to see you again, Doctor."

Bailey beckons in my direction. "Jingwen, may I introduce the splendid Lady Moraima Fox?"

The cold pool on the mountain disappears instantly, the cocktail's effect unable to compete with the woman who stands before me.

The Lady Moraima Fox turns to look at me, her waist-length red hair cascading over her shoulder, and the breath falls away from my chest. She is glowing with an aura, which emanates from the coral undertones of her cheeks and the veins under her skin, as if she was a porcelain doll in a collector's case, rotating under warm display lights. "Why hello, Jingwen." She speaks through her small, swooning mouth.

The breath falls away from my chest, because I last saw her effortless swoon resting upon a cushion of brown paper, in Liqing's clinic.

Huahua's bow-shaped lips pout on this woman's face, dressed in sheer gloss—still the deep orange-red hue of mandarin slices, parted in a curious grin. I search for scars on their border—ridges or distortions in her soft, fawn skin, which might imply they were sewn on like a patch in an old nightdress, but I find none. They fit, smooth as doeskin gloves, above this woman's chiseled jaw. This was the work of a professional.

She watches me, head tilted curiously to the side, no doubt waiting for a compliment.

"You look beautiful," I say, and a dull ache blooms inside my body.

I remember Usugi and Huahua in the Dove House, their faces swirled in shadows, pleading with me to help them—and then the girl whose name I never learned, who had trembled alone in the middle of a wheaten floor, before running into the night—and in that moment I know that if it's the last thing I do, I will help them make their faces whole again.

"Thank you." Moraima's voice clings to her throat, low and honeyed like molasses. She grins at Bailey, and I am racked with a sinking despair. If it were just the two of us in a room, I would dig my nails into the grooves around her lips and pluck them from her face, like sections of a ripe, skinned persimmon.

And then Moraima nods at the dais, where two more girls have appeared. Beneath their arched brows, their slender, hooded eyes are rimmed in coal. There is a slightly wild look about them, like deer in a public park who recognize a hound. These eyes have not been broken in the way Huahua's lips have. And if I squint, I can detect a faint, blotchy puffiness about their edge.

They sidle up to us, and I notice they have it too—a halo made from the faintest distortion of the air swells over their heads, like a ghastly lion's mane—but perhaps I am imagining things, and I've seen too many animal heads on fire for one night.

Moraima gathers the girls in her arms, with a laugh, and cradles the face of one in particular. "Brown eyes suit you so much better than blue. They match your hair."

I am dizzy suddenly, which is entirely unrelated to the Ancestry I've been drinking.

And in my head, I see a vision of Yue Liqing, with her slender, jade-like hands, standing over her operating table. A girl lies upon the table with her eyes closed, a smile upon the lips that will soon be discarded. And beside her, alongside her feathered scalpels and iron clips, two new lips rest upon brown tissue paper like manda-rin orange slices, waiting to be consumed.

Moraima leans in, so that her forehead touches Bailey's. "Doc-tor, shall we all get a drink together?"

She closes her eyes, mascara-heavy lashes brushing her cheek, and with a sigh, she tilts her chin up, Huahua's stolen lips parted.

"Ah, I would love to," Bailey explains, "but tonight I came as Jingwen's date."

He drapes an arm around my shoulders, his touch like air. I gasp when I realize he is still holding his Ancestry, the cool glass pressing against my cheek.

Moraima, recoiling as if he's hit her, draws her bottom lip be-tween her teeth. She bites hard enough that a pretty, ruby droplet, the size of a pin tip, wells from Huahua's orange-red lips. I want to tell her to treat them with more respect, because someday I will cut them from her face.

"Tomorrow then," she says softly.

"Tomorrow," he says, without a single emotion on his face. I can't shake the feeling he's gotten what he wants and doesn't need her anymore.

She tosses her hair, and her gaze settles on me, cool and full of wonder. "Well then, I'll see you tomorrow. Ladies, let's try the Ancestry. I wonder if it will be different from the Beauty, which we savored the last time we visited."

"Oh, it's very different," Bailey agrees. "I'm sure you'll like it."

The trio saunters away through the atrium. I see it even more clearly now that they are walking away—that slightly otherworldly glow that shimmers when they shake their hair and swing their hips. Each guest they pass seems to forget what they are saying, pausing mid-sip to crane their necks.

Bailey chuckles and slides his arm back from around my shoul-der, raising his Ancestry in a toast. The brown sludge at the bottom sloshes to the rim. He tilts the glass to his lips and drinks. "The three most beautiful bodies in Shanghai," he says, and then winks.

"But nothing, of course, compared to you. None of them could steal from the SMP."

I guess I'm supposed to be flattered.

Instead, I watch as Moraima cuts the drinks line with her two friends, laughing and running her fingers through her hair. The bartender faces her with the scream etched on his mask, his dancing stilled for a second as if she's turned him to wood.

"Doctor, when she said that girl's brown eyes matched her hair better than her blue ones, what did she mean?"

He grins. "Ah, another type of business dealing that goes on in Shanghai."

There is no music left in my head, and I don't even remember when the cocktail's effect faded. The silence pierces like water dashed over my face.

I know I must tread carefully. "Do you remember that first night we danced together, when my friend Huahua's lips were taken while she was dancing?"

He sighs, his breath fogging the edge of his glass, although the very edges of his lips are turned up in the corners. "Of course. How could I forget?"

"It's that sort of business, isn't it?"

I press my back against the wall to steady myself, hoping I am the only one between us who notices the quivering of my kingfisher earrings in my peripheral vision.

Bailey paces along the wall as he decides how to answer my question. His body falls in and out of patterned shadows. "Jingwen, I've only been in this city a few weeks, but I know how her gears turn. Let me see how I can put it. Shanghai is an opportunist's land—exquisite and cruel. More than wallets and hearts get stolen in this city." He winks, but the action comes off somewhat sinister.

I can only admire his eloquence—how he has answered my question without answering it at all.

My throat hurts from the vibration of the drums.

"And what part in it did you have to play?"

The words leave my mouth before I can stop myself.

Suddenly, I feel very small, surrounded by predators looking to dismantle me. There are over a hundred people in the Coeur de la Rose, yet I am the only one here of my kind.

Bailey narrows his eyes, the way a hunting cat contemplates whether to maim or kill a mouse.

And then he throws his head back and laughs.

"I certainly am an opportunist, but I'm not the one who sewed that dancer's lips onto another woman's face. That's not the type of medicine I studied. However, I've heard stories of a corrupt doctor in Shanghai who is skilled enough to perform such a procedure. She is notoriously difficult to work with as she's bought by the local gangs. However, sometimes I wonder what sort of things we could accomplish, if I could convince her to work with me."

The firelight gleams behind his eyes.

Tonight, I should not push too far. I look at the ground and tuck my hair behind my ears with a shy smile, careful not to betray anything. "Thank you for showing me your club, Doctor. It's been a wonderful experience, but I think I'd like to go home now. That way I can sleep before tomorrow morning's rehearsal."

"Fair enough."

Having finished his Ancestry, he sets his empty cocktail down on a nearby table. A hostess, wearing a garland of blue cornflowers, picks it up and walks away wordlessly.

"I just wanted you to know, Jingwen, that you've been a great asset to me."

He stands under the stuffed head of a European dragon with a scaly, flared snout, and the same candlelight appears to flicker in both their eyes. As I watch, his fingers stray to his vest pocket, where I know the smoke leaf lies tucked away. He taps the spot lightly.

Across the atrium, Moraima laughs at something one of Bailey's friends has said, her voice a honeyed melody for the colorless drums. I turn my head to catch her glancing in our direction—her delight transforming rapidly into despair when Bailey ignores her.

He leans in closer. "I've been waiting to meet someone like you."

"Thank you," I respond, but I am chilled to the bone.

He smiles, so widely it feels robotic. "Good. I'll be in touch. Come, my driver will take you home."

He starts across the atrium, to where that pair of silken black curtains flap in the wind, dividing the Coeur de la Rose from the hallway of mirrors that leads back to the real world.

CHAPTER ELEVEN

My grandmother's name means "beautiful, clear water." In Chinese, it's written 麗清, pronounced Liqing. She was born in a town shaped like an ox, with a lake for a heart. Her ancestors were geomancers who traveled the pastoral hills building towns in the shapes of omens, and in one of the stories her father told her, my grandmother was the reincarnation of her birth town.

Terrible things happened to the ox—raids from a warlord felled the trees that were its horns, and fires burned the white houses with curling gray roofs that made its body. Eventually, its spirit—a string of lanterns hung to guide passing ghosts, was extinguished by a malevolent demon, who wished the ghosts to be lost forever. And the town became a cruel place, a home to demonic fires that burned in cold places and disembodied heads that sang from the bottoms of wells. But that lake, its heart, could not be touched. And if on a night when the sky was clear, you gazed upon the skin of that water, you'd see the crescent moon reflected from the sky above, a perfect imitation. The way the moon swayed, you'd think the lake was laughing.

There is a pair of wings that hang upon the wall of my grandmother's clinic.

They were not always there.

When my mother first learned she was pregnant, she was a twenty-two-year-old bottle girl, working late nights at the Carlton Café by the water, and so she swallowed her pride and showed up at Liqing's door, to beg for one last favor. A few days after my birth, the clinic in the attic of the Cabaret Volieré became my home. During the day I wreaked havoc upon Blood Alley, chasing wisps of incense under the operating table and peeking into bars wearing my grandmother's nuo opera masks to scare the sailors. In the evenings, when neon glowed in the dark lanes under the Bund, I sat on the parapet above the Fantasio Café and blushed as I watched the showgirls whisper into their lovers' ears, wondering what kinds of things they were saying. I began to bring home broken things—martens whose legs were clipped by rickshaw wheels, alley kittens that were mauled by starving hounds, butterflies whose wings were torn by the neighborhood bullies. And Liqing would take my hands in hers and show me how to fix them with steel and pins as bandages.

For an entire spring, I'd perch by the sill of the window that was perpetually open and watch a mechanical butterfly flit around my head. In order to save it, we'd first had to cut its mangled, torn wings off. I hesitated before making the incision. Under my fingertips, I could feel the vibrations of its wing muscles, so furious and drunk with life.

"What if we make it worse?" I wanted to know.

And Liqing answered, "We might. But sometimes things need to get worse before they can get better."

I followed that butterfly everywhere through the alley, watched it nest in the beer-watered begonias that hung outside Irish pubs, sleep on the underside of gas lamps, and eventually mate with another, less colorful butterfly on the waterspout of a fire hydrant, before perishing one night upon the frost-covered windshield of a black Terraplane coupé. I ran upstairs to collect a jar so I might give it a deserving burial, but when I returned, the car had already driven away. That other, less colorful butterfly never returned, but for the rest of the summer, every time I saw a little green inchworm crawling along a dusty windowsill, I wondered if it was fathered by my butterfly, if it knew or cared his wings weren't real.

Before long, I began to learn the names of the gangsters who passed through the clinic, who would bring swords for Liqing to melt in her giant furnace and leave with limbs of shining silver. There was only one I was truly afraid of—a certain Wang Daojun, the leader of the Society of the Blue Dawn. He had one of those faces that never smiled, although he was handsome and tall, with thick, chiseled eyebrows. Liqing told me if I misbehaved, he could break open my skull like a melon using his silver hands, and so I always hid from him.

He married a young cabaret dancer named Li Aina. In the summer, the lovely Aina would bring me ice cream in outlandish flavors like lavender and stracciatella and flowers in pretty, ceramic pots— black peonies and exotic lilies shaped like stars with fiery centers. I loved her, in the purest sense of the word—how she would stroke my hair and share her expensive perfumes, which her husband imported from France and London.

But Aina, bright as the sun rising over the glistening river, could never understand her sullen husband, and young as I was, I ached at the way her face fell, when she begged her husband to go dancing, and he shook her off his arm. I imagined that she fell from the tower with the golden spire where the couple celebrated their wedding, eyes closed and arms spread like wings, into the river. No matter how she swam against the dark waters, she sank deeper and deeper, the champagne satin of her wedding dress pooling around her, until she sank right into the arms of a stranger she met one night at a summer solstice party at the Carlton.

He was the leader of the White Rabbits, a younger, hungrier gang. Rumor has it my mother once had an eye for him too, but he chose the bright Aina. And with their hands in each other's hair, on one of the rare nights where you could see actual stars bleed through the neon sky, they had their secret tryst in the freshly mown grass of the little cemetery on Bubbling Well Road.

It was Daojun, enraged by what he'd heard, who asked Liqing to replace her fickle heart with a loyal one.

Liqing chose the heart of a swan—those dazzling, slender-necked creatures that mate for life.

First, I watched the bird go down on the steel operating table, beating its great wings as Liqing wrestled a leather mask she'd sewn herself over its head, to pump its lungs full of ether. The wind raised by those powerful wings whipped my hair back from my face and sent my grandmother's anatomy diagrams flying against the walls.

Then, I watched the girl go down, and she didn't go lightly either. Tugging at my grandmother's arms, I screamed for her to spare my friend, as Aina kicked and bit my grandmother. At the head of the operating table, her husband stood impassive, smoking a cigarette.

Later that night, I watched Aina wake from the surgery, a wild glaze about her eyes and a swan's heart beating behind her ribs. She didn't know, but her first heart lay wrapped in layers of brown tissue paper in Liqing's kitchen, beside the caked and rusted stove. Like a doll she touched her hand to her breast, where a ropy scar would forever mark the brightness she once had. There were no flowers that summer to grace the little nightstand by my bed, but my grandmother dried and cured the wings of a swan, working in the late afternoon light of the clinic kitchen.

Given what I know now, I might surmise Aina's real heart was taken across the sea in a locked chest full of ice, where it was eventually sold on the end of a kebab stick in New York City, a dragon's heart captured from a fabled land.

I stopped bringing Liqing martens after that. The admiration I had for her hands faded like a bonfire doused by rain. I couldn't forget the glint that flashed in her eye when she lifted the swan's heart from a bowl of ice and set it down between the peeled-back ribs of my first friend.

And now every Friday night, when I push open the door to that little attic clinic, I see my grandmother, as mysterious as she has ever been with her hair bound in a handkerchief and her sleeves rolled to her elbows. She is performing surgery. Behind her, the wings she's taken hang upon the wall, held by crooked nails.

If you looked at her from just the right angle, they were *her* wings.

The door slams.

"Jingwen, you're late."

"I'm sorry."

The bones, packaged in their usual brown paper, rest on a corner of the sandalwood tea table.

I stare at the wings tacked upon the wall, the relic of my girlhood that no amount of burning incense will ever rid of haunting me. Liqing notices I'm lingering more than usual and glances up.

"Waipo, I've changed my mind."

She pauses, forceps and scalpels shining in her fingers, to indicate she's listening.

I close my eyes and I see Moraima Fox, sinking her teeth into her stolen lips, a pin drop of blood welling above the soft skin.

"I'd like to become your apprentice."

And then she starts laughing, her hands deep within the shoulder of a sleeping man.

"Finally, Jingwen. It's about time."

After I've delivered the bones, I don't go home.

I take the tram until the end of the line and walk on foot toward the silent fields at the edge of the university, glistening with night dew. Off to the sides, tire factories and flavor mills rest like silent giants, their rust-sprayed walls forgotten by the hundreds of migrant workers who are now gambling and drinking in the Badlands. The heavy aroma of burnt sugar hangs in the air.

As I stomp through the weeds, the heels of my shoes sticking in the mud, I hear the twang of metal against air, punctuated by soft breaths like the kind musicians take between cadenzas.

"Nalan Zikai!" I yell, standing amid the dead grass.

The fields fall silent.

I tear through overgrown weeds, ripping brambles and dried husks until my palms are raw and itchy. Under every barren tree, by every bridge that crosses the moving stream, a deep azure so clear I can read the expression on my face, I look for the shaman from the north.

"I know you're there."

I turn, around and around, but I can't pinpoint where the music comes from. The mouth harp's soft twangs change their direction of origin every few notes, as if he can control the source of the sound.

When I've finally given up and collapsed on a log, a voice says dryly, right above me, "Yes?"

I glance up the scratched trunk of a leafless quaking aspen. Zikai sits on the third bough up with his back against the trunk, one knee drawn against his chest. He is eating a plum, elbow propped on his knee.

He bites into the fruit with a satisfying crunch, before breaking into his maddening smirk. "You know, I've had girls chase me before, but never with a fury like that."

Although the cold has squeezed the blood from my face, I feel my cheeks reddening. Briefly, I wonder what kinds of girls have chased him and whether any of them are from Shanghai, before I force the thoughts away. I'm naturally competitive, but not all competitions are worth winning.

Across the field, a hawk owl swoops over the river, its feet grazing the dark water. In the campus' red-bricked dormitories, yellow-and-orange lighted windows stack neatly like Turkish delights in a French Concession shop display. Behind the fogged panes, I see the bowed heads of scholars, absorbing knowledge from heavy tomes.

"I'll accept your deal," I tell him. "I'll murder Wang Daojun, the leader of the Society of the Blue Dawn, and make it look like Yue Liqing did it."

He almost falls out of the tree and grabs a higher bough to save his balance. I am doused by a shower of dead leaves, which flutter off balance as if leaves could be drunk too.

"What prompted this drastic change of heart?" he asks, sinking his teeth deep into the plum again. Purple juice runs down his chin, and he wipes it away with his thumb.

I cross my arms over my chest. "Do you want my help or not?"

"Yes. Yes, I do." He finishes the plum and tosses the pit across the field. It falls into the water with a satisfying splash, sending a nest of starlings flapping into the night.

I cut him off before he says more. "Then come find me at the Paramount Ballroom tonight. I'm supposed to dance."

The night hangs still between us like a tightrope. When I exhale, the puff of my breath leaves my body like I've just spit away my soul.

I watch the thoughts churn in his head, as he contemplates the gravity of my invitation. He could ask me to talk right here, where he's established a territory for himself. But it's my turn to have the upper hand. I want him to meet me in my habitat that I know like the back of my hand—where I have already set the stage to revolve around me.

"Alright," he says.

The Paramount's spire rises toward the sky like a golden phallus.

They've carted ice sculptures before the front doors as well, nude Aphrodites rising from seashells and dryads with branches for arms. A group of young college students waiting for the doors to open are daring one another to cup Aphrodite's icy breasts, guffawing anytime a young man amongst them actually has the guts. What a resplendent night, full of blazing passions and sordid secrets.

I step over tulle costumes and discarded stockings turned inside out, which litter the dressing room's stained, mauve carpet. A row of girls perches at the long table, busy at work in front of a long mirror studded by vanity light bulbs. The room's aura more resembles a factory than a cabaret, only the girls are manufacturing themselves, dusting rouge and foundation over their cheekbones with thick brushes and coloring their puckered lips with every shade of red and pink.

With a sigh, I elbow aside shawls and half-drunk mugs of coffee. I'm wearing a black lace qipao tonight, and I'm feeling a bit fatalistic. I have just begun to color my lips bright red when Beibei plops into the chair beside me and begins to furiously pluck her eyebrows.

I try twice to meet her gaze in the mirror, just because I crave the company of a friendly face, but she ignores me.

Behind us, Zenaida and Arisha are fighting again, their chandelier earrings quaking like miniature of versions of the pyramidal candelabras that swing over the main ballroom.

"If you were really a Russian princess, then you'd be able to tell me exactly what the Romanov girls wore to the Costumed Ball of 1903 at the Winter Palace, and what crown jewels adorned their kokoshniks."

"That's not fair. Neither of us were alive in 1903!"

"But anyone who's spent a winter in St. Petersburg would know. You've never set foot in Russia. Your parents were poor refugees in Harbin, China, so stop telling the guests you're a duchess."

Their voices fade as they make their way to the dance floor.

I try one more time to catch Beibei's attention, when she tucks her tweezers back in her makeup bag and heads for the door. We try to step through the doorframe at the same time. For a second, she studies me, and I search for something to say.

Then, she bangs her hip against mine as she marches past. "What are you staring at?"

Perplexed, I drift into the hall like a splinter of dead wood on the ocean, ivory slabs and dizzying chandeliers sailing by.

The ballroom opens in layers of glass and crystal like a cavernous flower. Tonight, the velvet drapes and sloped couches make me think of viscera, soft and alive. Everywhere, the shadows seem to flirt with the light, swirling up to the ceiling along the helical staircase, like the inside of a conch shell, or a female sex organ.

I accept a dance with my lawyer friend, whom I haven't seen in a few weeks. After the insanity of the past few nights, I am relieved to have his company.

"Vilma," he says very seriously, taking both my hands in his. "I was worried you'd forget me."

"You're so kind," I respond. "There's no way I could forget you. How have you been?"

He hangs his head solemnly, as the dance begins. "I had two exams in the past week. That's why I couldn't see you."

I tug at his hands gently, to coax him to dance. After all, there are few dances I've never enjoyed. "I hope you did well."

He cheers a bit with my encouragement, and we dance thrice.

After the third dance, a soft purple light floods the dance floor, turning black dresses into red dresses. My lawyer friend bows to me.

That's when I see him.

Zikai has just walked under the giant, red yuletide bow affixed to the first-floor ballroom's entrance, wearing a suit. I can only recognize him by his long hair, which he wears half-bound behind his head, two small braids buried in his longer locks. He walks through the gilded ebony halls, his eyes fixed to the ceiling, using one hand to adjust a gray bow tie around his neck.

With a simultaneous pang of desperation, I realize that even within the Paramount's gilded walls, he has not lost his natural magnetism.

"I'll see you next week," I tell my lawyer friend, and I free myself from his grip.

Zikai starts up the staircase to the second floor, and I have to run up the stairs to keep up before I lose him to the crowd.

I jump into his path, slightly out of breath. "Over here."

He raises his eyebrows, no doubt alarmed to see me all dolled up, no twigs in my hair. A stray lock of hair frames the mole beside his left eye, and the small detail is infuriatingly distracting.

"What do you think of the ballroom?" I ask, raising my knuckles to a filigreed ivory panel and knocking on it. The entire wall sings with the reverberation.

Zikai strums the mouth harp hanging at his neck absentmindedly, a habit of his when he doesn't know what to say, and it briefly makes me happy that I've stunned him. "A waste of gold," he declares eventually.

I laugh. "Why don't you come up to the third floor? There's more to see."

He follows me up an even narrower spiral, to the ballroom's highest level.

The floor of the much smaller third-story ballroom is made of flawless crystal, with rainbow eggs of pulsing light suspended in the glass that threaten to burst from the weight of a dancer's foot-steps. On some nights, the eggs light up in variable patterns, which a number of critics disparaged in the tabloids for giving them the impression they'll fall through at any moment.

"On the nights that you don't dance, you must feel lonely," he says.

I think he's admitting he is impressed. There aren't many guests with access to the Paramount's highest tier—only politicians, se-lect gangsters, and friends of its investor, so being here makes it feel like we're sharing a secret. Shoulder to shoulder, we watch an army general of the Kuomintang, decked out in his uniform, dancing with Arisha, who floats about him like a sylph in a blue-and-silver geometric gown.

"Actually, the nights where I'm dancing are the nights I feel the loneliest."

Eventually, we sit at a small table by the third-floor balcony, which floats like a cloud over a dream world. Down below, colored wheels of lights fly across the second-story dance floor, like birds in a mating dance.

I bring us a bottle of rosé.

"It's pink and full of bubbles," I explain.

Zikai plays with the bottle stopper, carved in the shape of a square fan. His signature smirk tugs at one corner of his mouth.

"You've dragged me all the way out here to drink perfume."

We toast with a satisfying clink of our champagne flutes. The bubbles sting the roof of my mouth and the sides of my tongue, champagne fizz landing on my cheeks and my eyelids.

Zikai makes a satisfying sigh and leans back in his chair, grasp-ing the stem of his glass with just his forefinger and thumb.

I blink, the champagne bubbles popping like tiny fireworks against my eyelashes. In that moment, I feel it so deeply in my breast it hurts—my love affair with the fantasy worlds that only cabaret girls could mold out of light and steps—the very reason I became a dancer despite the fluff and duplicity. On the right night, when I've danced with the right stranger and seen the wonder glaze over their eyes, that magic still electrifies the air.

And I would do anything in my power to protect it.

Zikai clears his throat. "So, tell me Jingwen. What's your plan to kill Wang Daojun?"

And like that, the lightness of the evening extinguishes like a candle flame under a cocktail glass.

I set my glass back down. "She agreed to take me as her apprentice. After you injure Wang Daojun's silver arm, he'll come to her. During the operation, I'll asphyxiate him."

He flips the bottle stopper around in his hand. I note the similarity in shape to the fanned keys of his mouth harp.

"Does she trust you enough to let you that close?"

"Yes."

He nods.

"Okay then," he says. He tilts his flute against his lips.

"When are you going to do it?" I ask.

Zikai tosses the bottle stopper into the air and catches it again. "On Tuesday nights, Wang Daojun likes to frequent a club near the water called the Rue de Velours with his wife. I plan to ambush him there."

My throat tightens at the mention of Li Aina, my friend.

"Meet me there at seven o'clock," Zikai says. "Be the golden girl who saves him. Dress the part, play the part, bring him back to your grandmother."

"Does he know what you look like?"

"He's probably heard by now." He throws the bottle stopper again, and this time it soars so high, I am afraid he will crack a crystal panel on the ceiling. "And that's why I can't be seen."

I envision Wang Daojun's chiseled, unsmiling face the last time

I saw him in Liqing's clinic, watching as his wife's heart was fished from her chest like an oyster.

"After my grandmother has been stripped of her power—then what?"

Zikai shrugs, like I've asked something inane. "Then you go back to dancing here, butchering the Dance of the Qingniao under the moon when you think nobody's looking, whatever you like. There should be no consequences for you—if you pull off the kill correctly."

I roll my eyes over my champagne glass. "No, I meant what's the Court of Exiles going to do?"

"Ah." He takes a drink. "They're going to work on bringing the gods back."

"You need to be very specific. Otherwise, how can I trust the Court of Exiles will be less corrupt?"

"You don't." He tosses the bottle stopper again. "You take a gamble based on your beliefs."

I tip the champagne bottle into my glass, with too much force. A torrent of champagne rears up against the flute and leaps over the brim.

"I have one condition though."

Zikai snatches the bottle stopper out of the air but doesn't throw it again, to indicate he is anticipating my request.

"Those girls we met in the Dove House, who lost their eyes and lips. Help me get them back."

He laughs softly. "I thought you said they weren't your friends."

"I'm changing, I guess," I admit with a shrug. "I didn't know them well, but now I wish I did. Look—all this gold and crystal and light—you can call it a waste of money if it pleases you. But it's the world to me. And I'm going to save it."

"Deal," he says, taking care to study my expression, and I know that secretly, he's impressed.

He extends his hand over the table.

I grasp his fingers, and he gives my hand a firm shake. Then he breaks into a wide smile, scattering the tension that belies the moment before like dandelion seeds on the wind. "So, after drinking several bottles of this, do the guests turn into balloons that float away?"

He picks up the champagne, splashes more into our glasses.

I hesitate, not sure what he wants now.

He glances up, notes the suspicion on my face, and pushes my glass into my fingers. "I dressed up for you. You at least owe me the courtesy of finishing the bottle together."

I laugh then, allowing the tension from my shoulders to relax a little bit. "You know, I met another shaman. He was nowhere near as conversational as you."

"Really? I wouldn't think there's many of us in Shanghai."

With a silvery clink, we touch the sides of our flutes together.

I take a deep draught. "This one worked in a gentleman's club as a bartender."

Zikai laughs. There's a pleasant edge to his laugh. I wish he wouldn't stop. "Not a common profession for a shaman."

It only takes a few more rounds to finish the entire bottle. Zikai's cheeks are the faint pink of dawn clouds. We don't say another word, but I don't even notice the silence. My eyelids begin to droop, from the dreamy taste of champagne and too many adrenaline-fueled nights. I think I could listen to the jazz until the sun rises, in Zikai's silent company.

"I'll let you return to your work now," he says, after he's drained his flute of the last drop.

He rises to his feet, but I remain seated.

"Do you want to dance?"

I don't know why I ask, given the nature of the business we have agreed to undertake together. But dancing is the language I use to understand the characters who step into my life.

He considers it, and for a second, I stare into his eyes, which change from violet to brown with every pulse of the spotlights, without ever showing their true color.

"Okay." He slips his jacket back off and drapes it over the back of his chair.

Underneath, he is wearing a gray pinstriped vest over a white shirt. I walk over to the edge of the dance floor, and he joins me there.

We face each other, just breathing, until the next song starts.

The dance is a waltz. I reach for his left hand, which I grasp in my right. Then I take his right hand and guide it around my back. His touch is light but firm. I set my own right hand on his shoulder, and keeping the beat of the saxophone melody, I guide him through the motions of the basic waltz step. A practiced martial artist, Zikai does not have a hard time following.

"Dancing is not so different from fighting," Zikai remarks to me out of the blue.

"How many years have you been fighting?" I ask.

"My entire life. Since I could walk."

"I've been dancing for two years."

Soon, I lose track of the few dancers around us, their shadows grazing ours.

Patches of color break up our arms and faces. One of the managers, bored perhaps, flips the switch for the electric floor. I gasp as the floor lights up. Zigzags of color flit beneath our feet like goldfish. It feels like another world entirely, one high above the clouds ruled by irrational thoughts and furious colors. Under the dazzling shimmer of the silver chandelier, which appears to rotate with us, I close my eyes.

For a moment, I entertain the fantasy—that in another life we are a gangster and a cabaret girl, and the brush of our hands together upon the dance floor could've made for a fiery scandal we secretly delight in, rather than the brokering of a tenuous alliance.

Maybe I'm a little bit drunk, but I lean in.

Like an accident, our lips bump together. His mouth melts against mine, soft as butter. The whole world freezes for just a second. I drop his hand, and my fingers find the side of his neck instead. I am conscious of his fingers resting on my hips, his warm chest only a finger's space from mine.

When I open my eyes, I am staring into his, a fiery rust in the center, rimmed in green. In that moment, I think he is the most beautiful human being in the world.

The absurdity of the moment lingers in the air.

After all, kisses aren't to be given out like candies, not even to one you trust. And I'm not certain I trust Zikai.

Zikai breaks away first. The faintest of smiles tugs at the corner of his mouth, and then he walks to the balcony ledge and leans over it. Below, the couples twirl like colored pinwheels along a garden path. It's quite a different feeling, to watch a crowd of dancers from above. It becomes impossible to distinguish the dancers from each other—even Beibei, who stands out anywhere. I touch my lips, and my fingers come away red with my lipstick. My heart flutters softly behind my ribs.

That's when I see her.

Raven-colored finger waves held by a gold leaf headband and a black satin gown with a deep V in the back. A shimmering distortion of the air hangs about her. When she passes, the dancers drop their poses to stare, like pinwheels in a garden that has lost its summer breeze.

I grab Zikai's sleeve. "Look at that woman."

She glides between the columns of the second-floor ballroom like a specter, bathed in that otherworldly glow.

He narrows his eyes. "Who is she?"

"None of the other guests stand out this far away, but she stands out. Some part of her face was stolen from a dancer."

A sinking feeling returns to the pit of my chest. I search again for the magic I'd felt only minutes ago, swaying in Zikai's arms, but it's dried like a well in the sun.

"Are you alright?" Zikai asks me.

I push the balcony away, retreating back under the shadows of the hallway—away from the dappled dance floor. "Let's stop my grandmother from making more of her."

I'm breathing hard, but slowly, the fear drifts away. A fire has lit in the pit of my stomach, and it burns with a newfound realization—that I am no longer powerless.

For once, rather than battling his charisma with my own, I let my determination melt into his, to become something brighter.

Zikai follows, smiling gently. "You win and I win."

The woman is headed for the staircase back to the main ballroom, her hand placed delicately on the banister.

"I want to see who she talks to," I explain.

The main ballroom on the first floor is always the most crowded. As such, it is the locale where all the night's drama is to be expected. Tonight, the pillars are guarded by tea boys in all-white, carrying silver trays with special advent cocktails. Zikai pauses to sample a smoking cocktail in a Father Christmas–themed shot glass. Ahead of us, the woman has stopped by a VIP table by the orchestra pit, where a man dressed in a trim, navy suit has leaned over to whisper into the ear of a silver-handed gangster. With a lurch of my stomach, I realize the man is Bailey Thompson, surrounded by some familiar faces from the Coeur de la Rose.

At Bailey's elbow, the woman accepts a drink from another socialite dressed in a pink sequined dress and ermine stole, and they toast with their arms linked together. Bailey makes a comment, and she rests her hand on his shoulder, laughing merrily.

So they are together.

Zikai appears at my shoulder, having downed his advent cocktail. "An old lover of yours?" he guesses with a smirk. "And he's the one talking to your glowing girl. What will we have to do to him to get your friends' lips and eyes back? They were right—the affairs of Shanghai are resplendently sordid."

My cheeks grow hot. "Please leave with me so he doesn't notice me."

I don't bother to explain that Bailey is my date to the Firefighters' Ball.

Zikai shrugs and holds his arm out toward the door.

"Wait, let me get my coat."

I've never been more relieved to be buffeted by the stream of bodies passing in and out of the halls. A group of four dancers sweep past me without leaving much room, and I walk headfirst into the chest of Neville Harrington, who I didn't even notice tonight, making a beeline toward the second-floor bar to buy more drinks. He's left a familiar figure all alone in one of the lounges, who is smoking a Lucky Strike cigarette in between her crimson-painted nails, a red carnation falling out of her hair.

"Beibei."

I call her name.

She turns her head slowly, recognizing my voice. Beibei has a viscous quality about her movements reminiscent of melting candle wax, which creates the perpetual impression that she's bored of you. She draws the cigarette out of her mouth, dragging it along her oily lips, but before she can make a scene, I hiss in her ear. "That woman over there, she has the stolen lips of a cabaret dancer. Do you see it?"

For a moment, I'm afraid she won't—that she'll only ridicule me and draw Bailey's attention. Stooped over her shoulder, I can count the lipstick stains on her cigarette. She's taken seven drags on it, sucking the smoke as if it's Neville Harrington's bank account. Her eyes search the woman's face in the distant ballroom. Perhaps Beibei even knew the name of the dancer.

The dance ends with a blast of trumpet fanfare, and a row of small canons in front of the orchestra pit shoot cool smoke into the air.

"I see it," she says, so quietly I barely hear her.

I nod slowly. Beibei searches my face with her lively eyes, waiting for me to say more.

Zikai waits for me by the doors, twirling his mouth harp between his fingers. Outside, the gaggle of college students, bored of dancing, are molesting the ice statues once more.

"Stay safe," I tell Beibei. And I guess that's the closest I've ever come to wishing her well.

CHAPTER TWELVE

My grandmother lights her shrine in the early evening when the sun drops over the river. Kneeling before the terrifying nuo mask of a wizened hunter—forest-green mien with sharpened canines and the branching antlers of a stag—she arranges her incense sticks in a brass tripod. The incense smells like musk and pepper tonight.

I sit in the windowsill drinking coffee, as the smoke trails swirl around my head. The more I ignore it, the more it follows me.

"When I left my hometown to come to Shanghai, I brought these incense sticks with me," Liqing explains to me. "They were a gift from a traveling half-saint who stopped by the town, whom my father invited to stay in our house. I'm lighting them today in celebration of the journey we're about to begin together. All my career, I have dreamed of having an apprentice, and I always knew you were the right one to inherit my mantle."

On the clinic walls, demons glower through wispy clouds and frazzled gods ride on thunderbolts through the skies.

I force a smile. "I'm very excited to learn—*oww!*" The incense smoke kisses my cheek with a painful hiss, as if it can tell I'm lying, and I swat it away.

My grandmother rises to her feet from her knees, wincing at hidden aches and pains.

"Who will the patient be tonight?" I ask.

"A boy," she responds. "We'll be giving him a new arm."

The most fundamental of her operations. Of course. I've watched her perform this procedure hundreds of times throughout my childhood. Although I never held the scalpel, I could recite the order of the cuts she makes in my sleep.

We wait for the boy, and I watch her lay out her tools on a sheet of linen at the edge of the operating table—lovingly, the same way a dancer lays out her pearls and her headdresses when she is choosing her outfit for the evening.

Liqing smiles as me. "You know what the legends say, when the goddess Nuwa created the first humans, she was drunk. But when I operate, I make sure to remain sober. You don't drink at this dance school of yours that you attend in the morning, do you?"

"No," I promise.

For a minute, the only sound in the clinic is the muted tinkle of her surgical instruments, gently laid against the operating table through the sheet.

"Waipo," I say quietly, gazing upon the giant swan wings on the wall. "Did you know there are other surgeons in Shanghai trying to copy you?"

I remember the man from the Dove House with the mutilated arm—not quite silver, not quite flesh, but these two things rotted together—whom Usugi said liked broken things.

My grandmother straightens one of her scalpels. "Let them try."

She looks up, her eyes sharp under her eyelids, which have fallen just a bit lower in her age. She doesn't have to say anything for me to know.

"You asked the Blue Dawn to kill them."

"I didn't have to ask." She cleans her hands on a towel. "Those doctors failed. That makes them self-aggrandizers, not healers. There is no forgiveness if you choose to take apart a perfect, living thing and fail to put it back together in a better way."

She throws the towel aside.

"That's why you alone, Jingwen, are worthy of inheriting my legacy. You wouldn't fail."

I don't respond. When I think of the man's raw, mutilated arm, this time I imagine it as the doing of my own hands.

The boy arrives.

He is a small, scrawny thing, so thin that when he slips his shirt off, I can see his ribs through his back. Seeing him makes me think of Xiao Lei, when I made my first bone delivery when I was twelve. Xiao Lei had been his age then, an eager teenager who had given his soul to Wang Daojun in exchange for slick suits, gold, and power. If not for Liqing, this boy would spend his entire life at the docks, unloading shipments of watermelon off steamships for a faceless American businessman he would never even meet. But because of her, he'll get to live the glory days of a gangster.

At least, this is what she tells herself.

"Put him to sleep," Liqing commands.

I pick up the leather mask, connected to a bell jar that contains a rag dipped in ether. The boy leans away from me, one arm over his face, the natural human reaction when two strangers are about to cut your perfectly healthy limb away. I wonder if we gave him a chance now, he would change his mind. Wang Daojun certainly doesn't care. The boy's life is his after all.

"I'm sorry," I whisper, and I press the mask over his face before he can struggle.

He falls backward onto the operation table, where Liqing slides a pillow to catch his head. Soon he is sleeping peacefully, like one of the rich boys in Bailey's club. I secure the mask tightly behind his head with leather straps.

Liqing nods. "Next time, make sure there is something to break the fall before you do that."

She disinfects the edge of her saw, which she will use to remove his arm.

I don't wince when the saw blade meets the operating table with a heavy *thunk*. Despite being well past her sixtieth year, Liqing has retained the strength of a marauding army surgeon who once accompanied a young warlord on his campaign to conquer China's eastern coast.

Blood pools under the boy's body, and I soak it up in rags,

which I'll wash in the kitchen sink later. My grandmother leans over me to stop the bleeding with hemostats and clamps.

Liqing told me once that there are two ways to fear blood.

The first is to fear your own blood. This is the most primal fear conditioned into the human mind, a translation of the fear of death. A doctor with this fear will have nightmares, and that will be her greatest challenge. The second is to fear the blood of others. To miss that second fear, she explained, meant a doctor had no ability to empathize with others' pain. Then she laughed. She was kidding, she said. To miss the second fear, she explained, meant you were born to practice medicine.

In time, I learned I feared neither.

The summer I was thirteen years old, I stepped in a bear trap that soldiers of the British navy had set to prank sailors of the American navy, the iron jaws ripping through the flesh of my calf so that my shinbone was showing. Gritting my teeth, I had clambered up the staircase of the Cabaret Volieré back to my grandmother's clinic, dragging the trap with me. Liqing had to call one of the gangsters to break the trap open. I had stared up at Liqing with wide eyes, as she prepared the ether solution that would put me to sleep. "You aren't going to give me a silver leg, are you?" I asked, and she promised no, before she placed the mask over my face.

She kept her word. In fact, she mended the wound so well even now, many years later, I still run my fingers over the skin of my calves, looking for any hint of a scar. But I've never found any.

I didn't learn I lacked the second fear until many years later, on a hot summer night after I started dancing. There was a murder at the Paramount, a dance hostess shot by her scorned lover at the dance floor's edge. I remember her brains splattered over the walls and the polished, wheaten floor.

After the police scribbled a few haphazard notes and took the body away, the manager ordered Zenaida and me, the two newest dancers, to clean up the mess. With sponges and soap, we scrubbed the girl's brains and blood off the gilded walls. Zenaida's hands shook so badly, I took her sponge from her. I remember how she had looked down at my hands gripping hers, and mine did not shake at all. Zenaida backed away from me then, a wild look in her eye, and I went on cleaning. There was a bit of the dancer's skull lodged under an ivory filigree of a fleur-de-lis that I could not reach, and so I left it there. Sometimes, when I dance in that corner of the floor, I cannot help but glance up at it.

Liqing stores the boy's discarded arm in an icebox. Later, she will bleach the flesh off the bones, and the bones will trade hands through the cities of the world until they end up as powder, sprinkled in the tea of some wealthy New York lady.

"Jingwen, which tool should I use for the next part?"

I turn to her selection of tools, which gleam with a cruel sterility.

Liqing is watching me carefully. "Is something wrong?"

I've picked up a scalpel. There is a smear of red-orange lipstick on the silver handle, which does not come off when I run my thumb over it.

"Nothing," I say, setting the scalpel back against the linen. Instead, I select a pair of forceps with needle-thin tips, so that she might weave the boy's flesh nerve together with his silver ones.

"Good," Liqing says, "but next time, don't touch the blade. Even if you've washed your hands, you could contaminate the surface."

She begins to mold the shimmering silver matter that will become the boy's new limb, which comes from melted swords that the gangsters bring. My attention keeps wandering back to that scalpel, with the lipstick imprint. While Liqing is preoccupied, I pick it up again.

"What's wrong?" she asks, without looking up.

"There's a stain on this scalpel."

Liqing shrugs. "Must be some blood left over from the last surgery. Why don't you wash it off while I finish up here?"

I know from the way she's looking at me. We both know.

And so I stand before the sink in Liqing's kitchen, scrubbing at that orange-red stain until my thumb pads grow wrinkly. The sound of the sink water crashes like waves in my head. I think of how later tonight, once Nalan Zikai has injured the Blue Dawn's leader, as Liqing is mending his arm, I will quietly pinch the translucent tubing that allows him to breathe, and his breath will fail.

When I return to the operating room, having been unsuccessful in removing the stain, I lay the tool back with the others, careful not to let the blade brush against the unsterilized table. My grandmother's hands are nimble at work, a faint smile on her lips. It makes me think of how when I was a girl, she held my hands from behind as we mended butterflies—in my excitement, I never glanced up to see what her face looked like, but I wonder if she had the same expression.

For some reason, I feel a twinge of sorrow, at how we ended up here.

The Rue de Velours, on the roof of the Red Orchid Hotel, overlooks the Huangpu.

With a mint julep in hand, I lean over the crystal rail that encircles the roof. Sixteen stories below, the surface of the dark water shimmers, waves crashing over the wharves and leaving a shimmering trail of white foam in their wake. There is a full moon in the sky, its glow overshadowed by cabaret lights down the Bund.

Being an old-fashioned nightclub, there are no taxi girls to dance with, but instead a throng of bottle girls, dressed in sequined dresses with tall ostrich feather headbands. One girl brushes past me, all soft pink feathers, carrying a platter of steak and butter.

She walks to a table by the roof's edge, where a couple in fur-lined coats are spreading pâté over dinner rolls in silence. It's Wang Daojun and his wife, Li Aina. Daojun gazes at the skyscrapers of the Bund, some of their windows still lit, as he chews. They don't speak a word to one another.

Turning my back to them, I raise my drink to my lips. The mint leaf floating above the cocktail rocks like a sampan on the waves below.

There is the soft clatter of silverware before me.

"You're Liqing's little girl."

I freeze mid-sip, and an ice tube floats against the tip of my nose.

Slowly, I turn around. Wang Daojun is cutting his steak, holding his fork and knife the American way, while observing me.

"Mr. Wang." I curtsy to him with a smile. "Always a pleasure to see you."

Aina smiles up at me, a glassy emptiness drifting in her eyes. Somewhere in her chest, where Liqing's hands placed it, I know a swan's heart beats.

"You dance at a different cabaret, don't you?" the Blue Dawn's leader asks me, biting his steak off his fork. He chews without smiling, his eyes slightly narrowed as if I'm a small line of text in a book that needs to be scrutinized.

"Yes, but sometimes I like to come here to watch the waves."

A rush of wind blows out the candle on their table.

Daojun waves his silver hand to call a bottle girl over. "Hey, our candle went out."

I steal the chance to slip away. Wang Daojun has always had a way of staring at you that makes you feel like he can read your secrets through your skin.

On the other side of the roof stands a tropical aquarium, filled with bright angelfish and fighting goldfish with neon-colored, fanning tails. I am watching a fat silver goldfish swim through a feathery green plant when a pair of eyes blink at me through the glass.

A hand grabs my wrist from around the aquarium, and I gasp.

"Shh," Zikai hisses from where he is hiding. He is dressed in a silk shirt and dress pants to fit in with the Rue de Velours, the first two buttons fashionably loosened to expose a bit of his chest.

I nearly drop my glass. "I wasn't expecting you!"

"Don't draw attention to yourself," he mutters, glancing around nervously.

I roll my eyes and turn to face away from him, leaning my hip against the aquarium's side.

He whispers to me from behind. "Wang Daojun likes you. It shouldn't be hard to get close to him."

"When are you going to make your move?" My glass is empty, but I keep pretending to sip from it, ice cubes clattering about at the bottom. I wonder how long before Daojun notices.

Zikai sighs. "After he's drunk. Can you convince him to drink?"

I snort under my breath. "Why do you need him to be drunk? I thought you said you were the 'Highest Cultivator of the Middle Kingdom'?"

"I said someday," he hisses in my year. "Just do it."

Zikai releases my wrist, and I walk to the railing at the edge of the roof once more. Facing the river, I take a few deep breaths. At moments like this, I think I can smell the salty air of the sea, carried through the river. There is soft jazz playing in the dining area, but when I close my eyes, all I hear is the roar of water.

Squaring my shoulders, I walk back to the leader of the Blue Dawn. The candle on his table has been brought back to life.

He watches me approach, his shoulders bent protectively over his steak.

"May I join you?"

Wang Daojun pulls a chair from the neighboring table, his silver right hand gleaming against its back. "Beautiful night, isn't it? You can even see some stars."

Aina cuts her steak with a pretty smile and chews without making noise.

I sit between them, silently cursing Zikai for placing me in this situation. It's hard to look Aina in the eye, after what I know. A bottle girl brings me another mint julep, for which I'm thankful.

"I'll have another Syrah," Wang Daojun tells the girl, nudging forward his empty glass.

She nods and pours violet-red wine from a dark bottle without spilling a single drop.

"Do you read Classical Chinese?" Daojun asks me out of the blue, taking a deep draught of his wine.

"No."

My cheeks burn with shame, even though most Chinese cabaret girls cannot.

He indicates a framed calligraphy painting that hangs on the walls of a glass veranda.

"This scroll. I've been reading it all night. It extols the virtues of furniture designed by the French artist Maurice Dufrêne, but in Classical Chinese, like the old epics and war manuals. I find it entertaining. Do you know of Maurice Dufrêne?"

"Yes."

He makes an amused noise in his throat. "Oh? A Chinese dancer who is chosen by her partners for her native heritage knows contemporary French art, but cannot read the poetry of her ancestors?" He drums his silver fingers against his glass of wine, digesting this fact. "You know, I own a vase made by Maurice Dufrêne—it's my favorite item in my country manor—angular yet bold, the epitome of modernity."

It strikes me in that moment that he's bored, having a swan-hearted girl for a dinner companion who says nothing.

I raise my glass, tempting him to drink, and he takes the bait.

"I was chosen by the Paramount's manager, along with two other dancers, to pick new couches for the remodeled second-floor ballroom. A cabaret's furniture is more important than you realize—if the cushions are not comfortable, the guests won't stay long, and if the styles are not modern, the guests will question the establishment's taste. Knowing which designs are internationally popular is crucial for a cabaret girl—unlike Classical Chinese."

Daojun raises his hand to signal for more wine.

Syrah splashes into the glass like wings unfurling, and he searches my face with his piercing gaze. "Or, it simply means Shanghai has devoured you—stripped your identity away and melted French copper and English tin into your skin, the way a smelting machine made that bronze lampshade over there. But I don't disparage you for it. I've done the same." He opens and closes his silver hand. I can tell Liqing performed his surgery a long time ago, because the bulge of his silver knucklebones is larger than the detail she uses now. "It's what we must do to survive."

I fall quiet, unsure of how to respond. The first night I met Zikai, he'd said I was bowdlerizing the dance of the Qingniao. Was it shameful that until that moment, I didn't know what the Qingniao was?

"Let's drink to that then," I suggest.

"Hmm."

Another glass, followed by a sigh.

Wang Daojun begins to eat.

"You're friends with the dancer Li Beibei, aren't you?" he asks, stabbing a square of prime rib. I see he's cut the steak into neat pieces, all of them the same size, lined in rows across his plate.

"I guess you could say that."

"One of my top-ranking boys, Xiao Lei, has an eye for her. I'm hoping to arrange his engagement to her."

I snort my mint julep through my nose and hide my face behind my hand in a fake coughing fit.

Wang Daojun's eyes flick up from his plate. "Something funny about what I said?"

I clear my throat and recompose myself. "They wouldn't be a good match."

He raises his eyebrows. "Oh? Enlighten me."

"Xiao Lei is too serious for Beibei. She likes to play around with her men, and it takes a lot of wit to understand her. In addition, Neville Harrington, the lumber magnate's son, has his eye on her, and I'm afraid he's got a lot more money than any Blue Dawn gangster has."

To my surprise, Wang Daojun laughs. "You're exceptionally daring for saying that," he tells me.

I raise my cocktail in another toast. He lifts his glass and downs its entire contents. As the bottle girl refills it, he leans back in his seat.

"Some of my boys tell me I should consider you to be my next physician, after Liqing."

"I'm not a doctor, Mr. Wang. Just a dancer."

He nods, as if I've said something terribly deep. "Dance makes a venerable art, but the real movers of the world work behind the curtains. You remind me of Yue Liqing, but she's a realist, and you an optimist."

He toasts me this time, both of us throwing our heads back with drink, while Aina smiles blandly past us.

I wipe my lips on my hand. My lips leave a shining red imprint on the web of my thumb. The bottle girl comes to fill Daojun's glass a third time. Li Aina, who has finished her drink as well, smiles vapidly up at her. The girl refills her glass as well.

"How is Aina's heart?" I ask him.

He regards me out of the side of his eye as he stabs another piece of steak.

"Ah," he says, as if I've offered an answer to some deep quandary he's pondered for many years. "You resent me for it, don't you? After all these years?"

I wish Zikai would hurry up and injure him—before I say something that will result in my head rolling on the floor under the stars.

"Yes," I admit.

He wipes his mouth with his napkin and tosses it on the table. Then he drums his fingers on the tablecloth, lost in thought. "You loved my wife very much. She was like the mother you never had. I'm very sorry."

I lower my eyes and sip my drink, although the corners of my eyes burn with tears. "Do you prefer her this way?"

"Ah, Jingwen. I run the most successful gang operation in Shanghai, that spans four continents now. Do you know why I'm successful?" He leans forward so that we are eye to eye. I can see the shadows under his eyes, how unlined his face is compared to other men his age because he never smiles. The hairs on the back of my neck stiffen. "Loyalty. My men would die for me a hundred times, because we are united by a cause to become the greatest gang that rules Shanghai. Only as a united force can we stand up to the foreign powers that enslave our city. If it was one of my subordinates who I found fraternizing with my rival, I would've shot him dead on the spot. But no, it was my wife who betrayed me." He turns another glass bottoms up, not a single drop of red wine spilling onto his chin. "So, what can I do?"

In the reflection of the glass railing, a shadow moves behind us.

I hold my cool glass against my lips, to calm my nerves. "I saw her as a person," I say, without flinching, "and you saw her as a china doll to be displayed."

Zikai leaps across the table, his scimitar aimed at Wang Daojun's heart.

With less than a second to react, the gangster kicks his chair back and draws his sword from the scabbard on his back. The two blades clash in the night air with a ring as pure as water. In that momentary stillness, which lasts for only a second, I see the neon flashes of a hundred cabarets reflected in the metal canvas of their blades.

In the next second, wineglasses shatter on the floor with spectacular crashes like heavy rain on glass, and the guests seated around us flee from their seats, their screams muted by the music of clashing swords. I attempt to drag Li Aina with me to safety, but she refuses to leave her seat. And so I escape alone to a corner of the roof.

Zikai spins away from Daojun, and the next time I can see him clearly, he has brought his mouth harp to his lips with his other hand.

Cold mist thickens in the Rue de Velours, enveloping the rooftop club in its entirety. A cold wind blows around us and snuffs all the candles in the dining section. I find the railing and cling to it, just to have a sense of stability. Down below the hotel, the churning of the waves grows wilder, leaping high in the air with violent thrashes and dives.

The gangster and the shaman meet in the mist, Zikai's wolf tangled between them.

But the Blue Dawn's leader did not rise to his position with his wit alone. Their blades sing through the mist like silver ribbons. A lock of Zikai's hair, severed by Daojun's sword, flies into the fog, scattering like dust. It's hard not to be mesmerized by their shadows—Daojun's heavy-hitting technique and Zikai's precision, light as a ballerina.

And then Daojun plunges his sword through the smoke wolf's heart. It vanishes with a rasp like a sigh, and the mist begins to unravel around us.

Zikai brings his mouth harp back against his lips. A single, clear note echoes through the night air, splitting into three different harmonies that cause the air to shimmer and bend. The mist descends again upon the rooftop, thicker than before, like the skies being drawn down to the Rue de Velours. I can't recognize where Daojun's silver hand ends and Zikai's flesh one begins. All I hear are their muffled yells, as if they are dancing in a sea of cotton, and I can no longer differentiate between the two voices.

I brush my arm through the mist, as if I can clear it, but my fingers are swallowed.

And then I hear the crash of glass, and the glamour is broken. Daojun has cornered Zikai against the crystal railing, which cracked when he was thrown against it.

As the mist slowly thins, I am able to see the two of them more clearly. The sleeve of Zikai's shirt is soaked with blood. His scimitar has fallen to the floor, and Daojun has stamped his foot on the blade.

The Blue Dawn's leader stands with one hand resting casually on his hip, the other hand holding his sword angled up, so that the point rests just below Zikai's chin. With the blade pushed so far against his neck, the shaman has no choice but to tilt his head back over the railing, dangerously so. Knowing he is in total control, Daojun drives his blade a hair's width higher with a subtle flick of his wrist, forcing Zikai to lean back farther.

One push, and he will fall over the edge of the railing into the obsidian waves below. I envision the graceful way his back would arch, followed by the split moment of panic in his wide green eyes, playful even in their last moment, and the thudding of my heart twists into a dull ache.

I step between them, so that the sword runs along my neck as well.

"Mr. Wang, please don't."

I can feel Zikai's breath on the back of my neck as he sags against the crystal railing, his heart pounding against the ribs in my back. He's equally as surprised as I am that I've endangered my own life to try and save his. I'm not even scared of the cold tang of heavenly steel against my skin, blessed by demons or gods when the world was younger. All I can think of is the laughter being extinguished from Zikai's haughty eyes as his body is swallowed by the merciless waves, and that I can't bear it.

The leader of the Society of the Blue Dawn slowly looks from Zikai to me. Behind him, Li Aina remains sitting at the table, her chin cradled in her hand, and takes a draught of Syrah.

"Please don't what," Wang Daojun says quietly.

"Please don't kill him."

Free from the mouth harp's interference, the moon draws another tide to the wharves, torrents of water meeting the wet planks below with a soft hiss. As if a magician's blanket has been pulled from the Rue de Velours, the candles roar back to life all around us.

Daojun straightens, without altering the position of his sword. He is shorter than Zikai in stature, and his shoulders are no wider than Xiao Lei's. But his focused, unwavering gaze seems to pierce right through me. I am afraid that under the surface, he can read all the things I've hidden from him. "Don't kill this boy, who just tried to kill me as I dined peacefully with my wife? My trusted associates have recommended you to me as my next physician, but you ask me to spare a killer of mine. Well, I'd like to have a piece of your wisdom. Why not?"

Behind me, the pattern of Zikai's breathing changes, no doubt surprised at the turn our conversation has taken. For the first time, I am experiencing a true taste of Liqing's power, which has given me a chance. I'm going to use it to save the shaman from Hulunbuir.

I swallow, my throat too dry to talk. "Because you owe me."

Daojun almost drops his sword. Zikai, stealing his chance, almost makes a break for it, but Daojun recovers and drives the blade even higher under his neck.

The gangster's eyebrows are harsh, but the way they inflect at the corners is beautiful the way rough deserts are. "What on earth could I owe you?"

I stare straight back, my arms still at my sides, aware that I have no sword to fight with and no wolf to summon.

"For Aina."

Silence falls over the roof of the Rue de Velours.

"You, of all people, wish to barter lives with me?" Daojun shifts his focus onto Zikai, arched over the glass railing. The mouth harp around his neck has swung to the side, drawn toward the waves below. "Do you even know he who is?" the gangster asks me very quietly.

I glance at Aina, heartbreakingly pretty in a red felt hat, smiling through her glassy eyes as she draws a finger lightly across her lips to wipe the wine away.

In Shanghai, even your tragic memories can become a currency.

"You want me to serve you someday. Let him go."

Daojun scoffs. "What could you even gain from this?"

"This isn't about what I gain. It's about what you lose." And I touch my hand to my chest, where my human heart still beats, delicate and capable of treachery. "Years ago, you took something from me. It's my turn to take something from you."

Daojun does not respond for a long time. We stare at one another, and I refuse to flinch under the intensity of his gaze. Behind me, I hear Zikai's slow, labored breathing.

Wang Daojun sheathes his sword with an angry flourish.

"You aren't anything like Liqing," he tells me, his brows furrowed in a deep V on his forehead. "You act too much on your feelings, instead of what would benefit you. You don't know this boy or what he stands for. He is a shaman who has come to Shanghai to hunt your grandmother, and now he wants to mess with me. But I'll let him go, to teach you that lesson. He's your responsibility now. Whatever he does to my gang, I'll hold you personally responsible."

He steps around me and leans forward to confront Zikai directly. Although his height is only average, he seems to tower over the shaman. "The Court of Exiles is nothing more than a mosquito to me, buzzing about my head."

And then he clears his throat. "Come, darling, let's go dancing," he says to Aina with a honeyed tone. Daojun's wife stands and buttons her ermine stole around her shoulders. Glass crunches under his feet as he herds her away with one arm around her back.

I crouch beside Zikai, who only gapes at me, his chest rising and falling. "Why did you save me?" he asks.

At the roof's edge, near the green tank full of shining, fluttering fish, Wang Daojun turns around to look at me. So I stand again and hold his eye contact without wavering, until he spins on his heel, his coat flying behind him.

"He's gone now," I tell Zikai, purposefully ignoring his question.

He drapes his arm around my shoulders, and I do my best to half-carry him out away from the dining area, stumbling under his weight.

We ride the elevator down from the Rue de Velours in silence, the doors opening every few floors or so to admit bellhops pushing luggage carriers like silver birdcages, and waiters carrying steaming platters of lobster and rabbit braised in cognac. Nobody comments on the cabaret girl with the injured shaman standing in the back, little drops of blood staining the maroon carpet lining the elevator floor.

It is not until we are standing alone in the alleyway behind the hotel, just the two of us, that I exhale the tension I've been bottling in my chest. I feel like one of the little starlings that I've seen fly into the Bank of Shanghai's glass windows before fluttering down to the sidewalk like a discarded dance ticket. I don't know where to start comprehending the night's events.

"Well, fuck," Zikai says, falling against the wall.

He leaves a dark smear on the brick.

"Do you want me to look at it?" I walk around him, attempting to examine the extent of his wounds, while he shakes his head.

"I didn't expect him to be so fast. How could he be so fast?"

In spite of the situation we've landed in, I smile a bit—he could be bleeding out in an alley, yet all he wants to do is analyze his performance. He's purehearted deep down. "The Blue Dawn is the best gang in Shanghai for a reason."

"It's because of the silver arm." Zikai groans and digs his fingernails into the brick. "You know, I practiced years for that moment. I've tested my strength against rogue monks, pig-faced demons, tiger-riding shamans—just never a silver-armed gangster."

"Well, you'll have to put off your dreams for now. You might bleed to death."

He unbuttons his shirt and shrugs it back, exposing the tight musculature of his chest. I try to help him pull the shirt off, but he winces sharply when the sleeve abrades along the wound in his bicep.

I test the material between my thumb and forefinger. "Should I tear it?"

Zikai shies away. "No, this shirt was a gift from a traveling monk—rare silk from a blue silkworm that only exists in Wuzhen."

"Then why did you wear it to a fight?"

"Because I thought I'd win."

I assist him in easing the sleeve off the rest of the way. In the scant light in the alley, he turns in a circle, his chest bare minus the brass mouth harp, which hangs around his neck on a chain. Despite having suffered several gashes to his upper chest and back, his entire being still thrums with determination—so much I'm afraid to come close. In a city of jaded souls, I'd never met anyone so hopelessly obsessed with a desire to change something. I realize again, without being able to help myself, that despite being stupid enough to miscalculate Wang Daojun's abilities to great detriment for the both of us, Nalan Zikai is the most interesting person I've ever met.

"What are you going to do?" I ask.

The worst wound runs through the front of his bicep. The edges are raw and inflamed. When I press my fingers against his intact flesh, a few inches away, it purples from the pressure, hard and burning to the touch.

"I'll find a doctor, I guess, when they open at dawn." He snatches his shirt back out of my hand and throws it on. As he fastens the buttons again, I notice he is shivering from the wet blood that soaks his shirt. "Hey, city girl, I was impressed by what you did back there. You talked my life out of Wang Daojun's hands."

The compliment makes my heart flutter with joy, and then with shame at the inappropriateness of such a reaction. I have practically declared an alliance with the Court of Exiles to the leader of the Blue Dawn, and Zikai is bleeding profusely.

I try to match his pertness with a grin, but my mouth won't open the right way. "I told you cabaret dancers knew what they were doing."

He winks and offers me a salute, although I can tell from the veins straining in his neck that his teeth are clenched from the pain. Then he turns to go, and I watch his silhouette between the alley walls, his breath floating away in the cold air. I wonder for a brief moment why anyone would expend so much effort to appear unruffled and carefree when he is drenched in blood like that. It is so like him, so stupidly nonchalant, that I can't bear to imagine him crumpled in an alley later, wasting away from sepsis.

"Wait—I'll fix your arm."

He pauses, turns back over his shoulder. "Can you?"

"I'm my grandmother's apprentice, after all. I can close the wound."

He merely blinks back at me in wonder.

I bring the shaman to my apartment in the Old Chinese City.

"So this is an infamous Shanghai longtang alley," he remarks as we pass under a stone gate carved with snarling lions.

"The Old City is the best," I promise him.

The alleyway outside my apartment is crowded this hour of the night. Steam rises from bamboo baskets filled with braised ribs and crab shell pie. Old men in pajamas and sandals sit in plastic chairs on the street corners smoking cigarettes and drinking imported beer.

Upstairs, Zikai bites on a towel, and I thread a needle by lamplight.

It's not midnight yet, worshippers lining up at the Daoist shrine to purchase the little talismans of red-painted wood for scribbling prayers. People wish for everything—money, a rich husband, a high score on a university exam, more money. These hang like bunches of ripe fruit at the little shrines scattered in the temple courtyard, so heavy I'm convinced one day they'll pull down the temple's three grand halls, burying the jade and gold Buddhas under all those unfulfilled prayers.

"I hope they're praying for me," Zikai remarks.

I find my sewing kit and the bottle of turpentine under my bed.

"He really wants you to be his personal physician," he continues, as I dab blood away from the still-open wound. I notice the edges of the gash are razor straight, making it impossible to clot. Wang Daojun certainly keeps his heavenly steel sharpened.

I wash the wound out with turpentine, and Zikai bites down hard on the towel.

"He likes my grandmother," I note. "You can't deny she has influence and style."

Zikai stares up at the ceiling, his eyes screwed in pain. "I almost can't believe it," he says through the towel. "She has *that* much influence over the most powerful gangster in Shanghai."

I pierce the needle through his flesh and draw the thread through. He winces, and his knuckles turn white where he grips my windowsill. It gives me a dull, twisting ache in my stomach to hurt him like this, but I press on.

"I'm sorry if it leaves a scar. But I figure it beats bleeding to death before morning."

"I don't care," Zikai grunts through the towel.

It takes fifteen stitches down his arm to close the wound. He doesn't wince again, perhaps trying to hide the pain, although his occasional sharp breaths give him away. When I've finished, he examines the sutures with great interest, turning his arm left and right, in a way that makes me feel self-conscious. "Wow," he says. "I didn't realize you actually learned medicine from your grandmother."

I've never stopped before to think about how much Liqing taught me about medicine. But when I look down at my neat sutures, holding Zikai's skin together, I feel a strange pride in my work that disturbs me to realize.

I dress the wound in sterile gauze. "I grew up in her clinic watching her do all this and more."

"Thank you," Zikai says, without a single hint of his usual sarcasm. He glances up at me, eyes wide in amazement, and I pretend not to see.

As I put away my sewing kit, he slips his shirt back on. Although most of the blood has dried, he is still breathing very sharply. I draw out the cardboard box from under the bed, where I keep a few cans of preserved pineapple. I rip the top off one can.

"Pineapple? It's a working girl's staple in Shanghai."

He wrinkles his nose. "Sure."

I pass him the can and crack open a second for myself.

We eat in silence, him sitting on the bed and me against the wall. From the apartment on the other side, cigarette smoke seeps through the wall. I chew on the stringy rinds of fruit in my can, licking the sweet juice from my fingers.

When Zikai has finished, he drinks the juice at the bottom of the can with noisy slurps. Even with my sewing thread holding his skin together, he has not lost his sense of playfulness. It's equal parts bewildering and amusing—that nothing can ruffle his nonchalance.

I drop another ring of pineapple into my mouth, watching him slurp away with gusto. "You can sleep here if you'd like."

He sets his empty can down on the floor. Then, he lies down and tucks his good arm behind his head, taking a few seconds to fluff my pillow into a comfortable shape.

The rickshaws and taxis that fly by outside leave their shadows on the wall.

"I heard a lot of foreigners in the city are going to that Firefighters' Ball tomorrow night," Zikai says after a while. "Are you?"

"I'm performing at it actually. That bowdlerized dance you hated so much the first night we talked." I turn to smile at him, but he's staring out the window, at the sea of gray shikumen rooftops of the Old City.

"Who are you going with?" he asks.

I shrug, suddenly wishing we were discussing something else. Anything else. "Some rich businessman I met. They have nice hors d'oeuvres usually, and last year I heard they imported peat moss from Scotland for the decorations."

"It's the man we saw at the Paramount, isn't it?"

"Yes, it's him."

Another shadow flutters across the ceiling like a bird.

"Stay safe."

He scoots against the wall, and I lie down, leaving a body's space between us. Soon, his eyes close and his face relaxes into a peaceful expression. Finally, I hope his pain can go away.

I realize there are many loose endings to the story we have written tonight.

Wang Daojun still lives, and I have exposed my willingness to defend the shaman from the Court of Exiles. It won't be easy to get so close to him ever again. But that's a problem for another night, another time.

I lie awake for longer than I intend, listening to Zikai breathe. But his breaths are slow, the way a sleeping person's tend to be. Perhaps he is listening for mine as well.

CHAPTER THIRTEEN

By the time I awaken, Zikai is gazing out my open window at the alleyway outside. There is a morning fish market on Wednesday mornings, the sunlight shimmering on ice and freshly gutted fish packed in wooden boxes. Clearly, they do not care about Christmas in the Old Chinese City.

"Thanks for letting me stay the night, city girl," Zikai remarks as he ties his sheathed scimitar onto his belt. There are shadows under his eyes. I can tell he didn't actually sleep.

I push myself up into a sitting position.

"You promise you're going to see a real doctor, right?" I ask Zikai.

Under my window, automobiles and rickshaws flood the streets. A drove of traders in silk top hats and swallowtail coats march toward the Bund with their briefcases, blowing at steaming rice balls wrapped in bamboo leaves.

"Of course." He steps into his boots and knots the laces. "And then I'll think of a way to beat Wang Daojun. I'll admit it, I underestimated him."

The sunlight glints against the mouth harp resting against his chest.

I can't help but smile a bit at his diligence. "Focus on getting better first."

As soon as he's gone, I sit back down on the edge of my bed. The sheets are slightly crinkled where he lay, the way very calm waves disturb the Huangpu on a summer day. I'm left with the feeling that the events of the last night were just a dream. What of our pact now that we've failed? We can't outsmart Wang Daojun a second time, now that he's seen us together.

Yet, I can't afford to dwell.

Tonight is the Firefighters' Yuletide Ball, the largest event of the year in the International Settlement, where gangsters, politicians, and the city's most famous cabaret dancers gather in the year's most outlandish fashions for a night of gossip and posturing.

And I haven't prepared at all.

In the morning, I meet with a Parisian dressmaker recommended by Arisha—no doubt the same one every cabaret girl invited to the ball has gone to. She tells me I don't have time to try on more than four dresses, so I try on three, and I leave with the last one.

I then spend the afternoon in a French Concession salon, inhaling airy hair sprays that make me think of chemical factories and perfumeries at the same time, as I am fitted with the latest finger waves that stop just short of my shoulders. Across the salon, a pair of girls tease each other with rollers as their hairstylists whip perming cream in a bowl. No doubt they are the daughters of some European diplomat, also getting ready for the Firefighters' Ball.

The day ends in the alleyway before my shikumen apartment, where I wait for Bailey Thompson in my gown. A neighbor of mine, stumbling home drunk from a gambling den, flashes me a suspicious, horrified look, as if he's certain I'm a hallucination that has appeared in the dirty alley before his house.

At seven o'clock, Bailey's Packard Twelve squeezes through the alley, headlights throwing cracked brick and laundry lines into sharp relief. Bailey steps out dressed in a black dinner tuxedo with a white waistcoat and bow tie, his hair neatly gelled. This is the moment I've been waiting for—the moment I will be evaluated against the other dancers in our competition, and I am certain I have won—but for some reason I feel like Cinderella the moment she lost her glamour, primped and overdressed in a tattered street.

Bailey takes my hand, sheathed in white satin gloves that button up to my elbows, and kisses my fingers.

"Merry Christmas, Jingwen. You look exceptionally fashion-able."

I smile and turn in a circle to show off my gown. Champagne satin falls in a deep V down my back, which suddenly cuts to black silk below my shoulder blades. Two high slits along my thighs expose an under-layer of beige satin.

I am freezing, but a coat might crinkle the silk.

His driver takes us to the Astor House, situated by a curve of the Huangpu River north of the Bund. We don't talk in the car, although I notice Bailey is smiling to himself in that subtle way, as if I've amused him.

"Are you nervous about the performance?" he asks after a few minutes, resting the ankle of one leg upon the knee of another.

"No, I'm confident," I respond. To be truthful, I haven't even thought about the performance since that night in the Coeur de la Rose.

"Good," he says, and his smile widens just a bit more. "I have high expectations."

I observe his reflection in the dark window, and I recall our parting in his club before a bitterly jealous Moraima.

The ballroom's facade bleeds drama, a stark interplay of dark roofs and neon-lit colonnades. At the corners, Atlases and caryatids shoulder the weight of the ballroom on their heads, their closed eyes evoking the atmosphere of empires fallen, as if we are stepping through the tall double doors back through history.

The coat girl takes Bailey's jacket, and we walk between light blue walls decorated with nymphs and mermaids.

At the front of the main-floor ballroom, the blown-up portrait of an austere-looking man frowns down upon the entire ballroom. Bailey explains it is the prime minister of England, as the majority of the International Settlement's firefighters are British, and the fire department funded the ball. We are supposed to bask in the grandiosity of the prime minister, because he can afford to host lavish events in a city hundreds of kilometers away from his home—although his person does not happen to be in attendance.

I crane my neck to spy around the still-empty ballroom, but I do not spot any peat moss anywhere that might have been imported from Scotland.

Four Christmas trees guard the corners of the main ballroom, alit with glowing angels and stars. The sweet fragrance of pine carries all the way up to the second floor, where a series of circular balconies overlooks the main ballroom like opera boxes, split by baroque columns.

The first familiar face I encounter is Arisha, dressed in a gown made of silver crushed velvet with a swooping neckline, a crystalline kokoshnik nestled in her platinum hair. She slurps a roasted oyster out of its shell, arm in arm with the Kuomintang general I saw her with at the Paramount.

Bailey clears his throat as we pass. "General Chen. We met at the YMCA gala last week."

"Ah, yes. Dr.—?"

"Thompson."

"Dr. Thompson."

They shake hands. I watch as I receive a roasted oyster plated on a silver spoon from a passing tea boy. Bailey stands a lot more stiffly than he did in the Coeur de la Rose. I guess that he keeps his confidence carefully pruned like a rosebush, and he is a bit out of his comfort zone.

General Chen raises his eyebrows at me. "And this is . . . ?"

Bailey touches my back lightly. "Vilma Yue, the star of tonight's performance."

I smile as I slide the oyster into my mouth. The center bursts with such a gourmet flavor of cream and brine that for a moment I cannot find any words.

The general brings his hands together in a clap. "I've heard so much about *The Black Cat* and its folk-dance element. Thank you for showcasing our culture to our friends in the foreign concessions. I've gotten quite sick of watching *The Nutcracker* every year."

I swallow the oyster, lost in total bliss at how the plump body slides down my throat. "I look forward to performing for you, General," I say with a dazed smile.

Behind him, Arisha presses her thin lips together, her blue eyes hardened like frost.

I deepen my smirk in a challenge.

Bailey soon embroils the general in a reluctant conversation about camel routes across the Taklamakan Desert, and I turn so that Arisha and I stand with our backs to one another, both of us pretending to nibble at another oyster. "So how wealthy is he?" Arisha asks over her shoulder. "Do you think you've won?"

The hard crystals on her kokoshnik press into the back of my head. "Is money the only legitimate way to measure wealth?"

"How do you propose we measure it then?"

I shrug, closing my eyes to savor another buttery oyster. "Connections? Power? For example, Neville has a great inheritance, but if I asked him to procure powdered dragon scale by tomorrow morning, I don't think he could."

Arisha snorts her oyster up her nose but manages to transform the moment into a dainty coughing fit. "Powdered dragon scale? What are you talking about?"

"Dr. Thompson knows where to get powdered dragon scale."

I want to laugh at the statement coming out of my own mouth.

After what I've been through at the Dove House and the Rue de Velours, this night feels like a joke. Who cares if I have to wash Beibei's feet for the next year?

Arisha wheels around on her white satin pumps to face me and flashes me a puzzled look, as if she suspects I'm drunk. I smile through my mouthful of oyster.

Bailey presses his hand against my back with a wide smile. "Ah, and here is the director himself, Sui Feng."

Sui Feng has wandered over to greet us, dressed in plaid suit pants and a loose jacket, but with his shirt untucked. He bows to General Chen, his long whiskers threatening to sweep the floor. "A longtime admirer of yours, General Chen, since you fought in the ranks of the Warlord Kun. They say you might have even been blessed by a goddess of destruction herself."

The general claps for him as well. "You are quite the genius to reinvent the popular vaudeville show in the likes of Chinese folk dance. The Daoist myths are my favorite."

A sly look crosses Sui Feng's face. "You should look forward to the performance tonight then."

The general raises his old-fashioned to Sui Feng. "How did you conceive the idea for such a performance?"

Sui Feng strokes his beard between two thin, long fingers. "I've harbored a long yearning for the way things used to be," he says, miming a rainbow in the air. "You know, my life before I came to Shanghai."

Arisha bites into a caviar and crème tartlet, taking care to draw her lips back so that her lipstick won't smear. She doesn't seem to notice, but I feel it—the slightest edge to Sui Feng's voice, which chills the air. His name means "a wind that moves as it pleases." I've never thought to ask—where *did* Sui Feng come from?

"I'll go speak to the stage director now," Sui Feng announces. And he sweeps away, humming the opening song for *The Black Cat.*

"An odd fellow," the general remarks to Bailey. "But I like them that way."

Bailey laughs. "I have the best luck finding odd fellows like that. There appears to be more of them in Shanghai than the rest of the world."

More guests have filled the ballroom, eating seared abalone off toothpicks while gazing up at the domed ceiling, which is painted with deer-legged fauns and girls wearing nothing but ivy, over a layer of matte gold.

I note that this year, geometric dresses with sharp cuts and bold colorations are all the rage. Beibei, recognizable from a mile away, laughs on Neville Harrington's shoulder in choppy tiers of slashed emerald tulle, which blossom around her shoulders like a chrysanthemum. It's not her usual style, an inversion of the cold, sleek grace she regularly embodies. Only Beibei could look stunning in such a gown. Anyone else would look like a bunch of cilantro at the market.

And yet—all around I bump into blond girls with their hair dyed black, shoulders bare under a sheer, champagne gown. Under the fluttering silk, red velvet stilettos flash with every step. They are dressed the way I imagined Beibei at the Firefighters' Yuletide Ball.

I must admit, it's awfully clever of her to throw them off like that. Although I'm also surprised because I thought she liked the attention.

I drift along the crowd with Bailey, who waits patiently as I visit every tea boy dressed in white suits with red jackets. Their platters are piled with squash blossoms stuffed with ricotta and peach slices wrapped in braised meats. While I pop canapés decorated with duck liver mousse, Bailey explains to various wooden-faced politicians that he is attending the ball with the night's lead dancer. By the way, were they looking for a business partner in shipping exports? And did they know anybody in the Atlantic City night scene interested in opening a nightclub—no, not a gambling den, there's too many of those already—a radical, new evolution of nightclub.

Glancing up at the box lounges on the ballroom's upper floor, I catch sight of Wang Daojun speaking to General Chen with his arm around his shoulders, their heads bent together. Li Aina hangs behind him with one hand on the balcony like a princess locked in the window of a distant tower, making awkward eye contact with Arisha, who has no idea what to say to a swan-hearted mobster's wife.

Eventually, we bump into Neville and Beibei, who are drinking champagne with their arms entwined. Neville alone out of all the factory magnates and politicians does not show any interest in networking. Instead he makes silly faces at the exotic tastes of liver mousse and dressed-up gizzards, laughing at every word Beibei says. He's quite sweet and refreshing compared to the other socialites of Shanghai high society, I decide.

"Hello, I forgot your name," Neville remarks to me, as I slip my right glove off so that I may pick up a spiced Turkish meatball with my fingers, to dip in pomegranate yogurt.

"Vilma," I say, dropping the spiced meatball in my mouth.

Bailey extends his arm across me. "Mr. Harrington—even when I lived in New York, I heard of your father. My name is Bailey Thompson. I'm a businessman who would love to make your father's acquaintance."

Neville shakes his hand enthusiastically. "Oh, my father isn't at the ball tonight. He despises social functions like this."

"Fair enough." Bailey adjusts his bow tie casually. "When you're as rich as him, the world bows to you. But say, what times does your father frequent the YMCA on Thursdays?"

"Two p.m. to four p.m.," Neville responds dutifully, as Beibei slips a spiced meatball into his mouth. A dollop of pomegranate yogurt clings to his lip, and Beibei wipes it away with her thumb.

She giggles. "After completing his boxing lessons at the YMCA, the senior Mr. Harrington stops for an olive oil body scrub at the Turkish bath on Avenue Joffre. He asks for the full exfoliation treatment with extra virgin cold-pressed olive oil—the stuff they import on luxury liners from the Peloponnese." She narrows her eyes, the glow of her irises sharp like butterfly knives. "Because he can afford it."

I laugh and cover my face with my hand to hide it. The absurdity of the night feels like sobriety after a night of drinking. We are all sharks of different species, feeding on Neville Harrington's soft, sun-deprived skin. The guests might say they have come tonight to watch me perform with the East Sea Follies, but to me they are the greatest comedy of all.

Beibei winks at me as she licks pomegranate yogurt off her fingertip. "Anyways, good luck in your performance tonight, Vilma," she says to me. "I've heard many people have high expectations for you."

I curtsy the way they taught us at the ballet, slightly ironically. "Thank you. It must be a relief to have the spotlight shine on someone else for one night."

Beibei narrows her eyes like a wildcat, although on her it looks charming. "Certainly, I always hold my breath in case they can match me."

The Astor House's orchestra sits under a glass shell patterned like a peacock's spread tail. When the lights dim for the dancing to begin, rippling hues of green, blush, and twilight fall across the glass feathers.

I stuff one last wine-marinated olive in my mouth and accept Bailey's proffered hand. He leads me to the center of the ballroom, close to Shanghai's league of eligible bachelors, who have all chosen cabaret dancers and film stars as their dates. The familiar sensation of soaring lifts in my chest, as I stand amongst my fellow dancers in fairy-tale gowns, surrounded by the most powerful heroes and villains of the city.

The orchestra lifts their violins under their chins, and I hope for an Argentine tango, wherein Bailey will dip me back over his arm, prompting my silk gown to fall around me like water. But instead the melody blooms into a classical waltz.

As I take care to float upon my toes in Bailey's embrace, I do that thing which cabaret girls should never do—and I compare him to Zikai. I imagine what sarcastic comments Zikai would make about how the bite-sized appetizers are a cruel way to starve the guests, or how the gangsters' fitted dinner tuxedos are a disadvantage in battle. An odd nostalgia tugs at my heart. Undeniably, there is some part of me that craves spending the night at the Paramount surrounded by familiar faces.

After ten minutes, I am sick of dancing the waltz.

"Do they play anything here other than waltzes and quadrilles?" I ask Bailey.

He laughs. "The chairman of the Shanghai Municipal Council thinks that jazz is the root cause of societal atrophy. It's a sickness he is waiting to purge from the concessions."

I roll my eyes. "Well, it's boring."

Bailey points at the second-floor lounge above the peacock shell and lowers his voice to a whisper. "See, the chairman does not dance because he is arthritic, but he likes to watch from above. I think he would like it, don't you think, if Shanghai was a center for tailor-made deliriums like I want, rather than dancing?"

But it's not the chairman I notice. I see a different face staring out of the crowd, between two young girls who are stealing champagne out of their parents' glasses. Li Beibei sips whiskey with a bored look on her face, alone. Her elbow rests on the balcony's slender edge, the choppy, geometric silk of her dress pooling against her shoulder, her hand buried in her hair.

The orchestra begins to play another quadrille, which some of the older guests cheer for.

"How about I get us drinks?" I tell Bailey, dropping my hands from his shoulders.

He chuckles lightly. "Certainly. Al Israel—what do you say about an investigative expedition? I've heard there are beautiful flowers growing in the valleys of China's northern mountain ranges, which produce an assortment of highs much more fascinating than opium."

And he is quickly swept away by another business associate of his.

I climb the stairs to the second floor, my dress hitched in my hand.

Beibei lengthens her neck as I take a seat opposite her in the lounge. The emerald fringe of her gown falls along her collarbone. "How kind of you to join me, Jingwen," she says in her signature, viscous scoff.

She is so different from the laughing, twirling girl at the Neapolitan Gardens who demanded I drink rosé with her friend.

I fold my arms over my chest. "The waltz—it's kind of boring."

Beibei narrows her eyes, trying to assess my motive.

When she can't figure me out, she laughs, reaching for a white peach macaroon from a glass bowl on the lounge table. "Isn't it stupid? We spend the entire year anticipating the foreign concessions' Christmas balls, gossiping and building hype, but in the end— they're the most boring dances of all."

I can't help but grin. "Yes, the summer Venetian masquerades are much better—the ones the Italian embassy holds in the streets in late June. Last year, there was a lunar eclipse, and the skies looked like they were bleeding under the moon. Do you remember that?"

Beibei laughs under her breath, and for a second her eyes trace up to the dancing sylphs painted on the ceiling. A mischievous look shadows her red lips as she recalls some private, fond memory of hers.

Just then, I spy Arisha behind a Roman pillar, headed in a beeline toward us. Seconds later, Zina and the other Paramount girls come running. Arisha reaches us first with a sultry catwalk, clutching a folded sheet of paper in her hand.

"So, who won?" Arisha asks, brandishing the paper in the air. "I have procured a bank statement of exactly how much money General Chen has in his bank account right now as evidence of my standing."

"Of course you did," I mutter, prompting Zina to laugh with me.

Below us, the quadrille ends, and a momentary stillness seizes the ballroom. I find myself holding my breath even though I'm not dancing—the end of a dance is always sacred. And then the orchestra starts again—with another quadrille.

Like windup dolls, we come back to life.

"Oh? Let me see." Beibei holds her palm out, managing to look bored.

Arisha licks her pinky and unfolds the paper with her meticulous fingertips. "Don't wrinkle it, please."

Beibei's eyes rove across the page. I can see the printed digits reflected in her eyes, passing by like numbers falling on a stock ticker.

"It's Jingwen, Arisha, or me," she says, putting the paper down. Arisha scurries to cradle the bank statement in her hands.

Zina stomps her foot angrily, her stiletto tip ruffling the plush carpet fibers. "What? I'm not even in the running?"

Arisha adjusts the kokoshnik upon her head, the crystals reflecting the chandeliers on the ceiling. "We all saw you arrive with the Park Hotel's manager as your date. While he's certainly handsome and embezzles from one of the city's flashiest pieces of real estate, that's not even worth competing with."

Her hands fall to her hips. "Let's decide by evaluating the most expensive gift your date has brought you. For me, it was a bouquet with flowers from forty different countries. It even had a Peruvian sundew, a plant covered in spindly green hairs that eats flies."

Beibei's eyes slide onto me like honey.

When I don't speak, she twirls her hair around one finger. "Neville bought me a summer house on Hainan Island."

Zina gasps and covers her mouth with both her hands. A curl of her red-brown hair escapes a leaf-shaped pin and bounces at her cheek.

"Have you ever been to Hainan Island?" Arisha asks, her reaction more composed. But the jealousy bleeds through nonetheless.

Beibei picks up another white peach macaroon between her long, crimson nails. "No, but I'll retire there when I'm sick of the dirty air and the trolley bells. It's a beach. How horrible can it be?"

They look at me.

For a moment, I can taste the glory—a future where Beibei will pour me wine at the beckon of my little finger, and the other girls, upon my arrival on the dance floor, will relinquish the fine hands of their favorite playboys so that I can dance with them instead. In this future, power is sweet and guileless, like the delicate ivory that inlays the Paramount's walls.

But a twirl under a chandelier, and there might be a girl bleeding on the maple floors, whorls of darkness where her eyes should be.

It strikes me then—it's not enough to be loved by the guests and worshipped by the other girls. The real power I desire isn't over the dancers—it's over the face stealer and the people who do business with him.

Perhaps this is what Liqing has always urged me to perceive, with all her talk of puppets and puppeteers. Ironic that I've only started caring when my purpose is to unseat her.

I draw my shoulders back. "Dr. Thompson bought the Paramount Ballroom so that I could play the lead role in tonight's show."

Arisha scoffs, the jewels in her hair glinting under the chandeliers. "That's *romantic,* but it doesn't exactly scream rich, Jingwen."

I smile as I pop a white peach macaroon into my mouth, savoring the light, innocent sweetness. "Hear me out. Bailey's wealth extends beyond money—he has influence. Neville may be rich, but he can't tell a Chow Chow from a Shar-Pei, and he's twenty-seven! Come on, Arisha. He may have bought Beibei the fanciest beach house in Hainan Island, but when you live like we do, you get bored of white sand and palm trees real quick." I bat my eyelashes at Beibei. Even now, after I've given up my own flesh and blood to protect the other dancers, it feels good to taunt her. "After all, we thrive on competition and the attention of strangers. A man like Bailey Thompson though—he can devise social and political ingenuities like magic tricks—the other night he brought me to a speakeasy with cocktails that made you hallucinate orchestral scores and your grandparents' dirtiest secrets. Men like Neville, whose mother picks out his silk ties, can only be a player in the game—he'll never deal the cards."

And although I am bragging to win their veneration, I shiver nonetheless at my own words. "Bailey will bring me anything I want—make me the leading lady of any show I ask for, *as long as I stay by his side.*"

They're all staring at me now, their eyes wider than Daoist coins.

"What do you think?" I ask Arisha, licking the crumbs from my fingertips.

Only Beibei laughs behind her sealed lips, her eyes turning up at the corners like a cat's. She has started to line her eyes more heavily than most girls, I notice. I can't shake the feeling that she is the only one, out of all the girls, who truly understands what I have just said.

I turn to her and try to catch her tenuous gaze, adept as she is at just slipping out of reach. "However—I'd like to concede my victory to Li Beibei."

"What?" Zina shrieks and clutches my arm. "But I was about to ask you to request *Coppélia* for the spring season. I won't be jealous if you ask to be Swanhilda—I want to play one of the giant, life-size dolls."

Arisha frowns. "Jingwen, this whole competition was your idea!"

I reach out and rest my fingertips on Beibei's bare arm. "I'm yours. You can ask me to polish your toenails now if you want."

Beibei doesn't even smile at hearing her victory. She drinks from her whiskey with her eyes half closed, as the violins begin a dramatic crescendo on the dance floor.

I wish I could read what she was thinking.

"Why, Jingwen?" Arisha presses again.

It's a lesson my mother learned once, and my grandmother knew all along. In Shanghai, every gift has a price tag, and I am unwilling to pay the price of being Bailey's trophy.

I rise to my feet, layers of champagne and black silk falling to my feet. Although they still annoy me to no end, I can't help but feel a stab of nostalgic, painful fondness toward them. At the end of the night, I am glad to have them on the dance floor beside me in one piece—as familiar faces, as rivals, as friends. Conceding my inferiority to Beibei isn't so bad—if I can depose my grandmother from the Blue Dawn's favor and save us from being carved apart.

I shrug. "Without all of you, working at the Paramount would bore me to death. I'm glad I met you."

And I sweep away, just as a large puff of fire and smoke bursts in the air above the dance floor, raining sparks down upon the guests dancing below. The guests scream in delight as their hair and skin are shocked by the bite of fire. Down below, the man Bailey identified as the chairman of the Shanghai Municipal Council has walked into the center of the dance floor, dragging with him a silver microphone. "And with that exciting prelude, I'd like to introduce the Shanghai Fire Brigade of the International Settlement!"

A procession of men in black jackets and white hats march forward in single file to surround him, their rubber boots sticking to the dance floor.

The chairman continues reading from a sheet of paper. "Last year, these men put out three hundred eighty-two fires in the international concessions, assisted two hundred medical emergencies, and rescued forty-seven housecats . . ."

His voice fades behind the pounding of my heart.

The chair invites prominent members of the International Settlement to make speeches, and I return to Bailey's side on the first-floor ballroom.

He bends down immediately to whisper in my ear. "Al Israel, the owner of the Del Monte Club, has agreed to fund my expedition into the northern mountain ranges. He's a mad gambler, and he netted ten thousand American dollars last Saturday in Blood Alley, just by playing roulette."

I tear my attention away from the consul chairman. "For that strange fungus of yours?"

Bailey adjusts his bow tie. "Yes, I've identified a camel route through the Taklamakan Desert that avoids both the quicksand and the dust storms. We'll hire guides to meet us on the old Silk Road, and we'll proceed from there."

I picture Bailey in his designer suit, riding in a saddle on a camel's back, defying sandstorms with his sunglasses. "How much do you intend to collect?"

"Enough to load a small ship to New York. I have distributors waiting there. I'd love for you to join me at the docks for a little goodbye, of course—so I can show you off." He reaches down to tuck my hair behind my ear, and the movement chills my blood to ice. When his finger brushes my cheek, I can't shake the feeling I am being measured.

On the dance floor, the consul chairman takes the microphone back. "Any last words of thanks to be shared from the crowd?" he asks in his booming voice.

Neville Harrington steps forward to the microphone. The crowd gasps collectively, dazzled into shock by his beauty. He clears his throat and reaches into his breast pocket, from which he pulls a crystal pendant shaped like a heart, attached to a gold chain. "The firemen may have saved Shanghai from fires," he says, dropping to one knee. "But Li Beibei saved my heart. Will you marry me?"

Beibei covers her mouth with her hand, sheathed in a green velvet glove.

If I didn't pity him so much, I might have laughed at how stupid Neville is. For the rest of the night, it will be the joke of the town—Shanghai's femme fatale, captured by a lovestruck rich boy—who proposed to her not with a ring, but a crystal heart on a chain.

My soft heart almost feels pity for Neville, as I brace myself for Beibei's publicly staged humiliation. After all, she's already won. She doesn't need him anymore. At least his head is so far in the clouds, the insult might just bounce off him.

Beibei's face is still for a moment. I follow her gaze and realize she is looking at a dancing sylph on the wall, locked in the embrace of two other sylphs, wisps of clouds floating around their bodies.

And then she beams. "Oh Neville, it's all I ever wanted."

He fastens the crystal heart around her neck, and the ballroom erupts into thunderous applause—one thousand pairs of hands coming together under a gold-painted dome. A few of the women are sobbing, carefully dabbing their tears away with their pinky fingers, so as not to disturb their makeup. Any attention that might have been garnered by the fire brigade after the chairman's speech is instantly lost.

Beibei's face is still, but nobody notices. Soon, she and Neville are swallowed by clapping hands, which raise high in the air, like ghost branches waving in the air.

A hand taps my shoulder.

It's Arisha swathed in light blue silk, looking like one of the Paramount's ice sculptures come to life. "Where is Sui Feng? We're supposed to perform soon, and the man has disappeared!"

"There's a different matter I have to take care of first." I throw myself into the bodies on the dance floor, my wrist slipping through Arisha's hand as she attempts to grab me.

"Jingwen, wait!"

An eternity seems to pass as I sift through the crowd of applauding partygoers like the victim of a shipwreck, fighting the waves.

Beibei turns around in the center, buffeted about like a butterfly in a monsoon. As the crowd briefly drifts apart, I reach through and grab her elbow. "What was that about?"

She tilts away from me, the white heart pendant sparkling against her chest. "What do you mean?"

"You already won. You didn't have to accept his proposal."

She takes two steps back, slightly off balance, the sleeves of her gown fluttering like wings. The pendant resting in the space between her collarbones is so bright, I have to squint. "If I turned him down in front of all those people, all those people who have been drooling over us, living vicariously through our bodies— what would they have said? I made a love story for *them*. If there is no happy ending, wo would ever believe me again?"

"But if you marry him, you won't be a cabaret girl anymore. You'd be his wife."

The spotlights revolve in the sky with a dizzying velocity. I recall the spinning roulette wheel in my dream, stripes of pink and white turning faster and faster.

"I know that." She touches her throat where the pendant blazes in the cradle of her collarbones, as if she's choking softly.

Like a star, the brighter she burned, the faster it pushed her toward this inevitable ending. Just like my mother and Raoul.

But Beibei is not like my mother.

"What are you going to do then, kill him?"

She laughs at my joke, her voice the color of a vibrating wineglass flicked by a flirtatious pinky nail. Yet I hear the despair. She is seriously considering my request. It is both the funniest and saddest emotion I have ever seen in a nightclub.

I would miss her dearly if she became Mrs. Harrington of the beach house in Hainan Island.

I grab her shoulders. "You've gone too far. This is the only role you've played for a long time."

She tries to twist out of my grip, but I refuse to release her.

"Fight for your own happiness," I more or less yell in her face.

And then a large, strong hand is gripping my waist and pulling me away. Beibei falls backward and disappears into the chaos of colored silk and flying satin.

"What is this? A fight in the center of the dance floor? There's no need."

It's Bailey whose hands rest on my waist, hot and leaden. He leans down, close to my head. "Jingwen, I believe it's time for your performance now. Make me proud."

The performance—I'd forgotten all about it. Arisha is waiting for me in the dressing room. We were supposed to look for Sui Feng together.

Bailey's lips brush against my ear. I shiver.

"Good luck," he murmurs.

"Thank you," I say, my face expressionless.

CHAPTER FOURTEEN

By the time I shut the dressing room door behind me, I am greeted by the ordinary chaos that surges through the cast right before a performance. Rongyu rushes at me with her arms spread and her cheeks flushed.

"Jingwen, what did the elephant ask the naked man?" she asks me.

I stare at her, stunned. "I don't know."

"'How do you breathe out of that thing?'" She slaps her thigh and throws her head back, laughing so hard no sound comes out.

"Not now, Rongyu." I push her to the side.

Arisha beckons me over to the makeup table, where she is touching up her mascara.

"So did you find him?" I ask. Carefully shedding my ball gown like a skin, I change into my costume for the first act—an embossed gold robe with flowing white water sleeves.

The dressing room's walls are a soothing mauve color, broken by gold lines tracing the shapes of roses, which give it an air of ethereality. Around us, the girls of the East Sea Follies are transforming into goddesses and jade maidens, sweeping geometric ball gowns exchanged for flowing robes.

Arisha shakes her head. "No—not here, not backstage. Don't you find it strange that he would disappear like that before the performance?"

"No, it's exactly like him. I bet he's scaring us on purpose to sharpen our senses or something ridiculous like that." I pick up a coal pencil to freshen the liner around my eyes, so that my makeup will really pop against my gold robe.

But Arisha doesn't look convinced as she passes me my lipstick. "Never mind him for now. I still don't understand why you let Beibei win."

I smile at her with a tinge of sadness. "The type of power men like Bailey have has begun to scare me. I've been playing this game too carelessly, Arisha." I steal a glance at her, but I can't tell if she understands. "Plus, you and Beibei aren't my enemies." I smack my lips together to smooth my lipstick.

We rise to our feet at the same time. The costumes Sui Feng arranged for us are truly beautiful—flowers stitched with bright threads, dripping beads and ribbons.

"Shall we head backstage?" I suggest. "Hopefully that cursed old man will be waiting for us there."

The Astor House's theater can seat one thousand guests. Although I'm to perform there tonight, I have never seen the stage. Behind the wings, I riffle through the dark curtains, buoyed by the frantic bodies of the stage crew, who are dragging papier-mâché statues of sleeping tigers and many-horned animals into place.

"Have any of you seen Sui Feng?" I ask every passing body.

They all shake their heads. Several of the girls are lying on their bellies upstage, cautiously lifting the edge of the curtains to spy at the audience. I can hear the guests whispering down in their seats, like the low rumble of a mountain that is about to split.

My heartbeat quickens in my chest.

"This is Sui Feng's big moment," I point out. "Why isn't he here?"

Zina grips my hand. "Oh Jingwen, you'll just have to do it without him."

On the other side of those heavy velvet curtains, an announcer begins to speak. A spotlight flashes on, its warm light leaking under the curtain, and the girls run away giggling.

The stage manager walks past me cursing. "Where is that bewhiskered devil?" he mutters, no doubt referring to Sui Feng. He points at me. "You're on in three."

Arisha gives me a push in the back, and I run into the center of the dark stage, hidden from view by heavy curtains. As *The Black Cat*'s prelude begins to play, I drape one of my arms over my head, silk sleeve falling over my face.

The announcer says beyond the barrier of the curtains, "And now I present to you, the East Sea Follies!"

The curtain rises slowly, and a spotlight shines down center stage, bathing me in warm, orange light like the dawn sun. There is no concept of night and day in our version of the celestial mountains—only an eternal twilight. Behind me, a velvet backdrop depicts mountains with painted blue tips, green waterfalls cascading down their slopes.

I am Niang Niang, the Mother of Calamity.

In my immortal peach gardens, I leap between the sleeping beasts made of mashed paper and tree branches made of blue jadeite, twisting my sleeves in patterns the length of the stage—a shower of meteors across the sky and peach blossom petals falling about my body—mundane things for a celestial goddess bored out of her mind. I dance just slightly off balance to express Niang Niang's tedium, allowing my weight to tip me over.

As I dance closer to the front of the stage, I notice an aroma like grass but musky hanging in the air. I register the scent immediately. It's the smoke leaf I stole from Raoul Smith. Someone is smoking the fungus in the audience. I purposefully edge my dance closer upstage, taking care not to trip over the silk streamers meant to represent flowing, celestial brooks.

The theater is too dark to see the audience's faces clearly.

In the real performance, the next act will be the legendary Dance of the Qingniao, where Niang Niang transforms into a shimmering green-black bird who flies between the skyscrapers of Shanghai's entertainment district. But because the performance at the Firefighters' Yuletide Ball is a preview, we will not perform that scene.

At the end of the act, I shed my water sleeves to reveal that I am wearing a black sequined dress underneath my robe. I fit a pair of velvet cat ears upon my head, and the audience bursts into applause, shocked at my transformation.

The next number is a tap dance. As the curtain briefly falls, I run into the wings to exchange my dancing heels for tap shoes.

For the next scene, the chorus joins me onstage. We perform a standard vaudeville dance inspired by the seductive hunt of a cat. The chorus girls even have tails pinned to the backs of their dresses.

Displeased that I have chosen the lifestyle of a depraved show-girl, the Jade Emperor who lives in the sky will now send three gods to the Black Cat cabaret to bring me back. The first is the Insect God, played by a reluctant Rongyu, who bursts upon the stage wearing an eagle's beak strapped around her face, fake talons affixed to her nails and her skin painted blue. Even when she is drunk, Rongyu emanates a stage presence that burns like fire, a stark reminder that she is the East Sea Follies' true star.

As the chorus girls and I prance across the stage in our cat-steps, she lifts her arms to summon a swarm of locusts in the cabaret. I hold my breath, anticipating the rustling of black tulle wings as another group of chorus girls will leap across the stage, cutting through our foundation.

A loud buzzing rises, like waves crashing under the Rue de Velours, from the far end of the hall. Rongyu and I see it the most clearly, since we are facing the audience. The chorus girls never come with their tulle wings and gentle steps.

A cloud of black flies through the hall, thick like smoke. First I think it is an illusion, a trick of the light caused by cigarette smoke in the audience. But the cloud grows larger, trembling against the walls and rumbling louder. Then, I think it must be a cruel joke, some prank made by some gangster to frighten the foreigners.

The chorus girls stop dancing, having noticed our faces. They turn around just as the swarm of black locusts descends upon the guests, large as birds with pink veins shimmering in their wing membranes.

Rongyu screams and stumbles backward over a papier-mâché beast. I grab her hand and pull her toward the dark curtains leading offstage.

"We need to get out of here!" I yell at the others.

The locusts dive like obsidian bullets upon the audience, their wings trembling like harp strings. Rongyu and the chorus girls run after me.

At the edge of the stage, I glance over my shoulder.

Someone has flipped on the lights in the audience. The locusts have scattered along the hall, the cloud thinning into shining individual bodies.

A man falls somewhere near the front of the audience, a sword clattering out of his hand, a mountain of locusts attached to his chest. He lies on the floor in a growing pool of his own blood, and the light falls on a badge shaped like the sun clipped to his breast pocket. It's General Chen.

Arisha wrestles open the fire door that leads into an alley behind the ballroom. There, we lean against the wall, divided from the bloodshed inside the hall. I can hear our breaths, ragged and out of sync. I tear the cat ears out of my hair and throw them on the ground.

I don't think I will ever get over it—seconds before the most horrific slaughter I've ever witnessed in a ballroom, I was prancing about the stage pretending to be a cat.

"Sui Feng never came to the performance," I realize, although nobody seems to hear me.

"How could there be locusts in the ballroom?" Rongyu asks, wringing her hands.

Zina keeps pinching her own arms to confirm we are really awake. "Locusts aren't that large, and they don't normally bite people, do they?"

Rongyu bites her fingers to stop them from trembling. Her voice shakes when she speaks. "Did I cause that?"

None of us can find the words to respond.

The midnight sky glows reddish-pink along the horizon, warning of dawn rain. The air hanging in the alleys is heavy with wetness, causing the sequins of my dress to stick to my skin.

I fidget in my dress, wishing the disaster had happened one act earlier, when I could easily strip out of my robes into a leotard. "No. You didn't cause it."

A loud buzzing starts, low in the guts of Shanghai like the first whispering of a dreadful secret, which passed from mouth to mouth, exaggerates its intensity until it becomes a shout. The three of us stiffen, like forest animals who have sensed a predator, and the locusts come over the alley wall, a storm of angry wings and bullet-shaped bodies.

Rongyu grabs onto my forearm, and I instinctively clutch her back, never mind how we hate each other to the ends of the earth.

"Don't stand there—run!" Arisha yells, grabbing Zina's wrist and tugging.

We trip along the alley, passing under yellow squares of light that are windows filled with oblivious faces—playing pipas and rolling dice in the dead of Christmas night, drunker than the Tang poets. Yet they are safe inside, living in a wholly different world.

A dark form moves in front of me, and I only have moments to close my eyes and grit my teeth before we collide—a hurricane of warm body, tangled hair, and Parisian perfume.

I've run headfirst into Li Beibei. The rest of the girls pile up against me, and I clap my hand over Zina's mouth before she can scream.

"Jingwen," Beibei says, so calmly I wonder if she is even living in the same reality.

Her eyeliner is smudged, her green satin gown falling off one shoulder. Yet the heart-shaped pendant at her breast remains unsoiled—bright and resplendent in the dirty night.

"Beibei," I whisper her name no less, so relieved I am to see her—safe and whole. "Where's Neville?"

She scoffs, clawing her hair back with her red-painted nails. "You think I waited for him?"

"Jingwen, what should we do?" Arisha cuts in, her voice filled with panic.

I glance around at all of them—these girls I've collected in the dark, who look to me for an answer I don't have. We've outrun the nightmares of the Shanghai night for now, but we are still lost.

"We need to take these stupid costumes off," I decide, yanking off my tap shoes without bothering to unfasten the straps. The tight leather scrapes my finger raw.

Rongyu crosses her arms over her chest. "Sui Feng would never forgive us if we lost our costumes."

"I'm not saying to abandon them in the streets—take them with you!"

At last, Rongyu peels her hefty robes off her thin frame, and in an eye's blink, the locusts descend upon us. Zina screams and covers her face with her arms. We run as the buzzing rises over us, so deafening I can feel the vibrations in the hollow of my chest, growing until I cannot feel my legs anymore. I float through the alleyways like a limbless ghost, but I hear my footsteps like the beating of a drum.

I can see an intersection with Avenue Joffre at the end of the alley, bright headlights speeding across the alley mouth, tires rushing over the asphalt like water. Black forms dance in the periphery of my vision, threatening to reach us at any moment.

Between us and the avenue, the seam of closed-up storefronts is broken by a dark space where a Buddhist temple stands, hidden in the cluttered back street. The tall, red door is open a crack, bluish night inside beckoning through the space. The temple's presence exists like an abyss, devoid of noise and life.

The main road feels so out of reach, and I am exhausted.

"In here!" I yell, running to the temple and yanking the door wider.

The others slip past me, and I push the heavy door shut behind me. We press our backs against the bronze, our weight keeping the doors shut. Outside, the locusts roar past, making the temple walls shake with the beating of their wings. Zina sags against the door with her eyes closed, furiously sipping the night air.

Inside the temple courtyard, the black static of the streets is wholly absent. Silence envelops the grimacing lion dogs that guard each worship hall. The trees don't even shake when the wind passes through their branches.

"It feels like sacrilege to come here dressed like this," Rongyu remarks, attempting to pull her leotard up to her neck. Her voice feels uncomfortably loud in the silence. "Is there anyone here besides us?"

I drop my shoes in the path and turn in a circle, taking in our surroundings.

Five halls with sloping, brown-gold roofs circle the central courtyard, each guarded by two stone lion dogs wearing scarlet rosettes around their necks. Although the grandest Mahavira Hall rests quietly with its doors shut, a smaller hall to its left dances with life.

The light inside the Guanyin Hall appears to be flickering, swelling and fading as if the entire hall itself is breathing. Like a moth drawn toward fire, I head toward it.

"Jingwen, where are you going?" Arisha calls.

I hear their footsteps behind me as I enter the worship hall, whose doors are thrown wide open. Two long, red scrolls hang on either side of the entrance, covered in black calligraphy I can't decipher.

There are no worshippers inside.

She's there again, the Mother of Calamity, this time sculpted from gold. Her mouth is open in a damning scream, her hands raised beside her head like claws.

Behind her, a hundred gold statues rest in the wall like bees in a honeycomb—an entire pantheon of warriors and fairies, gazing down at us. They are vibrating with light, as if an electric current pulses across the walls, throwing each god's face into relief for a split second.

We stand in a row below the altar, staring up at the giant effigy, throbbing with energy.

"The light—it's moving," Arisha whispers.

I stare down the row of Guanyin's disciples as the light ripples over their faces. Their mouths are carved with harsh angles and angled eyes give the illusion they are watching us no matter which direction we walk. They seem ready to spring out of the gold to fly toward our necks.

"Something's weird about this place," Rongyu says. She is backing away slowly, her footsteps echoing with deafening clacks on the stone floor until she suddenly hits her ankle on the raised threshold. "Oww!"

I glance up at the goddess again. Her lips are drawn back to reveal fangs, her nails long and curled.

She's changed.

I turn and run out of the Guanyin Hall, the wind from my movement rustling the red scrolls beside the door as I sprint back toward the courtyard.

Rongyu scrambles after me. "Jingwen, wait for us!"

In the courtyard's center, a lonely stone incense burner rests in the night, with elaborate dragons for legs. A green smoke roils in the heavy air around it, turning gray in the bluish night. As I approach, the smoke extends toward me like a dancer's water sleeve—an invitation of sorts.

I lean out of the smoke's way.

It's the same smoke I sensed in the Astor House, the very smoke produced by Bailey's shimmering fungus.

There's a bucket of water left by a stone well in the courtyard, supposedly blessed by the Maitreya Buddha during the Han Dynasty according to an inscription on a plaque. I carry the bucket back to the burner, water splashing over my wrist, and upend the entire thing over the stone vessel—ash and incense sticks and whatever the source of the green smoke is. The incense sticks quench with an angry hiss.

"You just put out the sacred incense burner!" Rongyu shrieks as she runs down the steps of the Guanyin Hall with the others, covering her face with her folded robes. "Now bad things are going to happen to us."

"No," I breathe, clutching one of the pillars for support. The burner's drawn-out hiss has not faded yet. "I just saved our lives."

The flashing inside the Guanyin Hall ceases, leaving the entire temple even more still. But it is an uncomfortable stillness, like when all the gulls disappear from the riverside just before a storm.

A blast of green and red sparks tears the sky in the distance, and I jump. But they're just fireworks over the International Settlement, celebrating Christmas.

"What's happening to the city?" Arisha whispers.

"It's changing," I answer her, as I pluck a few incense sticks from the burner. There's nothing out of the ordinary about them—just wooden sticks with charred tips. "It's changing too quickly, and we're caught in the crossfire."

Beibei hangs behind us, oddly quiet.

"The Court of Exiles has finally made their move."

I gape at her as she paces along the stone path through the courtyard, the eyeliner smeared beneath her tear line like smoke. "How do you know about that?"

Beibei meets my gaze, a little bit rebellious. "I've been hearing people talk about it in the clubs for months."

She brushes past us, back toward the temple's main door.

Zina turns from Beibei to me, a blank look on her face. "What is the Court of Exiles?"

Arisha looks as if she's had a fine, hand-knotted Turkish rug rudely yanked from beneath her feet. There would have been no discussion of the Court of Exiles in the tabloids, no matter how widely she read.

I shake my head and run after Beibei.

She has opened the door, half her body out in the street when I catch her shoulder and turn her to face me. It takes a surprising amount of strength to move her. "Who told you about the Court of Exiles?"

Beibei wheels around to face me, and I see the gentle marks her teeth have left in her lip rouge, like footprints in dawn snow. She raises her eyebrows with an air of challenge, as if she is about to divulge an especially sordid affair of mine she has uncovered against my will. "I've known about the Court of Exiles far longer than you have, Jingwen."

She lets the door fall behind her.

"Wait!" I catch the edge, my fingers scrabbling against the smooth, cold brass.

The hinges protest with a high-pitched creak as I force the door open again.

"Go home, Jingwen," Beibei tells me. "Before you get hurt."

I follow her.

"How could you say that? Our fates as cabaret dancers are entwined with the rest of the city. We'll get hurt regardless."

Headlights rush down Avenue Joffre in the distance, punctuated by the laughing shadows of partygoers attempting to hail taxis. No locusts. No madness.

"Tell me what you know, Beibei!"

The traffic light swinging precariously over the street turns green, and a new rush of cars surges forward. Beibei's lithe form is swallowed by that sea of sleek, imported paint jobs and white headlights.

Soon, the other girls slip through the open door together with the incense smoke.

"What is the Court of Exiles?" Arisha asks again.

"I—" My voice quavers, but I hold my chin up and my shoulders down, thinking of my grandmother. The inevitable showdown between the Court of Exiles and the Blue Dawn is a fight Liqing dragged me into, and Beibei's warning has made my pulse quicken and grow hot despite the icy night air. The suggestion that the rest of the dancers might be hurt because I toyed too far with fire makes a unique pain well up in my chest—the same pain I felt when I held Usugi's cold hands in the Dove House. I can't drag them down with me. "All of you need to go home and not come out again until dawn. Please trust me. I'll take care of this mess."

Zina cowers from my suggestion. "What will you do?" she asks.

"Jingwen, let us help you," Arisha protests behind me, as I push Rongyu toward the bright lights and the happy-go-lucky crowds, yet untouched by the darkness spreading through the city's bowels.

But I shake my head. "Go, now!"

We split in three directions, our clothes tattered and makeup ruined, sweating in the winter air. But I don't go easily. I turn to stare at the space where Beibei disappeared.

The darkness of Shanghai outside the cabarets has always been my grandmother's world—a playground rife with gang politics and slowly-wakening goddesses, where I've been a reluctant guest. But now there are other dancers in it.

CHAPTER FIFTEEN

I can't bring myself to go home.

In the hazy twilight, the city streets feel the same as they always have. But in the shadows of taxicabs and leafless plane trees, I sense a hum of nervousness, like violin strings pulled taught under my skin.

Instead, I stop at a shikumen tenement beside a small, unkempt park—vine-ridden statues of mythical beasts around a mossy turtle pond.

There is an apartment on the third floor I am looking for.

I tap the door gently. "Beibei, it's me."

The peephole slides open, and I see a brown eye rimmed with smeared kohl. Then, the lock flips, and the door creaks open to reveal Li Beibei, who has changed into a night-robe of burnt orange silk, the waist ties loose at her hips.

Beibei is one of those women who radiates sexuality effortlessly, in the way her waist ties flutter at her ankles when she moves and her night-robe slides down her shoulder just a few centimeters. She's taken the pendant from Neville off.

She shifts her weight onto one hip as she looks me over. "You've never come to see me before at my home. I'm surprised you even know where it is."

"You told me once, when we were new dancers, and we tried once to be friends. You, me, and the Russian girls went for drinks in the afternoon rain. You said you lived past Yuehua Bridge, beside the small park with the turtle pond. One of the kids drew a rainbow on the side of the bridge with chalk and you thought it would wash away in the rain, but it never did. Third floor of the shikumen behind the bun stall, with a window overlooking the park."

I turn over my shoulder, where the rainbow persists on the bridge, faded to an echo. A gas lamp pulses softly over it. "There it is."

Beibei laughs softly. "Yue Jingwen, I'm impressed."

Reluctantly, I smile too. "Unbelievable, isn't it—we've danced together for two years, and I've never seen much of your life outside the Paramount."

Beibei edges the door open farther. "Come in then."

I hesitate briefly—my feet are blackened from running through the city streets. Even in the face of danger, I'd rather blister my own skin than scuff the bottoms of my tap shoes. After months of dancing under Evgenia Tsoy's tutelage, the sacred reverence that dancers hold for their shoes has been drilled irreversibly into my head. It's not until I see Beibei's own bare feet, in no better condition than mine, that I pad onto the soft carpet of her apartment, the worn carpet fibers filling spaces between my toes. The relief flows through my body up through my shoulders. I've never noticed how hard my toes ache when I release the tension in my ankles.

"There's a bottle of whiskey left from when I was dating the Scottish horse trader." Beibei slips past me toward the kitchen.

I remember the man, of course. Two summers ago—a fling hallmarked by bouquets of orange and pink parrot tulips, tossed carelessly about the Paramount's dressing room. He had red hair and liked to wear his shirtsleeves rolled to his elbows—the most carefree of Beibei's courtiers. He slept behind her back with a number of lovers, men and women alike, and teased her to violate him the same way. I think she liked that he wasn't afraid of her, unlike all the others that came before him, and after him.

I glance at the walls, situating myself in the center of Beibei's life beyond the twinkling ballrooms of Nanjing Road.

Her sitting room, drenched in thick orange lamplight, is hung with birdcages. They hang before a large glass window like tiered baskets of ferns in the Gardens of Babylon, some high and some low. In every cage there is a bird perched on a brass rod, mynah birds with yellow masks and knowing eyes, parakeets the hue of blue glaciers, a bird of paradise with a gossamer plume of a tail.

All these birds flit about their cages, cooing softly as they stir from slumber.

Beibei returns from the kitchen, carrying a bottle of whiskey by the neck and two lowball glasses pinched together in her other hand.

"Do you like them?" she asks, catching my gaze.

I approach the cage holding the mynah bird, by the large window. It swivels its head to follow my every move, yellow mask encasing its black eye. "I've seen one before, at a bar named the Dove House—a slender, white dove in a gilded cage. I thought it was real, but my companion pointed out its feathers weren't hollow. And then it opened its mouth, and I saw gears in its belly."

Beibei smiles. "I collect them."

She holds her index finger through the bars of a cage near her, and a little starling jumps onto her fingertip, turning its head to regard me through beady, black eyes. So does its master—haughty, enigmatic Beibei, whom I'd always viewed as too cold for pets and babies.

"I never knew you had this hobby."

Beibei removes her finger from the cage, and the starling hops back onto its perch. She smiles. "There are many things we don't know about each other."

It's the truth. Recently, all our masks are slipping away, and I'm not certain what I'll find underneath.

"Where do you buy them from?" I ask.

Beibei sets the whiskey down on a small table and unhinges the door of another cage, inviting a small finch with blue wings and a red belly to venture into her hand.

"They are all gifts. Their maker is an old craftsman from Tokyo, who left Japan out of sorrow when he fell in love with a young dancer from an Asakusa club. She was already married to a mobster, who swore to have him killed. Every Thursday night for four months, he would buy all my dance tickets—but he never wanted to dance. He just wanted to sit in silence—sometimes looking into my eyes. He said my eyes reminded him of her."

It's just like the love story between Li Aina and the White Rabbits leader. Listen to enough of the stories being whispered in the hour of drunks and fools, and you'll soon realize they're all the same—heart-torn lovers who set their minds on revenge, bitter military men who don't know what to do with themselves in an age of dancing, and tender poets overwhelmed by the philosophical chaos of the decade. We're all just tropes, acting out the same scripts over and over again.

Beibei strokes her finger down the bird's breast, and it coos under her touch. "He went back to Japan last year because he loved her too much—even if it killed him. I don't know if it did. All I know is that he made these birds while hiding in Shanghai, and he left them with me. He never taught me how they worked. I had to figure that out by myself. Like this." And she twists the bird's neck. It breaks apart, revealing a network of silver gears inside.

I cover my mouth with my hands instinctively. I can't believe how at ease she is, breaking the finch's tiny body.

She notices my hesitation and laughs. "Does it make you uneasy?"

I don't answer, and she gazes down at the broken, feathered body in her fingers—her expression one of utmost fondness, so tender the feeling morphs into pain instead. "You see," she says, stroking the bird's cheek with her thumb, "sometimes the gears get stuck, and they'll chirp the same note all night, unless I open them and straighten the machinery out. But don't worry, I can put them back together again. No harm done."

She clicks the bird's head back into place over its spine, and the finch flits out of her hand with a twittering song. Beibei laughs as it flies around her ceiling light, arousing all the other birds to cry from their cages, before returning to its own cage.

"But enough of my toys," Beibei says, latching the cage door. "You came to see me."

"Yes." I cross my legs in an armchair.

Beibei pours whiskey, and I close my eyes at the comforting splatter of liquor against glass—which sounds just like the rain in Shanghai alleys—never silent.

She pushes the glass against my hand. "Talk."

I open my eyes. Beibei lives in a less central location in the Old City, so her apartment is larger, with three distinct rooms instead of the studio layout in mine. She takes a seat on an old plush sofa missing one of its feet.

I sip my whiskey, and we listen to the birds sing. "How did you learn about the Court of Exiles?"

Beibei draws her feet up under her on the couch and raises her glass to her own lips. "One night, a few months ago, I danced with a man—I remember him distinctly because he wore a strange pendant on a red cord around his neck, which he said was a tiger's tooth. We danced three times, and then he took me outside to smoke cigarettes. He started asking me questions about you—lots of questions— where you danced, what names you went by, what kind of person you were."

She tilts her head to the side, her black tassel earrings quivering. "So I put my hand on his neck and told him I had a sudden craving for red wine. It only took four bottles, before he broke and told me everything—that he was from the Court of Exiles, an order of sha- mans who believed Shanghai had become corrupt under foreign rule. He wished to summon a powerful but uncontrollable goddess to the city to restore order. And you were a problem for him."

She traces her fingers behind her ear and down her neck, the way she'd touched this stranger. "Your grandmother—they said she broke the goddess's conduit, and because of her, they were having trouble reaching the goddess. And moreover, you had be- friended the shaman they sent to Shanghai and stolen him to your side, so he had to finish the job himself."

I feel my shoulders stiffening.

"Why didn't you tell me any of this?"

Beibei laughs softly. "Why would I? He came to dance with me, but all he talked about was you." She stares straight into my eyes, the cool brown of her gaze turning translucent in the lamplight, like a serpent's eye.

Outside, that characteristic fog begins to settle over the bridge, caressing the worn stone like a poison gas. The streetlamps and neon shop flicker weakly as they are smothered, the sky's color morphing from black velvet to the same cold silver as the Blue Dawn's limbs.

I drink more. "It would be pointless then, for me to ask for your help in the struggle that's about to unfold."

Beibei twirls a strand of her hair around her finger, the glass in her other hand. She looks like an advertisement in an American magazine. "You know Arisha wanted to help you. Zina would have followed suit. Why did you come here?"

"Because you've seen what I've seen. Because you listened to the man from the Court of Exiles, and you didn't question whether his story was true."

"Drunk men don't lie, Jingwen."

A kingfisher, with a golden breast and shining green wings, hops from one side of its perch to the other, setting its cage asway like a pendulum between us.

Beibei ignores it. "Which side are you on, anyways?"

"Ours." I rise to my feet and walk to the kingfisher's cage. The bird twists its head around to regard me, so I unlatch the cage door. "There will always be men in the streets of this city who convince themselves they're in power—gangsters, princes, millionaires. But it doesn't matter if the Court of Exiles brings their goddess back, or the concessions fall. There isn't truly a victory to be had. I think in the end, the city swallows every conqueror she's met. All we can do is protect the ones we hold dear."

The little bird flits into my hand, little tin claws digging into my palm.

"All I want, Beibei, is for the bloodshed to pass, and the cabarets to still rage with light and music."

I release the bird, and it flies to her, its shadow swelling on the carpet like a flame.

She opens her hand, and the kingfisher lands in her palm—tucking its small, fragile bones and mechanical heart into her fingers—not knowing that she held the power to break it.

I walk to the door.

"Good night, Beibei."

I go home and drag the box out from under my bed, where I've lain the dress Bailey gifted me. The sequins of the costume I wear cut into my knees, so I slip it off. In just my corset and underwear, I riffle through the layers of silk and tissue paper.

There is the handkerchief wrapped around a lobe of the shimmering green fungus I stole from Raoul.

Tonight, I've learned what the green smoke is capable of. And now Bailey has gathered enough money to fund an expedition to gather more, with a goal of exporting the fungus to America. But smoked from a pipe or cigar, how did it work? In the Neapolitan Gardens, would Raoul have been able to summon locusts onto the dance floor?

Making sure the blinds are drawn, I light a match, keeling on the floor with the fire cupped in my fingers. With my other hand, I pinch off an edge of the fungus. It crumbles into pieces between my fingers. I sprinkle the bits into an empty can that once contained preserved pineapple and drop the match in after it.

That grasslike, wild scent fills my apartment, quickly overriding the saccharine tang of pineapple syrup.

I close my eyes and breathe in the shimmering green smoke that ensues.

A silken high flows under my skin like water, nothing like the clammy, hot confusion of alcohol or the frantic, anxious butterflies of imported powders. Although I am aware I'm sitting cross-legged in my apartment, the wall stiff behind my spine, my consciousness expands. Suddenly, I am aware of spaces in the world around me I've never noticed before. I can feel the imprints of moths that have died kissing the hot incandescent bulb of my bedside light, the laughter of the cabaret dancer who rented this room before I did, when she allowed her lover to undress her.

And in that moment, I feel the presence of another woman, alone on a dark mountain far away. When she smiles, she has sharp teeth, which rise over the red horizon of her lips like snowy mountain peaks. She staggers like she is drunk when she walks between dead trees and empty forsythia branches, her silk dress torn and fallen in disarray. Twigs and dried holly stick in her hair, which is falling from its elaborate updo. She's not alone either. The night around her glows with the bright eyes of leopards and tigers.

She is a depleted shell of something vast and grand, slowly dried up over eons of time. But celestial beings like her do not simply die, and so she slowly goes mad in her jade gardens, waiting for a day the sun ceases to rise, which never comes.

I could recognize her anywhere.

After all, I've been seeing her around the city, and I played her character on stage tonight.

"Niang Niang," I whisper, and although she cannot see me, she can feel me through the layers of time and space that separate us.

She tosses her head back and laughs again, vise-sharp teeth shining in the moonlight. Behind her, lightning strikes in the mountains, which shimmer like blue velvet.

I am not the only one who has called to her. Around me, there are shadow footprints of other bodies—emperors in gold robes, who have sat on thrones in empty halls, curtains of beads trembling before their faces, who called upon her to burn down their enemies; warlords who marched through peat bogs with mud painted on their faces, who needed her help to drown their enemies; sect leaders of martial societies that kept the peace before any rule of law even existed in Chinese land.

But I also feel the broken-ness of her history. There is a piece of the puzzle that is missing.

Nobody can reach her anymore because part of her conduit is missing.

She hitches up her torn dress and walks toward me, just one fang showing between her red lips. To her, it's all the same—me, the warlords, and the emperors in their gold robes. As her voice rises to a high-pitched cackle, all the layers of consciousness I have crossed to reach her snap back together, until I'm sitting against the wall in my apartment once more.

The piece of fungus has burned out in the can, the sweet grass-like scent displaced by the smell of burnt sugar.

My hands shaking, I fumble to break off another piece of the fungus, just small enough to spend a little longer in that strange world. I strike another match and drop it in the can. The smoke is thicker this time, washing the room in a soft, iridescent haze.

I take a deep breath and close my eyes. The relaxing fragrance of the smoke washes over me. I exhale through my lips and inhale again through my nose. In my head, I can hear another heart pounding. Not far from where I am sitting in my room, another body is calling as well.

The god is short with wild, frazzled eyes and the body of a man, but an eagle's beak where his mouth should be and an eagle's wings sprouting from his back. In his taloned hands, he grips a mace and drum.

It's not my god, but I am drawn into his body nonetheless. Through the collapsed dimensions, I see Bailey Thompson's face, as he reclines in a leather chair in an office surrounded by Japanese paper screens, a hunger in his cool gray eyes that asks for the world upon a platter.

The god flies between the spires of the hotels and banks of the Bund, so swiftly it takes me a good minute to recognize the familiar streets and buildings. Bailey and I both recognize each other at the same time. I feel Bailey's panic as if it's my own. He doesn't want to be watched.

The god is flying to the Little Club, a small cabaret situated in a cove of restaurants and theaters in the International Settlement. He snatches a sausage from a grill, so quickly the hawker misses it with the blink of an eye, and perches on the roof tearing into juicy, oil-dripping meat. I feel Bailey urging the god to eat faster, but the god sinks his teeth into the sausage with extra gusto, making audible noises of satisfaction in rebellion.

When there is no meat left on the skewer, he wipes his mouth—that cruel eagle's beak, on the back of his hands, and soars down from the roof, wings spread like a paraglider. A man on the street glances up at the sky, pointing out a star to his companion, and I worry for a second that we'll be seen. Just then the god touches his mace to his drum, and a loud clap echoes through the air like the roar of thunder. The god, carrying us with him, glides around the tower at a speed much faster than the human eye can register.

Next thing I know we are inside the Little Club, brushing aside palm fronds in velvet-decked halls. There is a Christmas night happening at the Little Club, steaks and imported wine followed by a crème brûlée dessert. In the club, the god slides between tables set with silver cloths and filigreed plates. He smirks and touches his mace to his drum, before snatching the guests' forks out of their mouths, eating the prime rib and wine-grilled asparagus off the ends, and replacing the empty forks in their hands.

After he has sampled every dish of the seven-course meal and a couple flavors of aged wines as well, he jumps up into the club's rafters, where he sits on a beam swinging his legs in boredom. The band begins to play a slow jazz song, and the dancers on the floor come together. He is staring at one girl in particular, a cabaret dancer who briefly danced at the Paramount, who is known for her heart-shaped lips.

It suddenly comes together in my head. Right before parts of their faces were stolen, both Usugi and the girl at the Neapolitan Gardens mentioned they heard a roar like thunder. And there is no way a human could have taken their face so quickly.

As the realization dawns on me, I feel Bailey urging the thunder god to fly down from the rafters.

"No, stop!" I scream, as I'm hurtled back through layers of space and consciousness.

My eyes fly open and I'm back in my apartment. The fungus

has burned out again. I unwrap the handkerchief, intending to use more, but I realize there isn't much left. If I don't use what I have wisely, there will be none left.

Slowly, I close the handkerchief around what's left.

No, I need a better plan first.

CHAPTER SIXTEEN

see the news in the tabloids the next morning when I show up to the attic studio above the Lyceum Theatre. Sunlight dapples the polished wood floors, warming my bare arms.

Thirteen men were killed by flesh-eating locusts at the Firefighters' Ball. But when the Shanghai Municipal Police arrived to investigate, there was no sign of the giant insects at all. Rumor has it the guests experienced an episode of collective hysteria.

Jazz is the cause of societal atrophy.

"They didn't even play any jazz," I remark to the room at large, in an attempt to dispel the tension. I crumple the newspaper in my fist and toss it across the floor.

Rongyu huddles in a corner, her face white as she scans the first page of the *Crystal*.

The door hits the wall with a bang. Sui Feng staggers in, carrying his bags and muttering to himself under his breath.

I rise to my feet. "Where were you last night?"

He raises his eyebrows, eyes wide in confusion. "At the Firefighters' Ball, of course. We all were."

"You didn't come to the performance."

He shrugs. "Ah, well, I was busy." With a flourish of his arm, he turns his body to face the other dancers. "Come, let's practice. Opening night is less than a week away. There is much to perfect before then. Let's start with Act 2, Scene 3."

The other girls shuffle into place. In Act 2, the Heavenly Court tries to tempt the Feral Goddess back to her celestial home, and the three gods come down to Shanghai to find her.

I refuse to budge. The sun feels uncomfortably warm on my

back, the slice of white it would've otherwise cast on the studio floor eclipsed by my silhouette. "A swarm of locusts invaded the Astor House in the middle of our performance. Did you hear about it?"

Sui Feng waves his hand with a nervous laugh. "Ah, locusts, I hate those things. Especially when they show up in winter. Not enough crops in the field this far up north, so they go after the flesh instead."

Arisha breaks formation to face him as well. "Our script says that because the Feral Goddess will not go with him, the Insect God summons a swarm of locusts to wreak havoc upon the Black Cat. At the Firefighters' Ball, Jingwen refused to go with Rongyu, and at the part where Rongyu is supposed to summon locusts, the locusts actually appeared in the hall and killed people."

She shakes her head gently, as if she still doesn't entirely believe it herself.

"Coincidence is a strange creature, isn't it?" Sui Feng draws his cucurbit flute out of his pocket and plays a few notes with his eyes closed, bobbing his head enthusiastically to the beat.

Arisha and I exchange a glance.

Sui Feng ignores us, and after a while, I realize we have no choice but to let it go. He doesn't interpret the world as we do. Perhaps he knows something we don't, or he is simply an oddball we can't crack.

There is a strange energy in the air, an unspoken darkness which cannot be dispelled by bright sunlight spilling through the studio's wide, uncovered windows. The dancers wear forced smiles on their faces, and Rongyu stumbles over her part so much I am worried she will hurt her ankles.

Sui Feng makes her perform it again. "I want you to really channel the Insect God's energy," he demands. "After all, your salaries will suffer if we do not land a five-star review in the *Crystal*."

At last, Rongyu bursts into tears and runs out of the studio. I guess she never stopped blaming herself, after all that happened last night.

Sui Feng rubs his chin, looking puzzled. "Ah, she's having a bad day, no?"

He is met with blank stares. How do you explain to someone like Sui Feng that Rongyu is upset because she was first assigned to play an ugly god with blue skin and an eagle's beak, and then before an audience of Shanghai's most influential para-royalty, by performing that character, she actually summoned a cloud of flesh-eating locusts, which has now resulted in thirteen deaths?

I can only stare at him, stunned, until he beckons to me first. "Well then, I would like to see Jingwen perform the Dance of the Qingniao. I had a special dress made for you," he explains, drumming his fingers together. "I promise it's so stunning you will be the talk of the town for the next year."

"Shouldn't we make sure Rongyu is alright?" I ask.

"Is there a reason she wouldn't be alright?" Sui Feng asks lightly.

I catch Arisha's eye, and she returns an uncomfortable grimace, but nobody speaks up in Rongyu's support.

"I guess we can check on her later," I say finally, moving to my starting position in the center of the studio.

The other dancers look relieved to be out of the spotlight. They return to their patches of sun on the floor, content to be relieved of attention for a while.

I walk to the center of the floor and poise my arms overhead, taking care to check in the mirrors to ensure my lines are clean and straight. Sui Feng always enjoys playing the music for my solo with his hulusi, so I close my eyes and wait to hear the burbling melody that signifies dawn breaking over the towers in Shanghai. The Qingniao, poised on the roof of the Cathay Hotel, dances her final salute to the moon.

As Sui Feng plays the tune, I make the shape of the bird's head with my right hand and mime lifting the sweeping skirt that will serve as my train with the other. It was Evgenia, our former director, who stated a true performer does not let anything get in the way of her performance. As I spin in place, slowly bringing my silk train higher and higher, I refocus my mind so that everything falls away but myself as the Feral Goddess's familiar.

It's my first time dancing the part since I touched my lips to Zikai's under the watery light of the Paramount's upper floor.

Perhaps Sui Feng intended a different interpretation of the Qingniao's role as a character, but in my mind, the Qingniao is the embodiment of the goddess's nostalgia for Shanghai—her eventual understanding that the Jazz Age is only beautiful because it is impermanent. It doesn't matter that she was a goddess and we are ordinary girls. Niang Niang, like the rest of us, found that missing piece of herself the first time she stepped inside a cabaret and felt the thrill of swaying in a stranger's arms under a neon moon. It feels stark and profound, like red lipstick against pale foundation, or the fatal brush of a dancer's fingertips across her lover's wrist.

Deep in Shanghai's cabarets, humanity wears a different mask than it wears in high-rise offices and gas-heated homes. This mask is made of skin instead of suits, and it tears easily, so we adorn it with sequins like armor. Dripping in jewels, we come trying to fill the empty spaces within ourselves with the touch of others.

I open my eyes, and I see her again, cold and alone on her jagged mountain, red lips parted in a laughing snarl. The flowers are dead, the moon has fled, and she walks day and night, imprisoned in a dark wasteland filled with lightning and rancor, that used to be a palace.

The Mother of Calamity never finds that missing piece of herself in the Black Cat, because what she was really running away from was a part of herself. After thwarting locusts the size of ravens and rain that cuts like knives—there is no celestial being who has the power to end Niang Niang's love affair with Shanghai. She feels drunk off this realization.

Instead, it is her paramour, who must return to New Orleans, who spurns her fantasy. As he packs his saxophone in its black shell, he kisses her hand and begs her to come with him across the sea. She gazes into his brown eyes, holds his spiraled, coal-dark hair in her hands with painted nails.

But what will she be in New Orleans but an ordinary girl? She is used to being a goddess, feared and worshipped through the fables her subjects tell, able to summon the burning of cities at the beckon of her slender finger. China is the only place she can call home, and not even love, this new overwhelming power she's discovered, can outweigh that.

And so, the night after her lover's ship sets sail, black steam billowing on the ocean waves, the Qingniao appeals to the moon. As twilight fades to midnight, she remembers that she is a goddess of destruction. She chooses to burn down the city, after the dream she placed her trust in has failed her.

Niang Niang is vengeful, but the Qingniao is her sorrow.

The next morning, as the sun rises over a smoldering ruins, not a single cabaret left standing on the Bund, the Qingniao flies away, a lone shadow against the fading moon. And as she soars over the blackened wharves where neon lights used to twinkle, back in the direction of her blue jade gardens, a single, salted tear drops into the Huangpu's gray waters.

I finish the solo panting, my heart a thudding mess in my ribs. It frightens me even, how for a moment I forgot the others were there.

Sui Feng brings his hands together in applause, although he is the only one who claps. "You have shown so much improvement," he praises me, awarding me a rare smile that once would have made my world. "There is a surprise addition I would like to make to this scene. However, I will not tell you what it is until opening night."

The rehearsal ends, and the girls pack their bags in silence. By now, the sun has moved over the theater's roof, almost hidden from view. I squeeze myself into one last crescent of light as I change my dancing heels for a pair of tan leather Oxford heels.

Arisha and Zina follow me into the street, where I approach a food stall for crab shell pie with minced rose and sugar filling.

"Do you think Rongyu still blames herself?"

Around us, day traders and accountants who have left their offices for lunch slurp soup dumplings and beef noodles by the side of the road, their heads bent over their hands. A snake charmer, aware the lunchtime crowd comprises locals instead of tourists, sleeps against the alley wall, his cheeks warmed by the sun. Despite being one of the last days of the year, the sky is clear and sunny. A magpie flies across the sun, momentarily blocking the light.

I squint up at the sky, so blue it feels fake. "Yes, but it's not her fault."

Zina shudders and wraps her arms around herself. "Do you wonder if the other horrible things in the storyline will come true—hailstones the size of cows and rain that cuts like knives?"

"We could always hide indoors."

Arisha laughs a little at that. "A hailstone the size of a cow would easily break a building."

The hawker hands me a piping hot crab shell pie. Zina passes a one yuan note over the steaming baskets and points to a pie filled with sweet jujube paste.

I sink my teeth into my pie but immediately release my bite, as the roof of my mouth has been burned.

"Shouldn't we do everything we can to stop the performance?" Arisha continues.

I face her, outlined by the sun. The brightness that surrounds her makes me squint.

Dancing the Qingniao's solo awoke something in me, a magnetic desire to return to the stage. It makes me breathe faster, to think of the warm stage lights burning my skin, the dark eyes I can't see watching me. The euphoria that fills me then is intoxicating—this last time I performed in the studio, simple as the arrangement was—I didn't feel like I was playing a character anymore. I felt like a god myself.

I inhale the hot, floral aromas from my crab shell pie, which make me think of bouquets scattered after the performance.

"Our dancing didn't cause that bloodshed. I think it was a coincidence."

I squeeze my pie too tightly, and a dollop of hot rose sugar drips onto the sidewalk.

"But the timing was too perfect," Arisha cuts in. "Rongyu called for the locusts, and they came."

Another drop of rose sugar threatens to fall, and I catch it in my hand, burning my fingertips. The pain makes me gasp, and I quickly put my fingers in my mouth. "We worked so hard to perfect the performance—Sui Feng's right that there's never been a performance like ours before in Shanghai. We can't back down on a chance to showcase genuine Chinese mythology in front of the foreigners."

Thinking again of the stage, of grit and dust beneath my bare toes and dark velvet curtains swinging around me—I feel an urge to grin.

Perhaps I'm changing too.

I take a nap with the window open, the sunlight warming my belly as I lie on my back. In my sleep-deprived haze, I dream of my grandmother, whispering to me in a candlelit room. I realize I am lying across an altar, and she is an effigy towering over me, dressed in colorful Han robes.

I try to mouth her words back to her, but I can't get them right.

She holds my face with both her hands, a look of desperation crossing her face as she repeats the same line, over and over again.

It's not until I've already awoken, the sky darkening rapidly over the roofs outside, that I figure out what she was saying.

We are both gods.

By evening, I've thought of a plan.

The Paramount's gilded halls have been stripped of their ice sculptures and sequined gold bows, to be replaced by rosettes made from black tissue and pewter candelabras. For the upcoming New Year, the ballroom will hold a masquerade ball, its favorite breed of party.

After the dancing has begun, I shut myself into the dressing room. There is no lock on the door, so I push a few chairs against it. Although that won't do much if someone tried to enter.

Kneeling in the center of the room, I riffle through my makeup bag for the bit of fungus I have left. There will only be one chance to do it right.

One of the dancers has left a silver lighter on the makeup table.

I slide it off the table into my palm and strike the flame, which cackles into life. Whereas the night before, I remember feeling scared, this time I feel awake. The tiny, pugnacious flame warms my face. Holding it in one hand, I unroll the handkerchief that holds the remainder of the fungus.

There is only a small amount left. I do my best to separate the remainder in half. The piece I break off crumbles in my fingers, and I struggle to set it alight. The flame nicks my index finger, and I gasp.

Nonetheless, the fungus catches fire. The pieces flutter down onto the carpet, flickering with white fire, before slowly disintegrating into ashes.

Shimmering green smoke fills the dressing room.

I lean back on my hands, my head tilted back, so that I can admire the oily sheen in the air. It's beautiful, like the surface of a dark lake, never still, always moving. Like a mirage, the shimmer rises to the dressing room's ceiling. When I close my eyes, I feel a dust of smoke move across my body with a soft, ethereal caress.

As the silken high dives under my skin, I search for the thunder god. All it takes is a bit of familiarity to find him.

The Thunder God is flying amongst a patch of sky colored deep azure, but he sails down through the skies, eagle wings spread behind him. Although he comes because I called, he doesn't come quietly. Cackling, he skips down the wharves, pilfering sticks of candied hawthorns and mandarin orange slices from food stalls as he goes. As he slides the candied fruit off its stick with his teeth, he leaps along the abandoned wooden poles where a pier once reached into the river. The poles get shorter the farther he jumps. But with his wings spread, he sticks each landing on the balls of his feet. When he reaches the end, he brings his mace and drum together. A terrifying boom rocks the wharves, and he spreads his wings in flight.

A shadow flashes across my vision, and the laugh rings out from behind my corporeal body. I hold my head still, trying to catch the source of the sound. All of a sudden, I am aware that I inhabit two different bodies gazing upon the same lilac curtains and peeling walls.

He is somewhere in the dressing room.

I rise to my feet slowly. "Lei Gong," I say his name.

There is no response.

I throw open the wardrobe door, parse through feathered costumes, expecting to find him crouched in the back. A few moth balls roll along the wooden bottom. I walk in a slow circle around the perimeter of the room, searching above the wardrobe and under the makeup table. When I come to stand by the window, I pause and count to ten in my head. Then, with a sudden movement, I draw open the curtains, hoping to catch him off guard behind them.

That shrill, phantom laughter echoes again, coming from a location I cannot pinpoint. It starts to make me angry. I flip chairs and drag the drawers out of cabinets, searching for him.

I've turned the entire room inside out.

The smoke in the air thins. I don't think I have much time left.

"What are you going to do?" The voice comes from above. The Thunder God has materialized on top of the wardrobe, where he perches with his legs crossed as he jeers down at me. "You don't have enough of the fungus to hold me here for long. I've wasted more than half of your supply."

He seems very pleased about this fact.

As I look upon his face obscured by the green-black shimmer of the smoke, I wonder what Bailey has that I don't, which can convince the god to listen. The god laughs at me through the swiftly dissipating smoke, but for some reason I think of the incense in Liqing's clinic, which lit by her hand, always danced around me.

My entire life, I have cowered from demon masks on Liqing's shelves and the grotesque paintings on her walls, even feared the goddess I have tried to play in *The Black Cat*. I guess the answer should have been obvious all along.

Gods are puppets too.

It was never the gods I feared, but the people who pulled their strings.

I close my eyes, and this time, thinking of the Thunder God like a stole I can slip about my shoulders, I slip back into his body.

Cackling, he skips over the makeup table, taking care to smash all the incandescent bulbs along the vanity mirror as he goes. Glass spills over the table, falling into makeup bags and mugs of half-drunk coffee.

And then, simultaneously, I am both kneeling in the dressing room and soaring through the Bund. The Thunder God grabs the spires atop skyscrapers and twirls around them as he flies. I find I have to grit my teeth to fight the dizzying sensation of being thrown in circles. Like a fish leaping up a stream, we fly against the tide of Yuyuan Road, cars swimming upstream with yellow headlights.

On the roof of the Red Orchid Hotel, Wang Daojun is having steaks with Li Aina at the Rue de Velours.

The crystal railing remains cracked from where the Blue Dawn's leader threw Zikai against it. Having surveyed the scene, the Thunder God dives back down toward the river. His wings skim the river surface, and sprayed by the Huangpu's dark water, the Thunder God soars back toward the rooftop, his mace raised. The rest happens in the blink of an eye.

Daojun's eyes widen with horror as he realizes he is covered in his own blood.

His silver arm clatters to the floor.

The guests seated at the neighboring table scream and jump from their seats. The bottle girls drop their thousand-dollar champagne, which shatters upon the floor, white foam running in all directions. Amid all that, Li Aina smiles at the moon, her chin cradled in her hand, without blinking.

Chortling, the Thunder God steals a bite of Daojun's potatoes off his plate and leaps off the roof.

As I let him go, I feel the brush of another presence. Bailey is there, reclining in his leather chair, before sliding panels inked with cherry blossoms, the smoke's shadow dancing against the paper.

He smokes the fungus out of a proper pipe, his ankle propped on his knee and his neck relaxed on the back of his chair.

I come to my senses on the floor of the Paramount's dressing room, covered in broken glass.

The fungus has burned out, the shimmering smoke gone from the air.

I dust the glass shards off my body. It's a quarter to midnight. Daojun, having lost his arm, will demand to see my grandmother now. If I want to be there when she puts him under the influence of ether, I have less than an hour. But Bailey has also summoned the Thunder God, and I have no question that he intends to take another face tonight.

I fumble with the handkerchief, where the last of the fungus is wrapped. My time is running out. I hold the lighter against the black crumbs between my fingertips. The flame licks my skin with a searing pain, and I cry out. But the last of the fungus catches fire, and I let it flutter to the floor.

Holding my red and blistered fingers before me, unable to control the trembling of my wrists, I close my eyes and slip under the shining smoke's influence.

The Thunder God crouches amid the silver branches of one of the Paramount's chandeliers, which is swinging just slightly under his weight. He hums under his breath, seemingly delighted that none of the guests are intelligent enough to notice his presence. In his body, I can feel Bailey, who reclines in his leather armchair with his ankles crossed on his mahogany desk. The high feels like a heaven to him, and he is absolutely drunk on the power.

Before Bailey can react to my presence, I call the Thunder God back to the dressing room. The clap of thunder is drowned by the blast of horns in the orchestra shell.

I don't waste any time.

The moment he returns to the dressing room—after dallying in the hallways and knocking two mint juleps out of some playboy's hands—I enter his body and swing the mace around, at his own head. With a shriek, the Thunder God ducks under his arm and narrowly misses his neck. I don't know by how much because instinctively, I cannot bring myself to swing the mace at my own head.

"What are you doing!" he screams. He hisses with his jaws wide open, revealing rows of small, sharp teeth.

"Listen to me," I whisper, forcing his arm back around at his neck.

The Thunder God shrieks and charges at me.

I lift my arms to defend myself, but because my consciousness has melded with his, it's his arms that rise. We fall backward onto the carpet. The Thunder God's hands find my face, his skin leathery against my neck. I lock eyes with his dark, beady gaze, but I know it's Bailey who actually has his hand on my neck.

The Thunder God's carefully placed grip has cut the blood flow to my head, causing my vision to swarm with patches of black. Through the haze, the Thunder God draws a long, thin razor from his pocket, and I feel an icy sharp coldness against my lips. It dawns on me then what he's trying to do.

I scream and kick, but Bailey is much stronger than I am.

The blade slips under my skin like ice. For a long time, I had wondered—when the day came to be my turn, what would they take? When it's over, would I too forget how it happened?

"Jingwen?"

The Thunder God turns over his shoulder without releasing his grip.

Li Beibei stands under the doorframe, her red pagoda earrings trembling at her cheeks.

"What's going on?" she asks. Her gaze darts from the Thunder God's demonic mien to his razor at my mouth as I lie pinned on the ground. I taste blood on my tongue, warm like the regret that flows through my stomach when I realize that after I lose my face, I won't have a place in the Paramount anymore. Although we have done our best to sabotage one another in the last two years, in our worst moments, I got to see rare flashes of who Beibei really is—parts of her that her lovers know nothing about. Sometimes, enemies know one another better than friends. An irony, that this is what I choose to think about now.

The Thunder God grins at her.

"It was supposed to be you," he says. His beady eyes dance with glee. "But I'll spare you because *she* interfered. So you should run."

Leaning into her hip, Beibei breaks into a smile.

She walks toward us, her hips swinging in her signature cat-walk. The Thunder God leans back, mesmerized by her presence.

"I'm not running anywhere," she says. Her neatly drawn eyebrows, like ink strokes on a calligraphy scroll, make her eyes shine. "I want to be the one to take her lips."

A memory from our past crosses my mind. The first night I was hired at the Paramount, the manager introduced me as Vilma, the Shanghai-born girl with good English, who would have no trouble catching the attention of foreign guests. The country-born Beibei pegged me then as her enemy. After all, she was the dancer favored by foreign heirs and financiers. As I perched on the edge of my seat before the same vanity mirror before us now, dusting rose blush onto my cheeks, she had leaned in then and whispered in my ear that someday in my sleep, she would cut my lips away, so that I might never speak English to her boys again. How empty our threats seemed back then.

I wonder if she remembers that still.

"This is interesting," the Thunder God says. "This is not what I thought would happen."

Beibei thrusts her hand out, the way I've seen her ask for dance tickets from men who approach her to flirt.

Cackling, the Thunder God places the razor in her palm.

I close my eyes.

The Thunder God screams.

Beibei has jumped onto his back, her hands buried in his wings. Golden feathers scatter as she tears at his wings. He twists his torso around in an attempt to throw her off, and I roll out from under him.

The razor clatters onto the carpet, as he tosses Beibei aside like a doll. I reach for the razor and the Thunder God aims a kick into my chest. My back slams into the wall, shaking silk fans and paintings of milkmaids off the walls.

The Thunder God straddles Beibei's body and lifts his mace, intending to club Beibei's head. I grab a shard of glass from the floor and drive it deep into his wing. He howls, an unearthly shriek that shakes the thin chandelier hanging from the ceiling. I draw the glass back and stab again and again. Beibei, having wriggled free, picks up a jagged shard of glass and does the same.

We pummel the god's wings until they are torn like paper lanterns the morning after a dust storm, when sharp winds bluster through the alleys, whipping metal scraps and sand into a furious tide. I can see Beibei's red earrings through a hole we've torn through the feathers.

Unable to fight anymore, the god crawls along the floor on his thin arms and legs, a mess of tattered feathers trembling on his back. His ragged breath whistles through his lungs like a boiling kettle.

I no longer sense Bailey's presence inside him.

"I took you as a fair one." The small god scrambles back away from us, and eventually backs into the wall. The tattered wings on his back vibrate like those of the broken butterflies I use to patch together with Liqing. "Not vengeful."

We have clipped his wings, and there is nowhere he can fly to.

"This isn't revenge," I explain to the god, as I close the distance between us. "He's using you to hurt my friends, and he intends to export you to the Americas using the fungus. I don't know how much damage he has already done, but I'm going to stop him."

The Thunder God's beady, black eyes dart from side to side. "I have only done what I'm asked. After all, I am but a vessel for what the humans want. I didn't even make the girls bleed when I took their lips and eyes. I was merciful."

I grasp the largest shard of broken light bulb in my fist. My hands are shaking, so I squeeze harder. "I don't believe you."

He laughs in my face.

"You should have never touched the fungus. You've opened a box you can't close."

"Don't tell me what I can and cannot do."

The leather blue-gray skin of his face twists into a sneer. "You're already lost. You just don't know it yet."

And I plunge the shard of glass into his heart.

He dies laughing, his ribs contracting and opening against my hand. There is no blood that flows from his chest. The last of the fungus burns out as we pin him to the ground. And then his broken, unmoving body vanishes through the air, and just the glass shard falls on the carpet from where his heart once was.

Beibei blinks, her heavy lashes brushing against her cheeks. I close my eyes, and my legs threaten to collapse beneath me.

We just killed a god.

Only now that she and I are alone, with silence between us, do I realize how deranged I must look. There are chairs flipped on their heads, dressers knocked on their sides with all their contents spilled upon the floor, the curtains torn from their bars.

We face each other across the room, just breathing.

Beibei kicks the glass shard under the makeup table. "I want a glass of red wine," she declares out of the blue.

I draw my thumb across my lip, and my skin comes away red. Blood mixed with the chalky stickiness of lipstick. But I don't mind blood. The important thing is that my face is still whole.

"Thank you," I tell Beibei, fighting the urge to cringe. It feels strange to share such a deep, terrible secret with someone I've spent so long hating. "I couldn't have done it alone."

She shrugs. "If he was going to take both our faces, then I wanted him dead too."

If I had to bet on one person who understood the weirdness of Shanghai better than I do, it'd be Li Beibei.

Beibei picks up a tutu that has fallen on the carpet upside down, layers of stiff tulle stuck in the air. "Should we clean this up? How angry do you think the manager will get?"

I dust glass off the seat of a chair.

"I think we should pretend we were never here."

Beibei tosses the tutu over her shoulder, where it flutters back down to the ground. "Good idea."

I pat the blood away with tissues and lean over the mirror to reapply my lipstick, broken glass crunching underfoot. As I touch the soft, oily lipstick to the corner of my mouth, I hesitate.

It's hard to recognize myself in the mirror, my hair frazzled and sticking to my cheeks in places. Although the Thunder God didn't take my lips, my face doesn't feel like it belongs to me anymore.

I am wearing an expression I've never seen on myself before, but at the same time—it's strikingly familiar.

It's the same look my grandmother wore, after she took the swan's wings. When she stood over the swan's dismembered, vivisected body, like a golden effigy in a temple, holding power over a weaker creature. After all, is that not what I did tonight? Take away a living thing's wings, feathers flying down onto the ground as the Thunder God fell beneath my hands.

I quickly swipe the lipstick on, hoping the extra touch of femininity will change things. But the glory in my eyes does not soften.

So I look away instead.

"You look good." Beibei tucks a few flyaway strands of hair behind her ears. From most relevant angles, it just looks like we've had a few intense dances. We are bound together now by the shared killing of a god.

When I let the door fall shut behind me, it feels like we are burying a great and terrible secret behind it.

The spotlights in the ballroom shine brighter than I remember. I gaze up at the halls as if I'm seeing them for the first time—the gold geometry of the walls and the way the light catches on the chandeliers—it's all so beautiful, I hate that I could forget to notice it every night. I fight the urge to cry at how beautiful it all is.

Yet I can't have it tonight.

can taste the panic in Blood Alley tonight, a metallic tang like rust and stale beer.

The slender white bird outside the Dove House opens its mouth in a scream when I pass, metal gears twisting deep in its throat. The Cabaret Voliéré's tall wooden doors are open a crack, and through the slit, elongated shadows meet and fall apart on the far wall. High above the drunken guests, a trapeze dancer lies across a velvet hoop, dressed in a translucent white slip that flutters about her like an aura. She watches me pass from upside down, slowly drawing her fingers through her raven-colored hair.

I run to the top of the staircase, where the silhouette of a broad-shouldered gangster is tossing a dagger into the air. When he catches sight of me, the dagger slips through his fingers and clatters down the steps.

It's Xiao Lei.

"What happened?"

I reach down for the dagger.

Xiao Lei gets there first. His silver hand brushes against my flesh one. Up close, his face is blanched, his voice low and quiet. "It's Wang Daojun, our leader. He was attacked."

I bite my tongue behind my lips, so that I betray nothing.

"I'll see if I can help," I promise, and I push open the clinic's door.

Daojun sits on the operating table, unbuttoning his shirt with one hand. I thought he might look weak without the mightiness of his silver arm, but I am wrong. Under the silk shirt, Daojun's muscles are tight and hard. Frayed nerves of silver protrude from the flesh of his shoulder.

"Ah, and look, she arrives late from the cabaret." He removes his hat from his head and tosses it onto the coffee table. "Is this how you would handle your surgical appointments too?"

Li Aina perches on a chair by the window, her hands piled in her lap. The incense that rises from Liqing's shrine dances around her eyes, trying to tease a response out of her, but she does not blink.

She is staring at that pair of swan wings on the wall.

My grandmother walks out of her kitchen with a basket full of clean rags in her arms. "Jingwen, I wasn't expecting you."

I bow my head, trying to look demure, although I'm likely fooling no one. "I heard Wang Daojun was injured. I came to help."

Liqing ignores me and sets the rags down. Daojun, having removed his shirt, takes the time to fold it neatly with his one hand. My grandmother sets up the ether contraption, which will put him to sleep, and holds the leather mask out.

Wang Daojun is perhaps the only patient who she offers the respect of taking away his own consciousness.

Right before he slips the mask on, Wang Daojun stares directly at me. "Remember what I told you at the Rue de Velours the other night? This is what happens when you take pity on the wrong people."

I walk closer to the bedside. "Do you even know who hurt you?"

In response, Daojun glares at me so hard I can't help but flinch. But at the same time, I'm smiling. He has no idea, and it scares him more than anything ever has.

Liqing raises her eyebrows, silently wondering what I've done, but I don't elaborate.

Wang Daojun insists on fastening his own ether mask with one hand, while my grandmother holds it up to his face. But not even the greatest gangster in Shanghai can defeat the heaviness of sleep. He falls upon the table when the buckle is only half clasped, with a deep sigh.

Liqing jerks her head at me. "Tighten it."

I tug on the straps under Daojun's head, to ensure there are no leaks.

His old silver arm lies on the table, wrapped in a flower-patterned towel.

"Are you going to save that one?" I ask.

"No, we'll make a new one."

Liqing begins to trim the frayed silver nerves that have broken off with a thin pair of shears. Watching over her shoulder, I observe that outside of Liqing's handiwork, the sinews of Daojun's own flesh have grown and meshed around the silver connective tissue, forming hard knots in some places. Liqing has to tear the fascia off with forceps, which causes him to bleed. It's almost like Daojun's body, not understanding where his new limb grew from, tried to swallow the silver Liqing wove through his flesh.

"We need to debride some of the wound," Liqing explains, no mention of the grotesque knots in Daojun's arm. "I will mix a treatment to do the job."

She walks to a shelf stacked with glass jars of medicinal grasses and a collection of foreign solutions whose names I don't understand, humming lightly under her breath.

While she is away, I slide my hand under the translucent rubber tubing that runs out from Daojun's mask to the jar of ether. For so heavy a sleep, the gas that courses through the tube is as light as air.

The gangster frowns in his sleep, his dark, sculpted eyebrows knitting together. Unable to shake the feeling that I'm being watched, I lift my gaze. Li Aina perches on the edge of her seat with her legs crossed, both hands pressed to her knee. She blinks at me over the fur-lined collar of her coat, a blank curiosity written across her face.

All around me, there are frightening demons with brightly-colored skin and ungodly heroes with flowing hair like Zikai's gracing Liqing's walls, their snarls full of judgment—but Aina's is the only judgment I care about.

Staring straight into her eyes, I pinch the tube between my thumb and forefinger. The incense smoke, which formerly trawled around Aina's head, zips across the room to swirl around my head. When I exhale, my breath scatters the smoke. Although the clinic has never been more silent, I can hear my own heart beating in my ears, as loud as thunder. The sleeping Wang Daojun's chest rises and falls with greater intensity, which progress to lurching gasps. I pinch harder.

Holding my breath lest Liqing hears my panic, I allow my gaze to wander, until I catch my reflection in the window.

I am standing in that place Liqing usually does. Behind me, the pair of swan wings bloom like a nocturnal cereus, framing my shoulders like they are mine.

I hear the clatter of glass behind me, and brown, medicinal-smelling fluid lashes through the air the way rain flies after a car drives through a puddle. Little amber-colored droplets splash across my forearm and Wang Daojun's bare chest.

"What have you done?"

Liqing runs to the gang leader's side.

I release the tubing from my grip and step back. Time seems to slow down then, as the door is flung open, to reveal the yellow square of light of the stairwell beyond. Xiao Lei elbows his way through the clinic door, accompanied by three other Blue Dawn gangsters.

I watch his boots fall upon the carpet, his fists clenched at his sides as he approaches the operating table.

And then a ghastly howl tears from his throat, and when he wheels around, I see the pain etched on his face. His mouth is stretched in a grotesque yell. Grief and anger become the same thing when you've lost the part of you that matters most.

In that moment, we're all animals.

The gangsters reach for Wang Daojun, their hands pulling the mask from his face and shaking his limp body. Daojun's eyes roll back into his head. I realize in that moment that whatever he was to the Blue Dawn, it was something I've never had.

Xiao Lei draws his sword and points it at my grandmother, who gasps in shock. "How? You are a god who's never messed up."

Liqing meets my eyes across the operating table, and I stare back, betraying nothing.

"You will come with us," Xiao Lei says.

My grandmother does not resist. A curl of her white hair hangs down the middle of her face. "If you wish," she replies to Xiao Lei quietly.

She could give me up now. If she reveals it's my doing, the gang would kill me. After all, they have no reason at all to put me on trial the way they might give her a chance.

Liqing shakes her head at me, her mouth agape.

I watch them take her away, their footsteps retreating quietly down the stairwell, back into the drunk merriment of the Cabaret Volieré.

Eventually, it's only me and Li Aina left in my grandmother's clinic.

I walk to the shrine by the window, where tonight Liqing has placed a blue nuo opera mask with the snout and beard of a water buffalo, its eyes twisted downward in a condemning expression. The incense finally burns out, sputtering tiny puffs of smoke that dissolve in the breeze like dandelion seeds.

I pick up the mask, feeling the rough edges where the paint levels off and the poplar wood backing begins.

"You're free now," I whisper to Aina, although I don't know if I am speaking to her or the swan that lives inside her. I bring the mask back to the shelf where Liqing displays her collection, and I replace it in the one empty space.

Aina has returned to staring at the pair of wings upon the wall. I wonder if her disembodied swan's heart still longs for the body it separated from. If I was Liqing, I might have been able to put them together again.

I walk over to the table and pour a mug of rapidly cooling coffee. My hand shakes just a little, but I keep the stream steady.

When I am done, I push the mug in front of Li Aina. "I'm sorry," I tell her. "I wish I could have done something when it mattered."

She smiles and accepts the coffee, not minding that it is lukewarm.

I wonder briefly if there's a way we can become friends again—return to how things used to be. But I'm not sentimental. We've changed too much.

And I walk outside into the street, where the neon blazes so brightly there are no stars to be seen. A flashing sign shaped like a pink-and-white roulette wheel spins nearby, dizzying in its vividness. And I bury my face in my hands, and I scream.

My tears splatter upon the asphalt, tiny star-shaped blossoms to be trampled by tire wheels and footfalls.

I betrayed the woman who raised me from an infant, who saw in me talents that I never saw in myself. The night went exactly the way I wanted, yet for some reason it feels like I failed myself on every level.

I scream so hard that at some point, I realize I'm laughing instead.

When all the tears are gone, there is a feeling left in my chest, which I can only describe as lightness—as if I'm somehow rid of a burden I didn't know existed.

CHAPTER EIGHTEEN

n the Old Chinese City, I pay a water boy to fill my bath. He
delivers four jugs of hot water in a bicycle cart and empties them
into the stained, claw-footed tub I keep upstairs. It's a silly relic
I found for sale in a French Concession alley—I don't know why
the Europeans have a fascination with attaching chicken feet to the
bottoms of their bathtubs, but I've always liked the idea of sitting
in one, like a princess in a voyeur's painting.

I tie my hair into a knot above my head and stir the water with
my big toe. My skin turns soft and red, stinging from the hotness.
Gritting my teeth, I plunge my entire leg in and sink down into the
warm steam. The burning sensation makes me shiver.

There is a small window in my bathroom, through which the
sounds of the city night drift in, gossiping maids and schoolgirls
twittering like birds as they wander through the cramped alleyways. I rest my head back against the curved rim of the tub, the
little hairs at the nape of my neck blooming in the water like ink.

I wish the guilt I feel could seep out through the pores in my
skin, wash away with the water, which will eventually flow down
the drains that comprise Shanghai's guts into the Huangpu River,
to be buried in the depths of the ocean.

Too restless to relax, I grab my jewelry box off the little wooden
stand beside the tub and finger the various trinkets I've collected
through the years, holding each gem over the tops of my knees,
which rise over the water like limestone mountains. A deep ache
throbs where my joints meet the cold air, some product of sacrific-
ing many nights of my youth to twirling about in heels.

I lift from the jewelry box a pair of green kingfisher earrings that Liqing gave me for my sixteenth birthday, which flutter in the night breeze like they are real. Liqing told me kingfishers are an elusive little bird, which many empresses throughout China's history yearned to rear in cages, but whose swift wings always evaded their hands and nets.

Maybe that's all I'll have left of the woman who raised me—a little trinket worth a couple hundred yuan, that she probably didn't pay for anyways.

After I've washed my face with the hot water, gasping for breath through the steam, I dry off and change into a velvet, deep green–colored qipao that is easier to move in. My eyes are puffed up and swollen, but after staring in the mirror for a few minutes, I put away my palettes and rouges.

Then I set off to find Nalan Zikai, hoping he'll be where I expect.

I am the only rider in my section of the tram tonight. Like a ghost, I sit in the middle of the row of orange seats, buoyed about by potholes and cracks in the road, watching the hand grips swing on the ceiling above. I depart at the same white bus stop by the university at the city's outskirts.

The golden fields rest quietly in the night, the reeds bowing their heads as if in mourning. A dark figure dances amid the rushes, his white shirt forming a blunt contrast to the muted earth. His arm is a brighter silver-white than the sullen moon in the sky.

I stop and blink, certain I'm hallucinating.

The figure dancing in the field has long hair, a handful of it drawn into a high ponytail above his head. In between fight sequences, when the fluttering silk of his shirt stills, I note his sharp cheekbones and sculpted chin. No doubt, it's the man I danced with on the Paramount's third floor, his fingertips pressed lightly to my waist, glowing crystal eggs underfoot. But when his right arm arcs over his head, his skin blazes silver in the velveteen night.

Zikai moves with an air of fascination, at the way his own arm responds to his commands and weighs differently than flesh and bone. He stops suddenly, facing away from me, the sword tucked behind his back. In the dark, it's hard to differentiate where the blade ends and his steel hand begins.

"Good evening, Jingwen."

His voice is stiff, and he won't look at me.

"Your arm," I say.

He sheaths his sword, perhaps harder than he intended. The metal sings a loud, shrill note that echoes across the empty field. "Jingwen, I can explain."

I search for words to say, certain this is all a cruel joke he's set up.

"I thought you said the silver limbs were against your code of honor—that it was immoral because humans did not deserve to defile the role of gods."

"I did."

He turns around now, and I take a step back instinctively. His silver hand twitches as if he's tempted to reach for me, hurt by the way I recoiled from him.

"And now it's not?" I ask.

"Jingwen, there was no winning for me."

Zikai walks past me, his shoulder brushing against mine, to a secluded part of the field, where he raises his mouth harp to his lips and plays a forlorn note with his new metallic fingers. The note sings differently, like a diamond dropped in a pool of glass. The rushes seem to bend sideways, responding to his command. The song blooms in the emptiness, oddly alive in the dead field. "I don't expect you to forgive me, but this is the only way forward."

"You asked me to topple my grandmother from power. I killed Wang Daojun and had her arrested by the Blue Dawn." I barely keep my voice from breaking.

He lets the note sing out, harmonics splitting and flatlining across the deep night. Then he drops his arm, the mouth harp swinging between his collarbones on its gold chain. "I'm sorry."

"Zikai, I don't understand."

He won't talk to me.

I ramble on, still numb to what he's done. "Just now, I watched my grandmother try to mend Wang Daojun's arm. When she removed the silver, I saw that his flesh was sick underneath. It's like his body was rejecting the arm she gave him." A wind picks up in the field, making my teeth chatter. I wrap my coat more tightly around myself. The sky is overcast tonight, threatening to rain.

Zikai folds his arms across his chest. I can't stop staring at his artificial limb, the way the silver curve of his thumb fits in the nook of his flesh arm. He looks inhuman—not godlike, but something that transcends godhood—a new type of idol who is born to watch over the neon-laden gambling dens of Blood Alley. "How did you maim Wang Daojun?" he asks me.

"I inhabited the body of a god."

His eyes widen at my answer. "Which one?"

"Thunder." I walk over to a fallen log and collapse on it. My head suddenly throbs, and I hold my head in my hands.

Of all the people I've ever struck a deal with, I never thought he would leave me in the dust. Not with his rigid pride in the martial arts protectorate—his unwavering insistence that the Shanghainese were just glitter-obsessed sinners who would trade anything for drugs and silver dollars. He wanted to be better than them through his own hard work. I had respected that about him, even though I saw things differently.

It hurts even more to remember his warm, still-human embrace when we'd danced together—the sincerity in his eyes as he told me his vision of Shanghai, the secrets I felt like we had shared as we giggled over spilled champagne.

I realize then what the awful, raw feeling in my gut is.

Betrayal.

Zikai bows his head in thought, his silver thumb tucked in his pants pocket. "Did you do it with lingzhi, the fungus that grows in the Kunlun Mountains, which trainee shamans use to call the gods?"

I rip the browned husks of weeds from their stems and toss them into the field. "Yes. Bailey Thompson, the American doctor I met at the Paramount, is exporting the fungus to America. I stole it from him. He was using the Thunder God to steal those faces. I made sure he could never do it again."

Another refrain of Zikai's mouth harp trills into the weeds. A flock of starlings, startled out of a barren tree, flee into the night, their feathers darker than the neon-polluted sky.

Amidst my own pain, I feel a tenderness mixed with the hurt. It was his stubbornness that had shined so brightly—his refusal to break under Shanghai's satin-gloved chokehold, no matter how she pressed into his skin with insults of fashion and wealth. He, of all the princes, playboys, and starlets, had convinced me he could emerge unscathed. And although my grandmother and the Blue Dawn had claimed me as theirs, a small part of me had wanted to see him win.

But in the end, he was just like the rest of us.

Could I really blame him, when I had commenced my own drowning years ago?

"What made you go to her?" I ask, trying desperately to hold his gaze, while he refuses. "Tell me how it happened."

Zikai runs his silver hand through his hair. Beside his earthen eyes, the bright metal looks even more out of place. "When Liqing made those silver limbs for the Blue Dawn, she allowed the gangsters to cheat their destiny. It's like she clipped the wings off of birds and gave them to ordinary men, who have no business flying. In other words, she rewrote the rules."

He throws his arms out, his head thrown back to the skies, as if in supplication. "When the rules of the universe were written, the winners and losers were heavenly mandated. Some of us were destined to work on the docks, some of us were destined to wear expensive suits and export drugs, and I—a boy who grew up running among wolves and wild horses in Inner Mongolia—was doomed to never be taken seriously by the martial artists of China proper." He laughs brutally. "All my life, I thought if I just trained harder—if I defeated more enemies and learned from more experts, I could become the best at what I do."

He raises his silver arm again, flexes his fist before his face.

"When I was selected by the Court of Exiles, I almost dared believe I overcame the script that was written for me—by then, I could fight with a scimitar, raise the spirits of wolves to fight alongside me, shoot a hawk flying legions above in the sky. But none of that was enough to defeat your Shanghainese gangsters with their steel arms. The night Wang Daojun defeated me, I learned something—those silver-armed bastards didn't need to waste their life fighting for approval. They were powerful enough to stand on their own. Your grandmother was right. Her surgeries made men more powerful than gods. And wasn't that what I wanted all along? What did it matter if I paid for it with all the gold I had, instead of working hard until my sweat and blood were one?"

A cold wind sweeps through the rushes, whipping my hair from behind my ears. In the dormitories huddled at the center of campus, the lights in several windows snuff out, as more of the students go to bed.

I fold my arms over my chest in a feeble attempt to block out the cold. Fierce tears burn in my eyes, even as I remember Liqing's expression when the Blue Dawn led her out of her own clinic. "But what if my grandmother's actions came from a place of selfishness? Do you really think she's the answer?"

"You can be selfish and still change the world in the right ways," he says.

It hurts too much.

He was the one who showed me Shanghai might be a fairer place if Liqing was gone, and now he's turned on those beliefs. Myriad thoughts spin through my head. If I knew he'd gone to Liqing, would I still have killed Wang Daojun?

"Jingwen, I have a different plan."

"What?" I ask, although I'm afraid to hear him. Once upon a time, on account of his words, I found the rage and the foolishness I needed to destroy the glamour that ruled my life. And now I stand alone amidst the bits and pieces, having yet to determine whether the facade I shattered was made from crystal, glass, or diamond—and all the ways these things break differently.

"We'll take her knowledge and use it otherwise," Zikai says, a hungry edge returning to his voice. Even his cheeks seem to flush in the gray night. "Your grandmother was corrupt, but her knowledge isn't."

But I'm afraid of the way his words burn against the tender skin behind my ears, the promises they tantalize—the meaninglessness of his passion, when he might renege on his beliefs at any moment.

"How?" I whisper.

He takes a few steps toward me, and I am the one who cowers now, as if he is a ghost wreathed in flames, walking out of the weeds to consume me in fire. He clenches his silver hand, and the power in his fingers makes me wince.

"We can make the dancers whole again. You're brilliant, Jingwen. You know this city in and out. You can think of something. I'll help you, and we'll rewrite the rules."

That same frenzied determination, which had poured out of him the first night I saw him standing on the wall, now terrifies me.

"I don't know, Zikai."

I rise to my feet, the wind sweeping my hair around my face like a dark crown. I feel the Mother of Calamity's presence then, a dark, pliant embrace that drapes over my naked limbs in the blind night. She feels like the coolness of silk pressed against my cheek, offering comfort and erasure—an eager answer to my desire to sink away and resign myself to a role I've played my entire life, buffeted in a tide controlled by someone else's moon.

"I'm going to go," I say.

Then, I run out of the field back to the edge of the highway road, sticks and dried weeds crunching underfoot—back toward the Shanghai I know. I hear him breathing hard as I fade away, but he doesn't stop me.

CHAPTER NINETEEN

We rehearse *The Black Cat* one last time.

In the morning on my way to the Lyceum, I pause outside a smoked duck shop. A familiar face frowns down at me from a poster stretched between two poles, like a billboard in those photographs of Hollywood they like to hang in hotel lobbies. It's my face.

The shot was taken from the Firefighter's Ball, when I froze mid-dance, my eyes widened in shock at the bird-sized locusts diving into the audience. The caption reads, THE FERAL GODDESS CANNOT BELIEVE WHAT SHE SEES IN SHANGHAI . . .

Two women walk by with gold-foil shopping bags dangling on their wrists, wrinkling their noses at the rows of blackened duck swinging on the hooks.

"Have you heard of that show?" one whispers to the other in British-accented English.

The other giggles enthusiastically. "Yes, I saw the ads in the newspaper! I tried to get tickets, but it sold out instantly. Look at the lead dancer—her acting feels so real!"

I scratch my head, as the poster of my face billows in the morning wind.

It becomes effortless to slip into Niang Niang's skin. Once upon a time, I was plagued by an incessant awareness that I was playing a goddess of destruction who would come to burn down my home, but since leaving Zikai last night, I crave the senselessness of her wrath.

I dance through the first two acts as if a fire has been lit under my toes, hungry to lose myself in the fantasy. When I draw my arm over my face, the mirrors and the other girls disappear. I really am Niang Niang in the legendary Black Cat cabaret, sequins clinging to my hips as I twirl under frosted lights.

When I reach the end of the third act, where I perform the Dance of the Qingniao, Sui Feng yells in English, "Cut!"

For some reason, his voice angers me. He could've waited for me to finish my solo before stopping me.

I keep dancing, spreading my arms behind me like they are wings. The music rises to a crescendo. Imagining that the Qingniao is flying low to set fire to the roses in the Neapolitan Gardens, I turn under my arm and twine my fingers to the sky.

Sui Feng swings the stylus off the vinyl record that plays in the absence of the live orchestra. I feel the abrupt stop of the music like a hand is choking me. It only increases my annoyance.

Ignoring the silence, I keep dancing. Sui Feng grabs my wrist. "Stop."

I am surprised by the strength of his grip, given how frail he appears.

Breathing hard, I drop my arms back to my side. Sui Feng smiles without revealing his teeth. Slowly, I back away from him toward the line of dancers watching in the back. Rongyu looks especially frightened.

Sui Feng clears his throat. "I wanted to let you know that I have invited a number of special guest dancers to join the performance tonight. They will be added to the Dance of the Qingniao."

"What?" My heart feels like it's twisting in my chest. I don't understand why he would invest so much effort to ensure I can shine onstage alone—the biggest solo of my life—only to take it away from me at the last minute.

"The solo feels . . . empty," Sui Feng continues. "I think having additional bodies onstage could breathe more life into the number."

I draw the back of my hand over my forehead, and my skin comes away shining with sweat. "But the Qingniao dances alone."

Sui Feng twirls a finger through his long whiskers.

"In my original vision, she did. But I changed my mind. I think she will fly through Shanghai with a retinue of cloud maidens, who will dance in water sleeves."

"It doesn't make sense—"

He holds up a hand. "The decision has been made."

I dance my hardest the rest of the rehearsal—so hard Arisha pulls me aside during our water break to remind me I must conserve energy for opening night. But I shake her off. The reality is gutting—that I have spent all this time exceeding all of Sui Feng's expectations, to be cast aside now.

When the rehearsal is over, I follow Sui Feng as he begins to dust the windows of the studio with a feather broom. "Did I do something wrong?"

He raises his eyebrows as he continues cleaning the windows. A lot of the dust flies into his beard from his sweeping, eventually causing him to sneeze. "Of course not. You were perfect," he says, wiping his nose.

"I don't understand why you're taking my solo away."

I know I sound selfish saying it. We can only pull off a performance if we work together. Behind my back, I wring my hands together, ready for him to berate me.

Sui Feng smiles again.

"You'll see," he says.

And then night falls. The Lyceum Theatre's name lights up in flashing gold letters over the roof. Some of the girls climb up to the attic studio to watch the cars and bring the news back that traffic has been stopped six blocks up the road.

The buzz of pre-show nerves fills the air like the electric charge before a storm. In the dressing room, I dust my eyelids with the operatic red shadow used in bygone eras, when traveling casts of acrobats danced for emperors. My silk robe, loosely tied at my waist, flutters at my elbows every time the door bangs open and shut, and my heart leaps in my chest.

Zina walks around the performers' room, pouring cheap champagne from a convenience store around the corner.

"Look what I found, Jingwen! It cost less than the fancy Belgian cocoa powder you like." She thrusts a coffee mug half-filled with champagne out to me.

"Thank you."

I sip the chemical-tasting champagne in between coloring my eyelids. Without meaning to, I find that I'm making my face in the likes of the real Feral Goddess, the way I saw her with the lingzhi.

Arisha perches on the chair beside me and watches as I paint my lips a bright vermilion. "I've never seen you wear this kind of makeup before. Where did you learn it?"

I tilt my chin to the side and smile at my reflection, a new coldness in my stare that feels unlike me. It makes me feel powerful. "A dream I had, actually. Do you like it?"

Zina gasps. "It's not fair! My dreams are never inspirational."

"I haven't been sleeping well," I admit. "When I don't sleep well, my dreams become more vivid, more lifelike."

Arisha studies me like one of her magazines. "Jingwen, be careful on the stage."

I notice she has not finished her makeup—only her eyebrows are drawn. Beside me, decked in layers of rouge and glitter, she looks detached and ordinary.

I lay my makeup brushes back down and squeeze her hands in both of mine. "You don't need to worry about me."

One of the chorus girls clears her throat and taps my shoulder. "Umm, Jingwen. There's a call for you in the director's suite."

Zina's eyes widen. "The director's suite? Who could that be?"

I twist the cap back on my lipstick to keep it from drying. "I don't know."

I walk into the next room, where a black telephone vibrates atop a mahogany desk overlooking the street. The curtains are open, a draft leaking around the edges of the windowpane. Making sure to pull the door shut behind me, I settle at the desk, facing the French Concession dusk. The cold leather sticks to the bottom of my thighs.

I hover my hand over the receiver for three rings, before I pick it up. "Hello?"

"Jingwen."

It's Bailey Thompson.

There is a vision I have of him as soon as I hear his voice. He is lying back in his brown leather chair with a cigarette in one hand, his ankles crossed on his desk and his tie flipped over his shoulder. Behind him, the Japanese sliding panels are closed, and the smoke from his cigarette obscures the cherry blossoms hand-painted on the paper panels.

He clears his throat. "I called to wish you luck on your performance tonight. I was very pleased with how everything turned out at the Firefighters' Ball."

So we are still playing this game.

"Thank you, Doctor," I respond, my voice cool and even.

"You've seen the advertisements I put up?" he asks.

I stare at the gold vine pattern on the brown walls and continue like I am reading off a script. "I did. Thank you for convincing so many people to see our show. All the girls are thankful for your efforts."

He sighs. "I'm caught up in some late-night business and won't be able to make opening night. I'm sorry I haven't called in so long. I hope you've been well. You never cease to dazzle me with the way you shine at night."

I can't tell if he's making a reference to how we both inhabited the Thunder God's body at the same time.

"Mm-hmm," I say.

"Let's meet soon again at my club. There's someone new I'd like you to meet." His voice flows, low and honeyed like a river of molten gold.

I guess I've buried myself so deep, I don't know how to get out.

"Of course," I say. "I look forward to it."

"Good luck, Jingwen."

He hangs up, and the repeating tone of the empty line echoes in my ear. I replace the receiver back in its cradle. I don't know whether to feel relieved or worried that Bailey has chosen to skip the show tonight. But when I glance up, I see my faint reflection in the window wearing the goddess's face—pale and desperate, with angry, slanted eyes that arc toward the sun, bordered in red.

I grin and she grins, as if we're sharing a secret.

When I return to the dressing room, most of the East Sea Follies have finished getting ready for the first act. Rongyu is the last, coloring her eyebrows with a dull pencil at the far end of the makeup table. I rest my hand briefly on her shoulder as I pass. She makes a soft noise in her throat, and I give her shoulder a gentle squeeze. There will be more time to talk later, but for now, I'm grateful she came back.

I untie my robe and slip it from my shoulders. It slides to my feet like water. Arisha and Zina help me change into the embossed golden gown of the Feral Goddess. I roll the flowing water sleeves up to my elbows. "Wish me luck," I whisper, as I catch my own gaze in the mirror. Niang Niang stares back, her deep-set eyes unapologetic under slanted brows.

"Good luck," Arisha murmurs, fixing a slanted pin in my hair. "And I mean it."

"Jingwen, I'm scared of you," Zina says.

Backstage, the velvet curtains fall out of the sky. There is no wind in the theater, yet the curtains flutter as if there is an opening somewhere in the wall. I grab a fistful of velvet and immediately regret it, as a flurry of dust swirls into the air, making me cough.

Sui Feng stands in the center of the stage with his hands buried in the curtains, peering at the audience through the gap in the folds with a single eye.

"Are you ready, Jingwen?" he asks, breathless from excitement.

"Yes," I answer, although I don't really feel anything.

Sui Feng throws his arms in the air. "Then let's show them what we have."

I take my position center stage, silk sleeves draped over my body, dust between my bare toes. Through the curtains, I can hear the audience murmuring like the rumble of a mountain about to split. The lights darken on the other side, and the entire theater is washed in darkness.

A zither melody, meant to evoke the feeling of a breeze rippling through a field of fresh grass, flows across the stage. The curtains lift to reveal my gold robes and my coal-lined eyes shadowed in red. I see a flash of the audience before the spotlights flicker on, an ocean made of faces that extends endlessly into the dark night.

And then it's just me, bathed in gold light.

I tread the stage floor as if I'm dancing on clouds, colored smoke flowing out of the wings to provide the texture of an imaginary sky. Closing my eyes, I drag my silk sleeves around my body. I picture the goddess the way I saw her in my drug-induced dream, lithe with jagged white teeth and red lips, and then I reinvent her with childlike hope—bored, but not broken. Before emperors and warlords conquered nations through her avatar, what was she like dancing between jade trees and stuffing her belly full of immortal peaches, entertaining the dream of visiting other worlds?

Overhead, the spotlight persists, warm and fierce, illuminating the small particles of dust that fly and collide under its heat. I dance among my papier-mâché tigers, which sleep under snowy foothills with azure-tinged peaks. The dance passes too quickly, so much that I'm sad it ends.

And then the claves and the trumpets burst into song. The strobe lights flicker on, lighting the stage in blue and purple. It's time for the second act, where the Feral Goddess spies on the sequin-clad dancers in the Black Cat. When Sui Feng wrote the script, he meant to subvert the stereotype of the male voyeur, in a paradoxical shock to the audience—but I doubt any of the audience will understand. The only poets who come to vaudeville shows are already drunk.

Zina plays the role of the window, a member of the chorus who holds a translucent paper panel framed by cherrywood. Together we perform a lyrical duet, her the bridge between Niang Niang's kingdom in the sky and the hellish neon fires of Cabaret Row on Yuyuan Road.

At the end, I unravel the knot at my waist that holds my robe together, and I shed the water sleeves for a formfitting black sequined dress. The robe falls from my shoulders like I am stepping out of a real skin. The audience roars with applause, and I think I can smell the drunkenness on their breath. It flows through my body like ether, turning my lungs into wings that raise me higher into the air with every breath.

In a symbolic act, I raise my fist and shatter the paper window Zina holds.

Sequins drip off my body like water. The lights could cut me apart. Joining the chorus girls, I shake my arms loose for a swing-inspired tap dance number.

Rongyu meets my eyes from the wings, where she waits alone with her face and hands painted blue, an eagle's beak tied around her head. I sense the tension in her body, but I don't even remember why I was worried about this scene an hour ago.

I glide across the stage in a succession of ever-more-complex turns, steel bottoms of my tap shoes gliding over the painted floor, faster and faster—and when I reach Rongyu, I suddenly draw my arms into my waist, causing me to spin so fast I think I am making sparks on the floor.

Rongyu hesitates just for a second, her wide eyes brimming with anticipation, before she performs a one-handed backflip around me. But even a second of hesitation is enough to throw off the carefully choreographed rhythm of the scene. We end up colliding in the center of the stage, her arm crossing with my ankle while she is mid-flip, and she tumbles down, to land on her buttocks.

Sui Feng curses in the wings.

There are a gaggle of chorus girls waiting behind the drapes, grasping tulle fans meant to represent locust wings. He flaps his hands at them urgently, pressing them to enter the stage ahead of their cue.

They run to circle us, raising the fans behind their heads, and the stage becomes a sea of waving tulle.

Collectively, all the girls seem to be holding their breath.

"Please, oh, please," Rongyu is whispering under her breath, completely abandoning the choreography.

The number finishes with the chorus girls lying in an artfully arranged heap at my feet, while I reach toward the sky.

Buried under the tulle fans, I hear the girls release a collective sigh.

One by one, the gods continue to test Niang Niang's resolve. The Hail God, a trained circus acrobat, hurls slender fléchette darts across the stage, meant to symbolize knife rain, and I dance under them, whipping around in spins and leaps. Warm blood trickles down the side of my neck. One of the darts has nicked my earlobe without my realizing it.

The audience gasps with delight, unable to tell if it's on purpose.

There is one last sequence in the scene. I run up to the front of the stage and take off into a series of continuous turns, whipping my leg around my body to ride the momentum. The choreography Sui Feng made calls for ten, but I keep going, more and more until the balls of my feet grow hot over the metal bottoms of my tap shoes.

I close my eyes, and when it's all over, I can feel the wind from the audience's hands being brought together like a summer breeze upon my face.

In the final act, I raze the city down as the Qingniao. Sui Feng promised me he would have the most exquisite dress made for me, which I haven't seen yet. He has it delivered to the dressing room in between acts.

Zina, Arisha, and a few other girls crowd around as I tear the gold ribbon off the box. The dress flows like water over my hands, crafted from layered black gossamer with a thousand golden eyes sewn onto the train. I lift the dress from its nest of tissue paper, terrified I might tear it. The train is as delicate as a cape sewn together from a fish's scales.

Zina runs her finger along the gossamer. "Wow," she murmurs, batting her eyelashes in thought. "He was right. You really will be the talk of the town for a year."

I reach over my shoulder and unzip the tight, sequined gown I wore for the second act. "Help me into it."

Arisha holds the dress out, and I step into its depth. As Arisha pulls the shoulder straps over my torso, her knuckles brush my shoulder blade.

"You're so warm," she says, placing the flat of her hand against my shoulder. "You danced too hard."

Only after she points it out do I notice my skin is flushed. Her hands burn like ice against my bare arms. "I have never danced that way in my life," I explain, breathing hard. "I don't know why—it's like all the fear and anger I've been feeling took over, and it made me want to dance harder."

A knife-like cramp blooms in my ribs from talking.

Arisha smacks Zina in the shoulder. "What are you waiting for? Go bring her a cup of water!"

Sui Feng raps on the dressing room door from the outside. "Quick! Jingwen, you're on in three minutes."

I gulp the water desperately, my heart pounding loudly in my ears.

"You need to go now," Arisha says, taking the cup out of my fingers.

I refuse to let go, and she yanks it, spilling water over the edge. "Go!" she yells.

I dash down the darkened halls, where a few of the chorus girls are smoking in between scenes, the glowing red ashes at the end of their cigarettes resembling eyes staring out of nothingness.

When I walk onto the stage this time, the wood feels rough under my bare feet, still warm from the spotlights. A blue floodlight casts a cool, watery sheen over me, and the gourd flute begins to play.

The audience bursts into cheers at my transformation. I close my eyes as the spotlights dissect my body like a lover's hands, exploring every hill and valley. The black gossamer absorbs the heat gently, like I am lying on asphalt on a summer day. I pretend the warmth is a fire within the Qingniao's heart, about to be unleashed upon the city that dashed her dreams.

I grasp a corner of my skirt, lift it behind me like a peacock's train, and spin. The audience gasps as the thousand eyes of the Qingniao's tail fly open. I swirl my other arm down beside my waist, so that I spin faster. The eyes appear to blink through the gossamer folds, so that it becomes unclear if the audience is watching the Qingniao, or the Qingniao is watching them.

In the dark orchestra pit, the violinist stands and tucks his instrument under his chin. When the melody changes, I arch my back so my neck is tilted toward the sky, the fingers of my other hand forming a delicate beak and crown. The gossamer skirt pools around me, and I extend my arms like wings behind me, rippling my elbows and wrists the way a bird's bones would billow in flight.

I remember the Feral Goddess's eyes, staring back at me out of the dressing room mirror. Now, I feel her inside me, a soft, whispering presence that lines my insides with velvet.

Silk rustles behind the tall, dark curtains at the stage's sides. A row of bodies presses up on either side of the stage. For a moment I am confused because the chorus has finished their parts, but then I remember the unwanted guest dancers Sui Feng has invited.

As I arch my back so that the tips of my hair sweep across the stage, I twist my neck to get a clearer view of the dancers waiting in the wings.

We never even rehearsed together.

Sui Feng makes a signal with his hand, and they flow out onto the stage. They're wearing gigantic water sleeves in shades of gray and black, which billow like storm clouds over a lonely field. I inhale and close my eyes, as silk draws across my neck and wrists. Lost in the center, I twist and turn, trying to dance the choreography, but I find my arms tied in silk.

The fluttering clouds that extend from the guest dancers' shoulders cover me like warm steam exhaled from the vents of the Turkish bath on a cold night. The dancers weave through one another,

drawing their sleeves together in dynamic shapes that remind me
of wedding knots but also flowing, churning intestines. A strange
choice to intersperse such a sequence with the Dance of the Qingniao. It's not until I am engulfed in their tidal waves of silk that I
realize there is no way we can still be telling the original story.

Sui Feng has changed not only the choreography, but the storyline without telling us.

One of the dancers turns, the wisps of her bangs scattering on
her forehead, and then I see.

Her eyes are empty wells in the golden field of her face. Under
the billowing silk, the wisps of her bangs land on the edges of her
eye sockets like thirsty crows waiting to drink.

I try to scream, but the silk drags over my face, muffling my
yells. When I inhale, silk fills my mouth. I tear at the layers with
my fingers, but they won't break. The silk is so light, but it weighs
down on my face so heavily. I think this must be what drowning
feels like.

The air takes on a faint shimmer, which settles upon my face
like dust, trapped between the flowing sleeves like a poison gas. A
light, airy scent like grass drifts between the layers of gray.

"Stop," I cry out.

The silk tightens around my neck, and I am carried to the floor,
fighting to breathe.

As my consciousness fades in and out of clarity, the smoke over-
whelms my senses. Before me, there lies a beautiful face with a
pointed chin and a black mole at the corner of her mouth. The
mouth smiles, and pointed teeth rise beyond the horizon of those
dainty red lips like mountain peaks.

I call to her to help me, but she won't come.

Through her, I see the spotlight above me, bright like an interrogation light—a sun that rules the night sky.

When the drug wears off and I shake the vision away, I find myself
alone center stage. Although I remember myself lying tangled in

gray silk, I am standing upright. Soft, black gossamer flows down my legs like dark foliage, bright, gold eyes staring out of the thin gauze like fireflies lost in a forest. I wish I could shut all those eyes now.

The air is colder now, and the music has stopped. Around me, the lights are off and the stage is quiet.

The audience is silent. At first, I think they are in shock, perhaps high off the shining smoke.

And then I realize they aren't moving at all.

As the gray static of darkness settles, it dawns upon me that there is something terribly wrong with the audience.

Guts and blood shine darkly from the auditorium before me. There are bodies lying across the aisles, limbs torn from shoulders and ribs torn out of chests. Rivulets of blood trickle under the seats, carving crimson rivers through the sloped wooden floors to pool at the foot of the stage. I am standing upon a flood wall, overlooking an ocean of shining red.

It must be a dream I'm stuck in, the vermilion hue of blood melting into the maroon velvet of the seats, until I can't tell them apart. White ribs, cracked down the sternum, pulled upright like eagle wings spread in a fiery sky.

Someone clears their throat behind me, and I wheel around with a sharp inhale.

Sui Feng strolls casually across the stage to meet me, a satisfied look on his face. He holds a small incense lamp stuffed with the glimmering fungus between his fingers, which he shakes out onto the floor and stamps out with the heel of his dress shoes. Weak puffs of the glittering smoke shoot into the air and dissolve before reaching us.

"Little did you know," he says with a smile, "you were meant to be the watcher, not the watched. Welcome to the real show."

"What did you do?" I ask. My voice is hoarse, scarred by smoke.

He dusts his hands together, little flecks of fungus ash shaking loose from under his nails. The sound makes me think of applause, echoing weakly through the theater. "Shh," he urges me, nodding at the bloodbath in the audience. "The goddess has been released. Our work is done."

"The faceless girls," I realize. "They did this?"

"I know you've been experimenting with the lingzhi." He smiles at me. "The connection goes both ways. You brought the Mother of Calamity into you through your hard work playing her character, and you only made that connection stronger through your cultivation of the lingzhi. Now I've taken the part of her that grew in you, and I've sent it into the faceless girls, who were about to burst with their resentment. A beautiful dance we've made together."

"But why?" I ask, forced to whisper. "Why slaughter all of them?"

He walks past me to the very edge of the stage, his toes extending past the sharp descent into the crimson water below. If I pushed him, he would fall.

"Because they took something from me."

Sui Feng reaches into his shirt and pulls out an object he wears around his neck, which he allows to hang down against his chest. Then slowly, he turns around so that I can see. It's a round mirror, tied with faded leather cords died blue, orange, and green. The object is at once terrible and familiar.

I can hear the drums in my ears from that night, pulsing like my heart.

"You're the masked shaman who made drinks at the Coeur de la Rose," I realize.

Below the stage, two rivulets of blood flow together, the life force of two strangers who never knew each other becoming one.

He merely smiles. "Years ago, I was tricked into coming to Shanghai by a friend of your dear Bailey Thompson. He would loan me to his business associates, who were all club owners, and they forced me to perform party tricks like a monkey in a circus. I fell for the same folly all of you have—that somehow, if I pandered to him enough, he would take me to New York, where my sister was taken by American explorers when they came through my hometown as a child. But he never had intentions to help me. I was just a stepladder for him in his grand scheme to establish a cabaret empire fueled by shamanic flowers. I've planned this day for years, to make him and all his foreign business associates in Shanghai pay."

"Are you working with the Court of Exiles?"

Sui Feng throws back his head and laughs. "They're children compared to what I am. All this time, they've been trying to summon the Mother of Calamity the way you and Bailey summon lesser gods. But she cannot be reached that way—her conduit is broken. Something prevents her strings from being pulled. Instead, the trick was to make her the master, and let the faceless dancers be the puppets."

I remember those blank, white eyes stitched onto a dark, leather canvas, spooning bitters and golden powders into hardball glasses, while blue and red neon dripped down from above. I imagine how those nights must have passed, year after year, while he slowly realized his dream was a lie.

"I'm sorry they did this to you. But how will this fix anything?"

Sui Feng flashes me a wide, childlike smile, and for a moment he's once again the eccentric fool who showed up one morning with a charming agenda to make us famous, a mad twinkle of amusement in his eye. "You forget, Jingwen—I'm not the Court of Exiles. I don't strive to become the hero who fixes the broken world, like they do. I merely came to have my revenge, and I've had it. They'll die now, all of them who desecrated my magic. The city will fall within weeks."

So it was all a lie—the avant-garde show he'd pulled out of his sleeve, the dream he seduced us with, even the grand opening that was meant to catapult the East Sea Follies to fame and fortune. I feel stupid for believing he was trying to make me into a cabaret star.

A fléchette dart lies on the ground nearby, left from the duet I performed with the Hail God. I grasp it in my fist. "You used us."

Sui Feng gazes down his nose at me. "We aren't enemies, Jingwen. I recommend you flee this city immediately, look for work in Hong Kong. Don't you have a father living there? The goddess will take care of Shanghai."

I squeeze the fléchette in my fist, the raised vanes on the tail digging into my palm. "Shanghai is ours."

He throws his head back suddenly and cackles. And then he spreads his arms again and pitches forward off the stage edge. My breath catches in my throat without meaning to, but his body never falls in the sea of red below. Instead, his flesh and bones dissolve into white smoke, which soars high above the bloodbath in the hall as if admiring its work, before disappearing through an open doorway at the back of the theater, laughing still.

I'm left alone in the dark, wearing the most expensive gown I've ever been gifted, the sharpened dart raised in my fist. Below me, the red rivers continue to flow, pooling against the wall upon which I stand. Dark flies crawl on bare wrists and parted lips, humming softly. Around me, the long curtains that fall from the sky tremble, and the breeze ruffles the gossamer of my dress. I shiver from how cold it is.

CHAPTER TWENTY

run.

It's the hour of solitude, which rises just after most cabarets close, as the sun begins to paint the very last layer of the horizon. The cloven hooves of bled-out hogs reach from the shadows beyond butcher shops, and high above the neon pollution of the international concessions, the clouds roil like poisoned guts spilled across the night sky.

I take the tram to Blood Alley. Without needing to think, my feet carry me to the Cabaret Volieré. I run up the stairs to Liqing's clinic, but the door—which has always been open to me—is locked.

Why did I even come? It was the first place I thought of to go, just to sit in the dark surrounded by my grandmother's terrifying paintings—because although those snarling gods always frightened me, I'd always felt like they could never reach me. Because Liqing was not the type of woman ghosts and demons dared to mess with.

A deep twinge of sadness flares in my chest.

I don't know how to fight girls possessed by feral goddesses—not to mention saving them from the Mother of Calamity.

Closing my eyes, I press my forehead against the door, my palms heavy against the wood. I am truly alone now.

It takes a few breaths before I remember my conversation with Beibei in her sitting room, a forest of gilded birdcages hanging between us. She had asked which side I'd choose, and holding one of the pretty, mechanical birds in my hand, I had answered ours.

Even if the possessed girls don't remember me, I have to try and bring them back.

Outside, the alley is filled with shoulders in padded suit jackets, bumping into one another. I pass a row of neon roulette wheels outside a gambling den, flashing pink and white like candy. That's where I see her. A face swirling with shadows peeks out from around the sharp corner of a side alley.

I chase after her down the thin street, along dumpsters and damp, drained beer kegs. There is a limp body lying across the ground, white uniform shining with blood. I drop to my knees beside the sailor. There are lots of fights in Blood Alley, navy soldiers from rival nations clashing fists over street boxing and dance hostess girlfriends. I pat the sailor's face, but he gives no response.

"Help!" I cry. Seizing the sailor's wrists, I attempt to drag him back into the main alley, where someone might save him.

A thin form disappears around a bend in the grayish blue walls. I drop the sailor's arms and give chase. The shadow passes under a foreboding shikumen gate carved into a pyramidal crown, like the spire atop the Paramount, behind which ordinary underwear swings on laundry lines running across the alley.

I pause before the tall, stone gate.

"Come out," I whisper. "I just want to talk to you."

There's no answer. I duck under the gate into a short alleyway where the merchants have closed shop, rusted metal shutters hung over their stalls.

At the alley's end, a slender, dark form hops down from the wall.

It's a young woman wearing a plain black shift that flutters about her knees. She is wearing a pointed straw hat, which hides her face under the blue shadow cast by its rim. Slowly, she tilts her chin up, so that I can see her.

Her lips are a shining red.

"Usugi," I whisper her name. The last time I saw her, she was swathed in white ostrich feather fans at the bar in the Dove House, running her hands over her thin elbows as she told me her story.

Her gaze bores into mine, although her eye sockets are dark and empty. The goddess is staring at me through Usugi's mutilated face.

"Usugi, it's me."

A late December wind whips through the alley, knocking over pails and potted plants outside shop windows. Soft, glistening soil scatters over the asphalt, bringing with it the smell of old rain. Usugi's thin black shift blooms and withers with each howl of the wind. Although her shoulders are bare, her skin purplish from the cold, she does not flinch.

"Come closer," I beckon to her.

I reach my hand out, asking for her to take it. My fingers tremble just slightly, wavering before my vision as if they've become disembodied from my arms.

She takes a clean, cold step toward me, her leg bending and straightening in a way that's graceful but mechanical. The shadows mix on her face. We stand face-to-face.

But she doesn't take my hand.

"Please let her go," I appeal to the Mother of Calamity.

Usugi raises her hands until they are beside her ears, her face cast in shadow by the wide brim of her hat, and she begins to flutter her fingertips like rain.

Like feathers brushing along a violin string, a soft, breathy music fills the air. Slowly, Usugi extends her arms toward the sky, her crimson-painted nails quivering.

And then the rain begins to fall. Instead of splattering against the tin awnings over a flower shop and bun stall, the raindrops slash needle-sized holes in the awning. I glance down at my bare forearms to see glistening beads of red where the water strikes, although the night is too cold to sense any pain.

The feathered drizzle thickens until it nears a deluge, which soon makes a symphony against the metal shutters and tin awnings of the alley shops as the droplets slash through the metal. I scream as the rain makes a thousand cuts on my face and neck, but there is nowhere to hide in the alley. I turn away from the sky, blood clouding my vision.

And then, all at once, the rain stops.

Usugi's head is turned up at the sky.

Another body stands on top of the wall, his arm made of silver. When the wind blows, his long hair whips about his forehead.

It's Nalan Zikai, blood trickling down his forehead like sweat. He drags his sword over the rough brick of the wall, and it makes a screeching music that's at once terrible and beautiful. Usugi regards him from under the brim of her straw hat, shadows engulfing any emotion that might have shown on her face.

And then he leaps down into the alley. A cloud of dead leaves rises around him. Usugi steps toward him, her face shadowed by the straw hat. He points the tip of his sword at her breast, and she stalks around him in a loose circle. I rake my wet, heavy hair back from my face, and my hands come away red.

Usugi draws her hands back up, fluttering her fingers again. The music, like paintbrushes on harp strings, begins again. Zikai draws his sword back, aiming in a straight line for Usugi's neck. The asphalt runs with flowering rain, vines of red seeping into the cracks. As the droplets thicken, he leaps forward.

"No, stop!" I throw myself into Zikai's waist from the side, throwing him off balance.

"Jingwen, what are you doing?" he yells as we both fall.

The rain pierces my scalp like needles. It runs in my mouth, cutting my tongue when I speak.

"You can't kill her."

His chest rises and falls as he watches me with an expression of incredulity. Even now, it hurts to face him—a dull ache blossoming in the pit of my stomach when I remember his betrayal the last time we met in the rushes.

But I chose *our* side—me and Usugi.

"She was going to hurt you," Zikai says.

I hold onto his silver arm, which feels shockingly warm under my fingers. "That night in the field, you said we would find a way to make them whole again."

Zikai meets my gaze, the rain cutting down his cheeks. The earthen green tones of his eyes have cooled since he acquired his silver arm. I wonder if like Wang Daojun, he has begun to grow fevered knots under the surface where his silver sinews meet his flesh.

Slowly, he nods. "We will."

He lowers his sword back to his side.

Below the shadow cast by her straw hat, Usugi parts her lips in a sigh. And then she draws her arms up, to call for another volley of rain.

"We have to run then," Zikai tells me.

I hurry after him, covering my face with my arm as the rain lashes down. When my feet splash through the puddles on the ground, the water droplets cut through my ankles.

Zikai grabs my arm before I run into the main street, as a stream of cars hurtle past. I stumble back as the pipes exhale hot exhaust in our faces. The traffic light has just turned green, and the night smells like gasoline. Drunk patrons stumble after taxis, leaning against the doors to tip their hats at the cabaret girls giggling in the second-floor windows. Just another night in the Sin City of the East.

I turn over my shoulder at the narrow alley we just escaped. I can still see Usugi's shadow at the back, unmoving. Yet on the main street, the Shanghai night flows as if the small glitches of her shadows never existed.

The traffic lights change to red, their violet shadow cutting across Zikai's neck like a spotlight.

I follow him down the next alley, behind a row of bars with their back doors propped open. The darkness within smells like mint and orange peel. Shadows move deep in those gaping mouths, the conversation blurring like static.

"I was worried about you," Zikai tells me, sheathing his sword with a swing of his arm. Then he collapses against the cool, gray brick of the alley wall, his hair falling around his face. The moonlight brushes his arm in a soft, bluish glow. I turn away when I see the little mole beside his left eye, because the sight of it evokes too many memories.

"How did you find me?" I ask.

He sighs. "I had a bad feeling about this opening night of yours, so I came to check on you. I wasn't wrong."

A light flickers on in a distant apartment window, somewhere on the other side of the wall, and it makes our shadows stretch over the alley wall. I run my fingers through my hair to tease the curls apart. Although my fingers catch in the tangles, I'm numb to the sting. "Thank you."

Despite how much it hurts to know he saw my grandmother behind my back, I realize there's nobody else I'd rather spend this terrible night with. With him, I know that no matter how bloody and violent the night ahead gets, we'll make it to dawn.

I turn around and lean against the wall next to him. The soles of my feet sear from running through the city in high heels.

In this breath of silence, we are alone in a city where a deadly goddess rages in the bodies of possessed girls, and it makes me think of the first time we sat down together in the Dove House, strangers in unexplored territory.

He scratches the back of his neck with his silver arm. The sight of it annoys me less now. "So what happened at the show?"

I draw my foot through the dust, making meaningless swirls. "It was Sui Feng, the director of our show. He was that shaman I told you about in the Coeur de la Rose, who made drinks that let me hear music in my head. Turns out one of Bailey's friends tricked him into believing they would make him famous in New York, but they really just wanted him to be a bartender."

"Tricked into being a bartender," Zikai echoes. He closes his eyes for a second, his shoulders pressing into the brick wall as he sighs. A drop of rain, tinged slightly red, rolls down the side of his forehead into his brow.

I attempt to dry my hands and forearms on the Qingniao's dress. The black gossamer of my tattered costume feels damp, like wet tissues crumbling under my fingertips. "He said something interesting—the Mother of Calamity's conduit is broken, and that's why the Court of Exiles can't summon her. Instead, Sui Feng used us—me as the conduit since I was playing Niang Niang in the performance—to draw her into the faceless girls' bodies."

I expect Zikai to respond with a frustrated concession at Sui Feng's brilliance, followed by a detailed breakdown of how Sui Feng arrived at his conclusions, since they are both shamans after all.

"Huh," he merely says, scratching his head.

"That's all you're going to say? Is this what the Court of Exiles wanted too?"

I gaze up at the moon, resting behind thin clouds that soak up the neon light, moving sluggishly as if they're drunk.

"No," Zikai says finally. "If the Court of Exiles really brought Xiwangmu back, she would be controlled."

I recall how I'd filled the Mother of Calamity's body like I was trying on an oversized coat in a street stall—the way she'd felt like an old robe worn by many before me—emperors and warlords and men of power, all of them leaving an imprint of their sweat and ambition in the faux fur lining, shadows I could feel under my fingers in the way the fibers frayed. "If the Court of Exiles took over, who would be the one that inhabits her body?"

"The leader. I've never met him." Zikai shakes blood and water out of his hair with a stylistic toss of his head.

I scoff. "Yet you followed him, a blind disciple who's never met his god—no, not like a disciple even. Like a puppy taught to heel by its master."

Zikai laughs a little, raising his silver hand before his eyes to admire, before grimacing when he catches the look on my face. "I grew up believing romantic ideals. When I joined the Court of Exiles, I thought if shamans, who followed a thousand-year-old code defined by honor and justice, could rule the country instead of politicians, there would be less evil in the world. I dedicated my life to cultivating my practice, so that someday I could be a hero too. But now I've come here, and I've learned that those rules only work if people choose to play by them. I never thought about what I'd do, the day I arrived at a place they don't matter, and all of you have been learning to break rules for the same time I've been learning to uphold them. Now I'm the one who's a fool."

The moon moves again across the sky, and in the distance, the penthouse suite above a hotel eclipses its silver edge. In Shanghai, money can even buy the privilege of seeing the moon.

He sighs. "When I said I think you could take your grandmother's knowledge and make something greater, I meant it."

I study his face—the youthfulness of his dancing eyes, which has returned since that night in the rushes—the determined set of his cheekbones, pale in the cold—the mole beside the corner of his eye, covered by a loose strand of hair. "Do you really think so?"

"When I saw you at the Rue de Velours, I realized you had a gift of the tongue. I'd never seen anything like it. You could talk Shanghai's most careful man into doing anything, including sparing my life."

He reaches out with his silver hand then and takes mine—leaving our fingers loosely interlaced in case I choose to slip away. But I don't. I rest my fingers on his palm, impossibly light against the gravity of heavenly steel.

I remember the last time we touched hands on the dance floor, skin on skin—raw, sweat-tinged, nerves like electricity. Drawing my gaze away from hands, I look into his eyes instead.

Could I believe him a second time?

The stream of twinkling headlights from the street suddenly vanishes.

I bring my finger to my lips to signal to Zikai to keep quiet.

Lost in our conversation, neither of us noticed that we are no longer alone. Five girls have appeared in the mouth of the alley. They stand in a pyramid formation, almost like we are practicing a dance number together. I end up staring at the girl who stands in the front, as if she is a leader for the others. She is wearing a robe made of red silk, which leaves her bare shoulders exposed to the hungry cold, wisps of her hair fluttering in the wind like ribbons. The makeup under her eyes is smudged, like railroad tracks laid in the snowy hills of her cheeks. Lower on her face, the shadows roil where her lips used to be, like oil blossoming in water.

"Huahua," I say her name.

The corners of her eyes seem to smile, as if she recognizes my voice.

Although she has no lips to form words, she opens her mouth, and a note like a birdsong shimmers into the blue night. Thin rivulets of mist flow along the walls, like the dry ice they sometimes use in stage shows.

She begins to dance, rippling her arms around her body. The mist follows, like water sleeves. When she spins around, the mist lashes after her like a whip. Zikai shoves me out of the way and ducks under the curving length.

The other girls, hanging behind her, begin to dance as well. They are all missing their lips, but a breathy music flows out of their throats. I jump out of the way as the mist flows toward them like flowering vines covering an abandoned garden, snaking low to the ground.

"I promise not to hurt them, but we'll still have to fight our way out," Zikai warns me.

I nod and take a few steps back, to give him room. Blindly diving after him, I choose to trust.

Zikai brings his mouth harp to his lips, a cold intensity blazing in his eyes. The first note twangs like a low bell, slow and heavy. He walks forward, putting himself between the faceless girls and me. Tendrils of mist curl around his legs, flowing together and apart, until they finally settle into the shape of a snarling mouth and fluid haunches.

The smoke wolf rears up on its hind legs, the mist flaring down its spine.

Huahua extends her poised fingers toward Zikai and flicks her wrist. The mist swings through the air like a ghost pair of claws. Zikai raises his silver arm, to parry the attack, and the mist hisses when it touches the metal, but it cannot cut him.

Her brown eyes filled with wonder, Huahua tilts her head to the side. The Mother of Calamity has never fought against a warrior made of silver.

Zikai plucks one leaf of the mouth harp, and a second harmonic echoes up into the crevices under the parapets and the staircases leading up into the apartments—even the cracks in the brick. The wolf launches into Huahua's chest and sinks its teeth into her neck, although it lets go quickly as Zikai promises. She stumbles back, black plumes rising out of a wound in her shoulder.

The singing stops.

Slowly, Huahua backs away. The wolf stalks her, as the smoke rising from her shoulder curls around her thin form, a dark presence to contrast against the white mist she drew herself. She brushes her fingers over the wound, almost experimentally, and withdraws her hand with a sharp gasp, as if the darker mist could burn. Then, as suddenly as they appeared to us, the faceless girls flee, bare feet pattering through the alley back into the night.

Zikai drops the mouth harp, and it swings on the chain around his neck. "Please give me another chance, Jingwen."

I rest my forehead against the gray brick of the alley wall, trying to calm my breathing. "What do you propose we do then?"

Behind me, Zikai sheathes his sword quietly. The blade still whispers against its sheath. "The Mother of Calamity was sought after by every emperor in history because she does not kill through grand gestures. She slaughters in secret. We won't know how much damage is being done until it's too late."

The edge of a crack in the brick digs into my brow.

"Ironically, there is only one individual in the history of China who has ever outsmarted the Mother of Calamity."

I can tell from the way he grimaces who that person is.

"My grandmother?"

"Xiao Lei didn't want me to tell you when we first met. But there is a rumor among the wider martial artists' society that Liqing is able to make her silver limbs because she stole Niang Niang's gift of creation."

"How could a patron goddess of calamity have a gift of creation?"

"All dead things decay back into the earth, to grow again."

A drunk man staggers past the mouth of the alley, his tie loose around his neck, singing a love song about roses in the summer. We stare at him until he passes. He doesn't register our presence.

"How did my grandmother manage to pull it off?" I ask.

Zikai shrugs. "None of us know."

I kick a pebble, which skips down the alleyway with a clatter that feels deafening in the hour between dog and wolf. "I don't know how to feel about freeing her."

After all the emotional labor I burned through to convince myself it was the right thing to do, I don't think I could turn my back on that decision.

I couldn't stomach the guilt of facing her again.

"Let me be the one to deal with it for now," Zikai tells me. "I have a few contacts in the city whom I can use to gather information." He reaches into his breast pocket and retrieves a slender white object the length of my forefinger. The object is hollow, with a series of holes drilled into one side. Running his thumb over the length to remove a coat of dust, he holds it out to me.

"What is it?" I ask, without taking it.

"It's a bone flute. It will allow you to find me if something happens. Play a few notes, and I'll hear you, no matter where I am in the city." He opens his hand, so that the flute lies upon his palm—an offering. "Look, you're right to be angry at what I did. I went to your grandmother because my pride was wounded, and I hungered for power. I don't regret it, but it was selfish. All I can offer now is to use that power to heal Shanghai—and to help you."

I take note of the distance between us, and a memory flitters across my thoughts—of his arm around my waist and my head upon his shoulder, while soft, colored lights flew around us. The memory is hazy now, as if I'm recalling a night where I was drunk.

I accept the flute and turn it over in my fingers. It's warm, the temperature of his skin.

Out on the street, soft, feathered rain begins to fly down, stinging my eyes and my ankles. I flinch instinctively, expecting it to cut
my skin, but it's just regular rain. Zikai and I face each other in the
alley, both of our faces turned up to the sky. If I was a poet, I might
say that the silence stretched for so long, by the time it ended, there
was just the rain.

CHAPTER TWENTY-ONE

The sun crawls up the golden valley between the Shanghai Stock Exchange and the British Bank of Shanghai.

I walk through the mostly empty streets as the coldest hour sweeps the concessions. The city flickers like an aged neon gas tube—fleeting glimpses of wild girls in alley mouths, slain bodies crumpled behind dumpsters and Terraplane coupés. The Mother of Calamity devastates Shanghai like a gentle lover pressing kisses upon her partner's waist, through little hints left under cover of the dark. Just like her sordid affairs, bloodshed has been a part Shanghai's lore since the day the concessions named her the City of Demons. The new destruction is not like that—casual and forgettable—but the city and her inhabitants have learned too well to turn a blind eye to such dealings. The blood flows like a sunset, trickle by trickle through the alleys, washed in rain and piss and scattered under rickshaw wheels and leather shoes, until by the time there are so many bodies one cannot simply step over them while thinking about the stock exchange, there is only darkness.

But I'm not afraid of the girls who shed this blood.

They don't confront me again as I track their shadows through Shanghai's guts, turning bodies over and feeling for the pulse under their necks. I find drunkards who died with rosy cheeks and generals whose wallets overflow with Canidrome winnings. But I'm not here to plunder. Eventually, I turn over a body that has fallen in the middle of the sidewalk in Blood Alley, a dark stain running down her fishnet stockings. The trapeze dancer from the Cabaret Volieré.

I hold her cold body in my arms, as her wide, blank eyes stare through me.

Although I saw her silhouette in the Cabaret Voliéré's upstairs window every Friday night for a year, I never learned her name.

It's only when the sun has cleared the spires in the sky, ushering forth a cloudless day, that they vanish. Tram bells blare, and herds of businessmen pile through the Bund like deer grazing on a plain, as if the events of the last night never happened.

I go home and wash my face, flinching when drops splash over the edge of my washbasin onto my toes—but it's just sink water. After that I try to sleep, but sleep doesn't come. The sun's shadow moves up my bedroom wall, growing wider and darker. A part of me waits for the sun to set, propelling me to continue through my routine, the way a factory machine will continue to pass iron parts down an assembly line for new bolts to be screwed in, even if the iron is misshapen.

When the sun sets, I go to the Paramount because it's the place I know best—a place I've danced, and fought, and killed. I change into a white qipao sewn with orange, green, and blue chrysanthemums paired with a red coat. Before I go, I tuck the small white flute Zikai gave me into one of the pockets I've sewn to carry Liqing's money.

The sidewalk outside the Paramount has frozen with a layer of thin ice, which cracks like glass under the heel of my white leather shoes. Along the ballroom's crystal facade, the ice sculptures have melted somewhat, so that Aphrodite's alluring pout resembles a grimace, and half of her left shoulder is missing.

A face, pale with shadows, peers at me from around an ice sculpture, before vanishing around the back of the cabaret.

A pack of university boys laugh as they wander up to the front doors, nervous and self-conscious about their secondhand suits beside the socialites and royalty, none of them noticing that a faceless girl has passed.

Alone, I am going mad.

In the performer's room, I absentmindedly dust bronzer over

my jawline. Beibei slides into the chair beside me without speaking a word. Her presence makes the edges of the room grow sharper, like I've only now awoken from a dream.

After clearing a mound of ripped stockings, foundation-coated tissues, and orphaned earrings out of her way, she slides a pack of Lucky Strikes from her waist and strikes one with the antique silver lighter I used to burn the lingzhi. Then, as she leans down into her elbow, the hot end of the cigarette dangerously close to her eyelashes, she wordlessly holds the pack out to me. "I've seen the bloodshed."

I slip a cigarette from the box with two fingers. Beibei strikes the lighter, and I allow her to light the cigarette between my lips.

"And the dancers missing parts of their faces?"

Beibei nods, her black tassel earrings brushing against her shoulders.

The cigarette tastes like cloves, slightly sweet and full-bodied.

"What's happening, Jingwen?" Beibei asks.

"I had a part to play in it." And I tell her everything from the beginning—from my grandmother's role in the Blue Dawn's rise to my courtship with Bailey Thompson, and everything I witnessed in the Coeur de la Rose.

She listens wordlessly, her expression betraying nothing.

The usual chitter of the dressing room quiets, and I realize the other girls have gathered around us, makeup half done and hot irons still wrapped in their hair. They are all listening. What I don't expect is the relief I feel to tell them, as the two worlds I've simultaneously inhabited finally collide.

"I wonder how it feels to wear the skin of a god," Zina whispers when I've finished.

Arisha, ever the one to make astute observations, leans forward. "But Jingwen, how can we ever win against a god?"

There is laughter in the halls outside. Soon, the dancing will begin.

"I don't know," I admit.

The long mirror fogs up from the cigarette smoke, so that when someone clears their throat behind me, I cannot place the voice.

I turn, expecting it to be the manager.

There is a tall woman wearing a qipao made of plum-colored silk pacing before my door.

My mother.

The other dancers all turn to look at me. They all know who she is, even if they've never spoken. After all, she is a legendary first hostess, one of the original dancers at the now-defunct Carlton Café.

"I guess we'll go," Arisha says, putting her cigarette out in a glass of water. She walks out of the door, and muttering behind their hands about my mother's presence, the other girls follow suit.

Beibei is the last to go. She uncrosses her legs and brushes the slit of her dress back over her leg. And then she sweeps out the door. Beibei and my mother are both tall, but Beibei seems taller.

My mother stares after her, her thin lips pressed together.

"Yes?" I ask, turning my chair around to face her. I tap my cigarette over the glass of water, showering the surface with ash.

My mother stares out the window at another arrangement of ice sculptures along the ballroom's side, which melt in the day and freeze again at night, their faces and shapes changing with the sun. She folds her arms over her chest.

"I will tell you how to stop it."

I lean back in my chair, staring at her through the smoke. "Stop what?" I ask.

"The girls who are possessed by the goddess." She walks over to the window and runs her hands through the curtains. "In the summer, when the sun doesn't set until late in the evening, do you close these curtains? You shouldn't let so much sun into your surroundings, or your skin might grow dark."

I straighten. "You know about the faceless girls?"

"Yes," she says, tugging on the curtains and trying to pull them shut. "Raoul has been investigating it. These curtains don't even close all the way. You should really ask your manager to replace them before the days get longer. Voyeurs could see you while you are undressing—"

I cut her off. "Then why are you here? Just tell Raoul how to stop it."

I regret my words immediately.

My mother glares at me out of the corner of her eye. Yet she still makes me think of an ice sculpture, cold and unmoving.

"Sorry," I apologize, the words sticking to the sides of my mouth like dry cotton. "I want to know what you have to say."

I drop the cigarette in the glass of water. The fire at the end goes out with a soft hiss.

My mother drops her hands from the curtains. She comes over to me slowly, bumping into chairs and holding on to their backs as if she's sleepwalking. "Many years ago, when I was a little girl living in a backpack strapped to your grandmother's back, she hiked up the Kunlun Mountains with me and stole the Mother of Calamity's crown."

I remember the vision I had in the Coeur de la Rose, drunk on the cocktail named Ancestry—of my grandmother leaving my mother on an altar under the moon, her slender, bare feet making ripples in the cold green lake.

My mother reaches into my makeup bag and pulls out a dark, berry-colored lipstick, which she twists around in her fingers. No doubt the dancers of her generation did not wear lipstick of this color. I can tell she is telling the story through her gritted teeth.

"Waipo has the crown?" I ask.

"Yes," my mother answers. "But you'll have to convince her to give it to you. That'll be the hard part."

She doesn't know about Liqing's capture by the Blue Dawn, I realize. I briefly debate whether or not to tell her and decide against it.

"How did she steal it?"

"By offering me as a sacrifice to the goddess." My mother won't look me in the eye when she tells this part of the story. "The Mother of Calamity, who was formerly a patron goddess of Shanghai, fled after the concessions were signed to Europe and the Americas. She was bored, of course, after leaving the exciting life of a port city. So she asked to experience what it was like to be a child for a day, since she'd never been a child before. Your grandmother offered to hold her crown while she inhabited my body. You can't imagine how it felt, Jingwen, to have a demon slip into my body and do the things demons do—she tore apart creatures and other demons, and tortured men—things I witnessed with my own eyes and hands while unable to fight back. I think she enjoyed the horror I felt. Time passes differently for deities—eternities passed while she possessed me, and I've never forgotten. And you might have guessed—the moment the goddess had entered my body, your grandmother put the crown on her own head, and she never gave it back."

Whatever type of response she expects me to give, I soon find I'm not capable of giving it. I stare at her in silence, unable to process my thoughts.

"Why do you worship her then?"

"What?"

I sit before the mirror so I can rest my aching heels—dancing shoes were never meant for staying still. "When I saw you in the Jing'an Temple that night—you were praying to the Mother of Calamity, as Guanyin's incarnation. Why would you do that, if she hurt you?"

"I wasn't offering my blessing. I go that temple every week to curse her."

She drops my lipstick back in my bag and shoves it away.

"I'm sorry she did that to you," I finally mutter.

My mother shrugs, crossing her arms over her chest again. "That's why I'm telling you—so you can continue punishing her, after Liqing's days of glory are over. Promise me that. Never let the goddess fall out of our family's hands."

She lifts her head then, her eyes narrowed and her lipstick shining red. In that moment, she looks exactly like Yue Liqing, confident and unbreakable, as if she towers over the whole world.

"I promise."

I run my thumb over a red spatter on a corner of the makeup mirror, a stain that spreads the light within the glass beneath to form a rainbow, like the inside of an oyster's shell. The manager hired a cleaning crew after Beibei and I killed the Thunder God in the dressing room, convinced once of us had quarreled with a lover and killed him—although there was no sign of a body. The manager's been nicer to us since, frightened we might do the same to him. Still, they missed a spot. Like the small piece of skull wedged in the ivory filigree of the main ballroom, the Thunder God has his own memorial now. Maybe it will fade in time.

My voice comes out very softly. "Why did you become a dancer?"

My mother stares at me blankly.

"I don't really know much about you," I continue, as a bit of blood chips under my thumbnail, becoming lodged under there against my skin. I clench my teeth, my lips pressed carefully together, to make it clear I'm not being sentimental—just curious.

My mother walks around the room again, straightening her pearl necklace as she passes the mirror. "Your grandmother never wanted to teach me her surgeries, unlike with you. Maybe she saw something in you I didn't have, or she simply hadn't realized her mortality back then. I was just a pretty flower growing in her garden, whom she could cut shoots off of to give her courtiers and enemies, and I would grow back to be used again. In fact, I was the one who was supposed to marry the Blue Dawn's leader. I was young and pretty at the time, easily malleable."

I turn to look at her. "You were going to marry Wang Daojun?"

She laughs at the surprise on my face. "Perhaps I would've been that little swan-hearted girl you're friends with." Her silvery laugh drifts across the room, somewhere into the curtains like a butterfly that has accidentally wandered in, unable to find the way back out. "In those days, that's what most women aspired to be—the wife of a rich man who didn't ask too many questions about the secrets you were hiding. But Shanghai was already changing, and I felt it, so I gambled my life and became a dancer. It's the hardest thing I ever did—even harder than coming back five years later when you were born and giving you to her."

Despite my efforts to control myself, I must grimace, because a wry smile settles on her red lips. "Don't misunderstand—I didn't do it so you'd suffer like I did. Your father's wife was a powerful woman, who hired gangsters to have you killed. You were safer with her, under the Blue Dawn's protection." She looks at us in the mirror, and I follow the line of her gaze. Even if I don't want to, there are similarities between our faces—our wide-set eyes and prominent, rounded cheekbones. "Are you satisfied now?"

I nod.

She starts for the door.

"Thank you," I say after her retreating back.

She pauses for a second, and then keeps walking.

CHAPTER TWENTY-TWO

Abandoning my shift for the night, I run for the alleys outside.

Most of the stalls are shuttered down the lane, although a singular flower merchant continues to sell white dahlias for the couples that wander out of the Paramount, the flowers looking like they're unraveling too. From my waist, I draw out the bone flute Zikai gave me. The instrument glides under my finger pads, worn smooth.

I raise it to my lips and blow into the hollow space. A shrill, off-key note, which raises all the little hairs on the back of my neck, pierces the night. I wince from the dissonance. The flower merchant raises his head in alarm, but I don't have time to apologize.

Experimentally, I try covering some of the holes to see if that will improve the sound. The sound becomes even more high-pitched, a tortured screech.

"Jingwen."

Zikai leaps over the wall with a whoosh of air, using his silver hand as a lever. He dusts his palm off with a triumphant look.

Then he points at the flute in my hand. "You were playing it upside down. That's why it sounded so awful." Despite the somber way we parted last night, he is back to being his gallingly cheery self. I can't resist a small smile.

"Anyways, what happened? I was expecting to save you from some sort of danger, but this is as boring as alleys go in this forsaken city."

I'm breathless from blowing into the flute. "I found out what Liqing stole from the Mother of Calamity—her crown. If we take the crown back, maybe we can save the faceless girls."

He raises his eyebrows in response.

"How did you find that out?"

"From my mother." I fold my arms across my chest, a defensive maneuver that precludes the asking of more questions.

Zikai props his hands against the wall and bows his head, deep in thought. "Last night, you were hesitant to free your grandmother. Have you changed your mind?"

There is a lump in my throat, but I swallow past it. "We need the crown."

Zikai beckons to me and starts walking back toward the main street. "I know where to go."

He leads me to an alley I've never seen before, which only houses one establishment at the very end, shadowed by a roof that curls at the edges like a flame.

"What is this place?" I ask, running after him as he strides along with his longer legs.

He walks up to the establishment, which used to be a Japanese teahouse based off the architecture. Wooden statues carved from sandalwood guard the paper windows from the outside—beaked goblins wearing bowls on their heads and a god waving a leopard skin. Two red lanterns with long tassels swing on either side of the door, both carved with a single word: 霞.

I recognize the character for dawn. Zikai swipes his forefinger through the tassels trailing from the lantern as he walks past, which sends the lanterns into a furious swaying rhythm. He begins to sing a jazz song that has been playing in the clubs lately, although I cannot recall the name.

A heavy beaded curtain hangs from the doorway, under which Zikai has already disappeared. I brush apart the heavy wooden beads, inhaling the musky fragrance of sandalwood as I duck through.

The teahouse's interior swims into view. A beige-colored mat covers most of the floor, on which are seated a small number of men in suits. There is a long table at the back of the room, which is set with a feast of night snacks and tangerines stacked in pyramids.

The skeleton of a roast mackerel, picked clean, lies on a black plate in the center of the table. All of the men seated on the floor wear sheaths of gray-blue leather strapped to their backs.

This is where the Society of the Blue Dawn holds their court.

Xiao Lei sits in the center of the table like a king, drinking iced whiskey and eating melon seeds for dessert, presiding over the gang he has inherited. It looks like a scene from one of the Roman paintings hanging in the Astor House. All he is missing is a crown.

His hands in his pockets, Zikai strides down the center like it's a public garden, stepping over the outstretched feet of the gangsters. A few draw their swords, but Zikai doesn't even flinch. I follow like his ghost, but Zikai's presence is so loud none of them notice me.

With a second look, I realize all the gangsters gathered tonight are young boys, no older than Xiao Lei was when he first received his silver arm. One of them is the boy I operated on with Liqing. His eyes are puffy as if he's been crying. They stare at us like we have mistaken a lion's den for a rose garden.

Which perhaps we have.

Zikai smirks and then suddenly makes a lunge at the boys on one side. They flinch and scramble back into the shadows. He laughs to himself.

Xiao Lei, on the other hand, is not amused.

He watches Zikai's every move like a hawk, slowly chewing on a melon seed. When Zikai reaches the table, the shaman slowly raises his hands up in a display of surrender.

"I have a confession to make," he says casually, as if the two of them have been best friends their entire lives.

Xiao Lei spits the melon seed shells from his mouth into a small porcelain dish without saying anything.

Zikai takes his hands out of his pocket and rolls his sleeve up to his elbow. "First of all, do you like my arm?"

A loud crash shakes the room. Many of the boys jump. The plate with the fish skeleton has slid off the front of the table, breaking cleanly in two on the floor.

Xiao Lei snaps his fingers at the boys with a bored lilt to his voice. "Seize him."

Zikai holds one hand up. "There's no need. I came to turn myself in."

The boys hesitate, unsure who to listen to. They hover between their leader and this dauntless stranger, who holds none of the reverence they do for the Blue Dawn's rules and formalness. As such, they hang around Zikai, skulking over their indecision. A few turn to their leader for guidance, but Xiao Lei isn't looking at them.

He places another melon seed between his teeth. "What did you do, Nalan Zikai?"

The shaman from Hulunbuir bows, arms wrapped around his waist in a gesture of politeness.

"I killed Wang Daojun."

Xiao Lei blinks, his expression impassive, and then reaches for his whiskey. "Yue Liqing killed Wang Daojun," he says over the edge of his glass.

Zikai straightens again. Although he towers over Xiao Lei, who is seated, the Blue Dawn's leader radiates the same intensity as his predecessor. They appear on the same level.

"Yes, but I arranged for it."

A deep, cold silence stretches between them. Outside, the lanterns are still swinging, their unsteady light bleeding through the paper windows. I watch the condensation roll down the sides of Xiao Lei's lowball glass.

Xiao Lei looks from Zikai to me, and realization slowly dawns on his face. He narrows his eyes, in a way that reminds me eerily of Wang Daojun himself. "I warned you to stay away from him," he addresses me directly.

I bow my head, because now that Xiao Lei sits at the center of the table, it feels like the fitting thing to do. "I'm sorry, but after a while, what he said began to make sense."

Xiao Lei reaches for another melon seed. "What should I do with you then, Nalan Zikai? Are you here to propose your own sentence as well?"

I interject before Zikai can say anything.

"I need to talk to my grandmother. That's why we came."

Xiao Lei crushes the melon seed between his teeth, and the soft splintering of the shell echoes between his cheeks. He spits again. "Are you saying you're here to propose a trade? Nalan Zikai for Yue Liqing?"

"Yes," I say, at the same time Zikai says, "No."

We turn to glare at one another.

Abruptly, Zikai breaks into a grin and steps forward, right up to the edge of the table. The boys tense, gaze shifting from shaman to gangster, but Zikai's shoulders are utterly at ease. "I have left the Court of Exiles, and so we are no longer enemies."

Xiao Lei raises his eyebrows. "Oh, it's that simple to you?"

Zikai spreads his arms out to the side, one silver and one flesh. "There is no need to make life complicated. Given the chaos that has broken out since the masked shaman summoned the Mother of Calamity, which you are no doubt aware of, I propose we work together to restore order to Shanghai."

Xiao Lei laughs bitterly, the only thing that differentiates him from Wang Daojun. "What an ironic statement," he observes. "You killed my leader to displace Liqing for your bedamned goddess, and now you want to bring the old lady back. You think I'd help you?"

The smirk disappears from Zikai's face. I can't help but feel impressed at the charm he can switch on and off at will—the way his dancing eyes can extinguish their playfulness at once, and cool into stone—the subtle transformation I wish I could replay over and over again just to catch every detail. "I wonder why this teahouse feels so empty tonight? You can't fool me—more than half the Blue Dawn gangsters have flocked to new masters. They've left you because you can't compare with Wang Daojun. You need all the help you can get."

Xiao Lei rests his elbows on the table, his fingers interlaced. He stares at Zikai over his hands, their shared history hanging between them like a taught zither string. The silence stretches for so long, I worry it will crush them both before either can lift a sword.

I step in between them, my footsteps echoing on the cold floor. The shadows of the lanterns swing on both walls on either side of me.

"Zikai might be right—you can't compare to Wang Daojun."

The gang leader's head snaps up. For all the Friday nights he's spent cutting me dragon fruit at Liqing's behest, I never imagined he could be so cold.

I squeeze my hands into fists, willing myself not to shake. "But I think that's the point. You're *not* Wang Daojun. Wang Daojun was loyalty-inspiring, but he was also stubborn and infamous for his grudges. You can be different. Zikai is asking you for forgiveness— all you have to do is give it, and you have us as allies. Take us to my grandmother, and we will help the Blue Dawn's re-ascension to power."

Xiao Lei's gaze is an arrow aimed between my eyes.

"You are a cabaret girl. What benefit could an alliance with you possibly bring me?"

I hold my chin up, the way I've faced him all those nights bearing Liqing's trade. "We don't have silver arms, but we have access to the city's elite when they are most vulnerable. No gangster has made use of that before."

Xiao Lei makes a noise under his breath. He picks up a handful of black-and-white-striped melon seeds and lets them fall again, like a stream of pebbles. "You know, she's more eloquent than you think you are," he says finally to Zikai.

I close my eyes in relief. Beside me, Zikai snorts.

"There's a problem," Xiao Lei continues. "We no longer have Yue Liqing in our custody."

My eyes fly open.

"Bailey Thompson wanted her," he explains. "They had been working together for a while, but he wasn't satisfied to be her business partner. He wanted to learn her art. She refused to teach him."

"What are you implying?" I demand. Perhaps I am imaging it, but I think Xiao Lei flinches a bit from my raised voice.

A sudden hollowness opens in my chest, which deepens with no bottom.

Zikai stuffs his hands in his pockets with an exasperated noise under his breath. He begins to pace, back and forth along the table. "Money," he mutters. "He traded her to him for money, of course."

I turn to Xiao Lei, wishing for him to defend himself, but he's silent. His hand tightens into a fist on the table surface.

"Put me on the phone with Bailey now," I say.

CHAPTER TWENTY-THREE

X iao Lei shows us to his office at the back of the teahouse, a small room behind sliding panels, hung with vertical scrolls of bold calligraphy. A window on the far side overlooks a small garden of bamboo and weeping willows, a secret oasis buried in the city's guts. It's raining outside, beads of water dripping off spoon-shaped leaves into loose dirt. A wooden bridge provides cover for an artificial stream, around which the water makes small leaps and dimples where the raindrops hit.

I cradle the cool, ebony receiver in my hand while Zikai and Xiao Lei stand behind me, keeping a silent watch.

"Hello?" Bailey asks in his honeyed voice.

I hold my hand up. Zikai and Xiao Lei lean closer.

"It's me, Jingwen," I say, my breath creating soft static as it hits the receiver.

There is the rustle of silk as he adjusts the phone under his chin. "Jingwen." He mutters my name. "I was wondering about you. You're alive and well, I take?"

"Yes," I agree. "Am I not supposed to be?"

Bailey chuckles under his breath. "Alive and well is always the best condition to be in."

I can hear the soft patter of rain outside his window too. Perhaps we are not standing too far from each other. You could say the moment was romantic.

"Did you know there was going to be a bloodbath at the Lyceum?" I ask.

I can feel his surprise in the brief silence that follows.

"Of course not," he says, recovering quickly. "I would never want anybody to fall in danger, especially so many of my friends I invited to see the show."

Behind me, Zikai makes a disbelieving sound in his throat. Xiao Lei elbows him in the arm.

Bailey continues. "I was very sorry to hear about what happened on opening night. It turned out my partner betrayed me. I thought Sui Feng was an auteur—eccentric but wholly committed to his artistic vision. Turns out he had his own agenda."

"You mean you thought you were using him, but it was actually the other way around."

Any other man might've cowered then, but Bailey's voice remains a razor dipped in honey. "Wow, Jingwen. You are cold today."

I press the phone hard into my ear. "And what did it take to get my grandmother to sew those lips and eyes onto those foreign socialites?"

"She was a willing participant in that." He lowers his voice, as if he means to comfort me. "It hurts, doesn't it, to realize someone you loved so deeply could violate your beliefs anyways."

"I want to see her."

He shrugs on the other side, the silk rustling over his shoulders.

"Okay," he says. "Then come see her."

I turn around, hoping Zikai and Xiao Lei can affirm my own bewilderment at Bailey's eagerness. He's making it too easy.

"Wh-where is she?" I ask.

"At my club. Remember, I wanted to introduce you to someone."

Zikai starts mouthing something to me, but Xiao Lei shoves him aside and starts mouthing something different. I look from one to another, unable to decipher what they are trying to convey.

"Hello, Jingwen?" Bailey says lightly.

"Can I come tonight?" I decide.

"Sure," Bailey agrees. "I'll expect you at midnight. You know how to get in."

"Of course."

I place the receiver back in its cradle. It slides into place with a satisfying click. Outside in the garden, the boughs of the Japanese wisteria hang lower, weighed by rain.

"He's keeping Liqing at his speakeasy, behind the Fantasio Café in Blood Alley," I explain. "He invited me to go there at midnight, although I don't trust him at all. Why would he be so open about it?"

Xiao Lei is smiling to himself.

"There's another entrance to his club, which he wouldn't expect us to take—under the City God Temple in the Old City. An old passage connects the two. I recommend we go that way, take him by surprise."

Zikai folds his arms over his chest. "How do you know that?"

Xiao Lei's grin widens, a cold wryness written over his face. "Because before he bought the Coeur de la Rose, the Blue Dawn owned it."

***

The City God Temple rests at the center of the Old City, a palace of nine great halls with green-tiled roofs and red eaves that curl like a dragon's whiskers. Colored lanterns shaped like koi fish hang across the passages between the halls, where a permanent festival market has blossomed. We walk past an exhibition of bizarre stones and a thick crowd tossing coins at a troupe of child acrobats dressed in silk robes.

A moat still surrounds the temple, left from the days when the folk shrine was meant to shield a much smaller Shanghai from the dangerous marshlands. There are lilies growing in the green water, the temple's golden reflection wavering in the depths.

"Where is the rest of the Blue Dawn?" I ask my two sullen companions, who walk on either side of me, as far from one another as possible.

"We don't want to draw too much attention," Zikai explains. "After all, he invited you, not us. It would be a great red flag if you showed up with both a shaman from the Court of Exiles and the Blue Dawn's leader."

Xiao Lei scoffs under his breath. "There is no department in the twelve thousand eight hundred Daoist hells where the Court of Exiles and Blue Dawn would ever form an alliance—but it would certainly frighten Bailey out of his pants if we did."

"What if he has an army? The two of you will be outnumbered."

Momentarily distracted, I nearly walk into an expressionless man in a thin gray suit wearing sunglasses, who is twisting horses and lions out of balloons, while children clamor about him with coins in their fists. It is the liveliest temple I have seen, and yet there is no doubt—it has been a long time since the City God Temple served as a place of worship.

"We'll use this." Zikai produces the skinny bone flute from his pocket. "If any of the three of us gives a distress call, Xiao Lei's men will come down—provided they're skilled enough to hear it. You didn't train their ears very well."

Xiao Lei's fingers twitch at his sides, like he would strangle Zikai if he could. "This is Shanghai, not the grassland. We have no need to call for one another with a flute."

The passages under the quiet halls smell like candy. We pass barrels of rice wine flavored with cherry blossoms and shopkeepers hammering peanut brittle with flat wooden mallets. A noisy line curves around the courtyard, children yawning from sleepiness, as they wait in line for thousand-year-old tofu fried with scallions and sesame oil.

"I hate this place. It's such a tourist trap," Xiao Lei mutters with disgust.

"There are no gods left in the city," Zikai says. "What did you think it would become? I wouldn't worship a wooden husk whose knees have been gnawed by rats either."

We walk across a bridge shaped like lightning, lit by small, frosted orbs along the railing, through the moat. The doors of the shrine across the moat have been thrown open, revealing the dark effigy of a god in its depths, the stairs guarded by a pair of bronze tortoises whose downturned eyes appear jaded with wisdom. A child eating a candied hawthorn berry is sitting on one tortoise's back, slapping its carapace like a horse's flank while his parents scold him to get down.

I gaze up at the gold letters affixed to the shrine's front, which glow against the night sky. Deep inside the shrine, the statue of a generic-looking goddess carved out of camphor wood emits a light, flowery musk.

I grin, because we are old friends by now.

"The Niang Niang Hall," I declare.

I meet the wooden goddess's eyes as she gazes down at us over an altar piled with oranges and incense. A few red prayer cushions litter the floor before the altar, where a couple of elderly city dwellers kneel in supplication. Not entirely dead then—she still has fans in this part of town.

Zikai walks up to a handsome tin box standing beside the altar with a slit at the top, inscribed with fancy lettering. He shakes the box and scoffs. "Look, you can cast money to curse your enemies. What bullshit—the monks use that money to get drunk at Jingwen's club."

An elderly woman kneeling upon a prayer cushion shoots him a dirty look over her shoulder.

"This isn't the real shrine," Xiao Lei says to us softly. "It's a facade made for the public. Most temples in the city are just symbols—reminders of the gods' power so that people don't forget. But the real shrine is underground."

He strides around the wooden effigy, toward a doorway leading into a deeper room in the shrine. I glance around in case there are guards watching, but the temple has fallen out of favor with Jazz Age Shanghai. There are no monks to guard the hall.

A fluttering red silk curtain divides the altar room from the back. The sensation of the silk is oddly familiar in my hand. And then I remember the curtain in the Coeur de la Rose, which the coat girl stopped me from entering. This must be where the two places are connected.

Xiao Lei and Zikai are arguing on the other side. I step through. The room contains nothing but a square well with walls that rise to the height of my waist. There are ugly stone lions perched on all four corners, squat like toads, guarding the water.

"It's a well," I point out to Xiao Lei.

He nods, picking up a rope that runs over one corner. "When Shanghai was lost in the foreign concessions, the Guardians of Yama—which was the most powerful gang in Shanghai at the time—turned her shrine into a well to hide it."

"I've never heard of the Guardians of Yama."

"They don't exist anymore—wiped out by the Blue Dawn." Zikai walks in front of Xiao Lei, blocking him from view. "It's not a real well, of course—just a measure to ensure the monks never went down there."

I take the rope from his hands and swing my legs over the edge. "I'll go first."

Xiao Lei and Zikai exchange a glance. "Are you sure? Anything could be down there," Xiao Lei warns.

I smile at them over my shoulder. "After all, I'm the one who was invited."

I close my eyes and drop into the darkness. My feet hit the bottom with a gentle thud, the palms of my hands stinging from the coarse rope. When I glance up, all I can see is a small yellow square of the well room.

Before me lies a passage carved out of stone, lit by kerosene lamps hanging on rusted brackets along the wall, which extends infinitely under the City God Temple. If Xiao Lei is telling the truth, this passage leads all the way into the Coeur de la Rose in Blood Alley. I take a deep breath and enter the second temple.

There are demons carved into the walls, their mouths drawn into grimaces, their arms brandishing colorful staffs tied with flowing ribbons overhead. I trace a hand over their beards and detailed armor. Liqing would know their names.

Xiao Lei hits the ground behind me with a graceful *swish*, while Zikai lands with no sound at all.

"Don't they say the mark of a true martial artist is one who can land on water without making a splash?" Zikai asks.

"Shut up," Xiao Lei hisses back.

Chuckling, Zikai passes him, disappearing deep into the tunnel.

The first room we encounter has an arched doorway. Except for two torches flickering on the wall, the room is full of wooden crates with faded labels advertising ginger ale and Pepsi-Cola, stacked to the ceiling. I tear the lid off the nearest one, which is only half packed, and stifle a gasp. A dancer's entire face, lying on a purple cushion with a lace trim, gapes up at me, her lips just barely parted in a romantic sigh. I brush my fingertips along her cheek, which has been preserved in some way that it has retained its original softness and faint blush.

To my left, Zikai curses under his breath. He has just opened a crate which contains a long pillow, upon which rests a collection of disembodied lips quivering on white doilies. There are labels written in pencil under each: *summer cherry—small and puckered, hunter's bow—shaped like a heart.* They look like desserts.

I slam the box's lid shut.

"This is where Bailey runs his trade of faces."

Zikai beckons to Xiao Lei, who is hanging at the back of the room, with one hand. "Did the Blue Dawn know about this?"

Xiao Lei approaches us slowly, grimacing slightly.

"You knew?" I ask, although I already know the answer.

He sighs and runs his silver hand through his hair, in a manner that makes me think of Zikai. "Liqing was doing the surgeries, and she was with us. So we defended Bailey against the other gangs."

I cover my face with my hands. "Did you know about the other things too? His idea to install shamans in all the cabarets in Shanghai to drug all the guests for entertainment?"

Xiao Lei makes to touch my shoulder but drops his hand. "Daojun taught us to be loyal, not moral. It was wrong, and I played a part in it. As a leader now, I'd like to change how things are run. After this is all over, we'll ask Liqing to return these faces and lips to their rightful owners. We will burn the shamanic flowers. I'm sorry."

Zikai stands behind him like a shadow, one hand extended in front of him. He's gazing at his fingers with a look of astonishment. I wonder if he regrets allowing my grandmother to take his arm now.

I push past both of them, back into the hall. "Let's find her then."

In the next room, there is a stone altar, piled with incense and peach pits—but no goddess behind it. Scrolls with red ink calligraphy hang on the walls, the characters an ancient, primitive script that remind me of the neon lights in Bailey's speakeasy. A woman kneels on a prayer cushion before the altar, her hair hanging over her face. Although there are not enough torches to illuminate her features from afar, I recognize her white hair and cloth slippers immediately.

"Waipo!" I rush to her side.

She catches me in her embrace. Chains clink around her wrists, which are bound by handcuffs.

"Jingwen," she says, touching my face. Her eyes search mine, and I sense sadness in her expression. "You shouldn't have come."

And then I realize she is not alone in the room.

Bailey rises from a peach wood chair in one corner of the room, where he has been reclining patiently. "Finally, Jingwen, you have come," he says. "Although not through the door I expected."

He raises his eyebrows when Zikai and Xiao Lei rush into the room after me, drawing their swords in unison.

"Xiao Lei," Bailey says, recognizing the new leader of the Blue Dawn. "I thought we had an agreement."

"Not anymore," Xiao Lei says.

He and Zikai advance on either side of Bailey, their steps perfectly in sync.

"Well, that's unfortunate," Bailey says. He snaps his fingers in the air.

Footsteps echo in the hall outside, and a handful of silver-limbed gangsters burst into the room. They're wearing the Blue Dawn's insignia—a scabbard made of gray-blue leather on their backs.

Xiao Lei's eyebrows knit together.

Bailey smiles. "I'm sorry, but you don't have the charisma of your old leader. These men have chosen to join me instead."

In response, Xiao Lei lunges at him with his sword. The blow is caught by one of the Blue Dawn's gangsters. Soon my two companions are swallowed by a forest of silver limbs and dark jackets, Zikai's mist wolf leaping among them.

"Jingwen." Liqing whispers my name urgently, and I tear my attention away from the fight.

She buries her fingers in her white, unruly hair, and raises her hands, cupped, over her head. A brilliant white crown glimmers above her head, edges sharp as a knife, a ring of blue jade in the center. The crown is so bright, Zikai momentarily stops fighting nearby to gape at the object in Liqing's hands.

"No!" Bailey yells, as he runs toward us. "Stop her!"

The gangsters rush at us, swords drawn.

I want to warn Liqing to run, but there will never be enough time. Instead, I look at her, cast in the crown's brilliant white light, as she rises. It might be the last time I'll see her—the crow's-feet around her eyes that have deepened over the years every time she laughed, the way she seems to have shrunk a few inches now that I've grown older, and in the lines around her mouth—pride, and joy, and all the ways we've disappointed each other. I will myself to remember it.

But there is no wistfulness in her narrowed eyes.

Liqing smiles, triumph blazing across her face. "This is yours now."

And she places the crown on my head.

A blinding, searing pain splits my skull as the crown constricts my temples. I scream, holding my head, doing all I can to tear the crown off, but I can no longer feel the knife-sharp edges, sense the ice-cold metal against my skin.

Somewhere, on a cold mountain leagues away, she senses me receiving the crown. The Mother of Calamity, alone between blue mountain peaks rimmed by the gold eternity of a sun that never fully sets, throws her head back and curls her lips, revealing sharp teeth. At first I think she is screaming, until I see her thin shoulders shaking with mirth beneath torn silk. She turns to look at me, and for the first time, I am able to see her true form: a goddess of the virgin wilderness—deer's horns on her head, lion's teeth in her mouth, and the tail of a tiger.

She laughs because Liqing has bested her once again.

Behind her, a thousand glowing eyes open in the night, twinkling like stars. It's her entourage of tigers and leopards, watching from the distance. She falls to her knees, laughing so hysterically her entire body convulses.

A low twang echoes through the night, and like the snapping of a sheep gut string, it breaks the sky above the mountains. I find myself on my hands and knees on the floor of Niang Niang's temple, a throbbing headache all that remains of the crown around my head.

A few feet away, Xiao Lei is single-handedly holding Bailey's gangsters back, although I can hear his exhaustion in his cries.

Liqing smiles as we face each other on our knees, her calm brown eyes reflected over and over in the heaven-forged steel that clashes around her, like pools of still water.

I press along my temples gingerly, feeling for the outline of the crown, but it has disappeared into my flesh, something I can no longer remove. "How do I take it off?" I ask, my nails scrabbling uselessly against my skin.

"You don't," Liqing says, smiling harder, and she beckons over her shoulder. Zikai comes to stand over her, his sword raised over his head. "Now, do it, shaman."

I scream when Zikai brings the blade down at Liqing, but the blade merely falls through the chains tying her wrists.

Liqing flexes her freed wrists and rises to her feet. Her knees shake from the effort, and she uses both her hands to steady them. "Jingwen, I hope that someday when the time comes for you to die, you'll learn a bit from my example."

Having cast Xiao Lei aside, the gangsters who defected rush to surround her, forcing her back down onto her knees, their silver hands at her neck. It must be humiliating, since she is the god who made them, and now they have come to end her life. In the end, that's the greatest irony of all—the folly of all gods perhaps.

Bailey walks over slowly to where she kneels, a ring of blades pointing at her neck. The doctor from New York is holding an object in his hands. I recognize it as one of Sui Feng's mirrors, braided blue and green cords swinging from its border. The mirror reflects the torchlight in a blinding dance of orange flames and shadow.

I don't know what he intends to do with it, but I realize that I have the power to stop him. The feeling is both poisonous and freeing.

So I reach down, into the dark, cold space where the Mother of Calamity laughs alone, and I begin to dance. I spread my arms like the peacock's wings, behind me, and I envision all those glowing eyes blinking in the darkness of the sky, like the eyes of the Qingniao's train. As I unfurl my wrists, like a peacock taking flight, I find the place I am looking for.

This time, she is mine.

I draw the lightning down from the heavenly vaults above the stars, through the earth and the stone ceiling of the temple, toward Bailey. He only has a moment to look up before the light crashes toward his body. In that second, his face is thrown into stark relief, and on it I see written a childlike wonder, like a boy who has witnessed a storm for the first time in his life.

Bailey turns and catches the lightning with the mirror hanging around his neck. The light becomes so bright the walls tremble from its force, before it is reflected from the mirror's surface and plunges straight into the altar.

A chasm opens in the floor underneath the altar, like a grin in the earth, shaking the walls of the temple and knocking the scrolls off the wall. The gangsters, caught midfight, lose their balance. I fall against the wall as the scrolls crash around me.

For a moment, the entire room—no, the entire world—is still.

Then Liqing drops the sword with a yell, and she throws herself into Bailey, her hair flying wildly about her temples. The mirror on his chest shatters from the impact of her body, splintering into dust around them, and they fall together, as if in slow motion, toward that smiling ravine on the floor. The last thing I see is her face, her lips curved in a smile, before she and Bailey both tumble over the edge into the chasm, doomed to an eternity of falling into the center of the earth.

I run to the edge of the chasm, fighting the throbbing pain in my temples. Although I'm listening for her words—any last sign— all I hear is my own heart, thudding behind my ears. Zikai joins me, and behind him, the gangsters. It feels like we are all holding our breath, waiting for a sign of an ending.

The raging in my head slowly quiets down, like the tide after the moon has passed.

We stare at the blasted altar, the stone cracked in ugly, twisted ways, dust swirling in the air.

"She's gone," I say. For some reason my throat is dry. I can't forget the image of Liqing's face, moments before she fell over the edge. Her brows were knit, her eyes narrowed, like she was staring into the sun, and there was a certain fire set about her face, which I knew must have been the same face she wore when she defied a goddess for the first time.

My grandmother wasn't meant to die in peace. Her ending was to be loud, a celebration of the old rules she broke and the new ones she forged.

I drop to one knee, gaze down into the bottomless darkness, which spreads like the night above the stars, like the emptiness of a woman's face. I listen, but the dark is quiet.

"You didn't get to say much to her," Zikai observes. He moves to stand behind me, and I sense his warmth, like a mantle draped around my shoulders. "Are you alright?"

"It's what she wanted," I realize, unable to blink away the phantom of her gaze.

She may not have known how, or when, but she had always known. Someday, she would place the crown upon my head, and the Mother of Calamity would become my mantle to wear. I never shared her passion for surgery, but there were other ways to take from the goddess. My mother had asked for the same.

If we didn't use her, others would.

I've inherited a burden, and now I must choose what to make of it.

I back away from the altar. A strange feeling wells up in my chest—like sadness, but restless. "Why do you think he did that bit with the mirror?"

"Bailey?" Zikai shrugs, toeing the chasm in the floor. "Who knows?"

As if in response to our conversation, a darkness begins to roil in the crevice, bubbling like water that has begun to boil. I grab Zikai's hand and pull him back. A trail of black buds rises out of the abyss, sprouting out of the altar like cherry blossoms on a gnarled branch, wrinkled at first like an infant's skin and then curling open like sun-loving flowers in the garden of a god.

It's the lingzhi, which grows now upon the altar, so dark it shimmers green. It spills from the abyss onto the cold stone like wet ink landing upon a blank page. The wet, shining buds make me think of placentas, a birthing place in the shrine of a god.

So this is how it grows. The sight is oddly beautiful.

Xiao Lei grabs a torch from the wall, meaning to light the trail of lingzhi on fire, but I grab his arm.

"Leave it," I say.

"Are you being serious?" he responds.

The fungus blooms upon the altar, dark and shining like droplets of blood. I run my hand through the buds, the edges resisting the pressure from my fingers. The fungus is soft and velveteen in its natural form, cool to the touch.

I flash a hardened smile at Xiao Lei. "Things are going to be different around here now."

CHAPTER TWENTY-FOUR

arrange for my grandmother's funeral to happen by the water, where the bronze shadows of the Bund's towers lay in the waves, rippling like a dream. An unusual locale for death rites, but my grandmother never had a taste for obscurity.

As I collect the most gruesome paintings and masks from her clinic to send into the afterlife with her, I've dressed in white robes, more befitting the arhats who ride through the clouds on my grandmother's walls than a modern girl. Beibei ties a long strip of white cloth around my forehead, the ends trailing halfway down my back. She didn't ask questions when I showed up at her doorstep in the middle of the night, covered in dust and dried blood. She merely brought out the same bottle of whiskey we'd started and poured me a glass.

Later that night, I wrote a letter to my mother, explaining the situation. Although my mother doesn't respond, I know she will come.

Beibei tucks a frayed thread into my hair so it won't fall in my eyes. She does all of this without speaking because that is the sort of relationship we have—a silent understanding, grown from the horrors we've shared.

The last of the preparations done, Beibei leaves to dance at the Paramount.

I cry after she leaves, hot tears rolling down my cheeks as I draw the pins out of the swan wings on the wall. The pins have rusted now, their heads green and deformed. A few feathers drift down to the carpet as I lift the swan wings from their mount. But when I carry them across the room, they suddenly disintegrate in my hands, feathers and dust crumbling in the air until I'm left holding bones.

Without the feathers to dress them up, the wing bones look oddly like human arms, not unlike the ones I used to deliver for Liqing. I add them to my stack of Liqing's possessions, which might topple over if I build it any higher. Straightening briefly, I use my fingers to wipe away the tears.

Although Xiao Lei offered the clinic to me on behalf of the Blue Dawn, I refused. It's better to close old doors, I've decided, and open new ones.

Draping my winter coat over my shoulders, I carry Liqing's belongings down to the waterside in a box. The gulls are particularly vicious today, traversing the crisp afternoon air in figure eights.

My mother waits for me at the harbor, where she's built a pyre on a dock.

The harbor is noisy on a Saturday, steamships bellowing in the distance and dock workers swarming the waterfront like ants.

Wordlessly, I kneel for my mother to wreath my hair with green chrysanthemums. The river spray ricochets off the wet boards, peppering my dark curls with mud and salt. Then, I braid her hair with white ones, the petals fluttering past my fingers as the wind blows.

We don't speak to one another as we arrange the nuo masks around the pyre wood and scatter ghost money.

Although it rains that night, we burn the pyre.

The embers fall into the water, where they blossom like flowers for the space of a breath before they are consumed by foam. A haunting silence surrounds the orange and gold flames, which crackle and hiss in protest, but refuse to quench in the rain.

The gangsters come after midnight bearing wreaths of fresh lilies and chrysanthemums, which they hang on the pillars with their silver hands. Xiao Lei and Zikai come too and kneel at my side, where Xiao Lei slices dragon fruit in his silver palm and then lays the halves at the dock's edge, and when Zikai stands, he leaves rice wine and wrapped pork buns by my hands, which I eat without tasting.

As clouds float past the moon, mirroring the waves, they pay respects and leave. I smell salt in the breeze, see the crash of white foam on dark waves, and I close my eyes.

For a week, I kneel before the ashes of her pyre. The first three days, my mother stays with me, both of us kneeling on the sodden wood, which etches waves in my skin and makes my bones ache. And then it rains again, and after that she stops coming. It's just me, the wind teasing through the space in my billowing sleeves and cutting my flesh.

But I'm not ready to leave yet.

The heaviness that holds me before the pyre is manifold—anger that she sewed the dancers' lips and eyes onto the faces of ladies like Moraima, betrayal that even in her last moments, I was only part of a grander scheme she envisioned, regret that our shared blood was not enough to save our relationship.

I burn more ghost money, and each time the embers are swallowed by the waves. My sorrow turns to ashes with the rice paper, but I'm not ready to let go yet.

After the seventh day, I rise to my feet.

The chrysanthemums in my hair are dead. The rotting brown petals disintegrate in the wind as my knees shake from kneeling for so long. I press my fingers into my forehead, where the edges of Niang Niang's crown have vanished into my skin. The funeral rites have not brought me clarity, but they have given me peace.

Someday, I will make sense of the complicated feelings that cloud my chest—decide how to sort through the diagrams and shamanic relics buried in the dust of the clinic, whether I'll be able to use them to give the dancers their faces back, and then someday, sort through my memories of Yue Liqing herself—the healer, the matriarch, the human with the likeness of a god.

Time won't dull the wounds, but I'll get stronger.

And still, I have unfinished business with the city. I hail a taxicab to bring me to the City God Temple, where the familiar aromas of peanut candy and cherry blossom wine sweeten the air.

"Good evening, Jingwen." Nalan Zikai stands under the flared awning of the Niang Niang Hall, eating a plum off one of the trees. He's drawn his hair into a ponytail high over his head, the stray wisps hanging over his face. The large sleeves of his silk shirt billow in the wind.

"What are you doing here?" I am truly surprised to see him.

"Stopping you from visiting the shrine." He smirks and tosses me a plum, which I catch clumsily between my hands.

"What do you mean?"

"You don't have to put everything in order right away." He walks down the steps, giving the guardian tortoise's nose a pat on the way. "I know you haven't rested since the night of Liqing's funeral, and as your ally—I'd like to remind you that rest is important."

This close, I can count the sun-warmed freckles across his cheeks, see the fingerprints on the leaves of the mouth harp around his neck. When he ties his hair above his head, his cheeks look rounder. He looks younger, like a romantic literatus who wears his heart on his sleeve.

"I thought we were going to rebuild the city together."

He grins. "We are. But it doesn't have to be the day after your grandmother's funeral rites are over. You know, the plums that grow in this temple are truly delicious. It must be all the human blood spilt under these halls that the tree drink."

Transferring the plum to one hand, I reach out with my other and entwine my flesh fingers through his silver ones—the same way he'd taken my hand that night in the alleyways and asked me to trust him.

His eyes widen as he stares at the place where our hands touch.

"I understand now why you did it."

I exhale.

The moon is awfully pretty tonight, cradled between two eaves of the temple across the moat. It makes a gentle shadow of the pear trees in the courtyard, which seem to sway in the wind.

"You told me once that I've lived in Shanghai for so long, I've become neither Shanghainese nor foreign. I think you meant it to be an insult." I flash a sheepish grin as I recall how I dared him to outdrink me. Zikai's nose twitches, but he doesn't interrupt. "You're not the only one. Wang Daojun told me something similar the night you fought him at the Rue de Velours. He compared me to a lampshade."

His shoulders stiffen at the memory of that night, but he merely angles his head to one side, willing me to go on.

"Daojun believed that Shanghai eats us alive—all the factions who divided and conquered her. In her belly, we are digested together, and when she spits us out, we have the Old City's teeth marks in our waist, and the concessions' saliva in our hair. We share pieces of each other. The only way to survive in this city is to change—and my grandmother—whether she deserves reverence or hatred, was a bringer of that change." I think of the invisible crown that binds my forehead, the sharp edges buried under my skin. "She changed both of us."

In response, Zikai lifts my wrist up and flattens his palm against mine. I gasp at the sudden, sweet shock.

Our hands fit together—even though his fingers are just a bit too long, and he has no lines on his palm. My nails, painted red, glisten against the dark silver of his skin.

"We did survive," he whispers.

A breeze slips between us like a ghost, carrying the sweet, melancholy scent of pear blossoms.

I lean into his warmth, content if the moment lasted an eternity.

Zikai lets go and straightens, a mischievous smile turning up the corners of his lips. "What do you say—tonight let's forget about the possessed girls, the lingzhi, and Blue Dawn and go on a date."

The idea is so absurd, I balk. "And do what?"

Zikai shrugs, a stray wisp of his hair falling handsomely into his eyes. "Eat fruit off temple trees, listen to the street opera singers, sip cherry blossom wine on the bridge? Anything you'd like."

"That sounds incredibly indulgent," I remark, yet I'm dying to get started.

Zikai grins, and I realize I've never seen him like this—truly free of his long list of duties and burdens. "I think you've earned the right to be indulgent and carefree for just one night."

I raise the plum, still in my other hand, hard as a rock. "Is this even ripe? The skin is still yellow."

He shrugs. "The sourness keeps me awake at night."

I take a bite. The plum skin is overwhelmingly tart, the green flesh bitter and dry. I resist the urge to spit it back out.

Zikai laughs as I force myself to swallow instead. "Awake now?"

We buy a jug of cherry blossom wine from the temple market and sit on the zigzag bridge that runs across the moat, our legs dangling over the edge. I've seen so much water in the last week, yet I never tire of it. The water that surrounds the City God Temple is temperate and green with mold, in a way that softens it and gives it life. The reflection of Zikai's silver arm swims in the lazy ripples, glinting off coins sunken to the bottom.

"What are you feeling?" he asks me, untying the cloth stretched over the jug.

"Lightness," I respond, bringing my fingers to my breast and realizing there's a space in my ribs where I've held my breath for months—maybe years—and finally I've found a means to exhale.

"Lightness is a start." He drinks straight from the jug, droplets of light pink wine spilling in his lap, and passes it to me.

I take a swig as well, tilting my head all the way back to catch the sweet drops on my lips.

"So what do you think of Shanghai now?" I ask him when I resurface, and he uses his thumb to gently wipe a drop of wine off my chin. For a moment, I'm transported back to the Dove House, on the first night we drank together. I steal a quick glance at the trademark mole beside his left eye—it's still there, of course, unchanged.

What a history that has transpired since.

"Well . . ." he says.

I realize I'm afraid of the answer. He could say he hates it and plans to go back to Hulunbuir the moment we have achieved our plans. Or he could return to the forests in the south to keep fighting tiger-riding shamans and pig-faced demons, all the monsters from his stories that don't exist in Shanghai.

He sighs. "It feels like home."

My eyes widen as my heart begins to thud in my chest. "I don't believe it. What brought about this monumental change?"

"Well, precisely—you." He meets my gaze straight on, green eyes dancing, and I fight the urge to look away. "I like you," he says. "And I admire you as a firebrand. I think you will remake the city into something grander than it is now. You and Shanghai are one in my mind."

My heart swells with pride, to be lavished with his praise.

"Stay by my side," I implore him. "And help me make it come true."

I tilt my head back and inhale through my nose. The air is sweet with the sinful indulgences of the temple market across the moat, which smells like candy and steamed buns. On the other side of the moat, a firework show commences, colorful dragon's eggs and peonies bursting before the temple eaves.

Zikai folds his arms over his chest, frowning disapprovingly at the ruckus. "I'll never get used to it, how they derive such glee out of making noise at three in the morning."

I smile at the showers of fiery rain. "Well, you better, if you're going to stay in Shanghai. I think it's pretty."

A pear blossom flutters off a nearby tree and lands on the bridge. He scoops it up in his silver hand, taking care to straighten a few bent petals with his other hand.

"For you," he says, presenting the flower to me in his palm.

I grin in spite of myself.

A boy has given me a flower. What a silly thing to feel glee over, when boys have given me literal silver ingots and money before. Nonetheless, I tuck the dark pink blossom in my hair, behind my ear.

"Thank you," I add.

He leans down and kisses me full on the lips, his silver fingers brushing lightly against my cheek. It lasts only a second, a playful mark which burns upon my skin, before Zikai draws away with a smirk.

Another row of explosions sets off at the foot of the temple's main hall, a high-pitched whistle that peppers the sky with rainbow sparks.

"We're out of wine," Zikai observes, upending the jug over the moat.

"Let's get more," I say, pushing off my hands to stand. The flower nearly tumbles from my hair, and I tuck it more securely behind my ear.

I find I'm laughing effortlessly, even though nothing eventful has transpired. Zikai holds his silver hand out to me, and I place my fingers in his once again. Like children, we run across the moat. I experience that guiltless wonder again, like I've become a younger version of myself, chasing mechanical butterflies through the enchanted Shanghai night once more.

A few nights later, I meet with the Blue Dawn in a teahouse by the water, in a veranda floating on white pillars carved with clouds. A quiet mist hangs over the City God Temple's emerald moat, obscuring the lotus roots and dragon-scaled koi that hide below. The festival market across the way rages with life—a fire-breather charming the crowd with his throat bared to the moon, children running around gnawing candied wild fruit on bamboo sticks. The fish-shaped lanterns strung through the halls sway in the firelight, emblems of a ghost city come to life after midnight.

A waitress in a sleek, black qipao leads us to a set of dark, teakwood tables inlaid with gold phoenixes and flowering vines. We are the only guests tonight. I suspect this would be the case on most nights, as the teahouse is much too grand and solemn for the rowdy marketgoers. Like the nine great halls of the temple, it is left over from a different era. I take a seat facing the water, and Zikai and Xiao Lei draw out chairs on either side of me. A few other gangsters from the Blue Dawn join us, silent as the carved dragons on the pillars.

We decide to resolve the matter the way gangsters do—over a candlelit feast, the table set with roast fish and steamed buns filled with hot custard and melted egg yolks, a pyramid of tangerines stacked on a gold plate in the center.

Xiao Lei seems to think nothing of it, as he was raised in a gang. As far as he knows, this is how difficult decisions are always made, over good food and wine. I keep a sharp watch over the Niang Niang Hall, the underside of its roof lit dark gold by lanterns as Xiao Lei's men take guard over the shrine.

The tea is served in white and blue porcelain cups—a traditional tea set like they used during the Qing Dynasty, before it became fashionable to sip Earl Grey like Englishmen. Zikai is the only one who knows how to perform a proper tea ceremony, seeping the fragrant, curled leaves in hot water and filling our dainty teacups.

I pull a plate of fish—roasted until the skin is crispy in sweet vinegar—toward me.

"When you hold meetings like this," I say to Xiao Lei, hot steam rising off the fish's browned skin in my face, "is someone in charge of taking notes?"

Xiao Lei turns to me, his mouth slightly agape. He blinks, half expecting me to announce that I'm joking.

When I don't amend my words, he nods at one of his gangsters. "Ah Fang will take notes."

The boy, Ah Fang, scrabbles for a pen in his jacket and pants pockets but cannot find one. In the end, the teahouse's waitress takes pity and brings him a fountain pen and pad.

I dig my chopsticks under the fish's gills, to scoop the flaky white flesh from its cheeks, which I dip twice in the sweet vinegar sauce.

The gangsters observe me silently.

Fine then. I'll be the only one who eats.

"So, we have some matters to sort out," I say, chewing the soft white meat.

"I'd like to go first," Xiao Lei volunteers. He hasn't touched the food at all. "Jingwen, I still think we need to destroy the lingzhi."

He says it with very serious eyes. The lanterns dance within their amber depths, frantic like his heartbeat in his chest.

"Do you find the sight of it in the shrine unsightly?" I ask.

Only Zikai finds my joke funny. He laughs into a napkin as he wipes his mouth.

Xiao Lei narrows his eyes, and I remember his power as Wang Daojun's successor. The role suits him—it really does. I never could've imagined it the first night I delivered bones to him, when I was twelve years old, and he couldn't have been much older. "More men like Bailey will come across the sea, seeking what he did. Eventually, they'll get their hands on the lingzhi. The gang is powerful, but we can't stop them all."

I pour him more tea. My wrists don't shake. After all, we are equals now.

Then, I raise my own teacup in a toast.

"We're going to let them sell it," I respond.

The pen stops scratching where Ah Fang has dropped it, and Xiao Lei rises to his feet, his palms flat against the table. He towers over me, his shadow putting out a few of the candles.

Zikai's hand moves to the scimitar at his side.

I sip my tea as if nothing is wrong. "We'll let them sell it in New York, Paris, Amsterdam—wherever they want. Those who taste the lingzhi share in the madness it brings. That's how we'll keep the foreign powers in check—let them play with the gods. They won't be able to conquer us when they're drunk from it. And they're going to pay us handsomely. The profits we'll split between us, just like how we're going to split control over the city."

The longest silence passes as they ruminate on my words, and I ruminate on a chopped rice cake dish with pork and onions.

I cast a quick glance at Zikai. Perhaps this was not the rewriting of the rules he expected, but it is the one I have chosen.

Zikai rolls a tangerine between his silver hand and his flesh hand, before peeling it with his human hand. I wait to hear whether he'll stand by my side like he promised.

He offers me half the tangerine. "I think Jingwen's right that we can't stop them all. Bailey's associates still roam the bars on Blood Alley, and we couldn't kill them all before dawn, even if we tried. They'll flee across the sea when they find out what happened, and then they'll be back for more. I think that after the stories he's sold them, the lingzhi will be irresistible."

I smile then, before slipping a slice of the tangerine in my mouth. "That's the price of globalization."

Xiao Lei clenches his fists and sits back down. "The price of globalization, eh?" he spits.

"We could be the most powerful city in the world, if we played our cards right."

Xiao Lei shakes his head incredulously. "You're flirting with the guardians of hell, Jingwen. Do you know what happens if you misstep and fall into the departments of Naraka? They rip out tongues and skin there—they have whole departments just for boiling victims alive in giant cauldrons."

"I'm not familiar with the Daoist hell," I admit. "But I'm not afraid of change. The Court of Exiles was afraid of change, but the Blue Dawn always embraced progress. You wouldn't have silver hands if you weren't willing to take a risk. I don't think we can stop the world from changing. We can only carve out our place in it and do our best to protect what we love."

He bows his head, holding his forehand in his hands.

I divert my attention to a crab dish fried with green onions and butter. Two of the crab legs are stuck together by the fry batter, which I untangle with my bare fingers. I keep the larger leg, attached to the claw, for myself, and I place the other on Zikai's plate, as gratitude for taking my side.

After some time has passed, Xiao Lei lifts his head. "That other bit you said—we're going to split control over the city?" He raises an eyebrow.

"You, the Blue Dawn, and us, the dancers. The cabaret industry brings much of the city's revenue. Without the dancers, Shanghai would lose its sordid reputation, and with that, the money and attention that you and I both enjoy so much. After all, heirs and princes don't traverse the violent seas to visit the Blue Dawn's little shabby teahouse. They come to dance with us." I dust the crab shell stuck to my fingers over the edge of the veranda, into the emerald waters below. "You depend on us, more than we will ever need you. Furthermore, I'd like to remind you that the Blue Dawn caused this mess by supporting Bailey's trade of the dancers' faces—"

Xiao Lei cuts in. "We didn't *support* it—"

He falls silent when I wheel around to face him.

"You did. By turning a blind eye to Bailey's operation, you left us to be carved to pieces like sacrificial lambs. I haven't forgotten, Xiao Lei. You stood by and did nothing, even when I begged you for help."

I pause to let my words sink in.

He opens and closes his mouth a few times, before interlacing his fingers before him and choosing silence.

I pick up another buttered crab leg. "The dancers won't need the Blue Dawn for protection anymore. We're going to protect ourselves, and we'll have equal say as you from now on, in all of Shanghai's affairs."

"So you're forming a gang?" Xiao Lei asks.

"Not a gang," I respond, licking butter from my fingertips. "Something different—less punishing and demanding of people's loyalties. A band of dancers and we will take it upon ourselves to protect the cabarets using the lingzhi and the Mother of Calamity's power. I thought of a name for us already—the Court of Golden Flowers."

I say our name in English, letting the syllables ring out over the water.

"The Court of Golden Flowers," Zikai repeats after me. He runs his tongue along his teeth, tasting the name. "That sounds quite grand, but it's a bit old-fashioned, don't you think?"

"Shamans and gods are both old-fashioned," I retort. "We can give these things new meanings."

He stuffs a tangerine in his mouth whole. "That's true."

I reach across the table for a plate of wife cakes filled with candied rose petals and dried lavender. Xiao Lei can afford to pay for the real thing, not the hardened pastry shells dyed with food coloring they sell under the Jing'an Temple's north wall.

I grin at him across the table. "What do you think?"

He scratches his head with his silver hand, grimacing like he's in pain.

"I think you're enjoying yourself a bit too much."

I push the half-eaten platter of fish in front of him. "And you're paying for the meal, so you should really try to enjoy yourself more. There's nothing you can do to stop me anyways. I wear the Mother of Calamity's crown, heck—I don't even know how to take it off if I wanted to. You may have silver limbs, but I hold all the power of the Queen Mother of the West."

Xiao Lei finally picks up a pair of chopsticks. "I did promise you that I would lead the Blue Dawn differently than Wang Daojun did. I plan to keep my word. The Blue Dawn is content to share power with the dancers. We won't enact any of our campaigns unless we've shared them with you first."

I fold my arms over my chest. "Good. So, we'll convene here every week to exchange reports. Next week, we can divide tasks such as patrolling the docks and tracking down the remaining faceless girls. For now, I'll task your people to harvest our first bounty of the lingzhi from the shrine. Set a price for it, then call Bailey's contacts."

"The Society of the Blue Dawn and the Court of Golden Flowers," Xiao Lei mutters quietly. He's nodding in spite of himself. "I'll arrange it."

I imagine us here on a summer night, many months into the future, mosquitos circling our heads like stars and moths bumping clumsily under the lanterns. And we will talk again, business partners who share wine and feast as equals.

"And you," Xiao Lei says, nodding to Zikai. "What are you going to do?"

"You could kill me now, I suppose." Zikai throws his arms into the air, a stray curl of hair falling loose at his temple. "You've certainly earned the right."

When Xiao Lei makes no move to behead him, he shrugs. "No? Well, I've grown quite fond of Shanghai. I never thought I'd stay— the wine here is too sweet and the rooms too cramped, but I will stay at Jingwen's side as a protector and an advisor for whatever comes next. I've grown quite fond of her ideals, and I'd like to see what she builds. If you're going to play with the gods, you better have the counsel of a shaman."

"It will take me a long time to forgive you for what you did," Xiao Lei says, tight-lipped. "But I won't deny that you're useful." He turns to me. "And the girls with the mutilated faces? They are still running amok in the city. I don't think anything we've done yet has changed that."

"I'll give them their faces back."

Xiao Lei spits a fish bone into his silver hand. "Liqing didn't even know how. Do you?"

"I'll find a way."

I sound so confident he doesn't fight me.

On another side of the moat, the fire-breather's show finally ends, one last burst of flame turning to smoke between the sullen worship halls. The revelers in the courtyard cheer, their drunken breath turning the night air a pearly sheen, and another round of cherry blossom wine is passed around. A troupe of acrobats, dressed in colorful scraps with masks carved in the likeness of forest animals, crowds the fire-breather out of the square. A suona horn croons to the sky, and the acrobats tumble across the stones, brandishing moon-shaped mandolins and three-stringed lutes.

"We should be drinking wine," Zikai says, swaying his head along to the music.

Xiao Lei beckons to the waitress with two fingers. She nods without his having to say a word and ducks under a curtain back inside the teahouse. "Done."

The waitress returns carrying a black jug of sorghum wine, covered by canvas tied with red string. Xiao Lei tips the wine into little cups that look like they are meant for tea.

"Cheers to the new city," I say, holding my cup high above my head.

They raise their cups to meet mine with their silver hands.

The next night, I return alone to Blood Alley, where I spent my girlhood amongst gangsters. A new dancer lies across the velvet hoop in the Cabaret Voliéré, her fishnet tights soft between her toes stretched to the sky. Although I've told Xiao Lei I'm giving the clinic up, I can't help but visit one more time.

Most of Liqing's possessions have been burned, but a few relics still adorn the faded walls.

I light a dozen sticks of camphor incense, which I arrange around a brass burner shaped like a lotus. Curls of smoke twine in the air, following me everywhere I go in the clinic. I brush dust off the tea table, fix the cracked tortoise plastron on the shelf that has slid down onto its back. And then I line my high heels neatly under the windowsill and push the window up. The wind roars in, fluttering the few remaining paintings of horned demons and wild-eyed gods on the walls.

Throwing my coat down on the tea table, I climb outside onto the roof above the Cabaret Voliéré, where on many an autumn night, Liqing would recite pastoral poetry from her hometown. And I gaze out onto the city I call my home.

One street away, there is a party on a rooftop garden, ferns curling over the balcony and palm trees in glazed brown pots swaying in the breeze. A cabaret dancer is passing herself off as a Russian princess, dressed in a fur stole she undressed from a mannequin in a shop, laughing in the company of men with silver wristwatches. Someone is playing a saxophone, the golden instrument's neck curved like a swan.

Farther away, neon lights pulse over the Paramount Ballroom's crystal facade, illuminating the ballroom's name in Chinese: the Door to a Hundred Pleasures.

I close my eyes and I can still see the neon lights flash behind my eyelids. When I open them again, I realize I am not alone on the roof. A dark figure has approached me, wearing a red silk robe that has slipped down from one shoulder. Her feet are bare, her soles tainted with soot and asphalt. Although it is dark on the roof, I see her mouth in the light pollution—a bottomless chasm like the one I made in the goddess's temple.

She raises her fingers, and this time I wonder if the rain will fall over the entire city.

I rise to my feet and spread the wings I have taken from the Mother of Calamity. With a deep breath, I dance around her—the way the Qingniao greets the sun in the morning, after it has felled empires. I mean for it to be an invitation.

The rain doesn't fall.

Slowly, she raises her hands toward me, and I touch my fingertips to hers. The saxophone on the rooftop garden begins to play a tango. I lace my fingers through hers, and I pull her around me to the steps of the dance.

Our feet land upon the roof to the same rhythm. I find I'm grinning up at the stars, which cannot compete with the brilliance of Shanghai's night world. Over the edge of the roof, a quiet stream of black cars flows between the towers and nightclubs. When she dips me back, I see the red flash of cigarettes in the darkness, orange taxicab lights like little lanterns bobbing down a dark stream to guide lost souls to the underworld.

The dance ends, and there is soft applause on the rooftop garden.

The girl lifts her chin and blinks, turning her neck around to stare wide-eyed at the city waiting before her—the city that seems to wink back at her with its traffic lights, blinking green, blue, and orange.

One by one, I'll bring them back to us.

"Jingwen?" she whispers.

"Huahua," I say her name back to her.

CHAPTER TWENTY-FIVE

live in a shining metropolis by the water, where blood and wine run freely after dark, and sordid things are occasionally shut in pretty cages and hung on the street for onlookers to admire. In Chinese, her name means, "upon the sea." It's written 上海, pronounced "Shanghai."

There are other names too, in other languages—Mato. 神城. The Whore of Asia. A Heaven Upon a Hell.

It's the place you go if you wish to be changed. They talk about it in Montmartre poet's salons cradled in velvet, and deep in the torchlit villas at the Casablanca seaside. The stories, favored by romantics and desperados, always end in the same place. At a road in Shanghai that leads down a row of shining cabarets, to a palace made of crystal. This cabaret has a particular reputation, and not only for its facade, which resembles the white clouds of Venus bottled under glass. They whisper that you can dance with goddesses there—girls who are not ordinary girls, who inhabit the bodies of celestial beings like mink shawls loosely draped about their shoulders.

Tonight, a slender girl with eyes painted like a phoenix's and a thin waist like an aspen bough sips a Craven A cigarette by the doors, enjoying the cool night on her bare arms. When she tilts her chin back in a laugh, her eyes glow blue as if neon gas runs in her veins.

She smiles at me as I pass, our shoulders brushing together for a second, and I feel the goddess that trembles under her skin, cool and excited for a night of dancing.

I don't need the lingzhi anymore to call my goddess into my flesh. As I pass under the doorway, wreathed in vermilion streamers for the Lunar New Year, I close my eyes and invite the Mother of Calamity to join me.

When I cross the black velvet carpet to the dance floor, dressed in a gold qipao with a high slit in the side, I savor the wildness she brings. There is a new madness to my step, a spark to the jewels tangled in my hair, and an ancient magic that thrums deep in my bones, like the arrival of the first day of spring.

It's hot on the dance floor, so I welcome a light rain to fall from the lights—regular rain, not the type that will cut. It slides off the guests' skin and glistens on the maple floors. This rain that falls smells like dead leaves and the earth, scents akin to the blue mountain on which the goddess presides. The guests throw their heads back, laughing.

It's much better that way, to dance with a touch of the wild.

At the very edge of the dance floor, an enchanted girl smiles and places her hands on the shoulders of a stranger in a suit. Under the cap sleeves of her qipao, her veins glow with phosphorus, as if the stars beat under her skin—a girl made of the sky.

I grin up at the roving spotlights, which bathe my face in warm, dappled light. This is what Shanghai was always meant to become—an augmented reality that wakes at night. And no matter who you are or what nation you come from, you can don a glittering avatar and escape.

On the orchestra's stage, a girl sings in a red sequined dress, her hands cradling a crystal-studded microphone. Her skin, cool as midnight, makes a silken contrast with the silver spotlights.

She is one of the few girls present in the ballroom who remains untouched by shamanic magic, choosing instead to sing with her human voice.

In the front row, a lone silhouette rests at the table in the center, sipping whiskey from the guise of a goddess who likes to take the shape of a white fox. I could recognize her just by the way she breathes. Li Beibei traces her forefinger along the bottom edge of her crimson-stained lip, a pensive reverie lingering in her hips and the slender curve of her back.

The white fox and the girl behind it flash in and out of focus like static on an electronic television.

Of late, Beibei has been trying on the skins of many deities, including an arhat who wears the rainclouds as a veil and a warrior priestess who rides a white stag with reins of cinnabar. But her favorite seems to be this nameless goddess of the woods, a folk deity who immigrated to Shanghai from the pine forests near the Russian border, who takes the form of a white fox.

A crystal heart pendant rests between her collarbones on a black silk ribbon.

I pause by a column with a glass of champagne, to enjoy the performance for a minute.

The singer lifts her face, and her eyes connect with the Arctic fox sitting in the front row. It's Maia Kane, the jazz singer from New Orleans I saw with Beibei at the Neapolitan Gardens. Slowly, Beibei's fingers drift up to her neck to rest on the pendant. The crystal heart burns at her breast like white fire.

For a second, I contemplate which is the real Beibei—the one dressed in the face of a fox or the one who liked to smoke in the alleys behind the kitchen with the local rich boys, who accepted a marriage proposal from Neville Harrington.

She senses me watching and turns her head. The fox's slender face smiles at me, eyes narrowed with a wisdom that goes beyond both of our years.

I shed the Mother of Calamity from my body, to reveal my true face.

Beibei inclines her head in response and tips her glass to me, but the fox's sharp visage hardens over her face, becoming more solid— the nose slenderer and velveteen, the teeth sharper and hungrier.

And then I realize it doesn't matter which Beibei is the real one. In Shanghai, we are allowed to wear multiple skins, which we collect over our lifetimes and store away for when we need them. I'm glad I got to see her on the eve of the New Year, her cheeks glowing with a fiery happiness. I smile before I slip away, through the ivory halls that are my second home.

Across the street from the Paramount, there is a temple open to the sky, so brilliant it needs tall, dark walls to hold the light in.

The courtyard rests in darkness, but they are building a pagoda against the east wall, workers parading under a steel skeleton like ants carrying ladders and beams. In its full glory, the pagoda will have thirteen stories, and its outer walls will be embossed with phoenixes made from neon tubing and lotus flowers that blink after dark. A monstrosity, the tabloids call it, but I'm excited. Xiao Lei paid for it, a humorous bid to construct a flashier monument than the Customs Building in the Bund.

Around the courtyard's perimeter, the doors to the worship halls are thrown open. Inside, the rooms glow red like the chambers of a heart. There are girls dancing inside, their silhouettes constantly shifting through the paper windows. Once, tall effigies carved from camphor and river jade towered behind the altars, but since then they have been stripped and replaced with living girls.

Worshippers come from all over the world, bringing gold ingots and platters of exotic fruit. Some ask us for favors. Not all the girls are willing to perform unspeakable deeds—some draw the line at bloodshed and others only want to dance—but there are some who enjoy puppetting a god of destruction, or else inviting a god of destruction into their own flesh.

It's been a full two months since my grandmother gave me the Mother of Calamity's crown.

Signs of spring are waking across Shanghai—tiny green shoots on the gingko trees in the courtyard and wild garlic with yellow flowers pushing through the cracks in the pavement. We are still not done rebuilding the city, although a lot has changed. Shanghai is a city of open wounds, and the healing takes time to realize.

I pause by the Hall of Virtuous Works, where such a heavy quantity of the lingzhi burns, the entire structure is dark with smoke.

Amid the smoke, Huahua surfaces from her trance, laughing. Her eyes glow gold like a cat's. She has just left the body of a god somewhere outside Shanghai, giddy and refreshed to return to her mortal being. The shimmering smoke dances upon her skin, leaving a trail of light glitter.

She laughs despite not having a mouth, running her cherry-red nails through her hair, which is slightly mussed by sweat.

"Jingwen," she says my name in greeting. She lets the god go from within her, and her eyes darken back to their usual brown.

"A beautiful night," I answer, throwing open the peach wood window frames. Outside in the courtyard, the numismatic charms flap on their red strings, heavy in the boughs of gingko trees. The wind has blown a stray pear blossom over the wall. It dances across the short, stone pillars carrying the Mahavira Hall and comes to rest behind the ear of a door-guarding lion—a rebellious omen of spring in a fading winter.

A ray of light bleeds through the temple's tall, dark doors.

A visitor has arrived from outside, to ask of us a favor.

They come out of the dark to stand beside me—girls whose veins are writ in gold, whose eyes glow with yellow phosphorus and melted cinnabar. I think of how outsiders must see us—coldly beautiful and terrible, some with moving shadows across our faces.

They see us exactly as we are.

Living girls who wear the skins of goddesses.

THE END

ACKNOWLEDGMENTS

The journey to publication is a long one, and I am lucky to be surrounded by wonderful champions all around:

I'd like to thank Maria Heater, who chose my book from the Pitch Wars 2020 slush pile and started the ball rolling on everything that's happened since. Your mentorship then and friendship now are invaluable to me.

My brilliant agent Kurestin Armada, whose vision for *Daughter of Calamity* was the missing piece of my own vision. Thank you for your creative input and for having my back always.

My US editor Tiffany Shelton, who took this book under her wing and became its number-one champion. Since our first meeting, I have felt safe knowing Jingwen's story and the complex themes I sought to explore rest in your care. My gratitude extends to my publishing team at St. Martin's—Lauren Riebs, Laurie Henderson, Diane Dilluvio, NaNá Stoelzle, Devan Norman, Ervin Serrano, Rivka Holler, Austin Adams, and Sara LaCotti.

My UK publishing team: Bella Pagan, Georgia Summers, Holly Domney, Sophie Robinson [and more].

Thank you to Valle. Although we no longer share a life together, you were a real one for doing all the dishes during Pitch Wars.

Daughter of Calamity is my first book, but my writing journey began many, many years ago. I'd like to thank the wonderful writing mentors who have enriched my life, each of whom taught me something different, not just about writing but about artistry. The stories I tell come from deeper within my heart because of you: Jason Berry, Jeanne Cavelos, and Jonathan Ansfield.

Many may think of writing as a solitary endeavor, but as an

extrovert, this book could not have been written without the company of the many friends who accompanied me on late-night Discord sprints, in-person boba runs, and indulgent, sort-of wallet-breaking vacations.

First of all, the Pitch Wars Class of 2020. It wasn't easy to complete an intense writing mentorship during a global pandemic, but we did it together: S.A. Simon, Kyla Zhao, M.K. Hardy, Olivia Liu, Sara Hashem, Erin Fulmer, Hannah Sawyer, Nicole Magoon, Amber Chen, Lilly Lu, CJ Dotson, Kara Allen, Jessica Lepe. Special shout-out to my friends from Hellmo's Temple—Miranda Sun, Leanne Schwartz, Sara Codair, Jules Arbeaux, Ky Jackson. And of course the Discord bot Sprinto himself—you are the reason why I get anything done these days.

My friends from the Breakdown Space, who were there for me during the hardest part of this process—Sarah Mughal, Noreen Mughees, and AMKvita.

My best writing friend Sari Coritz and my mentees-turned-friends Tiera DiGiorgio and LJ Alexander—thank you for patiently listening to me rant about my Tinder and clubbing drama when I probably should have been writing instead.

To my best friends Lisa Takenaka, Preethi Siva, and Callum Rutherford.

I'd like to thank my dance community in San Francisco. In the depths of my revision despair, you were home to me. There is nothing more healing for me than losing myself in the music and the choreography together with you. In roughly the order in which I made your acquaintance—Tegan Barry, Catherine Chen, Lydia Chon, Lilli Lin, Angie Chen, Eliza Viera-Patron, Brianna Wu, and Q Zheng.

Additionally, thank you to Patali kusuma priya Tumuluri and Leah Kim for being my sanity and my rave fam. Please continue to send me memes for the rest of my life.

Thank you to Ki To for my favorite San Francisco adventures and late-night boba escapades, for imparting upon me your Gen Z wisdom regarding TikTok, makeup, and friendship, for approximately 60% of the songs on my revision and copyedit playlists, and for introducing me to the RIZE community.

As for the RIZE community—I have always found comfort in nightlife (if you can't tell by reading this book). Y'all were my safe haven in San Francisco as I struggled to come to terms with my divorce, my queer identity, and my first time living alone. Cheers to all the K-pop power hours and parking lot shots of AMF that have left beautiful, inerasable stains on my favorite jeans shorts, my memories, and my soul.

Lastly but not least, I'd like to thank the women of my family, who are beautiful in their flaws and complex in their histories. I admire you deeply for the sacrifices you have made and the burdens you have carried. Although we are estranged to varying degrees, I am constantly reminded of your strength, and I am proud to be one of you.

In particular, my sister Michelle Jiang, who has never left my side since day one. In the beginning, every story I wrote was for us. Because I had you, I have this career.

Rosalie M. Lin is a Chinese-American writer from the San Francisco Bay Area. She has, at various points in the past decade, graduated with a degree in Comparative Literature, pole-danced in two Beijing nightclubs and dropped out of a biomedical PhD programme, before seriously pursuing her original dream of becoming an author. *Daughter of Calamity* is her debut novel.